I Kissed a Girl

An anthology of sexy short stories

Edited by Regina Perry

BLACK

Introduction

2 4 6 8 10 9 7 5 3

First published in the US by Ravenous Romance
This edition first published in the United Kingdom in 2012 by
Black Lace Books, an imprint of Ebury Publishing
A Random House Group Company

www.randomhouse.co.uk

Addresses for companies within The Random House Group Limited can be
found at www.randomhouse.co.uk/offices.htm

The Random House Group Limited Reg. No. 954009

A CIP catalogue record for this book is available from the British Library

The Random House Group Limited supports The Forest Stewardship
Council (FSC®), the leading international forest certification organisation.
Our books carrying the FSC label are printed on FSC® certified paper. FSC
is the only forest certification scheme endorsed by the leading environmental
organisations, including Greenpeace. Our paper procurement policy can be
found at www.randomhouse.co.uk/environment

Typeset by Palimpsest Book Production Limited, Falkirk, Stirlingshire
Printed and bound by CPI Group (UK) Ltd, Croydon, CR0 4YY

ISBN: 9780352346742

To buy books by your favourite authors and register for offers,
visit www.blacklace.co.uk

Introduction

Katy Perry's hit song *I Kissed a Girl* brought bisexuality to the forefront. I admit I was amazed when I heard my neighbour's five-year-old daughter singing the entire song, never missing a word or beat. Alternative lifestyles are open for discussion – no longer taboo.

Since Dr. Alfred Kinsey released his first reports on human sexual behavior in 1948, society has been in the process of accepting that almost all healthy men and women have some homosexual tendencies. Instead of hiding these inclinations in shame, it's time to celebrate our desires and be comfortable in our own skin. No labels, no judgment – only enlightenment and tolerance.

I'm not suggesting that all humans are bisexual. As I have discovered, being aroused by an erotic story doesn't label anyone. I can get excited reading BDSM, but don't try spanking me in bed. Because I am passionate about same-sex erotica does not make me bisexual, but it has enhanced my ability to love and accept.

This anthology is a collection of lesbian first-time encounters. I am delighted with the diversity of this collection. I hope you enjoy and share my passion for exploring new boundaries.

Regina Perry

Freckles

by C. Margery Kempe

'You want me to do what?' Lea asked with surprise while Keegan grinned at her like a monkey. 'With whom?'

'Oh come on, Lea. Isn't it about time we tried something to jumpstart our sex life?' His words were lazily drawled, but she could tell by the quick twitch of his knee as his foot worked up and down that he was tense with fear she would nix the plan.

Oddly enough, she had also been thinking their sex life had become fairly moribund, but the solution that had presented itself to her was finding a new lover. Keegan just wasn't that interesting when you got right down to it. Despite her initial irritation at his suggestion – after all, wasn't he hinting she wasn't enough for him? – she was intrigued.

'Well, who did you have in mind for this *ménage a trois*? I don't want some random weirdo picked up at a bar.'

Keegan smiled, and at once Lea knew that he had been planning this for some time. 'What about Bridey?'

Lea frowned, trying to connect the name to a face. 'Is that the brown-haired mousy gal in shipping?'

Keegan laughed. 'No, the redhead, the one you said looked like an ad for vacations in Ireland.' He looked out the window toward the street as if to effect nonchalance, but Lea wasn't fooled.

'You already asked her, didn't you?' She wasn't sure if she was angry, but it had been convenient of late to act as if she were at times like this. *This is how a relationship goes wrong*. She felt a twinge of sorrow.

Keegan shrugged. 'I may have mentioned it in passing.'

Now he was playing with his dinner and Lea wanted to shout at him to stop, but she held in the urge and tried to concentrate on the question before her. Did she want to do this? Did she want to get into bed with Keegan and another woman? How convenient that he assumed that it wouldn't be a man. Two guys, now that wouldn't have required much debate at all. Bridey? Hmm – she remembered her all right: deep red hair, not quite auburn, milky white skin and a broad galaxy of freckles. Pretty enough for a girl, she supposed, though Lea had never given her much thought.

What would it be like? Lea had certainly showered with other women at the gym and dressed in close quarters on campus, but she had never touched another woman's body intimately. What would another woman's breast feel like? Would it be familiar or strange to run her hands along curves like her own? And touching another girl's clit! How would that be? Lea felt an odd prickle of sexual energy as she thought about it. Fortune favors the bold – wasn't that what they said?

Keegan played with his food, clearly trying to look at her out of the corner of his eye without being seen. Lea thought about the two years they had been together. It had been fun for a time, but it was never much more than that. Maybe this would be a breakthrough to a new level in their relationship, allowing them to share more intimacy. Either that or it could give her an out, right? *Oh, I can't believe you talked me into this! I'm breaking up with you.* Who could say which way it would go? At least it would be a change.

'All right, let's do it,' Lea said at last. Keegan grinned and jumped up from his chair to give her a bear hug, knocking over her water glass.

I hope I'm doing the right thing. Lea strained to throw her napkin into the spreading puddle of water.

That Friday night, they were all a bit nervous as they sat down to a light supper of salmon and steamed vegetables that Lea had prepared with a little soy ginger sauce. Nothing heavy; that was the theme. Bridey had arrived with a shy smile and a nice bottle of Shiraz. They were sipping it while they made awkward conversation around the table. Lea noticed that Keegan was drinking way slower than usual. She guessed he didn't want to miss a thing. But at the rate things were going, it was going to take about a week for anything to happen.

'So, Bridey, I hear your family's originally from Cork,' Lea said in a moment of inspiration. 'Have you been there?'

Bridey's face lit up. 'Every summer since I was twelve! My great uncle's farm is still operating, and we've got about three hundred head of sheep, mostly Galways, though we've got a few Cheviots as well. My cousins there all work in the wool trade. This sweater is one of ours,' she added proudly, fingering the soft grey of the wool.

'It's really beautiful,' Lea said with genuine warmth, watching the animated expression on Bridey's face. She really was a lovely girl. 'Do you knit . . . or, I guess it's weave?'

Bridey laughed. It was almost musical. She squinched her green eyes up tight and her red mouth opened wide showing small even teeth. *God, I have such a horse face.* It was hard not to compare herself to this other woman, but Bridey was oblivious to Lea's doubts. 'I'm absolutely hopeless! They tried to teach me carding and shearing. I just couldn't do anything right. They've all been doing it since they were babies, so they think it's dead easy, but I was all thumbs. There was no way they'd let me near the looms.'

Lea laughed along with her. It was easy to do. 'We had required home ec in seventh grade. We had to make a simple dress from a pattern. I was the only one who failed. It looked like some kind of torture instrument,' Lea admitted and the two laughed again.

Things went more smoothly after that. Lea realized she had been intimidated by Bridey's petite good looks. She felt large and oafish beside her, but as the wine hit her brain, her confidence returned. *All kinds of ways to be beautiful.* She admired Bridey's tumble of red curls and wondered what it would feel like to twine her fingers in that hair. The little rosebud of a mouth looked invitingly wet with a tinge of red wine painting it. Lea poured another glass. Wine was good. She had a feeling that tonight was going to be more than she had expected. *And why the hell not?* Best to be open to the possibilities, eh?

'So, how do you think we should proceed?' she asked,

looking from Keegan to Bridey, then back again. Both flushed with embarrassment but seemed relieved she had cleared the air. Lea tipped her glass up and let the last of the red nectar flow down her throat. Her whole body felt warm, and it was not just the wine.

'I want to see you two kiss,' Keegan said at last, his voice a little rough, so he coughed to clear his throat. 'And you know, whatever.'

'I've been looking forward to kissing you, Lea,' Bridey said, her voice barely audible, but sweetened with an extra blush. Lea felt a grin stretch across her face in return. She seemed to be filled with a glorious feeling of magnanimity for the world, although she had to admit, most of it was focused on Bridey at present.

She got up and took Bridey's hand and led her to the bedroom. Keegan followed, close on their heels. He sat down on the bench in front of the vanity. Lea kissed him softly on the lips before leading Bridey to the bed, freshly made in honor of the night with their very best set of Egyptian cotton sheets in a crisp, rich crimson. After folding back the duvet, she sat on the side, kicking off her shoes while Bridey did the same.

Not quite looking her in the face, she curled her arm around Bridey's neck and pulled it gently until she brought their lips together. The first touch was electric, and Lea parted her lips to thrust her tongue tentatively against the soft protuberance of Bridey's velvet lips. Her mouth was open at once, inviting the exploring tongue. Lea realized their eyes were closed, but it seemed like a teen's first kiss, sloppy and ardent, so the shut eyes was like part of the dare.

Now that they were face to face, Lea let her eyes linger over the freckles sprinkled across Bridey's nose and cheek. She ran her finger over the soft skin beneath the freckles while Bridey's bright green eyes opened to regard her curiously. Lea allowed her fingers to follow the trail of spots down her long neck to the white expanse exposed by her shirt. The valley of her breasts featured another galaxy of freckles. *I've never touched another girl's breasts*, Lea thought and with the thought, knew she had to know what it felt like, whether it felt different from touching her own.

She leaned in to take Bridey's lower lip between her own lips, moving her fingers to the front of the grey sweater, loosening the buttons from their companion homes until Bridey's blush pink brassiere appeared. Lea pulled back the wool far enough to slip her hand into the space between the soft sweater and the pink cups. Bridey gasped as Lea's hand circled the small tight mound of flesh. She heard an echoing moan from Keegan. Bridey's nipple popped up at once and Lea flicked it with her thumb. So tiny! She was accustomed to her own generous orbs, so Bridey's breasts seemed like little more than a beginning, tentative and uncertain.

Nonetheless, her ragged breath and the way she arched her back indicated pleasure, and Lea took this as license to roam further. She slipped the sweater the rest of the way off Bridey's shoulders, then with both hands she reached behind the girl's back and unhooked the bra, moving her hands back to the breasts and their eager nipples. Lea leaned in to allow her hands to circle the little mounds, unaware that her lips were open as her own breath became shallow. *Why does it excite me to handle another woman's breasts? Is it just curiosity?*

Even then, she knew she was going to have to feel those nipples in her mouth. Glancing over her shoulder, she could see Keegan, heavy lidded, content to hold his erection in his hand as he watched the two of them on the bed. Lea bent down and closed her lips around Bridey's breast. They both groaned. She flicked her tongue against the taut bud of the nipple and felt a resulting surge between her own legs. It was everything: the novelty of tonguing another woman's tit, the taboo feeling of it, the exhibitionistic joy of knowing how hard it made Keegan, of seeing his open-mouthed lust. She had never thought of herself as someone drawn to performing, but Lea was keenly aware of both their eyes upon her as she sucked away at Bridey's breast, moving to the other without hesitation.

When she felt a need for change, Lea moved back up to Bridey's lips, then pulled her own shirt off over her head and mashed their breasts together. Hers – larger, softer – pressed against Bridey's with glee as her tongue probed deeply into the gal's mouth. Lea fucked her mouth with growing excitement and finally pulled her down beside her on the bed. Kisses were not going to be enough, although the touching and kissing had made her feel drunk with desire.

Lea reached for the band of Bridey's jeans and popped the snap at the top, teasing the zipper down. At a distance, she heard Keegan groan as if he, too, wanted to join the fun, but for the moment, he constrained himself to continue watching and pulling at his cock. Impatient, Lea wiggled her palm into the polka-dot panties visible beneath the jeans. So warm! The heat was astounding. She wiggled a finger down between her lips and felt the slick wetness as a prize.

Bridey gasped, and Lea grinned. Bridey's eyes were as heavy-lidded as Keegan's now, her face consumed with lust. Lea stretched the jeans and panties out and brought her index finger back to the swollen bud of Bridey's clit. She began to swirl her finger around it, making lazy circles as Bridey arched back, eyes closed. Without much warning, Bridey was crying out, her clit pulsating with pleasure as she bucked beneath Lea's hand. Lea felt herself melt with wild desire.

She turned to shuck off her own jeans, before turning back to slide down Bridey's. No words of protest from the woman, but her own eager hands helping. Lea stared in wonder at the bright little bonfire, the patch of red hair at her delta of Venus, her little soft mound. Lea hesitated, but then bent her head forward to taste the soft wet lips between Bridey's thighs. It was tart and salty, but Lea let her tongue slowly run between the pink lips and playfully tease the still-turgid clit at the head of the passage.

The sight of Lea's head buried between Bridey's thighs was apparently too much for Keegan. He rose and crossed to the bed, kneeling behind Lea and resting his swollen dick on her ass for a moment as she continued to bob her head back and forth. It was a relief to feel his thick cock slide between her wet lips as she began to suck Bridey's bud. At least Keegan remembered to aim for her G-spot, distracted as he was by her ass being in the air at that particular angle, quickly gaining momentum as he slammed into her, clutching her thighs tightly with his fingers. Lea reached back with one hand to help along the orgasm that was beginning to bloom within her, stroking her own clit as she pulled at Bridey's with her lips. At the very end, her cries were muffled in Bridey's belly as she yelped aloud while Keegan continued to pump into her.

Without warning he stiffened against her, letting loose a groan of satisfaction that seemed to well up from his toes. Then he collapsed on her back, mashing Lea against Bridey, who looked less than pleased. 'Keegan, up. You're squashing us!'

Keegan mumbled something indistinct and rolled onto his back. 'That was the most amazing fuck I have ever had!' he enthused, rubbing his hand across Lea's back roughly. She tried not to let it set her teeth on edge, but she found it really annoying. Before Lea could do much more than wiggle into a more comfortable position between them, Keegan had begun to snore softly.

Bridey stared. 'Is he always like that?' she asked, her fiery eyebrows raised in surprise.

Lea nodded. 'Usually. But he doesn't always stay asleep for long. I can often wake him up later for a second round.' But she found it a bit embarrassing to see Bridey's look of derision. 'He's not that bad,' she added lamely.

'It hardly seems like you were satisfied,' Bridey consoled, moving her palm against Lea's cheek gently.

'I don't suppose there's anything you could do about that,' Lea said with a grin before Bridey covered her mouth with another enthusiastic kiss. This time it was Bridey who moved down to take Lea's breast in her mouth, hungrily sucking it in and giving a gentle nip to the rapidly hardening nipple. Lea closed her eyes and let the wonderful sensations wash over her. Bridey kept one hand on her other breast, cupping the soft abundance as her tongue and mouth worked away at the other until Lea was ready to dissolve in a cloud of bliss.

'Got any toys?' Bridey asked when she came up for air. Lea nodded at the drawer in the nightstand behind them, and Bridey rose up to investigate. She lifted up the beautiful glass dildo Lea's sister had mailed from Hong Kong and looked inquiringly at Lea, who grinned and flushed a little. Bridey grabbed the bottle of Astroglide and squeezed a generous portion onto the glass before pressing Lea back and drizzling more at her crotch.

Bridey slid her hand up and down the glass cock slowly as Lea watched, feeling the thrill fill her thighs. She supposed it was largely the sense of anticipation. When Bridey's hand moved to her wet folds, Lea could not hold back a serious groan of longing that wasn't quite drowned out by Keegan's persistent snore. As the lube heated up and Bridey's quick fingers increased their ministrations, Lea thought she was ready to come again, but Bridey withdrew her hand to guide the dildo slowly into Lea's aching cunt. She could feel the walls pulsate excitedly as Bridey thrust the tool slowly in, stopping and backtracking just a little until Lea thought she would die of anticipation.

When Bridey moved her other hand back to massage Lea's clit, she started to come, bucking her hips up involuntarily, crying out. Bridey continued thrusting the sleek glass in, poking at her G-spot while her fingers teased her clit. Lea kept coming over and over until she was breathless and gasping. When Bridey finally stilled her hand, Lea could feel her muscles still clutching away as the spasms slowed. Bridey left her hand on Lea's clit as she eased back down beside her, reaching for another long slow kiss.

'God, you are fantastic,' Lea said finally, looking into Bridey's green eyes. The freckles across her nose and cheeks were surrounded by a pink flush of arousal, as she grinned at Lea. 'I have never felt so good.' She ran her hand over Bridey's shoulder and the pale, nearly translucent skin with its galaxy of spots. Impulsively, Lea pulled her close in a warm hug, laughing with delight. 'What can I do for you?'

Bridey laughed, too. 'I think I'd really like to feel your lips on the little man in the boat again.'

'Would you like me to use my toy, too?'

Bridey shook her head and then lay back, looking at Lea expectantly. Lea decided to kiss her way down, nuzzling the soft valley between her small breasts and using her fingers to trace the soft roundness of Bridey's belly. Lea pressed her teeth onto the bump of Bridey's hip bone and reached for the lube to squeeze a little onto her red lips before working her fingertips around the area, spreading the rapidly warming fluid across Bridey's sensitive skin.

The look on Bridey's face was relaxed, yet the quick rise of her chest gave sure sign of her arousal. Lea walked her fingers down Bridey's thigh and pressed her legs open. She slid down the bed and moved her hands under Bridey's creamy cheeks, the soft round weight of them feeling good in her hands. Lea leaned forward to work her tongue up

Bridey's lips to the swollen bud, feeling her ass tense as the tip of her tongue touched her nubbin. She let her tongue make lazy circles around the clit until Bridey was moving with her, then greedily kissed it, sucking away while she massaged Bridey's soft globes with her hands. The movements grew more frenzied and before long, Lea was tightening her lips around the bud as it pulsated and Bridey called out, 'Lea!'

Lea slicked her fingertips in Bridey's wet juices, bringing them to her lips to taste, then inching up to lie once more beside her new friend. 'Was that all right?' she asked, suddenly shy, afraid that she had not been proficient.

'That was wonderful,' Bridey assured her, and they kissed again, more softly now, tongues meeting gently, hands on one another's cheeks.

'I'm glad Keegan talked you into this,' Lea said at last, closing her eyes and resting her head against Bridey's neck.

Bridey laughed. 'Talked me into it? That's a hoot.'

Lea yawned. 'What do you mean?'

Bridey twined her fingers into Lea's hair. 'I suggested it to him weeks ago. Ever since I saw you at the party at the Anchor, I haven't been able to get you out of my mind.'

Lea laughed. 'I'm flattered.'

'Are you interested?'

Lea raised her head and looked into Bridey's face. Suddenly she looked so much younger and unsure. She kissed her again. 'Very.'

Bridey kissed her back with enthusiasm. 'I'm so very glad to hear that, I was afraid – well, you know.'

Lea smiled and brushed a lock of the curly hair off

Bridey's forehead. 'It is kind of shocking,' Lea said, making her face look serious. 'I never fell in love with a redhead before.'

'Ee-jit,' Bridey said, then paused. 'Love?'

'Are you interested?'

'Very.'

'Good.' Lea snuggled back down into the crook of Bridey's neck. 'I'll give Keegan the news tomorrow.'

'Do you think he'll be surprised?'

Lea chuckled. '*I* am, so I suppose he will be. But I don't care.' She traced the freckles along Bridey's neck, then closed her eyes once more. Love was worth a little inconvenience, surely.

Who knew I'd fall for someone like this? Sleep overtook her while Bridey continued to stroke her cheek. Life was good.

Two's Company

by Louisa Bacio

Who says you need a cock to fuck? I think, rubbing my hands over Joanna's ass, feeling the voluptuous curves hidden beneath her tight jeans. Her breasts strain forward, nipples growing even harder. It's been coming to this for a long time: our first kiss.

We had been friends for quite a while – just friends. An undercurrent of sexual tension always lay beneath the surface. Way back in college while watching *Friends* on Thursday nights, Jo and I would cuddle on the couch. I would stroke Jo's long dark locks, inhale the lavender scent, and we'd talk about which *Friend* we'd most like to get friendly with. I loved the sweet naiveté of Joey, while Chandler's humor drew her. I imagined telling her it was Rachel, but I didn't quite have the nerve.

Jo always teased me that as long as she had known me, I'd always had a boyfriend – never a dry spell. Jo, on the other hand, dated sporadically, but always boned men. Still, I picked up on something – a connection. We left the tie between us unsaid, but a feeling still lingered that if given a chance, Jo would get with me. What Jo didn't know was that even though I always had a guy in my bed, sometimes I shared him with another girl.

I first got into women when I was in college. You know, during those *experimental* years. At least, that's the excuse most hetero women who experiment give themselves. I am the girl boys fantasize about – one who subscribes to nudie magazines just for the pictures. Actually, I picked up my first skin magazine to read twenty questions with my favorite author, Anne Rice, who's also known for her dirty stories written under A.N. Roquelaure and Anne Rampling. When all the college studs I knew refused to buy a copy of the mag for me, I trekked to the store myself. And after the curious looks from the male checkers who dared to dream about the hot brunette checking out naked pics of women, I decided to send out for a subscription. The writing was interesting, the advice columns entertaining, and the chicks downright delicious: big-breasted girls-next-door gave me something to fantasize about. Once, I even glimpsed a girl from my high school. The photo spread showed her in and out of her cheerleading uniform. Boy, had that homecoming queen grown up.

My college roommate, Mary Jane, inspired my initiation into bisexuality. My first adventure came in the form of a threesome. Mary Jane and I shared the same taste in men. It wasn't an outward appearance, because they all looked different. It seemed to be more of a persona or an intellect. To think back on it, I think we dated five of the same guys but only fucked a few of those at the same time. The first threesome was with Noah, a pretty frat boy with perfectly chiseled pecs who at first didn't quite know what to do with two willing chicks. In class, we used to tease him that someday we would double-team him; what he didn't know was that we actually meant it.

We played out our promise one Friday night. After a few drinks at home, we dropped in on Noah at his apartment. The tequila hadn't gotten us drunk; it was just enough to let our guards down. Noah's housemate answered the door and, with raised eyebrows, called him downstairs. Noah was dressed in a university sweatshirt and a pair of blue shorts, sans underwear. His sandy brown hair lay damp from his evening shower.

'Can Noah come out and play?' asked Mary Jane as she laughingly clasped my hand and looked back at me. 'Or is it too late?'

When two girls dressed in flimsy T-shirts and short-shorts show up close to midnight, there's not much to say. Noah's already wide smile got wider as he led us upstairs to his bedroom. His housemate looked like he had missed the jackpot at Vegas. Noah closed the door to his bedroom, and we slowly stripped out of our clothes. My Blondie T-shirt hit the floor, and I squeezed out of my khaki shorts. Mary Jane lost her clothing, first her Gap skinny T, then her denim shorts, and we both turned toward Noah. The three of us fit comfortably in his full-sized bed. A soft, navy plaid comforter rested beneath our bodies. Like a Benetton ad, Mary Jane and I complemented each other. For her slight build, I'm busty. Her pale complexion contrasted starkly to my darker, olive complexion. Noah was not the only one who noticed the difference in our physiology. While I was getting busy with Noah, I could see Mary Jane was just as interested in my well-stocked goods.

As Noah drank in the sweet-mustiness of my mouth, I felt a smooth tongue flicker over my nipples. I opened my eyes and caught the blond fall of Mary Jane's hair as she leaned over my chest. She glanced at me – almost as if she was asking my permission – and then her warm, soft mouth surrounded my areola. I closed my eyes and sunk into the pleasure of two mouths pleasing my body. A hand traveled down my stomach, then slender fingers lightly touched my increasing wetness. I felt a mouth settle over my nether lips. I once again opened my eyes. Mary Jane's head bobbed up and down as she focused full attention toward my pussy, and the white mounds of her ass rose in the air.

Noah stopped kissing me and checked out the action between my legs. The vision must have been too much for him, because he soon planted himself behind Mary Jane and started going at her doggie-style. Each thrust of his hips pushed her tongue deeper into me until the three of us soared into oblivion.

After our extracurricular activities with Noah, Mary Jane made it a point to invite herself into my bedroom at home when I had a male visitor. Yet we were never intimate alone.

Come senior year, Mary Jane particularly liked a new guy I was dating, Chris. We had only been seeing each other for a little while. He was a friend of a friend and pitched baseball for our college team. In those days, and

I suppose today, too, being in sports upped the *cool* ante. That he threw crazy fastballs racked up even more points. He was tall and lanky with jet-black hair and a tortured soul. On the outside, he might have been a jock, but inside he was a poet. Chris would show up at my place late at night, too drunk, with his car parked more-than-slightly askew. He wasn't a pretty sight and shouldn't have been driving, but I always willingly admitted him and his hefty cock *in*. One night, Chris showed up with another player from the team, Nathan. While Chris and I macked on each other and moved upstairs, Mary Jane grabbed Nathan and, last I saw, got busy with him downstairs.

Chris knelt above me, slogging his cock into my mouth. My hands wrapped around his ass, bringing him in even further. I felt his cock grow harder and longer with each stroke, but before I could finish him off, he pulled out and turned the proverbial tables. Let me tell you, there is something to be said for nimble fingers. If those digits can make a ball hum, they can make a pussy hit a home run. Chris gave the best finger-bangs this side of Memphis. I was in my second solo when I heard my bedroom door open, and Mary Jane and Nathan slipped in.

If Chris wasn't about to complain, I certainly wasn't. When four people fill a bed, it's a matter of limbs and licking. I took Chris out of my mouth, lay on my back, and pulled him inside me so he could fuck me silly, and then Mary Jane started to fondle my breasts while Nathan kissed me wildly. Yes, for the time being, it was all about me, but soon after, we changed positions.

The evening left me sore and sated – almost, because

even then there was still one thing I had yet to do: kiss a woman. Somehow, even though we touched each other, were breast to breast and mouth to snatch, Mary Jane and I never kissed. I had shared my bed more than once with a girlfriend but still hadn't fully given myself over to a woman. That abandonment was the final frontier.

Tonight starts out pretty slow. I shrug off my work outfit – blouse, bra, skirt, hose, panties, flats – and slip into sweat shorts and a tight white tank. Around the house, I love the freedom of going braless with no panties. Who cares? June gloom had finally lifted from the California shoreline and a Baja hurricane had pushed north, leaving the air muggy warm, as though we were in New Orleans.

Turning on the television, I catch a re-run of *The One With Frank, Jr.* – when the *Friends* get to pick the five 'freebie' celebrities they could sleep with. Slowly, I nurse some homebrewed sun tea, letting the coolness of the ice melt on my tongue. The doorbell rings, and the door opens. And in walks Joanna. She always does that, not waiting for me to open the door. With the falling evening sunlight streaming in behind her, I see the outline of her curves in her olive green Michael Stars T-shirt.

'Hey, Trisha, good to see ya, girl. What's on tonight?' She sits down next to me on the couch, her thigh touching my leg, and reaches across me to take a sip from the tumbler on the side table. Her breasts brush across my arm. She turns to me with tea glistening on her lips, and I think it is now or never.

I imagine my lips on hers – the first brush, the pressure

of my hands in her hair pulling her to me. They say reality may never measure up to imagination, but I'm ready to risk it.

She smiles, as if she knows what I'm thinking. I reach around her neck and pull her face to mine. Our lips meet, and I run my tongue across her lower lip, tasting the vanilla lip gloss. Her lips feel soft and delicate.

I thrust my tongue into Joanna's mouth and tighten my grip on her long dark locks. Our tongues intertwine, circling. Joanna's darts in and out of her mouth, almost as if playing hide and seek. *Ah, she's got a quick little licker.* Her free hand reaches into my shorts, pulling out the waist, past my partly shaven pussy, her fingers cold. She drags her closely clipped nails as she slowly strokes downward and raises goose bumps on me. I know she can already feel the come dripping down my thighs. *Oh, yeah, I'll give you something to slather over that pretty little mouth.*

One finger in, and I squirm. Two fingers and the moans begin to seep out. She presses me against the arm of the couch. I want to touch her. She kneels over me now and props open my left leg with her right knee, straddling my right leg, her arm deep into my shorts and her fingers deep into my cunt. I return the favor, unlacing my fingers from her hair, pulling down her jeans, making her shift her hips to wiggle them down and off. I had always admired her hips; her tan line is smooth and straight. She drips onto my fingers, as I stroke her labia, swollen now and more than moist. With both hands I pull her lips apart. The little bit of wet resistance sticking them together releases, and she practically gushes. I work my right middle finger up inside her and hear a whimper escape from Jo's pretty mouth bound with my own. By the time I'm in three-fingers deep, Jo can barely control herself.

'How do you like that, Jo?'

She responds by firmly twirling my clit between thumb and forefinger, and I arch my back as I come. Her fingers are relentless. She keeps at it, now releasing it and thrumming around my clit, teasing it fuller, lightly pinching and then stroking into the wetness of my slit, bringing it back up to moisten my clit, off center circles around and up, around and up, and I crest again. No more. I grab her wrists and pull her away.

I sink back into the couch and draw her to me. Her body feels so slight in my arms – her weight light against me. Both of us are considered petite. I think of that term 'lipstick lesbians' and gaze at the curve of her lips once again. She smiles in return.

I'd always been afraid to *go there* because of the labels. If I'm with a woman alone, suddenly that changes me, and I've got a new label – 'lesbian.' Truth, it's not about the selection of male versus female: It's about the person. Joanna's one of the most beautiful people I know – inside and out. The fact that she wants to be with me, well, it's hard to imagine. Then again, I've been told that I'm a pretty good catch, too.

'What are you thinking about, Trish?' she asks, taking in my sudden seriousness.

If she only knew the entire truth . . . 'Kissing you,' I say, 'and how long I've wanted to do it.'

Her lips come down on mine – gentle, soft, caressing,

and I sigh into her mouth. For some reason, this act of kissing her had worried me, yet it's so natural. She tastes slightly musty now, with a hint of sweetness lingering underneath. Our kisses grow more insistent, and I once again twine my hands through her hair, and rub my knee between her legs. She grinds her pelvis against my knee.

Moving to the side, I stroke her inner thighs with feather-light touches, feeling her skin prickle beneath my fingertips. Time to reverse positions. I push her back onto the couch to pleasure her. She opens her legs wider for me, granting me full access, and I gaze at her sweet pussy.

I lean forward and breathe in her scent. Her knees rest on either side of my body, and her fingers tease my already-erect nipples. I lightly take her swollen clit within my teeth and roll it – it's what I like, and think maybe she might too – apparently she does, as she moans and grabs my head. I swirl my tongue slowly around her clit, lapping up the sweetness that flows from her and push a finger back into her pussy. A little at first, twirling as I lick her, then a bit deeper and around, and with my free hand slightly lift her butt and keep her there. I pull out my finger and she grinds her hips toward me. So I push two fingers in, deeper, and circle into her again, all the while flicking her clit with my tongue and alternately licking up and down her nether lips.

Jo moves her hips with my mouth, bucking into my face with each rolling motion, her fingers tugging at my hair, timing and pushing against my fingers and mouth. *Yeah, who needs a cock to fuck?* And, emboldened, I say it aloud, 'Who needs a cock to fuck?'

Laughing and panting, Jo says, 'Don't take your mouth off me.' She pushes me back between her legs. And as I pull apart her lips again with my fingers and insert my tongue up inside her, she whispers, 'Not you. Not me. Not now – maybe later.' I smile without relenting and suck on her clit again until I feel her tremble uncontrollably beneath each caress, her legs coming together to stave off any more unendurable pleasure.

A first kiss and more: tonight, for us, is just the beginning. Later, there's always that dildo in my bedroom . . .

Champagne

by Inara LaVey

My eyes closed as a finger gently stroked my clitoris under the silk of my g-string. I squirmed with pleasure as the finger was replaced by the soft caress of my unseen lover's tongue – long, slow strokes up and down; warm and moist as he tasted my juices and then began to probe deeper inside me. I moaned softly as it slid in and out of me, impossibly agile, pressing against my G-spot, then flicking teasingly back across the clit. My climax slowly built as my hips lifted involuntarily to increase the pressure until –

'Jeannette?'

Darryl's voice cut though my erotic fantasy like scissors through thread. Snip. All gone, just like my interrupted orgasm.

'Jeannette, are you listening?'

'Mmm. Sorry.' I surreptitiously slid my hand out from between my legs. 'I was napping.'

'Well, we're almost there, so I think you'd better freshen up your makeup, so you make a decent impression.' He gave me a critical glance. 'Your mascara is smeared.'

Not bothering with a response – Darryl wouldn't listen anyway – I retrieved my purse from the floor of the car and pulled out a compact to make the necessary repairs on my makeup.

Darryl resumed his one-sided conversation. 'Now, Roux-Dubois is one of the few houses still exclusively owned by a family,' said Darryl as we drove through yet another small village in a cluster of them connected by acres of vines. 'They're part of a long history of wine-making royalty. We're amazingly lucky to have been invited to stay with them.'

Darryl was a self-styled oenophile, enamored with wine and all the minutiae that were part of its history and manufacture. He was also boring as hell, turning our trip to France into an excruciatingly dull series of lectures. Trapped next to him in our rented Mercedes SL2 as we drove through miles of beautiful vineyard-filled countryside, there was no escaping the endless stream of wine factoids that flowed out of him. I was sick to death of hearing about *terroir*, microclimates, hills versus flat, the right soil for the right grape, the virtues of cork versus 'the controversial yet increasingly popular screw top' (yes, he actually said that). I was expected to listen to everything he said with no feedback of my own that didn't consist of wide-eyed, 'Really?' 'That's so interesting!' 'Tell me more about malolactic fermentation, please!' I faked interest, the same way I faked orgasms. He didn't notice the difference, just as he hadn't noticed me quietly masturbating in the passenger seat next to him.

We'd started our tour in Bordeaux, visiting winery after winery of Grand Cru, Premier Cru and so-so Cru growths. I watched Darryl swirl, sniff, sip, swish, chew, swallow, and sometimes spit his way through countless glasses of Bordeaux, and all I could think was that someone who spent so much time and care on all the oral and olfactory acrobatics involved in wine tasting should really be more adept at oral sex. But even in the early days of our courtship, the sight of my naked body never brought the same gleam of lust to his eyes as a glass of Chateau Margaux. The culmination of the trip was the region of Champagne-Ardennes, northeast of Paris (which we bypassed completely) near the Belgian border. This was definitely my favorite leg of the journey. Rolling hills gave way to lakes and water meadows to the south, while to the north lay dense forests and the hills of the Ardennes. I also love champagne as it doesn't involve nearly as many facial contortions on the part of the taster, and we tasted the best.

We visited Veuve Clicquot-Ponsardin, Perrier-Jouët, Mumm, Laurent-Perrier, Piper-Heidsieck, Krug, and, of course, Moët et Chandon and Louis Roederer, where, respectively, Darryl bought a case of Dom and a case of Cristal. Heady stuff for a girl from a have-some-Beringer-White-Zin background. We also went to a number of smaller champagne houses, names not as recognizable, but the bubbly just as good. I spent the days pleasantly buzzed from morning till bedtime, a condition that made sex with Darryl almost bearable.

Today, however, I was lamentably sober as I listened to Darryl wax enthusiastically about our next and final destination: the champagne house of Roux-Dubois, where we were to stay as guests of the owners for the next three days.

'. . . absolutely flawless Brut in vintage years. A bottle

of Roux-Dubois '85 is actually worth more to collectors than an '85 Dom.'

'Mmm . . .' Not much of an answer, but I was too bored to come up with my usual chipper, 'Really?' I was also nervous. For Darryl, this was the zenith of the entire trip. I'd been dreading it since we touched down on French soil.

We'd met Monsieur and Madame Roux-Dubois, both in their late thirties, a few months earlier at a dinner party in Beverly Hills. Both had that impeccably put-together look that seems to be the natural birthright of the French; the confidence and ease of manner that made the simplest of outfits look high fashion. Monsieur Roux-Dubois was tall and lanky and so charming that one didn't notice that he wasn't really handsome. He had imperfect features – crooked nose, close-set green eyes, thin lips – that somehow worked when you put them all together.

Madame Roux-Dubois, on the other hand, was gorgeous, raven hair pulled back into the kind of sleek, chic chignon that would have been harsh on anyone less feminine. Her eyes were the color of bittersweet chocolate, made up in that sexy smudged I've-just-been-fucked-six-ways-from-Sunday look that I could never emulate without looking like I'd been sucker punched. Her lipstick was the perfect shade of true red and left no discernable smudge marks on her wine glass. I'd hated her on sight.

Once Darryl had discovered their profession, he put on his most charming manner and spent the rest of the evening wooing them while I sat silently at his side, feeling as awkward and unattractive as I had on my first date in high school. And the thought of being their guests for three days, not knowing any French beyond 'hello,' 'goodbye,' 'thank you,' and 'excuse me, where's the bathroom?' intimidated the hell out of me.

Darryl took a turn down a private drive, flanked on either side by – surprise, surprise – more vineyards. We drove through an archway into an expansive courtyard where a gorgeous eighteenth-century house nestled against the side of a hill, stones mellowed with time and weather, ivy and flowered vines climbing the walls. There was another building set off to the side of the house. Darryl nodded at it. 'I'll bet that's the winery.'

The front door opened and Madame Roux-Dubois stepped outside, casually dressed in slim-fit leggings, black ballet flats, and an off-white shirt that reminded me of an artist's smock. Very Leslie Caron, simple yet classic. She looked as if she should be on a catwalk in Paris or dancing with Gene Kelly.

Darryl saw her and his face lit up. He parked the Mercedes next to a sleek classic beige Jaguar and an incongruous little Fiat sitting side by side in the sheltered drive. He was out of the car almost before he'd shut the engine off, dashing to greet the lady of the manor without a glance back to see if I was joining him. I immediately felt frumpy in my boot-cut jeans and white Gap T-shirt and wished I hadn't eaten that chocolate croissant for breakfast.

Madame Roux-Dubois held out her hand and presented her cheek for Darryl's enthusiastic kiss. Even as she did so, though, her gaze flickered past him to me. Her eyebrows lifted, and she tilted her head as if in inquiry. She said something to Darryl, who turned and gestured for me to join them. I smiled weakly and reluctantly got out of the car as Madame Roux-Dubois came over, arms outstretched, a smile of what looked like genuine pleasure on her face.

'Mademoiselle Wilson,' she said in heavily accented English, 'it is a delight to see you again!'

I was immediately suspicious. Why would she be glad to see me? I was surprised that she even remembered my name. I chalked it up to good manners and awkwardly exchanged hugs. I come from a non-demonstrative family where hugs and kisses are saved for weddings and funerals. I just couldn't get used to the European custom of kissing cheeks by way of greeting.

'Thank you for having us to stay, Madame,' I said stiffly, hating the So Cal twang of my voice in comparison to the lilt of her French accent.

'Marie-Elise, *s'il vous plait*,' she said, putting a companionable arm around my shoulders to lead me into the house. 'And I may call you Jeanette?' She smiled at Darryl over her shoulder. 'And you will bring the bags, *oui*?'

The inside of the house was as impressive as the exterior – high ceilings, nooks and crannies everywhere, all sorts of interesting architectural details, and shabby chic décor done to perfection. Exactly what you'd expect to find in the 'At Home in France' issue of *Victoria Magazine* except without the overabundance of lace, tulle and twee china figurines.

'Are you hungry?' Marie-Elise asked as we walked up a curving staircase to the second floor, Darryl trailing after us with our luggage.

I shook my head, already feeling the size of a baby

elephant next to this French sylph. 'No, not really.' My stomach immediately growled in protest.

I blushed, mortified, but Marie-Elise gave me a friendly squeeze, her arm still around my shoulders, and said, 'The body doesn't let us lie when it comes to matters of food or love. We will have lunch before we taste.' She stopped in front of an open door. 'This will be your room.'

I stepped inside a cozy room dominated by a large cherrywood sleigh bed with a matching vanity and two small bedside tables. The duvet was white cotton, and I was pretty sure it covered a goose down quilt. Like the rest of the house, the room managed to be comfortably opulent, everything with the feeling of old, yet expensive.

'This is lovely.' I set my purse on the vanity bench as Darryl came in and plunked the luggage down in the middle of a faded Oriental rug.

'I'm pleased you like it.' She opened a door next to the vanity. '*C'est la salle de bains.*'

'She means bathroom,' said Darryl. Amazing how the man managed to imbue three words with that much condescension.

'I actually know that one,' I said, annoyed.

Marie-Elise's gaze briefly went from me to Darryl, but her expression gave nothing away. 'You must be fatigued from the drive. Perhaps you would enjoy a tray of food in your room? A bath and a rest before supper?'

I smiled gratefully even as Darryl jumped in, 'Oh, we've only been on the road for a few hours. I'm sure there's no need for that.'

Again, that quick glance from me to Darryl. 'If you do

not wish to rest, Darryl, you can take your meal with us, and afterwards I will be happy to give you a tour of the grounds.' To me she said, 'I'll have a tray brought to you. Dinner will be late. It will be a special evening, and you will enjoy it more if you're rested.'

And Daryl will enjoy himself more if he has you to himself, I thought as I ran bathwater in a tub large enough to fit a family of four. Not that I cared at this point. I was happy to soak in geranium- and sandalwood-scented water, covered up to my breasts in bubbles like a character in a Doris Day movie, and have some time all alone without Darryl's constant monologue. For whatever reason, our hostess was more thoughtful than I'd expected after the party in Beverly Hills. Maybe I wouldn't feel so out of place for the next three days after all, although I still felt incredibly gauche in comparison to Marie-Elise's sleek confidence.

I shut my eyes and sighed in contentment.

'*Excusez-moi.*' I looked up, startled, to see Marie-Elise standing by the bathroom door, which I hadn't bothered to close. She was balancing a tray laden with food. 'You do not mind if I set this down for you?' She indicated the ledge around the bathtub.

'Uh, no, I don't mind.' I slid a little further into the water until the bubbles reached my neck. She placed the tray within easy reaching distance. There was fresh bread, a slice of brie, butter, pâté, sliced peaches, and strawberries, as well as a full champagne flute.

'This looks delicious, thank you.' Another piece of my initial reserve slipped away in the face of Marie-Elise's thoughtfulness.

'It's what we're having downstairs,' she said matter-of-factly. 'I wouldn't want you to miss anything just because you're tired. Men do not always understand a woman's needs, and so we take care of one another.' She reached out and brushed a strand of hair back from my forehead, a gesture that took me by surprise, yet seemed quite natural. '*Appréciez-vous, ma chere.* I will see you at dinner.'

Alone once more, I picked up the champagne flute and held it to a ray of light filtering through the curtained window. Something Darryl had said came to mind: the smaller and more numerous the bubbles, the better the champagne. If that were true, this must be high quality, judging by the dozens of tiny bubbles streaming up through the pale gold liquid. I took a sip and tasted almonds and peaches, a creamy mouthful of ambrosia.

I could get used to this.

By the time I finished eating and got out of the bath, it was all I could do to dry off and crawl into bed, which proved to have not only goose feather quilt and pillows, but a down mattress as well. It was like sinking into a cloud, and I was asleep within minutes. Being surrounded by all that goose down, it wasn't surprising that I dreamed of feathers, or more specifically, feather light touches up and down my body, soft and sure along the curve of my spine, neck, arms and shoulders. There were bubbles in my dream too, tiny bubbles, like the silly Don Ho song. But these bubbles were inside me, a stream of sensations that centered between my legs and spread their warmth outwards. But they had no where to go, no point of release, so the sensation dissipated, leaving me vaguely dissatisfied when I woke up, my usual state whenever I had an erotic dream. Truth be told, I could never quite let go of my control enough either awake or asleep to feel that all-encompassing sensation of release that the French called *le petit mort*, another of the few French phrases I was familiar with.

I was lying mostly on top of the covers, one leg tucked underneath, but the rest of me was naked for the world to see had anyone chosen to come into the room while I slept. And when I saw that my clothes had been put away in the armoire, it was obvious somebody had. My first guess was Darryl, except he wouldn't have had the consideration to unpack my things. There was probably a maid or housekeeper, and I suppressed my initial embarrassment by remembering that Europeans didn't regard nudity with the American puritanical blend of prudery and *aren't-I-being-naughty-for-looking-at-this?* I hoped I hadn't snored, or worse, that the type of dreams I'd been having hadn't been obvious.

I looked at the clock and was shocked to see I'd slept for more than four hours. The sun had set, and it had to be close to dinnertime. Daryl had warned me earlier to dress for dinner, so I put on an ankle-length red silk velvet dress with a burned-out pattern of leaves. I'd brought it with me because I could crumple it into a ball, stuff it into a suitcase, and it would fall out into unwrinkled folds. The color and bias cut were flattering to both my figure and my coloring, and I found myself wanting to look my best. The only remedy for a disastrous case of bed-head was to sweep my hair up and back into a butterfly clip, but I wasn't displeased with the result. A quick spritz of Angel perfume, and I was ready to join Darryl and the Roux-Duboises.

I made my way downstairs and found Darryl on his way to fetch me. He was already dressed for dinner in one of his Italian suits. 'You look nice,' I said honestly.

His only comment on my appearance was, 'Good, you didn't wear jeans.' And then, 'Marie-Elise and Amaury are waiting for us in the dining room.' He walked away.

I trailed behind him, suddenly uncertain. Was I dressed inappropriately?

Once I saw the Roux-Duboises, my dress code apprehensions evaporated. Marie-Elise wore a simple sheath dress made of raw silk in a rich chocolate shade that matched her eyes, while Amaury had on a suit that managed to appear casual and yet extravagantly expensive at the same time. Both of them stood when I entered the dining room. Amaury strode across to greet me with a warm hug and the inevitable kiss on both cheeks. He was as unconventionally handsome as I remembered, and the admiration in his eyes was a balm to my ego after Darryl's dismissal of my efforts.

'Jeanette, *vous êtes exquisite*!' He turned to Marie-Elise. '*Ne semble-t-elle pas belle, ma cher*?'

Marie-Elise nodded. 'Very beautiful.' She joined us, touched my face lightly. 'Ah, the rest, it was good for you. You look rejuvenated.'

I smiled, grateful for the kind words. Amaury offered me his arm. 'Let me show you to your seat.'

Darryl, hovering next to Marie-Elise, immediately

proffered his arm to her. She cast me an amused, almost conspiratorial glance and allowed him to lead her to the dining room table, a massive thing that would have looked at home in a medieval castle's dining hall. It almost dwarfed the room, but like everything else the house, somehow managed to be precisely where it should be.

If my lunchtime snack had been delicious, dinner was an amazing culinary experience. Each course – and there were six of them – was matched with a different wine or champagne that complemented the dish to perfection. Everything was served in small, exquisitely presented portions that left one sated but not overly full. For the first time I truly appreciated the art of food and wine, perhaps because it was presented as a gift to be experienced rather than served to me as a lecture.

Now and again I would surprise myself and realize what a good time I was having – nothing like the social purgatory I'd been dreading. Not once did I feel excluded from the conversation. Indeed, the only person who seemed determined to converse exclusively in French was Darryl. Marie-Elise and Amaury, using a mixture of the two languages, would lead the conversation back into English so seamlessly that Darryl had no idea he was being manipulated.

I found myself enjoying the whole game of wine tasting as both Roux-Duboises gazed at me eagerly to see what aromas I could pick out, what flavors I detected, how each wine tasted differently when paired with food. Darryl seemed almost jealous of the attention I was receiving even though he was getting his share of it as well. 'Jeanette doesn't really understand the complexities of wine,' he said at one point, with a laugh meant to dismiss me in an affectionate yet belittling, isn't-she-cute sort of way.

'Then we will enjoy teaching her,' said Amaury, pouring me another taste of Burgundy matched with duck and sausage *casoulet*.

'I think she has an *affinité* for these things.' Marie-Elise smiled at me from across the table.

It was impossible not to relax and blossom under such a heady combination of rich food, excellent wine and attention. By the time we'd come to the dessert course, white chocolate mousse paired with a champagne tasting of lemons and vanilla, I was chatting volubly about anything and everything and thought our host and hostess were the most charming, fascinating people I'd ever met.

'Do you like this champagne?' Marie-Elise held up her flute and watched the streams of bubbles as they raced upwards.

I nodded. 'It's lighter than the one I had at lunch. This one's not as . . . as creamy in the mouth.'

'That's called 'mouth feel,' Jeanette.' Darryl put in his two cents.

Amaury nodded. 'They're two different styles. The one you had earlier was a Blanc de Noir, made entirely of pinot noir grapes. This is a Blanc de Blanc, which is one hundred percent Chardonnay and, as you said, much lighter.'

'They're both delicious.' I took another sip of the Blanc de Blanc and examined the crystal flute. 'Why do you use these glasses? What about the ones that are more . . .' I shaped my hands like a bowl, unable to think of the word I wanted. 'You know, the ones they used in old movies.'

'Ah, the champagne *coupe*.' Marie-Elise got up from the table, went to an antique china cabinet and brought back a shallow, saucer-shaped glass. 'Like this?'

I nodded.

'This has always been popular throughout history because it's pretty, but it's not meant to show champagne at its best. These,' she indicated the flutes, 'are designed to enhance the flow of bubbles and concentrate the aromas of the wine.'

Amaury nodded and took up the story. 'The original *coupe* is said to have been modeled by Sèvres from the breasts of Marie Antoinette. She was said to have the perfect bosom.'

I listened in fascination. How much more interesting was all of this trivia when told in delightfully accented and animated voices as opposed to Darryl's condescending monotone.

Marie-Elise took over again. 'Four white bowls were made and adorned the Queen's dairy temple at the Château de Rambouillet near Versailles. The dairy is still in existence today, as is one of the *coupes*.' She set the *coupe* on the table and turned to her husband. 'Amaury, I think it is time to open one of the '85 Bruts.'

I thought Darryl's eyes would pop out of his head and remembered the comment he'd made on the drive here about the value of the Roux-Dubois '85. I wondered why they'd be willing to open a bottle of what sounded like the equivalent of liquid gold for one visiting American wine enthusiast and his girlfriend.

'An excellent idea.' Amaury started to get to his feet, but Marie-Elise shook her head.

'*Je l'obtiendrai.* I can show Jeanette the *caverne.*' She turned to me and said, 'Our champagne cellars are dug out of the side of the hills. It is not as spectacular as the caves under Reims or Epernay, but we are very proud of our cellars.'

'*Est-ce que je dois aller avec toi?*' Amaury raised an eyebrow and looked at his wife. She smiled at him and shook her head.

'*Non cette fois. C'est mon tour, amour.*'

'Ah. *C'est bon.*' Amaury turned to Darryl. 'We shall fetch the champagne bucket and ice, perhaps step outside and enjoy a cigar and some brandy while the ladies do some exploring and bring back the champagne.'

I could tell Darryl was a little disappointed to be deprived of an excursion into the cellars with Mari-Elise, but brandy and cigars were a good consolation prize. I wasn't sure if I was up to a trip down or up any stairs after the amount of wine we'd already consumed, but I was genuinely intrigued to see the cave. And a small, childish part of me liked the fact that I would see and perhaps even touch the precious '85 Brut before Darryl.

I stood as Marie-Elise topped off our flutes with more of the Blanc de Blanc. I was pleased to find that while I definitely felt the affects of the alcohol, I was steady on my feet, even in my heels. I was still in control of my own personal Enterprise here.

She led me through a door at the end of the dining room, down a small hallway and through yet another door, a thick wooden one with iron hinges, opening onto the top of gently curving stone stairs. The light at the top of the landing was dim with nothing but blackness below, and I clutched the iron railing, wondering how I'd navigate the stairs without spilling my champagne. Marie-Elise, a few steps ahead of me, turned and gave me a mischievous grin that replaced the sophisticated woman with a fifteen-year-old schoolgirl. 'Drink some now and lose less to the floor.' She took a hefty swig of her champagne.

I laughed and followed suit. 'You read my mind.'

Marie-Elise smiled again. 'Ah, but can you read mine?' With that, she descended the stairs into darkness.

The further down we went, the more the temperature dropped and the dim light faded into inky shadows. I felt like a gothic heroine, going to explore the forbidden cellar against her own better judgment. I followed close behind Marie-Elise, catching the wafting scent of vanilla from her perfume. I liked it for the same reason I like Angel; with its honey and vanilla notes, it smelled like something I'd want to have for dessert. It was pitch black at the bottom of those stairs, and I bumped into Marie-Elise when she abruptly stopped. Champagne sloshed over my flute and spilled onto my fingers.

'Oh, I'm sorry!'

'No, I should have warned you that I was stopping.'

There was a small click, and light illuminated the first twenty feet of the room, which was better described as a subterranean cavern. The roof arched high above us, wooden supports following the curve of the ceiling. Racks upon racks of emerald green champagne bottles stretched as far as the eye could see back into the shadowed recesses.

'Wow.'

'Yes.' Marie-Elise nodded complacently, the Roux-Dubois legacy spread out before us. 'It goes back a quarter of a mile under the hills.'

I licked the spilled champagne from my fingers as I stared at the sea of bottles. 'It's like Aladdin's cave.'

'There is certainly treasure to be found here.' Something in her tone pulled my attention back to my hostess, who was watching me with an unreadable expression as I licked my fingers. I hastily stopped what I was doing, wondering if I'd inadvertently committed some unforgivable breach of French etiquette. But no, she didn't look angry. If anything, she looked – almost *hungry*.

'The truly wonderful thing about champagne,' Marie Elise took my hand in hers. 'is that it goes with almost everything.' She lifted my hand to her mouth and kissed it, her gaze never leaving mine.

The air seemed suddenly thicker, and I felt warm despite the cool temperature of the cellars.

'Do you know how champagne is made?' She let go of my hand with an abruptness that was as disconcerting as that brief kiss had been and walked over to the nearest rack.

'Um . . . well, Darryl tried to explain it, but – '

' – But you didn't really listen because he is boring, *n'est pas*?'

That startled a laugh out of me.

'Enthusiasts are often tedious,' she continued. 'When

one develops an enthusiasm, one can either inspire others by sharing this passion or push them away by being tedious. Listening to Darryl, I think he is one of the second types.'

I surprised myself by asking, 'If he's so boring, why did you invite him to visit you?' The champagne was having more of an effect than I'd thought.

She gave me an amused smile. 'What makes you assume that it was Darryl we wanted to have as our guest?'

'Well, I . . . I . . .'

Marie-Elise laughed at my expression. 'Now it is not so boring if one already has that same interest, as both Amaury and I do. But it's easy to see that Darryl has not yet discovered there is more pleasure in building the desire in another to learn than there is in thinking oneself. . .' She paused, searching for the right word, '*supérieur*.'

She'd hit that one right on the nose, I thought.

'Now Amaury and myself? We are much more interested in sharing our passions through experience rather than lecturing. *Par exemple*.'

She went over to a refrigerator behind a rough wooden bar and pulled out a half-bottle of champagne. 'This is our demi-sec, a sweeter style than the other two. I am very pleased with it. Try a taste.'

I looked dubiously at my half-full flute. 'I still have some of the other left.'

'*C'est facile*.' She drained her glass and poured some of the demi-sec. 'We will share.' She took a sip and held the flute out to me. Still holding the other glass, I took it and tried a small taste. Flavors of honey and apricots sparkled in the bubbles. It was delicious. I took another sip, more this time, and handed the flute back to Marie-Elise. She wrapped her fingers around both my fingers and the flute, holding my hand around the glass as she lifted it to her lips.

Her touch sent an unexpected frisson of warmth through my body, something about the firm grasp of her hand around mine. There was strength in those well-manicured fingers that made me wonder if I could pull away. Maybe it was the champagne, but I liked the idea that perhaps I couldn't. My face flushed with heat at the thought.

She gently stroked the back of my hand as she drank, a light butterfly touch that raised goose bumps all over my body. 'Here.' She lifted the glass to my lips and tilted it so a stream of champagne poured into my mouth. I swallowed, and she withdrew the glass, but not quickly enough. A few drops of champagne trickled from my lips down my chin, dripping onto the exposed flesh of my breasts.

'One thing we cannot allow with Roux-Dubois champagne,' Marie-Elise murmured in a tone as rich and decadent as chocolate mousse, 'is waste it.' Still holding my hand, she dipped her head to my chest and slowly licked the trail of champagne from my skin, moving from my cleavage up to my neck, her hair falling in a veil across her face as she did so.

My breathing quickened and my nipples stiffened in response as she gently nipped the base of my neck. I tried to draw back, afraid of the sensation that coursed through me at the touch of Marie-Elise's tongue on my flesh but found myself backed up against the wooden bar with no place to retreat. I felt her lips curve in a smile against my skin before her mouth resumed its leisurely path up to my mouth.

'*Je veux t'embrasser*.' Her voice caressed me as she traced the outline of my lips with the tip of her tongue. She kissed me then, a firm yet gentle kiss that tasted as sweet and intoxicating as the champagne. I felt her remove the butterfly clip and entwine her fingers in my hair, pulling my head back with a slight tug that made me gasp even as she increased the pressure of the kiss, her tongue like warm velvet against mine. Warmth coiled lazily in my stomach and spread throughout all erogenous zones.

My free hand involuntarily loosened its grasp on the other champagne flute, which slipped from my fingers before I realized what had happened. It hit the ground and shattered. Marie-Elise withdrew her mouth from mine and made a *tsk-tsk* sound. 'What did I say about waste, *ma cherie*?'

I started to apologize, but she quickly kissed me again, nipping gently at my bottom lip as she gave my hair another sharp tug. 'Shh. Don't worry . . . I will think of a way for you to pay for that.' Another kiss. She knew exactly how to use her teeth and tongue to elicit a response, not too hard, not too soft – just right.

'*Déshabille-toi*,' she whispered, her lips moving to my ear and sending another jolt of electricity through my body. She nipped my earlobe and repeated, sharply this time, '*Déshabille-toi*.'

I looked at her in confusion.

Marie-Elise gave a small laugh. 'Ah, I forget you don't speak French. Another thing to teach you.' She kissed me one more time, then stepped back, releasing both my hands and my hair. 'Take off your clothes, Jeanette.'

'What?'

'Now I know you understand English, *ma cherie*.'

'But – '

' – Take off your clothes.'

We stared at each other, the air between us crackling with sexual chemistry. I knew that if I acquiesced, I would be giving up control to this woman I barely knew. Common sense, and an upbringing by the equivalent of June Cleaver, told me to go back upstairs, plead a headache and go to my room for the evening. I knew if I chose this path Marie-Elise would say nothing to reproach act and me as if nothing had happened between us. But there was part of me – the part that was wet with desire and wild with curiosity – that urged me to give into the moment and do what Marie-Elise commanded.

I made my decision.

Setting down the remaining flute, I slowly pulled my dress over my head and dropped it to the ground, leaving a black Victoria's Secret Miracle Bra, matching g-string and heels. Marie-Elise's eyes darkened with desire, and she licked her lips as if contemplating a rich dessert.

'*Très bon*. Now stand very still.' She reached behind me and unhooked the bra in one deft movement only another woman could manage, then smoothly took it off. I shivered, both from the cool air on my skin and the heat of Marie-Elise's gaze. She gently traced a circle around each nipple before cupping my breasts – smaller without the miracle of Victoria's Secret – in her hands.

'You would have made a fine model for the champagne *coupe*.'

The g-string was next. She slid them down oh-so-slowly, her fingers caressing my legs as she did so. I lifted my feet one at a time and the g-string joined the bra on the floor with my dress.

'I want you to hold this.' Marie-Elise handed me the champagne flute as she leaned in and kissed me again. 'And you must not spill any. *Comprenez-toi*?' I nodded, hypnotized by her voice and the taste and feel of her lips against mine. '*Bon*.'

She dipped a finger in the glass. '*Goûtez-le*.' She brushed my mouth with her finger, inviting me to taste. I licked champagne from her fingertip, then caught my breath as she inserted it further into my mouth. Without thinking, I sucked on it, using teeth and tongue as if I were pleasuring a man. She made a noise almost like a little purr, withdrew her finger far enough to hold my mouth open as she kissed me fiercely, capturing my tongue with hers. I kissed her back, marveling at how well she knew what buttons to push, just the right amount of pressure on the lips, how her tongue caressed instead of intruded, the subtle movement of her other hand on the back of my neck hitting nerve endings I didn't know I had.

My knees were weak when she finally ended the kiss, murmuring, '*Tou goûtez comme le miel et l'épice*.' I wasn't sure what she said, but it didn't matter. She could have said, 'Come, let us go wash dishes,' and it would have had the same effect.

'And now I shall teach you a little about champagne.'

Marie-Elise dipped into the flute again, this time tracing a line of liquid around each of my breasts. 'After the grapes are pressed, the wine must age and go through first fermentation . . . ah, I said not to move.'

I tried to obey as her finger spiraled in ever decreasing circles until each nipple was anointed with champagne. My breathing becamc faster as she slowly began to follow the path of the liquid with her tongue. She took her time to reach my nipples, pausing now and again to continue the lesson. 'Before it is fully fermented in the barrels . . .' She encircled the aureole of my right breast with her tongue, her breath warm and teasing against the nipple. 'The wine goes into bottles that are then sealed with caps.' A light flick of the tongue against the nipple that I felt all the way down between my legs. A sharp tap against my bare thigh reminded me to hold still.

'The bottles are laid on their sides in racks to allow the *levure* . . . the yeast . . . to grow. It is what will allow the bubbles to form inside the bottle.' Her mouth closed around the nipple and it was by sheer force of will that I didn't move. There was something incredibly erotic about having to stand still while Marie-Elise teased me with her teeth and tongue; it focused my entire consciousness on the sensations coursing through me.

She ran the nails of one hand lightly down the small of my back, along the curve of my ass and hip, around and up between my legs. 'The *levure* dies before the champagne is ready.' She turned her attention to my other breast. 'It is called the lees and must be gotten rid of.' I gasped as she slowly slid a finger inside me. 'Mm, *tu mouilles*.' She pressed her hand against me, and I involuntarily arched forward, coming dangerously close to spilling the champagne. 'Be still.' She pressed harder and inserted another finger. My free hand opened and closed of its own volition as I made the rest of my body stay motionless.

'We get rid of the lees by what is called *remuage*,' whispered Marie-Elise against my breast as her fingers began to move inside me, and she stroked my clitoris with her thumb. 'The bottles are gently manipulated . . . turned and tilted on the rack, so that the lees collects in the neck. They are then ready for *dégorgément*.' She drove her fingers in deeper, moving them slowly as she continued to move her thumb in a gentle circle. My hips began to move of their own accord, and this time Marie-Elise didn't admonish me, but continued her ministrations with a gentle, steady rhythm as she took her mouth away from my breasts and drizzled champagne down my stomach.

'Traditionally a man with very large thumbs would remove the cap and let out just enough wine to dispose of the lees.' Her mouth followed the trickle of champagne down to my navel. 'Then sugar, and sometimes brandy, is added. This is the dosage and determines if the champagne will be dry or sweet.' Her mouth moved lower. 'The cork is put in and the champagne will age for at least two years . . . sometimes more. And all this time . . . the pressure continues to build . . .'

My breaths started to come in rapid, shallow gasps as the coil of heat in my stomach expanded, tiny bubbles of sensation rising through me as Marie-Elise's fingers increased their pressure and speed inside me.

'It is only when the cork is removed that the pressure is finally released . . .' With that, she removed her hand and replaced it with her mouth, licking me slowly and deliberately before suddenly plunging her tongue deep inside me. My hand contracted around the flute, and I cried out, hips bucking, bubbles of sensation filling my mind and body as I arched against her mouth in wave after wave of shuddering pleasure that seemed to go on forever.

I thought I might pass out, but Marie-Elise's arms kept me upright as her mouth retraced its path up my body. She held me until my breathing slowed, kissed me slowly, gently and murmured French endearments in my ear. I tasted myself on her lips and tongue, a tangy sweet, musky flavor and found myself wondering how she would taste down there.

Marie-Elise gave a sudden chuckle. 'Such a good girl . . . not a drop spilled.'

I looked down and sure enough, I was still holding the champagne flute upright. I was surprised the glass hadn't shattered in my hand when I'd come. I offered some to Marie-Elise, then finished the remaining champagne in one gulp.

Marie-Elise helped me back into my clothes, and we went back upstairs, making a brief stop to refresh our makeup before rejoining Amaury and Darryl in the dining room. My brief fear that Darryl would know what I'd been doing was quickly banished. Darryl's entire attention was focused on the bottle of '85.

Amaury, on the other hand, gave his wife a knowing

smile. 'Did you forget where we store the champagne, *ma amour*?'

Marie-Elise went to her husband's side and planted a kiss on the top of his head. 'Ah, but Amaury, you know that the fun is in the exploration.'

'True. So perhaps next time you ladies will allow me to join you.'

'Would you like that, Jeanette?' Marie-Elise stood next to her husband and looked at me. 'There is much still for you to learn about champagne.'

Darryl gave a laugh. 'Don't get your hopes up, Marie-Elise. Jeanette's not very interested in wine.'

'That all depends on the teachers,' I said and crossed over to join the Roux-Duboisrs. Marie-Elise kissed my cheek.

'And I promise you, Amaury,' she said, putting an arm around my waist, 'Jeanette will make a very good student. Now shall we open the '85?'

Get Thee To A Nunnery

by Samantha Jones

I get back to the dorm just after midnight. Regina's in bed reading. She reads a lot, mostly philosophy and social science, which she's studying while I toy with journalism. Regina is a serious scholar. I'm a serious party girl.

'Have a good time?'

'Okay. First date. Went to dinner, then his apartment.' I pull off my dress. 'Nice guy but much more a sprinter than a long-distance runner.'

Regina laughs. 'I guess that means the sex wasn't so good.'

'It started okay, then he just climbed on top and shoved it in and out and came before I was really into it. Then he said he had to get up early to study, so would I mind leaving? Typical man!'

Regina echoes, 'Men!' and giggles.

I slip off my bra, leaving the usual red, heavy-breast, strap marks on my shoulders. 'He wants me to meet his sister. What do you think that means?' While I rub the marks, Regina watches my swaying breasts.

'Probably a threesome.'

'But with his *sister*?'

'You know what guys are like.'

I put bra and panties in the laundry basket, pull on an

old T-shirt and go to the bathroom to prepare for bed. Back in the bedroom Regina has put her book away and turned off her reading lamp. In the moonlight, she watches me from the other side of the room as I climb into bed.

'Good night.' I pull up the covers, snuggle in, and one hand automatically goes down between my thighs. I'm still wet which means he turned me on more than I'd realized. Goddamn ignorant, selfish men!

My fantasy about taking on an entire hockey team in their dressing room after a game creeps into my mind and a finger touches my clitoris. *I'm naked in the team's shower room, surrounded by a dozen hard, hungry men with enormous erections. They kiss me . . . rub soap over my heavy breasts, between my spread thighs . . . want me more than life itself. Steamy water runs down hard chests and bellies . . . off urgent cocks . . .*

Regina's voice interrupts my fantasy. 'Hey, honey, can I ask you a question?'

I'm pissed. I want to come before I sleep and this is no time to chat with my roomie. But we've only been sharing for a week, and I don't want to seem rude. Also, I don't know her well enough to suggest that she let me finish masturbating before we have our girlish chat. 'If you must.'

'Will you introduce me to some of your boyfriends?'

'Of course. But you're almost twenty. Why don't you find your own?'

'Don't know how to flirt . . . never been with a man . . . wouldn't know what to do.'

I try to be reassuring. 'I promise you it comes naturally. Just lie back and open your legs, and he'll do all the work.

We'll talk tomorrow.' My finger has a mind of its own and goes back to caressing my clitoris.

Regina's voice is soft, scared. 'I don't even know if I'm heterosexual. How do you know *you* are?'

I chuckle. 'You just know. Like, you know by whom you watch and want to be close to when you're a little girl and later, when you're a woman, in a bar or restaurant or in the street. Is it boys or girls, men or women who make you feel funny when you look at them and they look at you? As much as anything, it's what you see in their eyes when you look deep. Are their eyes open to you? Can you see inside? If you can, and they can see inside you, that's how you know. It's eye access and the feel funny factor.' Suddenly I'm awake and curious. 'You're really still a virgin?'

'Oh, yes.' Long pause. 'Except for the convent, I guess.'

'How do you mean?'

'You really want to know?'

'Only if you really want to tell me.'

'Okay.' Her voice is soft. 'My dad's rich, and my parents didn't get along, so they sent me off to convents for schooling. Probably so they could fight in peace. Anyway, I was at a new convent for my last two years of high school.

'One of the first things I heard from the other girls – the girls in my class – was that the prefects liked to play with them after lights out. I didn't even know what that meant and none of the girls would tell me. You wouldn't believe how ignorant I was.'

I interrupt, 'What's a prefect?'

'Sorry. She's a senior girl given authority by the nuns to be in charge of younger girls in almost everything outside the classroom. Prefects are goddesses . . . have an awful lot of power.'

'Were you scared?'

'I suppose so . . . but I didn't really know what I was scared of. All I knew was once or twice a week, one of the prefects came into our dormitory after lights out and took some of the girls away for what the girls called 'playtime.' It was hours before they came back. Seems everyone knew what happened to them while they were away in playtime . . . everyone except me.

'For a couple of weeks after I got there, it was always other girls. I started to think maybe the prefects didn't like me. Maybe there was something wrong with me. Then, one night, a prefect came into the dormitory and stopped by my bed. She said I was to follow her. The head prefect wanted to see me.'

This is exciting. 'So what happens?'

'I'm feeling lonely. Can I come over to your bed? Then I'll tell you?'

I hesitate. 'If you want . . .'

Regina gets out of her bed, her slim body gleaming white in the moonlight, slips into my bed and lies down next to me. Our arms and hips touch. She's naked. I hadn't expected this.

She sniffs. 'You smell of sweat. And there's something on your boobs.'

'Oh shit.' I check my boobs. There's semen all over my nipples. 'Sorry. He decided to come on my boobs for some reason . . . thought I'd washed it off back at his place. Go on, please.'

'Only if you let me clean you up.'

'Okay,' I agree, without thinking.

Regina pulls my T-shirt up and before I can stop her, lowers her head to my breasts. Like a mother cat she licks the semen up, paying particular attention to my nipples, which harden under her lips and tongue.

'Jesus, Regina . . . I didn't think . . .'

She grins. 'Tell me you don't like that! It's sexy, right? Tell the truth.'

'Okay, I liked it. And thank you. Anyone ever tell you you're really weird?' I can almost hear her smile lying next to me in my bed. 'Now will you get on with the goddamn story?'

'When the prefect came for me, I put on my robe and followed her. I was terrified. Prefects didn't have to live in big dormitories like the rest of us . . . there were only three of them to a room, not thirty like us.'

Regina licks my ear. It feels rather nice.

'Anyway, when I got there it was dark, and they were all lounging on the beds . . . six of them on three beds. All in nightdresses. Really sexy, lacy, filmy stuff . . . like the rest of us weren't allowed to wear. They looked like those pin-ups you see in old magazines. I felt silly because I was wearing this respectable robe and regulation flannel nightie hemmed in pink roses like a little girl, and they all looked so grown-up.'

Regina's fingers tiptoe down my belly. It feels good, so I let them get all the way to my groin before I remember she's not a guy and push her hand away.

'Stop it, Regina. I'm not that sort of girl.'

'You don't like that? Tell the truth.'

I giggle. 'Have I screamed yet?'

She kisses me lightly on the cheek. I don't want to seem unfriendly, so I put an arm around her shoulders and stroke her hair, which is soft and silky even though she keeps it short. 'Don't get any ideas. But go on. This is really sexy.'

Regina's voice is soft. 'The head prefect told me to sit on the bed next to her. She was a really big girl in a filmy, shortie nightie, which showed her big boobs, and I could see her nipples underneath. I couldn't take my eyes off her nipples. She asked me how I liked the school. I gave her the answer she wanted; told her I like it a lot. She asked if I'd made lots of friends. I lied, told her yes. She asked what I thought of boys, and I told her I thought they were kinda scary, but I didn't actually know any.'

Regina's hand slides down my belly again. It's not intruding and feels natural, so this time I let it stay, even open my thighs a little to accommodate her. But I'm certainly no lesbian, and this is as far as I'm going.

'The head prefect said she hoped I'd be happy at the convent, and I was very pretty, and had a lovely body. Then she told me to take my robe off and drop my nightie so everyone could see my lovely body. I was so embarrassed, told her my boobs were still very small. She laughed and said she had enough for both of us. I looked around the room and all the other prefects were staring at me.'

One of Regina's fingers finds my clitoris and I jump. 'Don't.'

But she's gentle, and I'm already wet and hot and it

feels good, so I don't push her away. *But seriously*, I tell myself, *no further than this*.

'I knew I didn't really have a choice. The prefects had all the power. Besides, it was exciting being with all these big, powerful girls . . . the prefects who really ran the school. So I took off my robe and nightie so they could see me naked even though I was still embarrassed by my little breasts, even smaller then than they are now, if you can believe that.'

She pauses, her finger slips from my clitoris inside my pussy and back. 'You're still wet. Did he do this for you?'

'Who? What?'

'Your date. Play with your clit.'

'No . . . I guess he was in a hurry.'

'Do you like it?'

'Of course I like it. But don't expect anything more.'

She grins. Her teeth flash white in the moonlight. 'Of course not. And you can stop me whenever you want. All you have to do is scream, honey.'

Regina turns on her side and half sits up. One hand pushes my thighs wider apart; her tongue licks under both breasts, moves up to flick my nipples. 'I wish I had big breasts like yours.' One by one she takes my nipples in her mouth and sucks, making little squealing sounds like a baby eating.

This is nothing like messing around with boys and men who are always rough and in a hurry and seem to think the harder they rub my clitoris, the sooner I'll let them get their cocks in me. Sometimes I've had to fuck before I was ready just to stop some guy from attacking my clitoris like he was trying to rub it off.

Regina is gentle, knowing, patient. I close my eyes, and my body responds to her hand and mouth by joining her rhythm. 'Oh yes . . . go on,' I tell her. 'What happens next? That's nice . . . but nothing else . . .'

Her head comes back to share my pillow. Her voice is far away. 'The head prefect touched my nipples like this . . . and they got hard . . . hard like yours now. You want to know something? I liked it when she touched my nipples . . . then she licked them. I really, really liked it . . . it seemed so natural.' She whispers now. 'She asked if I wanted to see her naked and before I could answer she pulled her nightie off over her head. Her breasts were huge and beautiful, like yours. Each nipple and areola bigger than one of my breasts. And they were only inches from my face. Her nipples fascinated me. She asked if I was a virgin, and I told her I'd never even kissed a boy . . . never had a boyfriend. She asked if I'd ever licked a girl's nipples. I told her no. She asked if I'd like to lick hers.

'The funny thing is I *wanted* to lick them. I *wanted* to suck them. I really, really wanted to. I didn't *have* to. I wanted to. The next thing I knew, I was holding this lovely soft breast in my hands . . . just like yours, sucking on her nipple, and she was moaning and one of the other girls sat down on the bed next to me and put her hand up my nightie, first on my tummy, then between my legs. I was so ignorant . . . didn't know what to do so at first I kept my legs closed, then I opened up for her, because I wanted to . . . because I *wanted* to.'

Somehow it seems rude that Regina's having to do all the work, so I cup her little breasts with their hard, puffy nipples in my hand, one after the other. She whispers, 'That's nice.' Her fingers slip and slide delicately around my clitoris. I groan, tell Regina, 'That's what he should have done for me. The bastard.'

She giggles. 'Too late! Anyway, I ended up lying on my back on the head prefect's lap, her breasts hanging over me, and I held her breasts and licked them and sucked her nipples . . . while the other prefect played with my pussy.'

Regina slips a second, then a third finger inside me, and I groan again, angle my hips for her. It doesn't matter any more that she's a girl. All that matters is that she's making me feel good.

'Oh, that's nice . . . so what happens?'

She laughs. 'What do you think? They've got this pretty, innocent little girl who liked to suck tit. Didn't have to be persuaded or threatened. Liked it. So now they wanted to find out if I liked pussy too. Someone turned me over so I was on my knees and my head was in the head prefect's lap. She opened her thighs so her pussy was right there in front of my face. That's when the head prefect told me to lick her. So I put my tongue out and licked her – shyly at first because I really didn't know what I was doing, then with more and more enthusiasm. I wanted to . . . it felt incredibly natural, and it tasted quite lovely.'

I take Regina's nipple in my mouth, run my tongue around it. 'Did you really like it? I mean, like it a lot?'

'I loved it. I'd never even masturbated and there I was having all these incredible feelings with all these powerful older girls. I loved it.'

Her fingers circle my clitoris. I feel the beginning of an

orgasm somewhere way in the background, sparked as much by Regina's story as by her caresses. I'm breathless. 'Go on.'

'I got so excited, so horny. I went down on every one of them that night. One after the other. I was on my knees sucking pussy and boob, pussy and boob and they sucked me and slid fingers in my pussy. Sometimes I didn't know who was doing what to me. We kept going until long after midnight. I even had my first orgasm. First ever . . . and I adored it.'

Regina moves her fingers faster and faster around my clitoris, slides in and out of my pussy. It feels incredibly natural, like she really knows how to love the female body. My arm around her shoulder pulls her towards me. '*Yes . . . that's it . . . yes . . . oh yes . . . .*' My body tightens and a mini-orgasm grinds out of my belly and floods over me.

Neither of us speaks until Regina murmurs, 'It was the first time I'd been really happy in years . . .'

As if it has a mind of its own, my hand leaves her little breasts, slides down her body to her groin. 'That was wonderful, but go on . . . please go on . . .' She opens for me. It's the first time I've ever touched another girl between the legs, and I'm surprised by how wet she is already and how her clitoris is so hard and bigger than mine, like a tiny cock. I guess it'd had a lot of convent attention over the years.

'After that they sent for me almost every night. Sometimes alone, sometimes with other girls. Two or three of us girls did exhibitions for them. With dildos and strap-ons. Other times I went down on the prefects while they watched the other girls lick and finger each other. And they all loved to go down on me. I became the pussy princess of the whole goddamn convent. I looked like a skinny kid with almost no pubic hair, and all these big girls wanted to suck me. I eventually learned to multiple-orgasm and made a big performance out of it . . . lots of screaming and moaning . . . you know the sort of thing.'

'I know. I've been there,' I answer dryly. Regina pushes a leg between my thighs, rubs against my clitoris. 'Oh, that feels good. Keep doing it. Harder if you like.'

'They gave me presents and treats and when I was caught breaking school rules, I just got warned, never punished like the other girls. It was wonderful. For the first time . . . first time in my life . . . I was really happy!'

I start to ask Regina if she ever became head prefect at the convent but her thumb and forefinger are doing strange and wonderful things to my clitoris so I stop talking and tighten my arms around her and curl my body and come again, this time harder. *Yes . . . oh yes . . . oh yes . . . yes . . .oh Jesus . . .*'

She waits for me to finish before answering the unasked question. 'Then when I was head prefect in my last year, I could have any girl I wanted for playtime, to go down on me any time I wanted.'

I surrender. Being in bed with Regina is a lot more fun than my date plowing and grunting and coming on my breasts when he should have been worshipping my clitoris. I whisper, 'Would you like to go down on me now? I'd love it. You could show me if you want . . .'

'I thought you'd never ask.'

'Just keep talking.'

Regina slides down the bed, pushes her head between my thighs. I hold her head in both hands while her lips nibble my clitoris and her tongue slides into my pussy. She looks up at me, smiling. 'The girls were always too scared to say no, but I never forced it, you know. I never had a girl the second time if she didn't like it. But she had to try it. Convent rules. And I was the convent's all-powerful head prefect who made the rules.' She laughs to tell me she's joking. But I'm not at all sure she's really joking.

She circles her tongue around my clitoris, slips lower, thrusts into my pussy. I groan. 'But most of them really liked it. At least, they learned to like it. What else were we going to do? Hormones flowing in great tides in a convent, a girl's boarding school. No cocks, no boys within miles.'

I ask, 'But what about the nuns? From what I hear . . .'

Three fingers push gently in and out and Regina talks between licks. 'Hell, almost all of them were lesbians. That's why they were there. Sometimes we went to their cells, other times they came to the prefects' bedrooms. Sometimes, when they were feeling really horny and couldn't wait, they'd call us out of class and we'd go down on them almost anywhere.'

Her tongue flicks my clitoris, flicks again, and again. 'A lot of them liked to be whipped like they were being punished for being such sinners. Mother Superior herself, the venerable head nun . . . couldn't come until she was sucked off while being whipped. Not a pretty sight, I tell you. And when other nuns visited the convent, I'd bring girls to their cells, and we'd go down on them and suck their pussies . . . and . . .'

I can feel my orgasm start to grow like distant thunder. She pulls my lips back with both hands, thrusts her tongue as deep inside me as far as she can. In and out. In and out. In and out. Pussy to clit, back to pussy, to clit,pussy, clit, pussy. . . .

I collapse. '*Oh god . . . oh god . . . oh god . . . yes . . . yes . . . yes . . . yes . . . do it to me . . .oh yes . . . oh yes . . . oh yes . . . sweet Jesus . . . oh god . . . Regina, yes . . .*' I scream.

We lie wrapped in each other's arms. Regina nibbles my ear, asks, 'Does this mean we're dating, honey . . . going steady?'

I'm firm. 'No. We're just fuck buddies.' We giggle together. 'Meaningless sex, nothing more. Don't expect a diamond ring, you saucy thing, you!' I get up on one elbow to make a point. 'And don't think just because of what's just happened that I'm a lesbian. Because I'm certainly not!'

Regina reaches up, kisses me on the lips. I hesitate, don't know what to do. Then to my surprise, I kiss her back, just like she's a man. We fall back on the bed, our tongues touch and linger and taste and she slides her slim body on top of mine, and it's no different than with a man except that there's no rough, hungry cock pushing arrogantly at my groin, only another pussy, sweet and gentle, against mine.

'Fuck me Regina . . . please fuck me,' I whimper.

Later, Regina suggests shyly, 'Don't wash after you've been with your boyfriends and want playtime with me, okay? It really turns me on to lick his come off your nipples and know his cock has been in you only a little earlier. Never happened to me with a girl before.'

I run my tongue around her puffy nipple. 'You're a sick woman, Regina. But you give great head. Better than any of my boyfriends.' I kiss her lips; my tongue flirts with hers. 'Can I ask you a personal question?'

'Of course.'

'How do you know when you're lesbian?

'You really want to know?'

'Only if you really want to tell me . . .'

Lady's Maid

by K. Ann Karlsson

The fire in the grate cast a warm glow about my boudoir, creating subtle shadows on the carved marble mantel. I shifted in the deep copper tub, which had been set near the hearth, and picked up my glass of brandy. A small sip of amber liquid burned its way down my throat and spread heat through my body.

Brandy was not a usual drink for ladies, even married ladies, but my dearest husband had introduced me to the habit before his departure for the Peninsular Wars. It was a connection with him I couldn't bear to sever, even though brandy was not entirely to my taste. But the liquid fire felt good down my throat tonight. I fancied it drowned out the ache of missing Justin, but I knew that wasn't true. That ache was waiting, like a wolf among the trees. Later, when I was alone in my bed, it would pounce and reveal both my loneliness and my selfish desires.

Justin was, to my most recent knowledge, still alive and well. But I needed him. I needed his strength, his smiles, his calm patience and, most of all, his love. Tears pricked at my eyelids, but I blinked them back. Damn that nasty little Napoleon. And damn Justin for finding it necessary to lend his leadership to England's cause. *England*, I thought, *could not need him half as much as I.* Bloody damned war.

I sighed.

I had been soaking in the bath for some time, idly watching the fire while my maid, Moira, tidied the room and put away my clothes. We had just that afternoon arrived at Southerland Park from London. Town had grown thin of company and, therefore, of necessary distractions. In my rush to arrive in this wild part of Cornwall, I had preceded nearly all of the servants who'd been sent to accompany me. Without proper staff, Moira had been forced to ask two of the stable boys to carry up the hot bathwater.

Silence now filled the empty house like a heavy fog, and it seemed as if Moira and I were the only two souls alive in my husband's ancestral residence. Even Moira's occasional comment and quiet movements failed to disturb the deep hush that pressed in on me from all sides.

Moira and I had not yet established that comfortable intimacy expected between a lady and her maid. A burly coachman had recently enticed Higgins, my previous personal maid, to leave my employ for another household. But I couldn't find it in myself to resent the circumstances because on her wedding day, Higgins had looked content indeed with her new situation. And now I had Moira, who had most recently been an upstairs maid in the London house. I'd intended to interview proper lady's maid candidates to replace the happy Higgins before our departure from London, but for some reason I'd never made time to do so. Moira would do, I thought. Because what my new maid lacked in training, I'd found, she more than made up in immediate loyalty and overall good cheer.

'Lean forward, milady, so's I kin wash yer back.'

I was a little startled by Moira's low-voiced request. But I obediently set the brandy snifter down on a low table near the bath and sat forward.

'Where are you from, Moira? I don't believe I've asked you that before.'

'London, ma'am. And 'afore that, County Cork, it were.'

'Ireland.'

'Yes, milady.'

Moira's voice was low and sweet, with a lilting accent. She raised a steaming sliver urn and let the water sluice down over my shoulders. The sensation of heat, in contrast to the cooling bathwater, caused my nipples to stand out so suddenly I gasped. I wrapped my arms around my knees, and the brush of my erect nipples against my legs brought my mind back to Justin. How his mouth, cool, then hot, had dragged over the puckered tips of my breasts; how his large, demanding hands had felt on my body. A stab of longing shot to my core, and I pressed my lips together to hold back a sigh.

Moira put the pitcher down in front of the fire and fetched my favorite lavender-scented soap and a large sponge. I heard the splash as she dipped the sponge into the water. But at the first pass across my back, I jerked away.

''Tis sorry I am, milady. This sponge is a mite too rough for yer lovely soft skin. I'll use me hands then, shall I?'

It was an unusual suggestion, spoken softly. Higgins

would not have said it, but tonight, with Moira, it sounded just right.

'Yes, please,' I replied. 'That would be much better.'

The lavender scent grew stronger. Then Moira's warm hands glided over my back. The foam of suds between her palms and my skin felt silky smooth. A rush of pleasure flowed down my backbone to my womb, which heated and opened like a flower. I didn't know if the sensation came from the memory of my husband, or Moira's gentle touch, but a soft moan escaped me.

Her hands stilled but then continued to work soothingly over my back and shoulders. 'His lordship's been gone a long time, has he?' she said. 'How long were you married afore he left, ma'am?'

Water sloshed in the tub as I turned to look at Moira. Really look at her. She was about my age, or perhaps a bit younger. For the first time I remarked that our coloring was very similar, though our individual features were not. Her shiny black hair curled in tendrils from the steam of the bath, and framed a round and pleasant face. The candlelight had darkened her eyes, but I could see they were blue. Like mine.

Just now her eyes shifted away, and she returned her attention to the soap. 'I'm sorry, ma'am. 'Tis none of my affair. I just thought – '

'It's all right, Moira,' I said, feeling lightheaded and reckless between the brandy and the unwanted, uncomfortable sensations moving in me. 'You are perfectly correct. Lord Ravensdown has been gone for thirteen months, ten days and, let me see, about eight hours, I would say. And we were married just three days before he left, though I've known him since I was a child.' Tears threatened again. Three days had not nearly been enough time, but they *had* been lovely days, filled with pleasure and laughter. Until the outside world had intruded.

'Oh, ma'am, 'tis no great wonder that you miss him, then.'

I nodded slowly. 'Yes, I do miss him. More than I can say.'

She nodded too and then fussed with the soap some more. ''Tis just. Well.' She shrugged her shoulders. 'Sometimes a body craves another's touch. I could help ye with that, ma'am.' Her eyes, dark and mysterious, met mine. 'I know . . . things . . . to ease ye, body and soul. Things I can teach ye.'

I couldn't look away from her steady gaze. My mind had locked onto that word *touch*. There were whispers, always with a soupçon of scandal, concerning older married ladies who turned to other women for comfort. And for – other things. But the Duchess of Devonshire I was not. The truth was, I could never be unfaithful to Justin Southerland, Lord Ravensdown, and believe me, I'd had plenty of offers. I'd loved Justin my whole life, even before he'd inherited his title and vast estates. But this, this was not like those other offers. This was not a man making advances, but a woman seeking to ease my pain. I cleared my throat.

'What things?' I whispered.

Her face lit in a slow smile. ''Twill be our secret.' She stood and held out her hand. 'C'mon, then. I'll show you, shall I?'

She helped me out of the bath, then brought a towel that had been warming near the fire. She knelt in front of me and rubbed first my feet, then my legs. None of this was unusual, so I began to think I'd imagined the whole conversation until she stood and spoke again in a husky voice.

'Ye have a lovely body, milady. Strong, but womanlike too.'

'Thank you, Moira. I suppose it's all that riding I do to pass the time.'

''Til he comes back.'

'Yes.'

'Yer breasts are a picture, ma'am, if I may be so bold as to say. Yer husband must come close to heaven when he soothes ye here.'

I gulped as a clear memory popped in my head of Justin's face nestled between my breasts, his eyes glittering with passion as he molded the soft shapes in his large hands.

'May I?' Moira asked.

I nodded, breathless. She patted my chest dry with the soft linen towel, but then let it fall to the floor. Her warm, callused hand stroked down my skin until she cupped the slight weight of my breast, rosy from the warm bath. Her thumb moved across the nipple, and I sucked in air. I felt on fire where her fingertips trailed across the puckered tips. I'd never imagined that the fire of arousal, banked since Justin's departure, could now roar into flame at a woman's touch. Moira bent her head and suddenly my breast was in her mouth. I didn't think about whether it was right or appropriate for my upstairs maid to be touching me in such a way; my only thought was that she shouldn't stop.

Then I had another thought. I must see and touch too. I recognized something in Moira that bound her to me. It was as if I looked at her through Justin's eyes, in the way he looked at me. As a woman. As sexual and desirable.

The words that next came out of my mouth were ones Justin would have used. 'You must take off your clothes, Moira.'

She raised her head and smiled. 'Yes, ma'am. Come sit on the bed then, and ye can watch me.'

So I perched naked on the pale grey satin coverlet of my four-poster bed, and I watched as Moira Sullivan revealed her woman's body to me, piece by piece. When I told her I knew very little of lovemaking and seduction except what my husband had taught me in three days, her method became more like an instructional play. As she disrobed, she would say things like, 'yer man will like this' or 'the gentlemen love it when ye do this.'

Every movement was so fascinating and sensual I felt compelled to ask, 'How *do* you know these things, Moira?'

She looked up from untying her garter. 'I'm thinkin' yer not really wantin' to know *that*, milady.'

I stared. Her eyes held poignant sadness but with a hard glint of experience that squeezed my heart. I pictured any number of shocking situations where she could have learnt such things. 'Quite right,' was all I could manage in reply.

When she was naked, she joined me on the bed. We sat cross-legged and facing each other, and just stared for a few moments. She was broader of chest and shoulder than me, and her breasts were considerably larger than mine. Other than that, we were roughly the same height and shape. I had never seen another naked female body. Her skin was smooth and pale in the candlelight. The tips of her breasts puckered and drew up under my gaze. Was this what so entranced Justin when he looked at me? The endless fascinations of a woman's body?

She reached out and ran a finger down my leg, drawing a gasp from me. 'Has your man ever kissed that sweet cunny of yours?' she asked.

'What?' I frowned, vaguely affronted by the unfamiliar language.

She clapped a hand over her mouth, but then her eyes danced with such mirth I began to giggle. She lay down and propped a hand under her head. With her other hand, she beckoned. 'Lay yerself down, milady. I'll show ye what I mean.'

I lay on my back next to her, and her warm hand stroked up my belly, my breasts, down my arm and over my hips. As my skin heated, she began to drop kisses on my neck and shoulders. I moaned.

Here was an echo of what Justin and I had shared before he'd left, and I felt a moment of uncertainty. But the sensations were so different, I found myself easily tempted by the urgings of my body. Moira's skin was as soft as mine, contrasting with the hard point of her nipple that pressed against my arm. I reached to palm her breast but found my small hand unequal to the task. I turned on my side and used both hands, bringing the turgid point to my lips. Her cry sent a stab between my legs, and I felt a rush of heat and liquid there. Her skin smelled sweet but tasted salty; the combination enticed me even further.

'Ah, milady,' she said, 'that feels like heaven, it does.' Her fingers combed through my hair at the back of my head urging me forward. 'Take it a bit harder and roll it on yer tongue. Ah, aye, like that.'

She brought her hand up and caught my nipple in her spread fingers. She squeezed the point, and I writhed in pleasure, drawing hard on her breast.

A web of soft black hair, hers and mine, covered us. It was as if we were the same person split into two, and then merged back into one skin. We became a bundle of sensitized nerves locked together. The sounds of her pleasure drove me on.

She grasped my hand and pressed it down into the crisp curls below her belly. 'Here, milady.' Her voice was low and warm in my ear. 'This is where a man presses his big cock into ye. Ye've felt that, aye? When he stuffs ye full.'

Yes, I had felt the power of that deep possession. The pounding excitement, the race to finish. Justin had been large and hard. My heart thrummed at the intensity of the memory, the longing for something so basic, so primitive.

''Tis good, that,' said Moira. 'But there are other ways to enjoy yer body, milady. Softer ways.' Her words made me squirm, but her fingers tangled with mine and kept me focused on her velvety skin.

She dragged my hand further between her legs. 'This is me cunny. Me quim, ye see. And *this* is a woman's pleasure pearl.' She pushed my fingers onto a firm little nub of flesh. 'Ye rub it, and it grows hard, like a man's cock, aye?'

I'd never thought of such a thing. I'd scarcely touched myself even in the bath. To feel her sex was a revelation. I tentatively explored the slick folds and soft textures, growing bolder as I absorbed her sighs of pleasure. The points of my breasts were nearly painful in their engorged stiffness. I took the hard nub of the 'pearl' between my thumb and forefinger. She stiffened and cried out. When I hastened to apologize, she laughed.

'No, ye've not hurt me. 'Tis a stab of good. It feels sharp but sweet. Here, I'll show ye.'

She sat up and knelt between my legs. Her white skin glowed in the candlelight, contrasting with the dark, damp curls between her thighs. She pushed my knees back and I confess to a blush as she studied my nether parts.

'Ah, milady. Such a pretty hole. So ripe an' pink.'

My husband's face flashed again at that moment, and I understood it was because I'd recognized a similar expression – excitement, arousal, desire. That look had been a prelude to unimaginable pleasure. My belly quivered in anticipation, my hips twisted. A small smack of her hand landed on my bottom. I froze in place.

'Hold ye still, milady. Ye'll want to enjoy this.' Her fingers trailed heat through my curls, her thumb circled the little pearl, then grasped it lightly and pulled. I cried out, clutching at the coverlet. Her eyes flicked up to mine. She plunged two fingers inside me, still teasing the nub, stroking it with her thumb. Lightning flashed in my head and my whole body stiffened and shook. The sensation was not unfamiliar; Justin had also used his long fingers to bring me delight, and I felt a twinge of conscience as

Moira's hand moved inside me. But it had been so long ago, so *long*. My womb clenched around her fingers, and I gritted my teeth against the pain-pleasure. She removed her fingers and bent low between my legs. Her breath burned hot on my curls, then the wet heat of her mouth surrounded that tight little nub.

'Ah, Moira, it's too much,' I cried.

She looked up then, her face framed by her tumbled hair and the V of my thighs. 'No, milady. Yer strong, and beautiful, ye are. Ye must ride it out.' She bent her head. 'Savor it.'

Justin had also attempted to kiss me in this most intimate way, I remembered, but I had shyly pushed him away. And, uncharacteristically, he'd relented, promising to revisit me there later. I now regretted refusing him as Moira lapped up my honey-flow like a cat at the cream pot. Her fingers dug into the round cheeks of my bottom, holding me still while her tongue plunged deep inside. My hands fluttered about until Moira placed them gently on my breasts. I licked my fingers and drew the points of my nipples tight, playing with my breasts' soft weight, pushing the mounds together.

Our quiet sighs and groans blended as she worked her fingers in my slick passage. Her hot-cool mouth on that secret place was nigh unbearable, and her tongue darted everywhere at once, now sharp, now soft and fluttering. The sensations built in me until the muscles of my legs and abdomen grew tighter, harder as I strained towards that wicked mouth.

She pressed the point of her tongue against my pearl

and swirled it round and round just as three of her fingers plunged into my quim. I could not be still now as I rode her clever fingers to completion. Her hand drove forward again and again. The lightning fire in my womb burst into a ball of flame, burning a path up my spine, stealing my breath completely. I arched my back in ecstasy and my moans turned to wordless cries as my passage rippled and released over and over and over.

I sprawled on the coverlet, limp and damp. Moira crawled up from between my legs. Her heavy breasts swung between us, and I lifted my hands to shape them. I could feel the tension in her, and it sparked my own as she knelt over me.

'May I kiss ye, milady? So's ye can taste yer own sweet juices.' Her voice, husky and panting, stabbed at my core. I put my arms around her, and she lay flat on top of me, the soft mound of her pubis pressed to mine. She was light and silky smooth, so unlike my huge bear of a husband. Her eyes glittered with passion.

'Kiss me, Moira,' I whispered. 'Please.'

Her mouth tasted of citrus and musk. Of me. The scent was earthy, pungent. I plunged my hands into her hair to hold her closer. Her tongue licked at my lips and chin and throat. We were wet with sweat now, slick and sliding. She turned, and we lay again on our sides, facing each other.

'Put yer fingers in me, milady, and I'll show ye how to bring me off.' I slid my hand down over her hip and she lifted her leg, her knee forming a triangle. My hand dipped into her wet folds and she moaned. She reached for my sensitive flesh, but I pulled away. Even as I did, I found myself eager to see what Moira would do next.

''Tis like a game, see, or a mirror,' she said. 'I'll do something to ye and ye do the same to me.'

'Hmm. I think I like this game.' I mimicked her pose and then moved my fingers inside her. She gasped but then pushed my hand away.

'Me first,' she said sternly.

I stilled. 'All right.'

She swirled one finger in my passage, then lighted on an interior spot that made my sweet cream pour into her hand. My hips jerked in rhythm as she pressed and released her fingers. But then she stopped. My eyes slammed open to glare at her.

'Your turn, milady,' she said. And damned if she didn't have a dimple showing in her cheek. Hmm. I *did* love a challenge.

I slid my middle finger into the depths of her dripping cunt, turning my wrist, seeking that same spot. When her whole body tensed, I pressed inward. Her hips kicked forward, and a frown of concentration appeared on her face.

'Like that?' I teased, enjoying myself, shoving two more fingers inside her.

'Uhnnh. Jay-sus, milady. Sure an' ye're a quick learner.'

Her accent had become thicker, her voice dark and throaty. I made to pull away, but she grabbed my wrist, locking my hand between her legs. As she pumped on my fingers, body slick, breasts bouncing with effort, I pulled her hand back between my legs with my other hand. I drove her slack fingers deep inside me, tangling them with my own.

Then Moira started to come apart. Her body convulsed, a hot flush bloomed under her skin, and she squeezed her eyes tightly shut. Her high shriek pitched me into an identical climax, and we writhed together on the bed in utter abandon, soaking the coverlet with our sweat and come.

I must have dozed for a while, but when I came awake it was to Moira stroking my hair, my head pillowed by her breast.

'Why did you show me these things, Moira?'

After a long pause she said, 'I could sense ye had need of it, ma'am. I had need too. I miss me man. He was there with your'n. I was there too. 'Tis where I learnt what I know.'

I sat up to stare down at her. 'You mean you followed the drum?'

She snorted. 'Aye, I was a camp whore, more like.' She put her hands under her head so her elbows splayed out on the pillows. 'But then I met Patrick Sullivan, ye see. He was good to me.' Her mouth lifted in a small smile. 'We even got married. When they went into Spain, though, he said I was to come back to England.'

'Where is your husband now?' I whispered.

Moira looked away then, and I thought she wasn't going to answer me.

'Dead,' she said. 'Killed just after I left. At Ciudad Rodrigo.'

I gasped, and the tears that had threatened earlier now

spilled over. But Moira sat up and brushed them away from my cheeks with her fingers.

I shook my head and reached out to her. 'Oh, Moira.'

''Tis all right, milady.' She took my hand, almost shyly, and squeezed it. 'But I wanted ye to know. I've shown ye these things for yer own sake, milady. For yer kindnesses. To take away a little part of yer loneliness. I know, ye see, what it means to feel so lonely ye want to die. Though it may mean little from someone such as I, 'twas what I could do for a great lady such as yerself.'

Her deep blue eyes looked steadily into mine. 'And 'twill be our secret,' she said, 'I swear 't.'

The next morning, I was sitting at my escritoire in the library, taking stock of the previous evening's events when I heard the front door bang open. I frowned. Who could –

'Cassandra! Cass, I am home.'

'Justin!' I ran to him and was at once engulfed in his arms. And though I could scarce see him for the tears in my eyes, he felt large and strong against me. I pressed close, breathing in the wind-dusted, travel-stained scent of him.

He cupped my face and looked down into my eyes. 'Damn, it's good to see you, my girl. I've missed you.'

He stroked my jaw with his thumbs and bent his head. His mouth swept over mine, molding and shaping our lips together. I clutched his lapels and pressed my tongue to his. His hands slid back, tightening in my hair as our mouths slanted and sucked. After several dizzy moments, Justin pulled back.

His whiskey-colored eyes twinkled into mine. 'I see you've missed me too?'

'Every minute of every day,' I whispered. I looped my arms around his neck and drew him back down to me.

After a discreet interval during which Lord Ravenswood and I had some opportunity to become reacquainted, I heard a scratch on the door and Moira entered. Her eyes twinkled in her pleasant face as she asked, 'Shall I fetch some tea then, ma'am?'

'Oh, I think only brandy will do for this occasion.'

'Yes, milady.'

Justin raised an eyebrow. 'Brandy, my dear? At this hour?'

'Of course, Justin. I want to celebrate.' I pulled him close in another hug.

Then I did something I'd never done in my life. Over Justin's shoulder, I caught Moira's eye and winked.

And of course, dear reader, you know she winked back.

The Tiger's Tale

by Kilt Kilpatrick

That evening, lying underneath the mosquito nets, Elspeth could scarcely believe it had happened at all. All night she slept feverishly, slowly tossing and turning on the mattress of their great oak and satinwood four-poster like a ship lost in a tempest. She even dreamt of Vijaya's tiger.

Vijaya had said tigers were the guardians of sleep, and could ward off dark dreams, but still her slumber was troubled with nightmares of fire and thunder. But mostly she dreamt of Vijaya's beautiful smiling face, resplendent in her green silk sari and short *choli* blouse; trembling at the sense memory of those skillful, tender hands on her, undressing her, touching her

First Vijaya slid her hands into Elspeth's rich auburn hair and freed it from the delicate little combs to cascade down to the nape of her neck. Then, with patient, nimble fingers, she undid the myriad mother-of-pearl buttons down the back of the gown and slipped it off Elspeth's shoulders. Vijaya marveled at Elspeth's smooth, pale Celtic skin adorned with thousands of tiny red freckles as she methodically unlaced the hooks and eyes of Elspeth's gold- and cream-colored sateen corset and set it aside, then had her raise her arms so she could pull off her pretty French camisole as well.

Elspeth watched in fascination while the beautiful young woman knelt and unbuckled both her soft leather boots, and lifted each of her calves in turn to pull them off her feet. Vijaya quietly directed Elspeth to pull up her chemise. Elspeth obeyed her servant; she bent down slightly, and gathering it in both hands, lifted the silken folds up to her thighs like the curtain on an art exhibit, exposing her long legs.

Vijaya reached up to the tops of Elspeth's stockings and smoothly rolled them down and off. She paused a moment, then looked up, meeting Elspeth's gaze at last. The bare moment seemed to stretch on into forever. She kept her eyes locked on Elspeth's and at last reached up again to take the elegant, lacy chemise from her and gently tug it down, until Elspeth was as completely unclothed as Botticelli's Venus, and just as radiant. Then she slowly rose and took Elspeth by the hand, laid her down on the large feather bed and sat down beside her. Elspeth looked up at her for a clue to her intentions, but Vijaya's only expression was a serene inscrutable hint of smile.

From the nightstand she lifted a portly glass vial out of its pan of hot water and poured the warm sesame oil into her hands. She took her time, beginning by tenderly cradling the arms, massaging the fingers, palms and wrists and giving long, unhurried strokes down to the shoulders. Then she rose and repositioned herself at the top of the bed, nestling Elspeth's head in her lap in order to better anoint the crown of her head with oil and trace out swirls back ad forth, well up into her scalp, down to the line of her jaw and chin and across the brows of her eyes to the temples. Elspeth closed her eyes and her lips parted involuntarily with faint sigh. Vijaya gave soft little tugs all along the ridges and lobes of her ears, and put drops of warm oil on the tip of her little finger to carefully tickle the opening of her ear canals.

Elspeth could feel the pleasing warmth from Vijaya's bare midriff as she leaned over her, stretching out to rub her collarbones, reach down her flanks, and run her hands in broad clockwise circles across her abdomen and chest. She felt her breasts swelling and her nipples stiffening as the young women's skilled hands passed over and around them. She swallowed, her breathing becoming deeper and more ragged. Vijaya's reach extended nearly to the bottom of her belly, fingertips just grazing the thatch of curly red hairs there.

'Could you turn over for me now, *Bahanji*?' Vijaya whispered. Elspeth opened her eyes, smiled sleepily, and did as she was asked, resting her head on her hands. Vijaya meanwhile stood and came over to the foot of the bed to work on Elspeth's feet and ankles with more oil, as she audibly groaned with pleasure. After they had received sufficient attention, Vijaya progressed up to the calves, her upper legs, and her thighs. Elspeth shuddered at her touch. Quietly, Vijaya rose onto the bed, and carefully straddled Elspeth's legs just below her soft round buttocks.

There was a pause and the faintest of rustles, then Vijaya's hands returned to Elspeth with a firm slow slide from her sacral dimples all the way up to her shoulders, where she kneaded the muscles with a surprising strength. This she repeated twice more before stretching herself down to lie on Elspeth's back. With a jolt that ran through her body like lightning, Elspeth realized Vijaya had stripped off her *choli* and was naked from the waist up; she could feel the points of the young woman's breasts rubbing against her shoulder blades.

Vijaya softly rested her cheek against Elspeth's, and they lay there together companionably. Then Vijaya raised up just enough to bring her lips to Elspeth's ear. Her whisper tickled. 'Do you love me, my sister?'

Elspeth nodded, and her voice cracked 'Yes.'

'And I love you too. *Bahanji*, your heart needs to be ravished. I will do my part, but we must find you a lover as well.' She played thoughtfully with a stray lock of Elspeth's hair. 'We shoul– ' She gasped in mid-sentence and shot upright.

Elspeth's husband stood like stone in the bedroom entryway. His eyes were flat and cold; his hands were clenched into hard, furious knots.

Of all the innumerable trifles she left behind in coming to India, Elspeth missed the sea the most. She was born in Scotland, in the village of Blackwaterfoot on Arran, a green and rocky isle in the Firth of Clyde with more sheep and burren-rabbits than people. As a girl, she played along heathered hills and standing stones, in storied sea caves whose mossy walls were still engraved by Viking and Pictish graffiti, on Neolithic dolmen graves with a patina of lichen. On the clearest days, she could see Ireland.

She was a lovely ginger-haired girl. Her modest family recognized her potential at an early age and sent her to live with her aunts in Edinburgh, city of a thousand chimneys, in order to groom her into the sort of suitable wife who might attract a reasonably well-off gentleman of means for a husband. She was tutored in proper language and etiquette, subtleties of protocol, domestic skills, and the art of dutiful silence. She was forbidden to speak or sing in Gaelic. In the fullness of time she grew into an exquisitely striking young woman with a pale, soft beauty of the kind so favored by Dante Gabriel Rossetti; she gloried in long red hair, the very slightest dusting of freckles, and gentle eyes possessed of a sweet sadness so lovely you could almost forgive a man for wanting to keep her in a permanent state of unhappiness.

Clive Archibald Godfrey was the man who fixed his eye upon her. When her aunts, through various behind-the-scenes machinations, brought the seventeen-year-old girl to his attention, he found her most desirable as a prospective wife and mother. On first perusal he was not an immediate choice for a romantic assignation; though tall and strong and perhaps not unhandsome, he was somewhat horse-faced with a high forehead and an unfortunate overbite that could only be partially mitigated by his handlebar mustache. What was more, he exhibited a highly fastidious deportment, unyielding Anglican piety and a slightly peevish temperament that did not endear him at social gatherings.

Elspeth's aunts nevertheless thought him a most promising candidate for their charge, and they strove to assure

Elspeth that any awkward stiffness was merely a superficial disguise for his fine inner qualities. In their judgment, any shortcomings he may have possessed in manly pulchritude, charm, or sparkling wit were amply compensated for by one salient feature: He was, above all, ambitious. His father in his time – before his untimely death from consuming a surfeit of canned oysters at a summer picnic – had been with the East India Company and profited well from the Chinese tea trade. The younger Godfrey in turn was eager to make his own fortune as a colonial bureaucrat in the British civil service office of the Raj.

Their courtship and subsequent engagement was brief and unremarkable, consisting in the main of pleasant chaperoned outings in the country and church functions and tense interrogatory visits with Elspeth's future mother-in-law. Events culminated in a small, lovely wedding ceremony appropriate to their class, and Clive indulged Elspeth's wish for a weekend honeymoon in Blackpool. It was there by the seashore that they consummated their vows with the physical act of love, in great solemnity and earnestness.

Then in very short order, they bid Britain farewell, 'possibly for quite some time' as Clive put it, to begin their new life in India. From the great port of London, Clive's mother saw them off most imperiously while Elspeth's aunts, their long work done at last, cried and waved goodbye over and over as their ocean liner bore the happy couple off to another world. For more than seven thousand miles they steamed the seas, and it seemed they also sailed backwards in time as well, past France and Spain, though the

Pillars of Hercules at Gibraltar, across the wine-dark Mediterranean; into Egypt and threading down the Suez canal into the Red Sea, past Arabia and the African Horn, and out again through the strait the ancient Arab navigators called *Bab-el-Mandeb*, the Gate of Tears.

Then across the Arabian Sea, until they at last caught sight of the mountains of India.

'The Jewel in the Crown,' murmured Clive uncharacteristically as they looked out over the railing towards the harbor of Bombay. Despite the insufferable heat, Elspeth shivered with wonder and anticipation, and perhaps more than a little trepidation. Elspeth never forgot that overwhelming first moment when they disembarked, or the dreamlike carriage ride towards their new home. They had left the Indian Ocean only to dive into an ocean of Indians. It was not just that there was a sea of people; the whole of creation was here, in a kaleidoscopic frenzy of sight and sound and smell: gods and filth, spices and incense, stench and sweat and urine and feces, silk and gold and dust and rags, festivity and suffering. Always and everywhere the clamorous opposition of a dozen scents, a hundred voices, a thousand bright colors, everything mingling with wild abandon in uproarious profusion. Holy rivers flowed in an infernal heat, as though in the Hindu cosmos, the heavens and hells had collided long ago, leaving their ten-armed divinities to shrug and say: This is India.

Ten years passed. As hoped, Clive's ambition and single-mindedness paid off handsomely. He threw himself into his career with great élan and advanced rapidly in the colonial administration, and each new promotion meant moving to another fine house in another exotic locale on the subcontinent. Regrettably, the days were not unqualifiedly halcyon for the two of them. For Elspeth, though, it was a period of unparalleled sights and marvels, subtle pressures mounted. She could not shake the apprehension Clive did not love her so much as he admired her, in the way of a useful, well-crafted tool or a conversation piece on the mantelpiece. And despite years of dutiful effort and doctoral supervision she was unable to conceive, a deficiency Clive found difficult to forgive, particularly since he himself took such care to follow a strict daily regimen of Dr. Pritchard's Healthful Turpentine and Calomel Compound to prevent melancholic blood.

Elspeth increasingly regarded herself as a lifelong pilgrim through successively dreadful circles of hell, since circumstances beyond her power had taken her from her island birthplace. Sooty, smoky Edinburgh had offered nothing but unending hours of study and strict training. London had vacillated between fogbound dankness and a falsely merry, gilded marketing of her own person. She hated those days of stiff competition with English society women, outwardly all courtesy and elegance; at heart, rapacious and cruel as predatory birds. The twisting, reeking thoroughfares of Bombay and Delhi were squalid circuses of the most dire, crushing poverty, and her only diversion were the dreary social functions of other colonial wives, who in the large were either dull matronly figures or disdainful patrician social climbers no less unpleasant than their London equivalents. In princely Hyderabad, more Arab than Hindu, elephants and camels roamed the streets and cruel-faced men strode about with open swords in their hands. It was no place for a woman; with Clive so frequently called away by the extended absences required by his work, she spent long days and nights there concealed behind screened windows, a cloistered prisoner in her own home.

So it was with no small relief when Clive's career brought them out of the teeming cities and north to the Central Provinces, to the lush forests and beautiful wild places of Madhya Pradesh. Now they had gained a fine large house in the country, complete with a handsomely appointed garden, stables, a carriage-house and a contingent of servants. In anticipation of good sporting, Clive acquired two hunting dogs, fierce black *metzgerhunds* he named Sampson and Goliath. Elspeth began to dare hope that the vicissitudes of her fortunes were finally improving. One morning in the sitting room she expressed her longing to go explore the wild countryside of the region, only to have Clive respond that he had an announcement and a surprise for her. She looked up from her book of poetry, struck with a twinge of apprehension – surely not another move so soon, especially now that prospects seemed so full of promise . . .

'Truly?'

'Yes, my dear. Now that we have come into our own – and indeed, it is no idle speculation or mere bombast to declare that my efforts may even yet earn us a knighthood or baronet, or other title into the peerage – it is time we learn to comport ourselves in proper fashion. To that end, I find it most unbecoming that you gallivant around the countryside unescorted like an undisciplined schoolgirl.'

Her heart dropped, and she struggled to compose herself to give a reply.

But he continued. 'So, then, I have someone I should wish to present to you, and that person is here with me now.'

He clapped his hands sharply and in came a young Indian woman. She was lovely; perhaps a few years younger than her. She was dressed in a simple but lovely sari of green silk with delicate accents of gold. Though her arms and midriff were bare to the eye, there was nothing unbecoming about her attire; indeed, she was elegance and poise personified. Her eyes were bright and happy. Slender jangling bangles garlanded her forearms. A tiny perfect vermilion *tikka* dot decorated her forehead and a delicate little gold ring her nose. Her flawless skin was of the dusky cinnamon complexion the admiring natives called 'wheaten,' and her hair was sleek and midnight black, tied in a long braid.

'She was a temple dancer in Tamil Nadu, but since then she has foresworn heathen ritual and done fine service in English households. I daresay she will be good for both of us, in service as your new lady's maid. And yes, I judge her a most suitable companion to accompany you on all your reconnoitering.'

The girl put her hands together in a gracious *namaste*, and wonderfully, broke into a delighted smile and a light laugh, as though the meeting was her heart's fondest desire. He beamed and presented her with a flourish.

'This is Vijaya.'

'*Bahanji*, what song is that you are humming?' Vijaya asked one day as they reclined, leisurely picnicking on a hilly meadow overlooking forests of teak and *sal*. When Clive was at home, Vijaya took care to respectfully address Mrs. Godfrey as *Memsahib*. But when they were by themselves and carefree, Vijaya delighted in calling her *Bahanji*. Sister. Elspeth smiled at the sound of it. Vijaya was not shy and demure like the village women; she did not keep her gaze down or her voice soft, or her opinions to herself.

From the first, they were inseparable. During the monsoon season, or when the summer heat grew too unbearable, they enjoyed leisurely days reading aloud to one another, or playing cards and backgammon. Some days they would simply talk, entertaining themselves for hours telling stories and laughing together. But on their favorite days they went on long strolls, explored the local markets, and set out on bold expeditions out into the wilds, as they were today.

Elspeth paused in her sketching – in recent weeks she had taken up watercolors. 'Was I? How very curious. I was so engaged with my drawings, I hadn't realized.'

'It went like this,' Vijaya said, and mimicked the tune.

Elspeth's eyes brightened as she recognized the melody. 'Oh! Yes, of course. It's a song I sang as a girl on Arran:

'Cluinn mi na toinn, an aosda ceòl nan t-uisge
Is aithne dhomh gu math an t-òran sin
An nochd, tha me gafa eadar talamh is an fairge

'Ach thig mi dhachaigh arithist
Fodha an gealach, thig mi saor . . .'

Vijaya had never heard Elspeth sing before, and the haunting lilt of her voice speaking strange words stirred her deeply. 'It's . . . beautiful, and yet so sad, too. What does it mean?'

A strange look crossed Elspeth's face. 'It's a song sung by a *selkie* – a seal-woman who has become trapped on the land by a fisherman's love, bound to remain in human shape forever. She looks out over the ocean in the moonlight and listens to her kin there, singing to them. She says,

'I hear the waves, the ancient music of the water
I know well that song
Tonight I am caught between land and sea

'But I will come home again
Beneath the moon, I will be free . . .'

Vijaya sat up and wrapped her arms around her legs, cocking her head to one side and closing her eyes while she listened and pictured Scottish islands far, far beyond the black water. At last, she said, 'Did you know sometimes, your voice changes? I like it.'

Elspeth smiled sheepishly. 'It's my Scottish burr. My aunties spent years beating it out of me so I could become a woman fit for fine English society. But it seems I am just a fraud for all their best efforts. I am no English lady.'

'And I am a very misbehaved Indian girl. Once I was a *Devadasi*, a handmaiden to the *Tridevi*: the three great goddesses Saraswati, Lakshmi, and Parvati. We cared for the temple, performed the rituals and *pujas*, and danced *Bharatanatyam*. The upper castes would have us give our blessings at the weddings of their children. It was considered quite auspicious.'

She smiled at the thought, but grew rueful. 'But the old ways are fading, and now all consider us no better than whores. So I serve the English. But I am not properly dutiful or industrious or respectful. I am quite impious. I do not know my place. I know I am a poor servant.'

'Poor, indeed!' Elspeth said, laughing. But then her face grew earnest. 'I have servants aplenty, Vijaya-ji. But I have never had a friend. Would you be my friend?'

Vijaya leaned over and touched her cheek. 'I am already your friend, *Sanam*.' Elspeth smiled and looked away, suddenly feeling bashful. The two of them lay back on their picnic blanket and for a time watched the clouds companionably. Presently, Elspeth felt her courage grow enough to ask an impertinent question she had been ruminating on for quite some time.

'Vijaya?'

'Yes?'

'Do you – have a lover?'

Vijaya rolled over and regarded her before answering.

'Oh yes, *Bahanji*. As beautiful as Krishna, and as red as the sun.'

Elspeth looked at her in surprise. 'Vijaya! Who is this man?'

She kept her face inscrutable. 'Oh, it is no man.'

Elspeth stared and hesitated. 'What – whatever do you mean?'

Vijaya returned her gaze unflinchingly. 'My love, my heart's desire . . . is – a tiger.'

Elspeth was unconsciously holding her breath. Now she let it out with a sharp exhalation and threw a twist of grass at her. 'Cheeky girl!'

Vijaya sat up and continued. 'By moonlight I go to the garden and sing for him. He stalks out of the jungle mad with love for me. Oh, he is so magnificent, *Bahanji*, so handsome! His eyes are bright as carnelian stones, his nose is as broad as an axe, his face is orange and black and shot with white blazes. He weighs five hundred pounds and he fears neither elephant nor maharaja. I embrace him and we make love right there on the estate grounds. Or some nights he takes me his secret honey-scented love-bower in the jungle. Oh, such a marvelous lover, my sister.'

Elspeth smiled indulgently and shook her head. Vijaya was given to the occasional burst of the most outrageous fancy.

Vijaya gave her a playful push on the shoulder. 'Oh, you are so serious. Come! When we get home I shall give you a proper Indian massage to help you forget all your troubles.'

'That does sound marvelous. It's fortuitous that Clive

is away until tomorrow. I should hate to think how scandalized my husband would be to find me in such a compromised state.'

They laughed.

Peacocks woke Elspeth in the morning with their half-human cries. As consciousness returned, realization descended on her: where she was, and her terrible loss. She rolled into a fetal ball, cried and shook in her bed. Her head felt thick and there was a queer taste in her mouth. On the nightstand was a bottle of McGillicuddy's Patented Laudanum Tonic. Something was wrong with the room; all her watercolors of the Indian countryside had been replaced by a thick wooden crucifix and a pair of oil paintings depicting Christ the Good Shepherd and Jesus praying in the garden of Gethsemane. In the mirror, her wet, teary eyes looked like raw oysters.

When she had collected herself as best she could and done some needful things, she wiped her tears and came down to the dining room where her husband sat at breakfast, reading his paper over a plate of smoked haddock Kedgeree. She sat down at the table without a word. The news from home was vexing him more than usual. He fumed over Welsh nationalists demanding recognition of their native tongue. 'Bloody Taffies and their Celtic gobbledygook! They should conduct themselves as *a conquered people.*'

Elspeth forbear to mention that she spoke only Gaelic until she was six. He sneered at the announcement of more dinosaur fossils discovered in the Wyoming Territory; Clive trusted paleontologists as much as freemasons and was convinced *Archaeopteryx* and Neanderthals were Prussian hoaxes orchestrated by Von Bismarck to sap British morale. Finally, Jack the Ripper had killed yet again in Whitechapel.

Clive threw the paper down in disgust, then straightened his collar and cleared his throat. He folded his hands and regarded Elspeth gravely. 'My dear, we must speak seriously as man and wife.'

He frowned, marshalling his thoughts. 'My dear, we are servants of the Empire, as well as Christian soldiers on the front lines of spiritual warfare, crusading into Lucifer's very suzerainty on Earth. Demonic forces walk freely here. We must never forget that these people are their thralls.'

He made the approximation of a smile meant to be reassuring. 'You must not despair or blame yourself too harshly for falling under the spell of . . . that woman. Strength of will is not a gift given to the fairer sex. But dearest, now you must fight and redouble your effort, despite your feminine weakness. The apostle Paul warns us against those women who exchange natural passions for vile affections that contravene the order of nature.

'This Jezebel, this heathen demoness who insinuated herself into our lives has bewitched you – India has bewitched you – but my angel, with prayer, faith and strict discipline, for as long as is required, we can drive the devil out of you. It is my husbandly duty to correct you, and I will not be slack in my moral responsibility. Do stop your infernal sniffling, Elspeth,' he snapped. 'Wipe your eyes and cease your childish behavior this very instant.'

He furrowed his brow and gave a deep exhale to preface a serious new topic. 'Now. What is more, we must take great pains to ensure that this . . . singular incident . . . remains our own private disgrace, with our good name and reputation unsullied. And I most solemnly promise you, I will protect you from that evil succubus and ensure that she never lays a finger on you . . . or anyone else again.'

Elspeth strived to keep her voice from quavering. 'Clive, darling, please listen to me. You mustn't do – '

'Enough!' Clive shouted. He stood and rang the servant's bell, then tugged on his waistcoat and collected himself. 'I have contacted Rev. Abernathy, and he will be coming by this afternoon to begin your spiritual discipline. Do make yourself presentable for him. And I must forbid you from leaving the house until such time as we are convinced you have been spiritually buttressed.'

'No!' She burst from the chair and rushed at him, striking at him viciously. She struck him three times before he managed to seize her wrists. Two of the groundsmen appeared in answer to his summons. 'Take Mrs. Godfrey upstairs and see to it she is given three spoonfuls of her tonic.'

The men nodded and pulled her, sobbing and kicking, up the stairs. There was a dreadful commotion from upstairs, but in a few minutes' time there was silence and the servants returned. 'The *Memsahib* sleeps now,' they reported.

The footman found Clive out on the grounds with his rifle, shooting any little grey *gilarhi* squirrels unfortunate enough to enter his sight. 'Are the three Rajasthanis here?'

'They await your pleasure even now, *Sahib*.' Clive lowered his gun.

'Good. Have them meet me on the veranda.'

He had grim work to do now. The turbaned desert trio appeared up to the task that lay ahead. Their bearded leader was grizzled and had but one eye. His second was wire-thin and hatchet-faced with long creases cut into his cheeks. The third towered over them all, a dark taciturn juggernaut with mighty thews like a djinn. All bore heavy curved daggers in their belts to defend their honor. Clive cleared his throat and spoke with authority. 'She is called Vijaya. The peasants have seen her take refuge at the Lakshmi shrine to the east of the village, the one on the old road.'

'We know the place,' spoke the grey-beard. 'And we have seen the harlot parading herself without shame or decency.'

'You do well to humble her pride.'

'Virtue is its own reward.'

'Lastly, to earn your money, it is imperative no one ever learn of this incident.'

'Have no fear for your honor. Shame burns well, and ash cannot tell tales.'

Clive permitted himself a cold smile. 'We understand one another.'

The men departed, and Clive returned to his sullen shooting. After his brooding had subsided, he returned to the house and ascended the stairs. The servants had closed the shutters and lower the gossamer mosquito netting to encourage Elspeth to sleep more soundly.

He stood unmoving, watched her sleeping form while

black thoughts twisted in his head. Then he regarded the new paintings, their Redeemers somewhat sinister-looking now in the ill-lit room. He straightened the crucifix hanging on the wall, and casually lifted the bottle on the nightstand. Perhaps just a nip would remedy his melancholy. He took the smallest swig, then a deeper draught. He nearly choked. It was only water. Stunned, he turned to the bed and lifted the netting away, and stretched out a quavering hand to his wife's prone figure beneath the bedcovers. Grasping the sheets, he pulled them away suddenly. Beneath them were nothing but pillows, rolls of clothing – and her wedding ring. His wife was gone.

Miles away at that moment, Elspeth sprinted past fields of wildflowers and splashed across rivulets, lungs on fire and muscles aching, hoping (now in vain) that her escape was still unnoticed. She had been terrified slipping out of the bedroom and skulking around her own house in only her nightgown, scarcely believing that her clumsy ruses had worked and certain she would be discovered at any moment. She had to crouch for two hellish minutes at the base of the stairs while two of the maids puttered around the corner. From a closet she quickly snatched breeches and a pair of Clive's big riding boots. Then carrying them she made her way to Clive's study and closed the door behind her. Her mind was racing to devise a plan. Quickly she pulled on the pants and stepped into the boots, then frantically ripped away the bottom of her nightgown to fashion a shirt.

She scanned the roll top desk for money, the keys to

the carriage house, clues to Vijaya's whereabouts, anything that could help her now. In the top drawer she found a scattering of erotic postcards featuring Parisian courtesans, and a black, coiled shape that for an instant she took for a scorpion. It was a service revolver. Elspeth jerked her hand away as if it might bite her.

She frantically rifled about the rest of the room, all the while desperately trying to think where Vijaya would go, how she could get a horse from the stables or somehow seize control of the carriage . . .

Movement from outside made her duck out of sight. She crept to the window and cracked it open. She could hear Clive's voice. 'She is called Vijaya . . .' She listened in rapt horror.

Minutes later, she chose the simplest option: she waited until the coast was clear and darted from the front door and into the trees. Then she bolted for all her heart was worth. She knew taking the dirt road to the village would eventually lead her to the old caravan route and Lakshmi's shrine. But she knew the lay of the land well enough now to realize that if she cut through the hill meadows and streams, and cut through the neck of the forest, she might reach the old shrine in time.

But she did not reach it in time. When at last she glimpsed the peak of its little stone roof she bounded down the hill, whipped by branches, and out of breath, and charged through the underbrush into the roadside sanctuary, she came to an ungainly abrupt, jarring halt against a stone pillar, transfixed with shock. The killers had already found Vijaya.

The giant and the hatchet-faced man had seized Vijaya, stretching her arms apart between them. The giant also clutched her neck in an iron grip, forcing her to kneel, forcing her head down as she wept and pleaded. Their leader stood before her, emptying a jar of lamp oil upon her. She shrieked with each douse. The greybeard turned at Elspeth's intrusion, a furious gleam in his eye. He held a lit lantern in his other hand.

Elspeth had no time to think of her hasty plan, only to react. She drew herself up and affected her most imperious manner. 'Release her!' she commanded. 'I am the *Memsahib* Godfrey!'

The one-eyed man's evil glare did not waver for an instant. 'We know well who you are, woman. Get back to your husband or we will drag you back to him ourselves.'

Elspeth matched his awful gaze, rooted to the spot. Her false exterior became something else, something true and even darker. She hunched her shoulders and bent forward in a slightly predatory crouch. 'Let her go now . . . or I will kill you all.' The three were dumbfounded at this transformation, then their shock smoldered into low mocking laughter. She began to raise her hands.

There was a rumble and flash of movement that caught the grey-beard from his side and dashed him across the room into the side wall. Lantern and oil jar shattered and he burst into screaming flame, illuminating the room.

A tiger wheeled to face them all, his eyes blazing in the fire-light like a god's. The great animal snarled, and stalked rapidly towards the two men. He batted at the shrieking hatchet-faced man like a cat playing with a mouse. With a single swipe, the man fell twisting away, clutching what remained of his throat and face. The big Rajasthani released Vijaya and held out his arms in pure raw fear, cornered. The tiger crouched and leapt, catching the turbaned giant in an embrace, and clamped his jaws on him. His smothered scream was cut off by a soft wet crunch, and he collapsed to the flagstones.

At length the tiger released his prey, and nonchalantly circled to regard the two women. He raised his head, sniffed the air, and made a deep chuffing sound. He observed them for a brief eternity; then, without warning, padded out past them and bolted away into the jungle, gone again.

The entire affair had lasted no more than a dozen heartbeats. Elspeth stared after him for long disbelieving moments, then came to her senses again and ran over to Vijaya, now gasping on the floor. She cradled her head and stroked her hair, sobbing and kissing her drenched forehead. Vijaya trembled. 'Oh, Elspeth, I was so terrified, so sure they were – they would . . .' She looked up at her and beamed. 'But then *you* were there, so brave . . . become the wargoddess . . . Mother Durga, riding on a tiger.' Elspeth looked at her, eyes wet with tears, wordless, full of love, her heart bursting.

How long they remained there on the stone floor holding one another, no one could say. But at last Elspeth peered around anxiously, suddenly aware of the terrible stench of blood and burned flesh. 'We must get away from here, darling,' she said, lifting them to their feet. She anxiously looked out at the road, the jungle, the sky. What now? She had no idea. 'But where can we go?'

Vijaya raised her head from Elspeth's shoulder. 'I know.'

In the branches overhead, langur monkeys leaped and chatter-barked at them. Now Vijaya had taken the lead, and Elspeth's hand, leading her deeper into the jungle. 'Where are we going?' she asked.

'We are following my tiger.' Vijaya smiled, as if this were the most natural explanation in the world.

Elspeth went along in a daze, her exhaustion finally taking its toll. *This is a dream*, she thought, *too much laudanum elixir.*

'*Bahanji*, trust me a little longer. We are nearly there. Pray to the moon now. She is a goddess and understands. She smiles on lovers and thieves, and those who must travel by night.'

Elspeth smiled at the thought.

She was very nearly asleep on her feet when Vijaya whispered into her ear. 'Beloved, look – we are here.'

She focused her bleary eyes on great masonry blocks, stone turrets adorned with intricate pendants and finials. They had arrived at the ruins of a temple courtyard adjoining an enormous pool of water ringed with fragrant pale lotus flowers. The crumbling stone walls were clutched by banyan tree roots and overgrown with flowered garlands of creeping liana vines, but on their ancient panels, bas-relief gods and nymphs could still be seen coupling in series of acrobatic exuberance. Night-blooming jasmine perfumed the air. Tiny frogs and cicadas serenaded them. Twilight was dyeing the sky, from cerulean to peacock teal to star-studded indigo. Above it all, the silver-tinged ring of the moon shone like a diamond necklace. 'A honey-scented love-bower . . .' Elspeth marveled.

'Come,' said Vijaya, pulling her by the hand with a smile.

The moon waited for them in the water, beckoning them to join her. They undressed and hand in hand, lightly stepped down the flights of baked brick steps into the cool water. *This must be how the selkie felt,* Elspeth thought, *throwing off her human shape to return home.*

They laughed and squealed; it felt delicious to wash off the sweat, grime and oil. Elspeth watched as Vijaya wiped the excess water from her face, then met her gaze with a coy half-smile. Treading water, they drew closer to each other, reaching out to touch fingertips, then grasp hands. They pulled one another in close until their hungry bodies touched; then tentatively, slowly, leaned in until their lips met as well. Elspeth felt dizzy, electrified, transcendent, and kissed her with a passion she scarcely knew was possible.

They released hands to embrace each other all the tighter; Elspeth clasped Vijaya's sweet face with both hands to kiss her, and Vijaya in turn wrapped her arms around Elspeth and held her tight. They spun round and round this way, then Vijaya broke free and swum to the stone steps. She left the pool and knelt on the steps, turning to entice Elspeth out with a beckoning finger and a lascivious look. The Scotswoman followed her gladly, and Vijaya tugged her up and over to the mossy flagstones. They felt soft as a velvet carpet when Vijaya sat down and pulled Elspeth down after her.

'Lean back,' she urged, and cradled Elspeth in her arms. With her left hand she tenderly pulled Elspeth's forehead back until Elspeth's head rested on her shoulder, then nuzzled her neck with abandon. Her right hand snaked around to caress her lover's breast and slyly play with her firm nipples. Elspeth closed her eyes and moaned. Vijaya continued to ravish her neck, but let her right hand trail down her torso, and slip the fingers between her legs. Elspeth shuddered, she reached back to grasp Vijaya's head, latched on to her bronze leg with the other hand for dear life. As Vijaya continued her ministrations, Elspeth eyes clamped tight, her mouth opened involuntarily, she began to writhe and tremble, shaken by the first orgasm of her life.

Vijaya cooed softly and shushed her, gently kissed and stroked her hair, bringing her back down again. She rested her head on Elspeth's and looked up at the jewel-glazed moon, thoughtful. 'We must go to somewhere without crucifixes or karma, my love.' She mused. 'Somewhere beautiful and disreputable on the other side of the world . . . Tahiti? Hawaii . . . San Francisco, perhaps. But first I must make an offering here.' She reached around and hugged Elspeth tightly, squeezing her in a firm grip. 'You must not be frightened now, *Bahanji*. Open your eyes. Can you see them?'

Elspeth felt a prick of unease, and gasped. Across the pond, bright eyes at the water's edge glowed and long, dark shapes moved. Tigers. 'Do not be afraid,' Vijaya reassured her in a firm voice. 'He is coming.'

From the dark of the temple ruins, a great shape

approached them. It crossed the pillared courtyard through alternating bands of moonlight and blackness like a Kinetescopic show. It appeared low and powerful at first, striding silently on all fours. In the crafty half-light, now it was a tiger – *their* tiger – no, now something else, then a tiger again, but when at last it emerged before them it was a no beast at all, but a man. His hair was wild and comely; his skin was the darkest shade of dusk. He was naked and unashamed, with a lean, powerful build that spoke of strength and feline grace. His handsome face was both ancient and ageless, his eyes glittered in the moonlight. 'They call him Vaghadeva,' Vijaya murmured reverently. 'He is the Tiger God, and my lover.' He drew closer still.

Elspeth never felt such a potent mix of fear and wonder. 'What does he want of us?' she asked softly.

Vijaya held her tighter. 'He hungers, and I must make an offering to him. But you have both saved my life this day, so you are my gift to him. And he is my gift to you.'

Vaghadeva said nothing, but took another step, standing before them. The dark shaft of his penis rose in an offering of his own. Vijaya reached forth a hand to cradle it, and with her other gently raised Elspeth's chin to it. 'Now open, and take him in your mouth,' she instructed. Elspeth obeyed, and opened wide to let Vijaya feed her. His phallus tasted musky and delicious.

Elspeth kept her arms locked at her side, using no hands but Vijaya's to sheath him in her mouth, while Vijaya supported her chin and worked the shaft back and forth. The god raised his head and growled his pleasure. He reached down to stroke both their heads with sacred carnality. The temple dancer directed the formerly respectable colonial lady how to make her obeisance to the idol before her, kissing and sucking upon the head, licking slowly up and down the shaft, tenderly kissing the testes, as Vijaya cupped them for her.

Then, responding to some unspoken command, Vijaya pulled Eslpeth's mouth away. 'It is time,' she whispered, and took her place behind her mistress. She sat supporting Elspeth's body as before, but this time had Elspeth hike up onto her lap, and lifted Elspeth's legs up and apart.

Vaghadeva knelt down, locking eyes with her, and took hold of her ankles, setting them on his broad shoulders. Elspeth gave a swift intake of breath as she felt Vijaya's fingers on her vulva, opening her for him completely. She was lost in his unearthly eyes as he bore down and filled her, Vijaya's hands guiding him in. The sensation made her eyelids flutter like butterflies; her breathing turned to gasps, then groans and a low animal growl. Vijaya brought her wet fingers to Elspeth's mouth and she suckled on them between gasps, tasting her own juices. Vaghadeva brought his face closer as he thrust into her with a deep, steady rhythm. He did not kiss her but seized her neck with his teeth, making her cry out with pleasure and clutch his head with both hands. He wrapped his arms around her thighs and pulled himself into her deeper still, while the two women covered his neck and cheeks with their kisses. Elspeth's head arched back as her body was wracked with her climax.

But the god wanted more sport. He allowed her legs

down again and without warning stood and hoisted her entire body, effortlessly turning her around in his arms until she faced down and away from him, her legs splayed out behind him. Vijaya came up to support her and Elspeth wrapped her arms around her neck, and they kissed fiercely while he suspended her by her hips and took her. When he finally deigned to let her down again, it was with surprising gentleness, placing her carefully down on her hands and knees. He placed his hand on her neck and carefully pressed her down, running his other hand beneath her to lift her rear. He laid his hands on her hips and entered her again.

Vijaya moved forward placing her lap below Elspeth's head, cradling her face in her hands. Then she spread her legs, and worked two fingers into her own exposed slit. She pleasured herself for a few moments, then brought her honeyed fingers to Elspeth's lips, rubbing them there and inserting them into her eager mouth. Elspeth sucked her lover's nectar as readily as she had her own. Then Vijaya hooked her hand into Elspeth's auburn hair and tenderly but insistently pulled her face down into her waiting sex.

She first whispered soft, urgent directions to Elspeth: 'Now kiss me, use your tongue, lick me. Yes, that's it, my love, just like that,' then just sighed and bit her lip as instructions simply became unnecessary.

Loud menacing growls came from the jungle behind them, interrupting their lovers' games. Two bristling, rippling muscular shapes with black coats and devils' eyes tore out of the undergrowth; teeth bared, snarling and vicious. It was Samson and Goliath, Clive's prized hunting dogs, and their master emerged behind them, rifle at his hip. The women scrambled to grab their clothing. Vaghadeva stood like a statue, glaring his displeasure. If he recognized what a gun was, he gave no sign.

The Englishman strode forward, barely able to speak his rage through clenched teeth. 'You've made a fool of me . . . sapphist! Fornicator! Filthy harlot!' He spat the words.

Vijaya and Elspeth clutched their clothes, knelling on the flagstones. The Indian woman said nothing, trembling with fear, but Elspeth looked up and met his gaze with defiance. 'Return home, Clive. You and I are finished.'

'You are my wife!'

'I am nothing of yours any longer!'

His wet bloodshot eyes reflected pure pain. 'I loved you . . .'

'You misspeak, sir. I was never the object of your love. You do not love me – you admire me, in the way of a useful, well-crafted tool or a handsome conversation piece on the mantel. You made me a porcelain doll in a curio cabinet and called it love.'

'That Jezebel has stolen your reason and made you play the whore with this black bastard – and degrade yourself with her sinful filthiness!'

Vijaya clung to Elspeth, wide-eyed.

'She did nothing but love me,' Elspeth said, 'and for that you would had have her killed.'

His voice was steady, soft, and deathly calm. 'I would follow the scriptures . . . and deliver such a one unto Satan for the destruction of the flesh, that the spirit may be saved in the day of the Lord Jesus . . . Deliver all of you . . .' He raised his rifle and trained it on Vaghadeva's heart. 'You first, you black devil, then your concubine. And you shall be last, Elspeth.'

Elspeth withdrew her hand from her bundle of clothes, pulling from the breeches pocket the item she had borne with her throughout the long day's ordeal: his service revolver. She aimed it at his head with a resolute grip. 'Clive, this business is at an end now. Put down that rifle and return home. We shall not trouble one another again.'

Clive blinked, hesitating. His arm did not waver, but tiny rivulets of sweat tracked down his forehead. Vaghadeva's eyes locked in on the Englishman, unwavering and unafraid, but his stance dropped almost imperceptibly into a fighting crouch. As he did, his dark handsome form changed and broadened, hands became claws, and his dark skin and mane of onyx hair became a fiery red-gold coat shot with black flames. Warrior became beast, man became god.

'Devilry!' hissed Clive.

The Tiger God leaped at his adversary. A thunderclap and lightning flash split the night and echoed off the ancient stone courtyard, sending blossoms of wild parakeets to flight.

Three weeks later, the Nagpur *Colonial-Telegraph* ran a small item reporting the tragic circumstances of the Godfrey incident. A local colonial administrator had gone into the jungle to rescue his wife, who had run into native trouble of some kind. Lamentably, his salutary ordeal would end in a most pyrrhic victory. He never found his beloved wife. His hunting dogs returned home without their master. His body was never found, only tatters of his bloody jacket. It was believed he was killed by a rogue tiger, a large male Bengal also responsible for the deaths of three natives earlier that day.

Happily, his sacrifice was not entirely in vain. Mrs. Godfrey emerged from the jungle the next morning, shaken but alive and well. Understandably however, the loss of her husband affected her greatly, and the widow Godfrey announced her plans to sell the house and depart the subcontinent in short order.

The wealthy young widow discouraged many a would-be suitor by declaring earnestly that after her husband, she could never love another man. But in a rare display of Christian forgiveness, the now quite wealthy young widow spent a sizable sum to purchase one hundred thousand acres of jungle-forest and prohibited the hunting of tigers there. That business complete, she left India to begin a new life somewhere in the Americas, some said San Francisco, accompanied only by a loyal servant.

Passions, Like Storms

by Nola Erus

Twilight on campus, and Heather knew she should prepare to leave. The walk home would be comforting at this hour, but in minutes day would slip away completely, and a moonless night would make the walk frightening, dangerous.

Prudent by nature, Heather considered her mother's warning to be safe on this little campus, but a new sense of experimentation grew within her, and she sought something more dangerous. She yearned for something with possibilities, which had not yet (perhaps never would) occurred to her mother. Heather sought Amber, the tiny redhead who helped catalogue books in the International Studies Department, the girl with the sassy way about her, whose eyes delivered devilish suggestion every time they gazed at Heather. Heather had felt them on her, had spurned the glances in the beginning, but every day she allowed herself a better glimpse back at the diminutive vamp in tall black boots.

Tonight, as always, Amber moved in and out among the stacks of magazines and books, decades of dust collectors, her dyed bob bouncing as she passed, spewing obscenities the likes of which Heather had rarely heard, certainly not from other women. As she worked, Heather watched or listened, grunted agreement or confusion, as Jason, Amber's dark shadow of a boyfriend, dozed on the sofa in the center of the room. It was Jason whom Heather had noticed first, tall and lean, dark and brooding, his sensuality like a primal come hither, and she had detected a connection there, but every day that she worked in close proximity with Amber, Jason fell deeper into the shadows of her fantastic hopes. Where once she had dreamed of his hands on her shoulders pulling her to him, his lips to suck her plump cushion smile, his hands on her breasts, now she thought about Amber. While she had entertained virginal hopes of his taking her in various positions she'd heard described by her friends, Heather now envisioned falling, rolling, oozing into new positions with Amber, the girl light enough for her to lift yet made to be in charge.

Heather smiled to think of how they would look to Jason, each with her own attributes to share. At five feet, ten inches, Heather was a giant in the eyes of some men. In the minds of others, Heather's body elicited daydreams of models drunk on vodka willing to enact sordid fantasies. Coupled with her alluring height, Heather's quiet disposition caused some men to presume her a snob while others imagined her stupid, but everyone she knew treated Amber with a certain reverence. Heather could stand like a statue, be treated with as much compassion, but Amber, like a rocket in miniature, commanded attention, and – though many were dismayed by her filterless approach to life and conversation – none would ever presume she did not know exactly what she was talking about. Heather, willowy tree of a girl, was the perfect submissive, and Amber, the shrub, was dominant in all she did.

Concentrating proved nearly impossible as images of Amber standing over her piqued fantasies within Heather. Sometimes Heather reminded herself to consider moral avenues, the need for feminine companionship rather than shared ecstasy, everything her parents had taught her. Other times, she asked herself what they could possibly have known, the two of them only with each other for twenty years; never another lover for either, never a lover to share between them. 'Heather bores so easily,' her mother often said, and Heather knew it was true. Amber represented more than danger – she represented purest, unadulterated pleasure.

'Are you even listening to me?' Amber's smoker's rasp at her shoulder caused a prickle across Heather's skin that pushed itself up and across her chest, peaked nipples imagining breath there. 'You haven't given so much of a grunt in at least five minutes.'

Heather smiled back at her, nodded and cleared her throat, 'Every word. Everything between your lips beckons me.' She'd meant it as poetic parody, but as soon as it had escaped her mouth, Heather cringed a little even as she grew dewy and taut at Amber's smile, a devil's curl at the corner of her mouth.

'You should stop flirting with danger, Heather. You'll get burned.' Moving to the window, past the tall shelves that divided the room, she added, 'I was saying we should all head out. The weather looks bad.' And as if to punctuate her words, a loud boom of thunder struck and shook as Baron Hall responded to Nature's wrath. Another boom, in the distance, and then total darkness. These buildings, old and weathered, were scary denizens on any night, but on a night like this, they would be absolutely sinister.

Sensing her distress, Amber rescued Heather, 'We'll walk with you. We'd drive you if we could, but you know us, always on foot.' That was the way it usually was on this rural campus, little luck for a ride, but Heather would be happier for the company. Especially Amber's. In the dark, a glint from lightning outside, Heather saw blue flashes across Amber's pale skin, ached to touch and stroke it, wondered if what happened in the dark, unexpected and confusing, could be brushed away, never broached again.

Did Amber feel eyes on her? Moving closer to Heather, she said, 'You could come over, you know. There's safety in numbers. Jason would protect us.' A sly giggle at this, and Heather thought she felt the brush of fingers at her thighs. She never saw the motion, but suddenly Jason was awake and talking to them both.

'Oh yeah, it'll be great, Heather, but let's get out of here now before the bottom falls out. We might beat the flood home.'

And with that, the stage was set: Heather, Amber, and Jason headed out together into the night, tumultuous skies overhead, heat and pressure in the air, and a hint of possibility like a fragrance on the night.

Six blocks from the building to the edge of campus, and another six from that edge to the house on the hill, restored by an art professor, Victorian in period pink. Heather shivered to see it, a glow of lightning behind. In the dark, it rose out of the hill like a movie set, Norman's house in *Psycho*, but in the daylight it would be warm and inviting.

How often had Heather imagined stepping in, finding her way upstairs, fingers trailing the banister, listening for the sound of Amber's sleeping breaths, finding her way into Amber's room, her refuge, peeling sheets back to expose pert breasts, that flat tummy, the ring at her navel? Heather knew the shiver that ran up her spine could not be described as fear so much as anticipation.

Opening the door with a shove of his shoulder, Jason smiled broadly, his teeth gleaming in the dark. 'You can stay the night, if you want. We'll put candles out, play some music. You play?' His eyes at her neck, her chest, caused Heather to halt her breathing just a moment. Such an interloper to her fantasy, but always she remembered need for him, however slight.

And Amber was pushing against her now, her chest at Heather's back, beneath shoulder blades. 'Y'all let me in. I'm not standing out here all night.' Heather turned to let her pass, and the breath that passed through her was forceful, labored as the breasts she had fantasized about stroked just beneath her own, and it seemed that Amber slowed them there, her eyes searching Heather's for invitation.

Broad pine panels, glossy in the dark. Shining hardwood floors. Billowing pillows substituted for sofas and chairs throughout the room. Candles everywhere. The room was not so different from how Heather had imagined it. On the looped rug in the center, fireplace to his back, Jason lowered himself to the floor, pulled Heather's hand to guide her down to sit, too, as Amber stepped behind her, fell to her knees with a slow rubbing caress across Heather's torso.

'Jason'll keep you company while I make the tea, light the candles. He plays acoustic. You'll like it. It'll help you relax.' Brush of fingers, childlike hands in her hair, lips at her cheek, just below her left ear, and a sudden thud of fear in her chest.

Go now, Heather thought, *leave and this all goes away. Stay and you've made a bed to lie in*. Heather set a challenge for herself: five minutes and she'd be gone, but if she hadn't left by then, whatever happened would be retribution or reward. She thought about her father's lectures, near sermons: 'The company you keep builds your reputation.' Her heart counted moments in the minutes.

Five minutes came and went as Jason began to play the Fender he carried everywhere. A song Heather recognized from childhood, something her uncle had played, by REM. Jason's eyes on her, she panicked to think of Travis, her boyfriend, at work, expecting to call her when he came home, perhaps check on her early in the storm. Jason's lips, glossy in the glow of candles, each lit by Amber's delicate hand, as he sang were like conjure magic to her, 'You don't really love that guy you make it with, now do you? I know you don't love that guy 'cause I can see right through you.' It was as if Heather were on trial, yet Jason smiled – sweet, low thing.

Amber was near her in minutes. 'We've thought of inviting you before.' Just that. No more invitation than this to a house, but a low pulse pushed through Heather, beat in her heart, flared through her chest, heated at hips, the meeting of thighs, in her tight jeans. Insistent, pulsing need at her clit. Taut aching at her nipples. Beautiful, seductive fear in her heart. Need, all-consuming, everywhere.

Amber slid to position in front of Heather, and just over that shoulder, tank top revealing crimson bra strap, satin silky beckoning, Heather saw Jason as he saw her, a show in the making, an actor in a role, this a new scene for each of them, and clearly, Amber was the star. 'You have no idea how wonderful this can be.' Flat statement of fact, but her touch was pure, dynamic energy as Amber reached to cup Heather's face, pull it to her for one deep vanilla-flavored kiss. 'But I bet you've thought about it.'

The glitter of night and candle in Amber's eyes was pure ignition for Heather; her lips moving in were kindling, and now they were kissing each other. Deep, wet, lustful suckles, Heather tugging at Amber's sweet cupid bow mouth, and Amber trailing fingers to breasts well larger than her hands.

'Oh my God.' Breathless exclamation, and Heather wasn't sure which of them had said it, but she reveled in the vibration passing through them with its utterance. Heather's hands at Amber's thighs, mysterious electricity. She'd run her hands over her own thighs countless times, moved her fingers up and under, found delight between soft, wet petals so often hidden beneath girlish panties, but never had Heather felt the thighs of another girl so intently, with such passion, with such purpose. Smooth, warm, firm things, naked to her touch, short denim skirt pleading for Heather's exploration.

Amber breathed deeply, sucked the moment in, whispered, 'Heather, find me.' She pulled her hand down

Heather's arm to force that hand up her skirt, to say *do as you please.* Fingers following instruction, Heather gasped to feel a wetness there at the tops of Amber's thighs, then the secret so poorly hidden that Amber wore nothing to keep her sweet, juicy peach from the world. A giggle in Amber's chest to see the surprise on Heather's face. 'I never wear panties when we work together, baby, just in case.'

And Heather could no longer pace herself, hold back from her desires. Dark as they were, forbidden, frightening, she plunged her fingers into the wet crevice at the meeting of Amber's firm legs, felt Amber from the inside out, explored deeply, then retreated to find that precious pearl at the gate, to stroke and tease and fluster Amber, to have more of Amber than she had yet dreamed.

From his place on the floor, Jason watched as the two made love, Amber opening her thighs wide, motion that pushed her skirt to her hips. Heather falling back to the pillows behind her, her hair – an auburn cascade he longed to touch. Amber's fingers at Heather's buttons, jeans opening slightly, then Heather's kitten-like crawl from them. Amber's hands pulling them, her bottom, round pretty thing, in the air so that he could see her pink, wet, smooth-as-silk pussy. He could kiss it now, surprise her with his tongue, but he knew this was not for him yet, knew these two meant to discover one another before he joined the party. Patiently, he sat and watched as Amber stripped.

A gasp as she looked down at Heather's pussy, soft thing with curls, such a virginal offering, and there a tongue peeking through to surprise and tease her. Again, 'Oh God,' and they both laughed, right before Amber lowered her tongue to find her groove in Heather's haven, sweet solace of her wet, peaceful shore. Amber's tongue like waves in lapping need. Heather's coos met in time with her unfastening of buttons on the shirt that belonged to Travis. She shivered to think no one had kissed her here before he had, no one else since until now. And sweet as he was, Heather was thrilled to discover how much better Amber was at this than Travis. Her tongue in practiced motion. Her hands sliding up Heather's torso to push the shirt from her shoulders. Her fingers resting there on puckering nipples, then pressing, and pinching, and teasing them.

Heather found herself in motion too, new response to growing, evolving feelings, sexuality in development, sensuality only now tapped by this sweet key, the tongue in twisting, hopeful motion. Lifting hips, rolling motion, Heather pushing herself up to find Amber who sought her, and all the while Jason's rise a pressure there between his thighs, a need insistent to his core, his hands finding flesh all his own to stroke in time as they created harmony with moans and coos in lust.

Heather now nude as Eve on the pillows hummed low ecstasy, long legs pleading for something more than just a tongue on her clit, pushing high to pull Amber in, and Amber wondered if she could drown here, intoxicated in this ecstasy. 'You're beautiful,' she whispered in the dark, candle flames inspiring reflections in dance across Heather's body. And Heather rose, her heavy chest bouncing as she reached to pull Amber's black T-shirt from her narrow body.

'Let me see you, pretty girl,' Heather purred, and for a moment Amber wasn't surc she was Heather's first, but then she realized from the expression on Heather's face – part shy expectation, part bold inspiration – that Heather was completely drunk on something she had never tasted before. Arms high above her head as Heather pulled that shirt from her, Amber awaited other kisses at her nipples, breasts firm but not large, inviting in their perky youth, and when those lips and teeth, that tongue, touched her nipple for the very first time, Amber felt her lust growing to orgasm, knew she'd come soon from just this, the build and suckle, the feeling having Heather gave her, the perfect unity of their beautiful bodies on this storming, dark night. A thrill, too, to know that Jason watched in lust, his hands on his flesh, stroking ecstasy from his shaft, his head, his cock in rhythm even as he ached to join them.

And now their mouths, searching each other, Amber's tongue across Heather's teeth, straight from braces, one slightly turned out, Heather's in Amber's cheek, there to the right, and both of them swooning into each other, falling into decadent loving, lust for each other. Amber in Heather's lap, legs tightly crossed at the feet, and Heather rolling Amber to the floor to show her the pleasure she had shown her, just a hint of times they could have together. 'I've never done this before.' Shy blue eyes peeked at Amber from beneath long auburn hair, wisps like a curtain between them. 'But I have dreamed about it.'

'Heather, you don't have to do anything you don't want to, but you shouldn't be shy either. Do to me what makes you feel good – it'll be so good for me, too,' and Amber fell back then, her skirt exposing her swelling pink petals. Heather sat there for a moment, amazed to have this opportunity unfold in front of her. Her fingers there now, touched tentatively to watch shivers pass through Amber.

'Seeing your sweet pussy is very different from touching it in complete darkness or in my dreams.' And with that Heather kissed this girl, her sweet Amber, fully on her pretty lips, there between her thighs, felt her tongue offer its virginity to that hardened jewel there, that clit pulsing for her, wrapped her tongue around it to suck it into her mouth, to pull sweet nectar from her. Amber's smile ran deep within her, played along her arms, at her elbows, at her rising nipples, found its way to frolic at each stroke of Heather's hungry tongue.

'Touch yourself, Heather.' Jason offered his insight into the situation, knew Heather might not do for herself what she would do for Amber.

But Heather replied quite simply, 'Come closer, Jason. Look again. I am touching myself, and so are you. Come closer.' Jason rose to join them, having ached for this invitation, and Heather raised herself to kiss his cock sweetly, one plump kiss to the head, the soft sweet stroking tongue to the shaft, as she moved her hand to stroke Amber's tight pussy.

'You've got such a lovely cock, too,' Heather said, a hint of tease in her voice, 'and I've dreamed of having it in me.' She looked over her shoulder coyly, subtle hint that Jason followed as he lowered his jeans to the ground, slid out of them, and took his spot behind her, 'I do play, Jason, and I'll be so happy to play with you, but this is Amber's night.'

Jason halted though he ached to touch her, and then Heather reached behind to touch his throbbing flesh, 'Come play, Jason, but save the best for Amber, my pretty, pretty girl.'

And now she leaned forward, resumed kissing Amber's sweet clit, stroking her own, as Jason pushed himself into her. Heather felt a shudder build in her, slowed her pace to focus on Amber, knew she would wait to come until Amber did again, and then she and Jason would show Amber, their girl, her sweetest rewards, flowing them to her.

Amber's growing need pushed her hips to Heather's mouth, and as Jason pushed his cock into Heather's tight pussy, she returned the favor by squeezing her tongue into that angel's space, sweet nectar, fragrant pool between Amber's twitching legs, in and out, in and out, as Heather enjoyed tantalizing new sensation at the tip of her tongue. Amber moaned to feel such joy, to know she had inspired something new in Heather. And Heather moaned to feel how tight Amber could close sugared walls on such a slim thing as this cherry red tongue. Flash of lightning at the windows, splashing rain in puddles on the porch, and now thunder that echoed their rising need.

Jason's hands at Heather's hips, then slow circle to her own flushed jewel where he rubbed faster and harder as she licked more furiously at Amber's fiery clit, and Amber reached to twist nipples that swayed against her thighs, each stretch of her arms seemingly making her pussy tighter, tighter, tighter like a vise. Jason's hand in Heather's hair, so tempting to him before, as he twisted her locks to make reins, to pull her head back, but she pulled forward tenaciously, more determined than ever to feel Amber's kiss flow into her mouth, spread across her face, her cheeks, drip to her chest, bobbing there against Amber's thighs.

'Oh my God.' A cry across the thunderous night, part joy, part howl, and Heather felt it echo through her, sensed it spreading through Jason as he bucked and thrust into her, Amber trembling beneath that ecstatic tongue, and now Heather could contain herself no longer, purred deep growling need against Amber's sweet wetness, moaned, collapsed, and suckled as her pussy tightened against the deep, needful drill of Jason's cock, his hands at her shoulders to keep her there as her body tightened to squeeze him out, and Amber rose to come to her, sweet Heather, her new lover.

Amber's bucking thrusts subsiding to coos and flutters, her body pouring ecstasy into Heather's sweet mouth, and Heather's responding with sweetest flow was more than Jason could bear and now he exploded into Heather, she who had instructed him to save the best, gave her everything he had in the moment, and together their howls and coos were echoed by the thunder, reflected in the lightning, and drowned – as they were in each other – in the rain.

Crawling up to Amber's shoulder, exhausted but joyful, Heather laid her head there, closed her eyes and rested, as Amber stroked her pretty hair and Jason leaned back on his knees to watch the friends. He would lie beside them soon, but just now he wanted to enjoy their peace. And as Amber kissed Heather's forehead, then her lips, Jason thanked the stars for storms.

When I Taste Like a Waste I Breathe

by Farrah J. Phoenix

More and more, the office building roof is becoming my refuge. An escape from the consistent inconsistency of a failing company and the constant droning of incompetent co-workers. It is hard enough dealing with my own negative distortions without dealing with the onslaught of idiocy from power-tripping bitches who have no hope in hell of excelling.

Up on the roof I am free to slip into the mindlessness of my fantasies. Up here I am relaxing in the sun on a beach in Maui. A deliciously tanned surfer massages my feet while I read a magazine. The article is about my ex-husband undergoing a radical penis-ectomy after contracting a flesh-eating disease from the snatch of the redheaded bitch he ran away with. Surfer boy and I laugh together before folding into each other's embrace under the watchful eye of Mother Nature.

Up on the roof, everything is possible.

I unbutton my blouse, exposing the smooth curvature of my voluptuous breasts. The sun caresses my yearning skin like a lover's seductive touch. I've been craving warmth, my body aching daily from its absence. Closing my eyes, I give in, allowing the rays to enfold me as a lover should.

I am just thinking of heading back to the office when I hear the squeak of a rusty hinge behind me. Turning in place, I see her. I have seen her a few dozen times in the building hallways, the elevator, and the ladies' washroom, and each time I couldn't help but stare.

She is the image of sensuality, with dark flowing hair that caresses her neck softly. Her eyes are deep and dark with a devilish twinkle that speaks dirty desires to me. Her skin is smooth and tanned – breasts, perfectly perky. Everything about this mesmerizing creature draws me to her, but I can't speak. I want to tell her how beautiful she is, how captivating, but when she smiles at me my body burns, and I can't find the words.

Each time I see her, an intense craving to touch her bubbles up from my tummy. Running my hands along her curves, feeling the heat from her soft skin as I press my mouth to hers; the thought sends a chill up my spine. I yearn for an opportunity to know the feeling of her skin against my lips, her body urging me to continue. Tracing a slow line down her stomach, my hands delicately following along, eliciting cries from her honey sweet lips. Watching her gasping breaths as I discover a world unknown between her smooth, responsive thighs. Exploring every inch of her goddess form, becoming as one as we respond to each other's touch, a sweet yet foreign desire constructed from the mere sight of her.

'You discovered my secret,' she purrs.

Watching her walk towards me is like watching an exotic dance. Her tight body moves rhythmically. The bounce in her tits, the swing of her hips, invoke tiny eruptions deep within me. With every step, I become more aroused. How could a woman cause such a reaction? I have been with men all my life and have enjoyed all the pleasures a penis can offer. Yet I desire her.

'This would be a great place for a midday fuck, don't you think?' she poses with a laugh. 'That would definitely help me through the rest of the day.'

I laugh nervously, nodding in agreement; visions of her naked form start to build.

'Smoke?' she offers.

'Oh, no, thanks.' I watch as her soft, wet lips wrap around the end of the cigarette. Her breasts heave as she inhales. My body aches.

'So, how do you make it through the day here?' Her eyes bore into mine. I feel exposed. Like she can see the dirty thoughts I have about her. I turn my gaze away and start to talk. I can feel her watching me, the movement of my lips, my breath, my breasts. My body blushes.

No more than a few sentences escape before they are silenced by the luscious lips of my desire against mine. Shocked, I go numb. When I taste, like a waste, I breathe and the moment is gone. Her warm, wet lips pull away from mine.

I want her. I want to sample her, to feel her.

'I've been wanting to do that for a while now.' She nibbles her lower lip, staring deep into my stunned eyes.

Intense heat rises up from inside me like a raging inferno of repressed sexual desire.

I grab her by the back of her neck, pulling her close.

Our mouths devour each other. Her lips are soft and sweet, like nothing I've experienced before. The fire blazes.

I feel her hands on me. My face, my neck, shoulders, breasts. Blood surges like lava flow between my legs. I draw deeper into her mouth.

Our lips release. She traces her tongue around my jaw bone, behind my ear. I moan as my body responds.

Frantically, she rips at my blouse, exposing bountiful bosom.

We paw at each other like lionesses at war, removing clothes, caressing curves, indulging in our sensual desires.

Exposed, we rise to our knees, drawing our bodies together.

Hard nipples and soft breasts meet.

I run my hands over her arching back. Cries of pleasure escape my mouth as her lips and tongue discover.

She grinds her hips towards me, pressing her velvety sweetness against mine.

My body erupts.

Grabbing her ass, I pull her to me. Our mouths meet again. She presses forcefully against me, pushing me to the ground. Her hand slides between my legs. Spine tingling vibrations burst forth, enveloping my body in pure, erotic bliss.

Echoes of intense passion reverberate off neighboring buildings as she explores the inches of my body. The strands of her hair dance over my naked skin, fueling my veins with electricity. Slowly, she ventures across my stomach, over my hips and back to center, her tongue landing softly on the wet velvet her fingers have been massaging. The warmth of her tongue against my clit, the movement of her fingers on my g-spot, set my body ablaze.

My heart beats faster than it ever has. Muscles in my back, thighs and pussy twitch and contract. Each flick of her tongue drives me wild. I want to hold on to the moment. My mind fights with my body to resist the urge to overflow in ecstasy.

Her moans of excitement increase the passion, increase my desire, increase my bravery.

I caress her head and guide her back to my lips. My arms wrap around her slim, silky form. I inhale every delicious taste of her mouth. I have never felt so connected to someone. I want to taste more.

Rolling her on to her back, I straddle her, grinding our throbbing desires against each other. Her eyes close, her lips part as she breathes in our lust. I run my hand softly down the center of her chest, watching as small goose bumps follow.

Leaning down, I kiss along her breastbone, squeezing her gorgeous tits at the same time. I trace the outline of her breasts with my tongue. Her hard nipples beacon me. I close my lips around the peaks of her breasts, gently licking and sucking as the beautiful body beneath me writhes with joy.

Her blissful cries entice me to continue.

I want to please her. I want to feel her ecstasy flow out all over me.

Slowly, I spread her legs with mine. Nestling my head between her heaving thighs, my tongue teases her clit as gasps of breath emanate from her parted lips.

Liquid joy mixes with my saliva as my tongue darts out to brush her nerve endings. Her taste is sweet . . . clit full and throbbing. My fingers creep inside her tight, wet pussy while I continue to probe her with my tongue. Fingers and tongue work in tandem to send her into sensory overload.

When her body tightens, my fingers squeeze; she cries out in sheer bliss. I kiss her tummy as it twitches rapidly from her orgasm.

I am overwhelmed with desire as hers subsides. Grabbing me, she frantically rubs my clit until my insides surge with rapturous delight. We lay together in our euphoria, waiting for our bodies to cease shuttering.

Sunbeams caress our skin as our breath slows back to normal. I smell the scent of unbridled, passionate sex. Images of our bodies entwined flash through my mind. My desire continues to twitch as a reminder that this fantasy was real.

Silently we collect our clothes, slip our panties on, secure our bras, and cover up the evidence of this afternoon's frolic.

Slipping my arms into my blouse, a pain rises from my stomach. Then a thought: *Could I love this goddess?* She could not possibly love me. My mind races, pain growing stronger, eyes starting to moisten. I feel silly. How could I feel this way about a woman?

The touch of delicate hands on my body pulls me out of the rampage of negative distortions shooting through my head. It's her, standing in front of me, buttoning my blouse slowly. She takes her time, purposefully running her fingers over my skin as each little button is put in place. My body shivers; my breaths become erratic.

Her beautifully radiant eyes meet mine. She smiles sweetly before placing her lips on mine once again.

'So, would you like to come over tonight?' she asks sheepishly as she grabs my hand and guides me to the roof door. My mind and body explode with joy.

'I would love to.'

Quietly we leave our secret place, entering a new world of possibilities, eager to discover.

My New Roommate

by Jen Bluekissed

Joelynn, my dorm's resident assistant, pulled me aside. 'Lenora may not have mentioned it to you, but she's gonna move out next semester. She's having trouble coping with school and losing her father at the same time.'

'Oh?' I sat on the couch adjacent to where the RAs watched TV when not helping the dorm residents sort out issues. Crossing my legs and forcing down a gleeful grin, I said, 'So I get to have a double-sized room all to myself next semester?' Lenora's quirky habits coupled with her erratic behavior had been bothering me for months.

'It depends. If you want to pay the higher single-room rate, the university'll let you stay where you're living now with only you in the room. If you can find yourself a roommate, then you'll keep the double rate.' She reached for her mouth. Joelynn quit smoking two weeks ago. She smiled when she realized I was watching her pretend to reach for the cigarette she didn't have.

'And if I can't find a roommate but can't afford to pay the higher cost for a single room?' A sensation akin to heartburn welled up within me. Everyone I knew who wanted a roommate already had one. My student loans were already taken out for the whole year. I couldn't afford to pay the single-room rate.

'Then the university will match you up with someone in a situation similar to yourself. You may not get to stay in this dorm. It's likely you'll have to move into another girl's room. Or maybe she'll have to move into your room.'

'Will I know if the university has put me up with another girl before winter break if I don't pay the additional money for a single room?'

'Maybe. Maybe not. I really don't know,' Joelynn said.

'Hi. I'm Ruby, but everybody calls me Ru,' I said to my new roommate's father. Extending my hand, I forced my lips upward in a polite gesture.

Even though it was January and bitterly cold outside, the trips up the stairs with Cami's fridge, microwave, and boxes caused droplets to form near the top of his balding head. I had already introduced myself to Cami, but she was somewhere near the ground floor carrying a box.

'Hi. I hope you have early classes.'

I didn't know what to say while Mr. Stydle caught his breath. After an extended awkward silence, I climbed the ladder to my loft and sat on my bed. 'No, not really. After three years of college, I know better than to sign up for morning classes. The earliest one starts at eleven. I have a couple of night classes that get out at nine.'

He raised an eyebrow at me. 'So you're a night owl, then.' It wasn't exactly a statement, but the words didn't hold the right inflection for a question either. I didn't feel I needed to justify my choice of class schedule to a stranger's father, so I allowed silence to fill the room until he left to carry the next load of boxes up the four flights of stairs to the dorm room. If Cami was half as anal about stuff as her dad seemed, the semester would drag. Only after I sat alone for a few minutes until my new roommate returned with another box did I realize that they hadn't hauled any lumber up the stairs yet. I hoped she also planned on hoisting her bed onto a loft. The room would feel too cramped if her bed stayed where it was, low to the ground.

The morning wore on with Cami and her dad lugging her possessions to our dorm room. Not only were both of them sweating, but I was overly warm too. The hot water heat our building used caused the temperature to rise as the day progressed. I was used to the heat in the wintertime, as most of the girls in the building were, but I wondered if Cami knew how ungodly hot our room would get. For her sake, I opened a window. The cold air felt good as I walked back to my loft and climbed the ladder.

'You were in one of my freshman English courses, right?' Cami said. She flicked her long blond hair behind her shoulder.

'Yep.' I dangled my legs over the side of the loft. 'Don't think we've ever actually had a conversation, though.'

'I was sure I knew you from somewhere.' She locked the dorm door before continuing the conversation. 'My dad says you have late classes. Mine start at eight every morning. Organic Chemistry kicked my ass last semester. I hope I don't seem like a bitch, but if I'm going to pass

Organic Chemistry II this semester, I'm going to have no life. I'll live in the room and the library if I have to.'

Cami's voice flattened as she droned on and on about how much she hated the professor. She rolled her eyes and sat on her bed. I silently sulked because she hadn't lofted her bed, but I wasn't sure she noticed I didn't care about Dr. Wildaguarde. My attention was on myself until I saw her lift her tank top above her head. After removing her tank top she wore nothing above the waist except a black sports bra. The window was still open, but it felt like ninety inside our room. I wanted to take my shirt off too, but I wasn't sure how she'd respond. She wiped the sweat from her forehead with the back of her hand. 'Everybody talks about how this building's heat is all out of whack, but this is ridiculous,' Cami said, wiping away the sweat. Mascara and eye shadow smeared across her face in an ugly line.

'You might want to look in the mirror,' I said. Her appearance helped brighten my mood.

Cami walked to the sink and washed her face. A sloppy amount of water splashed onto her sports bra and down the front of her jeans. I continued watching her without saying much. 'I usually stay up pretty late,' I finally said when she turned to face me.

Without explaining herself, she removed her shoes and unzipped her jeans. I guessed she was removing them because they were damp, but she didn't replace them. Cami was quick about undressing. Her skin was light and freckled. She wore pink cotton underwear, the black sports bra, and socks. I didn't want to stare; we'd both have to change in front of each other over the course of the semester, but my eyes remained fixed on her pink underwear. Her legs looked freshly shaven, and I felt both comfortable and awkward while she stood in front of me. What a tease.

'How do you concentrate in here? It's horrible how hot the room is,' she said. 'If I'd have known how bad it was, I'da asked my dad to pack me an extra fan before he drove out here to help me move.' Cami's nipples were erect and poking through the bra. Maybe a new roommate wouldn't be such a drag after all.

I didn't know what to do with my hands. Seeing Cami stand below me almost naked sent a bolt of desire through me. My hands wanted to busy themselves. 'Do you care if I take my shirt off too? You're right, it's oppressive in here.'

My hands trembled as I lifted the knit shirt over my head. Thank the stars I'd worn a decent bra. My old, yucky ones were in the bottom of my underwear drawer for when I really, really needed to pay the laundry gods. One long brown ringlet of hair fell between my breasts. It tickled, but I didn't remove it. My heart beat rapidly in my chest while she watched me remove the shirt, but then she turned away and leaned over and clutched her Organic Chemistry book. 'I've got to study before class begins on Monday. I felt like I was always a chapter behind last semester.' She trudged to her small, wooden desk and sat. Her body was opposite the open window, and I could see her reflection against the glass as well as her live profile from where I sat on my loft.

'Oh,' I said. 'You mean you're going to study now? It's Friday night. Don't you want to hang out or something?

Unpack your stuff? Watch a movie?' I felt like saying, *Invite me to take my pants off too?*

She combed her straight, sleek hair with her fingers before tying it into a ponytail above her neck. 'Maybe tomorrow. When organic chemistry is on the brain, I gotta study. If I don't, I'll be kicking myself on Monday.'

I regretted removing my shirt once I realized Cami meant business. Was she freaking kidding me? Even if I wasn't attracted to her, a get-to-know-your-roommate session should have been first and foremost on the schedule. I turned down offers from my friends to party that night because I wanted to be nice and offer to help Cami get to know the other girls on the floor. 'Okay, but I have to ask you a few questions before you really get serious about the studying,' I said. 'My last roommate, Lenora, drove me batty because she had a few habits that drove me nuts. I need to know you're different,' I said.

Cami opened the drawer to the desk. Her expression was odd, like she expected something to be in the drawer, but she hadn't unpacked any of her stuff yet. 'Okay, so what's your big pet peeve, then?' she said as she furrowed her brow at me.

'Well, Lenora's boyfriend used to hang out here all the time. It was like he lived in the room too. It got super old.' I leaned against the wall and stopped dangling my feet over the side of the loft. 'Do you have a guy?' I tried to be as cool about the question as I could, but the sound of my own voice as I asked the question sounded odd. My voice held a nervousness I hadn't anticipated with Cami.

'Nope. The last relationship went sour, and I've sworn them off altogether.'

What kind of an answer was that? *Throw me a bone here.* I glanced at the clock and regretted I hadn't asked all my friends where they were going for the night. Some of them were out bar-hopping, but my twenty-first birthday wasn't for another two weeks. I thought about calling a few of the others, but found my butt glued to the top of the loft. It was as if Cami held me there even though she was trying to study. 'Okay, well, if you're going to study, I might as well pop my ear buds in and catch a few tunes.' I turned up the volume to my iPod and climbed down the ladder alongside the loft. On second thought, maybe I would pay a visit to one of the other girls' rooms down the hall. This chick was hot, but she was boring as hell.

'Where ya going?' Cami said as she raised her nose out of her organic chemistry book.

'To Stacy's room. She usually has a movie on the tube on Friday nights.'

I watched Cami as her face revealed her desire to tag along with me. She scrunched her nose up and opened her mouth without saying much of anything. Then she returned to organic chem.

'You wanna meet Stacy and the other girls on the floor who don't get wasted on Friday nights? We're not as lame as you might think. The movies are usually pretty fun, and normally there's popcorn.' I wondered where Cami's friends were, but then I remembered she'd told me while her dad had been down a flight of stairs that most of her good friends had a house away from campus. Her dad was pretty strict and wouldn't help her buy a car, so she was grounded on campus unless her friends wanted to pick her up. If they were anything like the rumors circulating around school, they would already be drunk by this hour. From what I'd heard, she ran with a pretty wild group.

Cami tapped the eraser of her pencil against her cheek three or four times before wrestling herself away from the textbook. 'I guess a little fun time won't hurt.' Turning her head and scanning the room for the location of her shirt and pants, Cami smiled. 'What movies do y'all watch?'

'Just about anything.'

Sunday night, Cami insisted she needed to go to bed early. I wasn't ready to sleep, so I allowed her to turn the lights out and listened to my mp3 player while I thought about the upcoming semester. Most of my professors were known for being easy, but one of them was notorious for giving huge research projects. I'd seen a copy of last semester's syllabus, and my mind rolled through the possible topics. I didn't want to pick anything too time consuming, but I did want to learn something in the process. Homoeroticism in Shakespeare's plays was one possibility. Maybe the influence of the Greeks on Shakespeare's works? Losing myself in Elizabethan England, I removed my ear buds and pictured the Globe Theater of Shakespeare's day.

What brought me out of my daydream was the sound of quiet, heavy breathing. Cami's inhaling and exhaling sounded too rapid for her to be asleep. My ears perked when I realized Cami obviously thought I was asleep or couldn't hear her over my music. She was touching herself. The moonlight through the open window lit the shadows in the room, and even though I could barely see her, I knew she was reaching between her legs. Having lived with other roommates before Cami, I wasn't naïve enough to think she'd never reach for herself when she assumed I wouldn't notice. This time, though, realizing my roommate was pleasuring herself affected me differently.

I knew all the other girls were straight. With Cami, I wasn't positive. I wasn't sure if she was maybe bi or what, but she just gave me different vibes. Although she hadn't mentioned a boyfriend, I was fairly certain I had seen her on the arm of a guy once or twice around school, but not in a long time. What was Cami thinking about as she stroked her clit and pressed her finger into her slit? Who was she thinking about? In that moment, I hoped she was thinking about me. Cami hadn't been shy when removing her clothes earlier, and she still slept in her sports bra and underwear. Our room's temperature stayed inhumanely warm. I was hot, and I wanted to taste her.

Cami whimpered as she climaxed. I pictured her soft lips, how moist and gentle they would feel against mine. How wonderful it would be if I could part her folds with my tongue and explore. I wanted to be the one to cause those quiet sounds. The sheets rustled across the room, and I assumed she was about to turn over and fall asleep. Instead, I watched as Cami reached under her bed for a toy. Once she was on her back again, the toy disappeared under the sheet. There was more movement from her bed as she used the object. I assumed it was a dildo, because the toy was silent as her figure pulsed, shrouded in the moonlight from the open window.

Figuring she wouldn't notice, I removed my bra, then slowly glided my fingers down my body while I listened to her whimpers resume. Closing my eyes and imagining her nipple in my mouth, I licked my lips and parted my sex with my fingertips. Cami's noises became louder while she thrust the toy into her flesh, and I clamped my own lips tightly so I wouldn't be tempted to join her in sounding out my pleasure. Gently squeezing my clit between my fingers, I felt the warm and slick moisture against my hand. Just as I almost reached orgasm, a jolting, obnoxious noise caused me to bolt upright in bed. Cami did the same.

'What drunk asshole pulled the fire alarm in the middle of the night?' I said in a mutter as Cami flipped the switch to her bedside lamp.

She stared at my exposed breasts. With a smile, Cami's face gleamed an expression similar to how I imaged she'd look when opening the first present on Christmas morning. From below me, her eyes remained on my breasts while the fire alarm continued blaring. In a quick movement, she dropped the sheet draped over her chest. When had she removed her bra? Cami stood slowly, hunting for a robe. I was surprised she hadn't slipped her underwear back on like I had before standing. Even though the fire alarm still rang loudly, all I wanted was to touch her. Still highly aroused from nearing orgasm a moment earlier, I would have given anything to take a hammer and smash the fire alarm to pieces.

'Damn freshman,' I said while climbing down the ladder

from the loft. 'The RAs will be here any minute to make sure everyone's okay.' I found my clothes and dressed quickly while I watched Cami cover herself with the robe and her winter coat. I found mine and bundled up.

'I know.'

We walked into the hall together and then down the stairs with the other girls living on our floor. Within moments we were outside. At least a half hour would pass before we'd be allowed to return to our room. The temperature outside was around zero before wind chill, and I felt my arousal disappear. I regretted not finding a hat and gloves before leaving our room. Cami had been smarter; she was bundled head to toe. 'Put your hands in the pockets of my coat,' she said. 'How'd you find a winter coat without pockets?'

'Don't ask,' I said. Her pockets didn't help the temperature of my hands much, but they did keep my exposed skin from the wind. I could smell the fruity shampoo she used in her hair, and I showed my gratitude by smiling. 'Thanks.' Taking a step closer to her, I pressed my pelvis against her butt while I stood behind her.

Another girl from our floor tapped me on the shoulder. 'I have a spare set of gloves in my pocket if you want to use them.' She held the gloves in front of me.

'Thanks,' I said, trying to keep the sourness out of my voice. Not wanting to offend this chick, I removed my hands from Cami's pockets and filled the gloves with my hands. Cami frowned when she turned to face me. Her lips looked disappointed, and her eyes held a wanton expression.

* * *

Once we were back inside the room, both Cami and I removed our winter gear. I closed the open window and sat on her bed. 'Did you really swear off guys?' I said after she sat next to me. Rubbing my hands together to warm them, I waited for her response. She looked at her shoes and drew in the corners of her mouth in a tight line.

'That question was pretty random,' she said. Fumbling with her shoelaces, Cami didn't look at me.

'Well, I want to know,' I said. 'The thing is . . . I'm attracted to you. I don't want you to be weirded out or anything, and if the feeling isn't mutual, that's cool.'

She finally returned her gaze and looked me in the eye. 'I think we both know what we were doing before that fire alarm went off.' Cami's face flushed as she continued talking with me. 'I don't really have to study organic chemistry as much as I've let on. When you're in the room with me, I feel different. I saw how you were looking at me, and when I closed my eyes in the dark and thought about you, I just wanted to imagine you and feel the electricity in the air that I felt when you watched me remove my shirt earlier.'

She was making sense, but in her own way she was babbling. I touched her jaw and leaned toward her. The scent of the aloe lotion she used earlier in the morning on her face and neck mixed with the scent of her arousal as I moved in closer. I closed my eyes and held my breath as I pressed my mouth against her moist lips. Cami stopped talking mid-syllable, and she pressed her lips against mine. I felt giddy when Cami's tongue touched mine, and I knew she wanted the kiss as much as I did. A big chunk of me wanted it to stop. What if we hit it off okay right now, but then in a month or two we broke it off and still had to live in the same dorm room together? When Cami tugged gently on one of my long, brown ringlets of hair, I stomped my apprehension back into my gut and kissed her back.

Cami's breathing changed, and just as I was about to pull away from the kiss, she lifted her other hand from her side. Touching my breast through my clothing, Cami explored my mouth more deeply. Neither of us was wearing a bra from the sudden jolt of the fire alarm, so I could feel the warmth of her hand through my shirt. I wanted to keep going, to return her touch, to wind up in a full-fledged romp on her bed. Instead, I stood up and stepped away from her.

'What's wrong, Ru?' she said, suddenly looking hurt.

'Nothing.' I stepped back a little further. 'It's three in the morning, and you have an eight o'clock class. We have all semester to get to know each other. I don't want you to be exhausted all morning. You don't have the luxury of sleeping in like I do.' Winking at her, I turned away and flipped the light switch so that the room was flooded with darkness. 'If you fail Organic Chemistry on account of me, your dad'll really flip.'

Cami whined under her breath, and I recognized the sound as the same one she emitted earlier in the night while touching herself. I climbed up into my loft, and she lay back onto her bed and turned off her lamp. I wasn't sure how long I stayed awake while listening to her breathe. My mind raced through what just happened.

I kissed a girl.

We both liked it, and now we had the rest of the night and the rest of the semester to deal with it. The feeling of my hands in the pockets of Cami's jacket, the softness of her lips against mine, and the sound of her breathing filled my consciousness until I fell asleep.

Her alarm clock rang loudly at six thirty the following morning. With my pillow over my ears, I drowned out the sound of the buzzer and groaned. I could learn to love Cami as long as she wasn't one of those chicks who hit snooze twenty times before finally getting out of bed. I sighed in relief when I heard her shuffle out the room with her shower supplies in hand. Smiling as I drifted back to sleep, I remembered I'd kissed a girl. Her last words before leaving the dorm for the shower were, 'Ru, it's gonna be a long day while I wait to see you again. I want to finish what we started.' I was instantly horny.

During all the new semester's classes that day, I thought of nothing but being with her.

After both of us finished classes, Cami and I sat inside the dorm room and faced each other. She flashed me a wicked grin and said, 'I want to explore you.' I felt her tug at one of my long, brown ringlets before she broke it apart with her fingertips. Throughout my life people pulled on my curls, especially in elementary school. I usually batted people's hands away from my hair. This time was different. I wanted her fingers in my hair. The little twirling motion she made with her fingertips reminded me of the other curls I wanted her to explore.

I lifted my shirt over my head and watched as Cami mirrored my action. She unhooked my bra, and I unhooked hers. My heartbeat thumped in my chest as I felt the heat rise up into my cheeks. Cami's mouth found mine, and she lightly kissed my neck as she cupped my breast. I reached into the elastic of her lounger pants, pushing the waistband over her full hips. She unbuttoned my jeans before freeing me of them. With a flurry of activity I was naked, and she was in nothing but her panties, lying on her back. I straddled her as soon as she lifted her hips off the bed, pushing her panties away from her pelvis. Grabbing onto them with my toes, I yanked her panties down her smooth thighs and took her nipple into my mouth. It was hard against my tongue, and I lightly nibbled it, enjoying how it hardened in my mouth.

As I opened my legs and rubbed my open, moist flesh against her mound, she whispered in my ear. 'I'm so glad you're my new roommate. Don't stop.' She inhaled quickly, and I liked feeling her body move against mine. I slipped my tongue into her mouth, paying attention to how her body tensed under mine. She began panting. 'You're good with your mouth. I want it.'

We were both sweating. Cami drew arousal out of my shy personality, and I felt like I was in heat. 'Stay like this,' I said as I turned my body around. I needed her to lick me as I sucked her. Too eager to take turns, I handed her a small pillow and knelt over her head. Burying my tongue in her fuzzy mound, I found her clit. My lips kissed her inner lips, then I sucked her. I almost forgot about how badly I needed her until she reciprocated, and we sixty-nined.

If my mouth hadn't been busy pleasuring her, I would have told her then and there how good it felt. Cami knew just where to lick. It was as if I was instructing her, but she didn't need instructions. I moaned while continuing to suck her clit. Chemistry, my ass. She'd been studying how to pleasure me. Oh. My. How many fingers was she plunging into me?

I used one of my fingers to explore inside her wetness, but I couldn't concentrate on what I was doing. Cami's mouth and fingers rocked the orgasm through my body before I could even try to hold it back.

Stopping the sucking, I changed to flicking gently at her clit while trying to replicate what she had done with her fingers. She moaned as I found the right spot inside her. I teased her clit with my tongue once I realized what Cami liked. My pleasure over, she began speaking softly. I could barely hear her.

'I want it. Don't tease me anymore,' she said.

Cami's thighs moved on either side of my head as she came. She moaned her gratitude while I changed positions again and lay over her face to face. Our slow kiss tasted a little like me and a little like her.

'I'm glad you're my new roommate too,' I said before catching my breath.

The End of the World

by L.A. Mistral

Katherine knew only one part of her was fragile. The rest of her was tough. She knew that too. She'd been riding horses for about five years. She'd started with a course in college and continued after she graduated. There was just something about the sweaty, svelte power of the horse and the earthy musk of hay that slipped inside Katherine and stayed there, keen to come out.

She rode Western style, took to the training immediately and could now ride with the best of them. She loved sitting on the horse as it galloped around barrels or gathered calves for penning. She felt she would fly with just one more puff of air. Many of the other girls were afraid of it, for the risk and the loss of control. But that's exactly what Katherine liked about it.

Katherine was ready for something new. She just didn't know what.

The risk and uncertainty made her weak in the knees. Sometimes the thrill of barrel racing did that. One time just the power of a glance almost broke her bones. That glance came from Dora. Dora, 'of auburn hair and alabaster skin,' as Katherine liked to call her. Dora's skin was so translucent that it had just a slight tinge of blue, like you could see inside her. But you couldn't, really. Dora was quiet. She hardly ever looked anyone straight with her hazel, half-opened eyes. *Like the color of the Ionian Sea just before a storm*, Katherine thought. She'd cruised there once and stood for a long time on the balcony lost in the lazy flow of the amethyst and emerald contours of the waves. Katherine had felt like she was at the end of the world. Dora's translucent skin perfectly complemented Katherine's own olive-tan complexion and eyes as dark as her Arabian horse.

She'd never recognized these feelings so clearly before, and they were so different from what both excited and bored her about men. Most of them talked endlessly about business or sports or both simultaneously. Their bodies were different, but she always felt they were an alien presence. What was worse, men treated her body like a football – grabbing instead of fondling and forcing when she was most willing to surrender. When push came to shove, she'd take grace over strength any day.

But that was not to say she didn't enjoy fucking men. She liked it just fine and had the swollen, extravagant, permanently polished pussy to prove it. Yet Dora didn't exhibit gentleness. She could be rough. Katherine had seen how Dora used the crop against the flanks of the horse. Dora was sweet-tempered but firm. She took control of eight hundred pounds of muscle and instinct with the flick of her wrist and the snap of a tooled leather crop. *It's not the crop*, Katherine thought. *It's who holds it.*

Dora had skin like the inside of an almond, and Katherine's skin was like the brazen, bronze of the outside.

Sometimes, just for an instant, Katherine imagined how Dora's skin might look and feel pressed against her own. If she'd let her mind wander, she imagined what her skin might taste like. She sucked an almond in her mouth once just to think about it and was scared to feel how she trembled.

Katherine drew in her breath like she did when she was excited and reached down to smooth between her legs. She was wet already, and her pussy lips felt all pure and puffy. By now, Katherine could slide the width of her hand inside there. She slid the side of her hand back and forth, harder and harder. Angels ascended and descended into her own wide-open, reddening wings. Katherine sucked air between her teeth to keep from screaming. As she opened her mouth in the middle of one silent scream, something snapped inside her, not in her body but like the ancient Mayan calendar prophesy, one era giving way into another – the end of the world, the beginning of something new.

The next day she watched Dora again, bouncing up and down on a wide saddle, her spread legs fitting her blue jeans thin and tight as a breath. The chaps held her ass like a tanned-leather lover. Dora's hair flowed like a dark, red bandanna. Then her horse faltered, confused by some command, and stopped. Dora's momentum jolted her from the saddle and spilled her into the dirt. It all happened so suddenly that Katherine couldn't react immediately. Other riders came over to check on her, and when Dora stood up, they all knew she was okay. Dora limped out of the corral to wipe herself off, and Katherine met her at the dressing rooms. Relief made Katherine less cautious.

Katherine hugged Dora lightly and was glad when Dora responded by pressing back, just slightly, like she was answering a hard question on a test. After splashing water on her face, Dora glanced up at Katherine. It was just a glance. But Dora's emerald, oceanic eyes stared one moment too long, one moment with too much longing. Dora's glance asked a question and Katherine answered back.

Katherine took a hand towel and wiped the remaining mud off Dora's face. It was more like a face massage than a cleansing. 'You look like a raccoon,' Katherine said, caressing Dora's cheek all the way down to the bottom of her throat, 'but a lovely raccoon, a very lovely . . . .'

Dora leaned into Katherine's shoulder and started to tremble. Katherine could feel Dora shake and her voice crack, 'It's just the f . . . fall,' Dora stuttered, 'It was so startling.'

Katherine held Dora, her head falling into Katherine's breasts and Dora's long auburn hair covering her face like a shawl. Dora breathed harder and harder against Katherine's nipples and she felt herself stiffen. Soon, she too, was panting. She began to kiss the top of Dora's head. Each time she did, Katherine smelled the rich, malty smell of turf. Dora let out low whimpers, then lifted her head, took hold of Katherine's shoulders, and drew her mouth into a kiss.

Dora's kiss wasn't timid, and it sucked Katherine's soul out through each cell of her body and gave it back again. Her tits ached to be twisted. She felt the ache from beneath her belly all the way up to her throat. One feeling flowed into another: the love-gut-ache, the down-low-ache, the fear-thrill-ache, the suck-full-tongue-ache, the empty-pussy-ache, the skin-full-fuck-ache. Her mouth became dry, and she pulled Dora's mouth even closer.

'Let me get dressed,' Dora said, 'and we'll take a walk.'

'I don't want this to end.' It wasn't a plea. It was a promise.

'Don't you worry,' Dora answered, 'it's only beginning.' She slipped on a short, blue dress, her hips flaring out like fireworks, and tall cowboy boots. She still carried her riding whip. Katherine had on a skirt with a Western-style snap-buttoned shirt with long sleeves.

'The guys really go for a dress like this,' Dora said. 'Do you think women are different?'

'I think men, or *boys*,' Katherine emphasized, 'go for what is revealed. I think women like what is concealed.'

'Like my pendant?' asked Dora, touching the gold necklace she wore. The locket had slid slyly down between her breasts. 'You can get it if you want.'

They both stopped near the end of the paddock where hardly anyone ever went at that hour. Dora wasn't wearing a bra and Katherine bent over and kissed her breasts lower and lower until she found her large, dark nipples. They were as dark and stiff as Moroccan olives and then she sucked on them.

Dora flicked the riding whip carelessly against Katherine's thigh, and it drew them to kiss again.

'Gee, you'd better be careful with that thing,' Katherine said, trying to be nonchalant. 'Someone could get hurt.'

'Only if they want to get hurt,' she joked, her mischievous smile spread like a sunrise across Dora's face. It was as if the whip was a language she used when she had no words. It was the way her skin spoke to skin.

Dora was exploring. Katherine could feel it. Only Dora was more sure of herself.

Katherine and Dora continued their walk through the empty paddocks, arm in arm. The slanting sun of a late summer sunset warmed Katherine's legs, exposed by her short skirt. Dora urged Katherine into a stable door and kissed her there, then turned Katherine around. Katherine bent over and held onto the edge of a hay crib while Dora lifted up Katherine's skirt with her riding crop and flipped it over hips.

'Umm, now I like this,' Dora crooned as she caressed her fingertips over Katherine's panty-less crotch. Her fingers made circles, swirls, and secret Mayan signs. Katherine's slick cunt was already evidence of an elegant openness for the play to come. The sunlight on her skin and the sting of the whip on her raw skin made her feel so ripe, so naughty, so wanton.

She wanted Dora to take her like that – rough, uneven, and raw. Katherine felt like she'd jumped off a cliff, so she might as well enjoy the fall. Dora bit on Katherine's shoulder in slow sips and tapped her whip against Katherine's thigh. The whip tapped a Morse code up and down the smooth slaloms of Katherine's inner thigh. Dora tapped out long syllables of longing, and she tapped out staccato sentences of ache and desire. Katherine instinctively understood this new language and was dying to answer. She whirled around, grabbed each side of Dora's face and plunged her tongue into Dora's open lips where it swelled deep inside her mouth. Katherine's whole body ached to be inside Dora now, skin for skin and soul for soul.

The whip's tapping got harder as Katherine's mouth got bolder and harder against Dora's lips. Dora's mouth felt like an incendiary device.

'Your wide lips, so red, so beautiful,' breathed Katherine. The whip awakened something strong and delicious, and Katherine reveled in her surrender. Dora seemed to be an expert in the unspeakable properties of leather. She was an expert in the teasing, pleasing and teaching that leather can bring in the right hands. 'That feels good,' Katherine whispered heavily, 'just like an extension of your hands. Please . . .' Katherine panting harder now, the words came out only in single syllables, 'Please . . . take . . .me . . . now!'

Dora turned her around and pressed Katherine's body against the half-filled grain trough next to the stable door. Then she pressed herself against Katherine's back and bottom and kissed the back of her neck, breathing heavily into her ears. 'I'm going to get your permission, okay?'

Just the fact that Dora asked got Katherine excited. She bent lower over the feeder and spread her thighs even further apart. Her full mouth formed a perfect 'O' as she sighed heavily. Her ebony eyes shone like dark stars in an evening of arousal.

Katherine's consent stoked Dora's desire. A moment later, Katherine felt the smooth tongue of the leather whip ripple across the inside of her thigh.

'Okay?' Dora asked, still pressing against her backside and breathing in her ear.

'Yes!' Katherine chanted back, stretching out the syllable like she wished Dora would stretch her.

Dora did just that, brushing the lips of Katherine's pussy with the wide handle of the whip, unfolding her cunt lips and teasing her with the thick end of the whip along the length of her pussy. Katherine's cunt frothed and steamed. The closer Dora pressed the whip toward the opening of Katherine's cunt, the more aroused she got. Katherine thrust her bottom back harder and harder. She wanted to cling to the whip, to feel the sharp, teasing lips of the whip nip and nibble, biting into her skin.

'Okay?' Dora asked again.

'No!' Katherine said. It wasn't a protest. It was pleading.

Sweat pooled behind Katherine's neck and shoulders and her own special syrup surged like the sun dawning between her legs. Warm rays flooded down her inner thighs as she tried to take the whip inside her. She wanted any part of Dora inside her now. Katherine's whimpers and moans were the best prayers she could offer. No other words would do.

The whip peaked into her and her pussy opened like King Tutankhamen's gold enshrined tomb when Howard Carter gazed into it for the first time. A new world unveiled for Katherine. Her body was a universe just awakening.

Dora felt something new too. She watched as Katherine's pussy blossomed, then closed like the petals of some dew-drenched flower aching for light's brilliant, blissful advance. They both felt the end of their old world and the beginning of a new one.

That was enough, at least for now. This adventure was not over, not by a long shot.

Dora withdrew the whip and lay against Katherine, kissing her over and over. 'I wasn't teasing you,' she said. 'I needed to know what I liked too.'

'Did you find out?' Katherine asked her, turning around now to face Dora's sultry, sea green eyes.

'We'll find out together.'

Katherine didn't need to answer. Their bodies said it all. They tasted each other even in their sleep . . . the only cure for ecstasy – exhaustion.

Show Me Yours

by Lucy Felthouse

I felt I'd fallen on my feet with my university digs. Despite having a two-bedroom, I'd never had to share. I was incredibly lucky to have all that space to myself, and I'd always made the most of it. All that changed when Celeste arrived. She'd come over from France on a placement, gaining experience of the English language for her degree.

It was up to my university to find her somewhere to stay. Ever the cheapskates, their own property was the cheapest option; therefore, she ended up in my room. I knew it wasn't like I had to give up my bed or anything, but I'd gotten so used to my own space that I felt affronted having anyone share it.

When she arrived, though, it wasn't so bad. I was expecting a language barrier and awkwardness, speaking only the most basic French myself, but it turned out that she spoke better English than I did.

Celeste settled in quickly, and we got on famously. Just as well, since we were living in such close proximity. My main problem with the situation was the lack of privacy. I'd always been able to go to the loo with the door open, or wander around in the buff – difficult habits to break. Not to mention masturbation. I'd taken that *totally* for granted. No more slipping into bed with my Rampant Rabbit for a quick session before sleep time – even if Celeste was asleep, that damn noise would wake her up!

After a few frustrating wank-free weeks, I was at bursting point. As we were both always popping in and out of the dorms all day, there was no guarantee she wouldn't come in any minute. Finally, I got so desperate I decided to take the risk. Having no boyfriend at the time, it was the only way I could get any relief. I was sure she had a lecture at twelve for an hour. I planned to do it.

I skipped over to the window and closed the curtains, but not before peeking out across the courtyard to make sure Celeste wasn't around; I had visions of her coming back to collect a forgotten book or something. The coast was clear – excellent.

I drew back from the window and cursed as my top caught the handle of the dressing table drawer – Celeste's dressing table. I untangled myself and went to shut the drawer, until I saw what was inside.

The saucy minx had a dildo! One of the thick, veiny lifelike things, complete with balls. I was astounded. Here was I, desperate to masturbate, and yet she was finding time to use this bad boy! Or was she? Just because it was there – after all, she was in the same predicament as me. Perhaps she used it in the shower, with the noise of the running water to drown out her cries.

I was lost in reverie – images of Celeste standing under the shower, stuffing herself with this monstrous synthetic cock when the door opened.

Startled, I shoved the dildo behind my back. I must

have looked like a kid caught with her hand in the cookie jar. I suppose I was, in a way. Celeste walked into the room, frowning at the dimness and flipped on the light.

'Liz? What are you doing? Why are the curtains closed?'

'N-nothing,' I stuttered, mentally fumbling for an excuse, 'I have a migraine coming on. I was going to have a lie down.'

Only a partial lie. The second part was true.

'Oh, okay,' she said. 'I'm sorry I disturbed you. I just came back to change. I spilled juice on my jeans.'

Damn. She was going to come to the chest of drawers. I shuffled hastily out of the way, hoping she'd think it was she who had left the drawer open. No such luck. She hesitated as she noticed the drawer and turned to me.

'Why is that open, Liz? And what are you holding?'

Her face registered annoyance, then, after a beat, amusement, as she thought about what I could possibly be hiding. I thought desperately for an excuse, then gave up. After all, I hadn't really done anything wrong. I hadn't been snooping; the open drawer had been a genuine accident. It was just my curiosity that had gotten the better of me and left me holding the dildo.

I held out my hand. Celeste's eyes widened. I held both hands up in surrender, not thinking how amusing my pose would look to a bystander.

'Look,' I began, casting around for the right words, 'this looks bad, I admit. But it was an honest mistake.'

'An honest mistake resulting in you examining my dildo?'

Touché. 'Celeste. Listen.' I explained what had happened, sticking to the migraine explanation, as opposed to the

I'm-desperate-for-an-orgasm one. ' . . . and when I saw your dildo, I was just curious. I'm nosy and I'm sorry. I never should have touched your stuff. I won't do it again, I promise.'

Celeste's eyes narrowed and I tensed, believing she was about to start ranting and raving. Aren't the French renowned for their tempers?

'Do you have a dildo of your own, Liz?'

Wondering where this was leading, I answered, 'Not a dildo, no. A vibrator. A Rampant Rabbit.'

'Really?' she squeaked. 'I have never seen one of those! Show me!'

It was all getting a bit weird, but I figured I wasn't in a position to argue. I handed Celeste her dildo and went to fetch my own toy. I presented it to her, feeling like a naughty schoolgirl forced to turn out her pockets by a teacher. My vibrator fascinated Celeste. She turned it over in her hands, looking at the buttons and fingering the bunny ears.

'Show me how it works,' she demanded, handing it back to me. 'If it is good, I may get one of my own.'

'Well,' I said, 'you press this button here and the bunny ears vibrate, and this button here makes it faster – '

'No, I said *show* me, not tell me.'

'I don't know what you mean,' I replied, though it was slowly dawning on me where this was going, 'I'm not . . .'

'Come on Liz, don't be scared. Show me.'

Celeste walked over to me, took my hand and led me to my bed where she pushed me down and sat beside me. By now, I was seriously panicking. I'd never had so much as a drunken snog with a girl before, and yet here I was about to use my Rampant Rabbit in front of her?

Of course, Celeste and I had seen each other naked; living in the same room it was kind of inevitable. But that wasn't sexual. Or had it been for her? Despite her never mentioning a boyfriend, I'd never got the impression she was gay. Perhaps she'd kept it from me because she didn't know how I'd react. Or maybe she felt she didn't know me well enough yet. Could she be bi?

I didn't get the chance to voice any of the questions flitting through my brain as Celeste spoke again.

'Liz.' She tucked her long dark hair behind her ears, looking at me through her lashes. 'Come on. You've seen my passion, let me see yours.'

She *was* coming on to me! Her hand found mine, and she lifted it to her lips and began to kiss and nibble my fingertips. I was frozen to the spot. My brain struggled to keep up with all the information that was being thrown at it. I'd just processed the fact that Celeste was a lesbian, or at the very least bisexual, when I came across a question. *Was I?* I'd been with guys, though not very many, but I'd never really thought about girls in that way. Or had I? Reading magazines, I'd always appraised girls' bodies, but in a more analytical way than a sexual one. So I thought.

As Celeste continued her ministrations on my fingers – she was now sucking them – I thought, *what the hell?* I wasn't *anti*-girl, after all. Plenty of girls partake in lesbian encounters at university and then go on to have straight relationships for the rest of their lives. They just see it as experimentation, so why shouldn't I?

I gently removed my fingers from Celeste's grasp, put my vibrator down and began to unbutton my blouse. Following my lead, Celeste started to undress. Within seconds we were both down to our underwear. She was wearing a matching black set, which looked striking against her pale skin. Her figure was lithe, almost boyish, narrowed at the hips with small but perky breasts.

She pushed me so I was lying down on my bed, then began to tug at my pants, which didn't match my bra. I rarely paid attention to such details. Celeste didn't seem to mind and discarded my underwear without a second glance. Then she handed me my Rabbit.

Wow, I thought, *this is it. My first girl-on-girl encounter, and I am totally unprepared!* I tried to tell myself it would be fine. I was just using my vibrator in the same way I always did; it would just be in front of an audience, that's all. By now, I was wet. Whereas I was worrying, my subconscious was obviously relishing the situation. My clit was tingling with anticipation, and my pussy lips were slick with juices, which squished as I parted my thighs.

I slid the head of the vibrator down between my folds, swirling it up and down my vulva, coating it in my juices. Celeste watched, enthralled. She was biting her lip and looked as though she was restraining herself. Did she want to touch herself? Touch me?

Seconds later I changed the angle of the toy and positioned it at my entrance. It was by now lubricated with my natural fluids. I pushed it inside, gasping as it stretched my vaginal walls and feeling it all the more keenly as it had been such a long time. When it was in as far as it would go, I pressed the button to switch on the vibrating ears. I positioned them on my sweet spot and groaned as the vibrations shook my clitoris into ecstasy.

I half-forgot that Celeste was there as I felt my orgasm approaching. She wasn't trying to get involved, as I first thought. She was merely watching what I was doing. I slowed things down – not wanting to come too soon – by moving the ears temporarily from my clit and penetrating myself shallowly with the shaft of the toy.

I felt my orgasm subside a little, so I put the Rabbit back in its original position, not wanting to lose my climax altogether. This time it built up much more quickly, and I felt the familiar tingling building up in my abdomen. Celeste, clearly realizing what was happening, didn't move a muscle. Only another woman can understand how fickle the female orgasm can be.

I began to twist my wrist back and forth, flicking the bunny ears across my clit and back, a surefire way to get me off. Sure enough, I felt the contractions begin, and the wave of intense feeling which signaled my climax. I tensed involuntarily as the waves rolled over me; then relaxed as they subsided, quickly tugging the toy off my clit, suddenly sensitive. As my breathing and heartbeat slowed, I opened my eyes.

Celeste was sitting at my feet, looking shell-shocked. Was she horrified? Disgusted? Our eyes met, and she grinned, dispelling my concerns.

'Liz, that was really sexy. That thing looks magnificent! I am definitely going to get one.'

Reaching into my bedside drawer for a condom, I replied, grinning, 'Why don't you test this one first?'

Defining Lines

by Regina Perry

I'm not a sun goddess, but I do aim to keep my skin bronzed year round, so I frequent a tanning salon in my neighborhood. I also play for a girls' fast pitch softball league, swim on the city team, and teach yoga. I pride myself on my athletic ability and toned muscles. I'm conscious of my body and want my physique and skin to be at its best in a swimsuit and leotard.

Entering the salon, I encounter shelves of tanning accelerators. The names of the various bronzers sounded like something from a brothel: Love Potion, Enchanted, Dark Secrets, Spellbound and Stolen Darkness. Enya croons *Wild Child* in surround sound as I search for the attendant. When I conclude the place has been abandoned, Ginger, the owner, pops around the corner, beaming her vivacious smile.

'Hey, Ava, how's it going?'

'Great, except for this stupid shoulder injury I got from pitching in last week's softball game. Now, I can't even demonstrate downward-facing dog. Guess I'll get a lot better at *describing* positions until it heals.'

'Ah, that's too bad. How long did they say it would take?'

'Six to eight weeks,' I answer, rubbing my shoulder.

'So you'll be out of softball that long too?'

'Unfortunately . . . guess I'll catch up on my reading.'

'I'm sure you'll find something entertaining to occupy yourself with.' She winks. 'Been dating anyone interesting?'

'Nah, I don't even get asked anymore.'

'What? A fit, gorgeous brunette like you! You've got to be kidding.'

'Well, Rusty was killed in Iraq, and after that, I just had no desire to be with anyone else. I'd try to go on a date, but the whole time all I could think about was Rusty. I guess word got out that I was one boring date.' *I need to get over this. Everyone is sick of hearing me whine.*

'Oh, Ava. I had no idea you'd had a loss like that. I'm so sorry.'

'Well, it's been two years. It's time I moved on.'

'You should go out with me and my girlfriends some night. Find someone new.'

I wrinkle my nose. 'Pick-ups have never interested me much. Rusty and I started dating in high school. We were planning to get married as soon as he got back.'

'After all this time, you still don't think you could fall for someone new?'

'Actually, I do think I'm ready now if the right person came along. Question is: How do you find that *right* one?'

'If you're not willing to get out there and look for love, then I guess you just have to hope and pray it knocks on your door.'

'Doesn't sound too promising, does it?'

'You never know . . .' She smiles. 'The stand-up is ready for you.' Motioning with her head, she directs me toward the back hallway.

Entering the dressing room, I'm overwhelmed by a fresh coat of scarlet paint. The octagonal tanning booth fills half of the four-by-eight foot area. I set down my bags and turn toward a newly installed full-length mirror. The booth had been completely remodeled. A shelf stocked with tissues, wet wipes, and deodorant jutted out from the wall beside the door, with several hooks underneath for clothing. I inhale a fusion of tropical fruit, chocolate, and coconut.

I tune the radio to my favorite station, then undress as Usher sings *Love in This Club* like a serenade for me alone. I drape my clothes over the hooks and place my jewelry on the shelf. The new plush throw rug emblazoned with a brilliant red and gold sunburst cushions my feet. I slip on my bikini bottom and lather on the accelerator. Attempting to apply it to my back, I feel pain rack through my body. Yoga training had given me the flexibility to reach between my shoulder blades, but not with this shoulder injury. I crack the door and call for Ginger.

'Yes?'

'Would you mind helping me a minute?'

'Sure, no problem.' She skirts around the counter and moves toward me. Her five-foot, two-inch body literally bobs when she walks and her blond ponytail swishes from side to side. Perky describes her best, from her cute, freckled nose to her perfect little butt that sways with every step. Her nipples, poking through her thin cotton tank, slant upward.

'Whatcha need, Ava?'

'Do you think you could rub bronzer on my back? I can't reach the middle with this bum shoulder,' I plead, standing behind the door.

'Of course.'

I turn away and open the door wide enough for her to enter. Facing the wall, I wait while she warms the bronzer in her hands. Slowly she massages it into my skin, beginning at my waist and inching her way upward. I'm surprised by the tingling sensation of her touch as she works my muscles.

'Oh Ginger, you should be a massage therapist. That feels so good.' I relax more with each swirl of her hands.

'Actually, I'm enrolled in the school of massage.'

'Great! You're wonderful already. I'd say you're ready to graduate.'

'Thanks. I really enjoy it too. I love the feel of skin and muscles beneath my fingers.'

'Mm.' I place my hands against the wall for support, relishing every moment. I'm acutely aware that my boobs have swung forward, dangling freely.

'Most people tan nude. Do you wear your bottoms?'

'Yeah, I want to see my progress. Gotta have something to compare it to, you know.'

'Cool. I think bikini lines can be so sexy – a piece of art, if done right.'

'Oh, yes.' I'm quick to agree.

'Just your bottoms? Not the top?'

'Right. I don't want any strap lines. Besides, I love golden skin on my breasts. Do you tan nude?'

'No, I'm with you, Ava. I want to see my progress.'

'Top too?'

'Yes, but I tuck the straps inside the bra cups.'

'Oh, how clever.'

'May I sneak a peek?'

'What?' I tense, standing straight.

'I want to see your tan line. I'll just pull down your bikini a little.'

'Oh, sure. Okay.' I relax into my previous stance.

It's strange, being half-naked with a woman in this tight space. But it's been so long since I've been naked with anyone, I'd probably feel strange with a man too.

Ginger slides her hands to my navel, working her fingers in small circles. Then she slides her thumbs inside the band of my bikini pushing it down about an inch, lowering the suit all the way around. I can't believe my reaction. My groin contracts, and the sensation tingles all the way down my inner thighs. There's a butterfly in my pussy that won't go away, no matter how hard I fight it. *What's wrong with me?*

'Mm . . . nice lines,' Ginger gushes, 'and you take such good care of your skin. It's so smooth and supple.'

'Th . . . anks,' I squeak. *Can she tell I'm aroused?*

She continues to massage me, concentrating on the newly revealed inch at the top of my bikini. She slithers her hands back to the front along my waist, then enlarges her circular motions upward until she's brushing against the underside of my breasts. A moan escapes from my throat as I press my body into her hands.

'Did you get enough of the bronzer on your breasts?' she asks.

'Uh . . . I . . . I'm not sure.'

She pushes her buttocks against the door, and I hear the lock click. A trickle of wetness drips into my crotch. Ginger squeezes a few more drops of bronzer into her hands, then widens her circles on my stomach until she's kneading my breasts. By reflex, I rest my back against her. She pulls me tighter to her chest, and I feel her nipples protruding against my back. Her hands cup my tits as her thumbs flick across my nipples, intensifying the pressure and speed. It has been so long since I've been touched, I'm near orgasm. My head falls back to her shoulder, my back arches and pelvis thrusts heavenward. I tingle with desire. When she slides her hand down my stomach and pushes inside my bikini, my inner thighs quiver and knees buckle.

Using the pressure of her fingers, she turns my body to face her. I peer at her through half-closed eyes and face my own bare-chested reflection in the mirror behind her. The shock of watching Ginger examine my nakedness titillates me even more. She rolls her tongue across her parted lips. The moisture makes them glisten. She grips me at the ribs, sliding her hands beneath my breasts, pushing them higher. She lowers her mouth and captures a nipple between her teeth before sucking it deep into her mouth. Her tongue circles my areola, around and around, then flips up and down across my nipple. I squirm in ecstasy. She moves to the other tit and equalizes the pleasure.

'You really have sensitive tits, Ava.'

'Yes,' I whisper, shaking.

Her hands move down my side, her fingers slip beneath the bikini's waistband and push it downward. She pulls it down far enough to expose my pubic hair in front; the back of the suit cups beneath my butt cheeks. She teases me, tickling my bush with her fingers while she sucks from one breast to the other. The pressure of the bikini excites me. I savor the suspense of waiting, anticipating what Ginger will do next.

Her hands move to my backside and my glutes tighten as she molds them in her hands. Her flawless round ass juts into the reflection of the mirror. I consider touching her private parts. Desire builds within my groin; I want to explore her naked.

I begin to pant when she grips the bikini and pulls it down. Coolness hits my exposed pussy, and I suck in air. She slings my bottoms to the side, positioning herself under me. Sliding her arms between my thighs, she spreads them as my back slides down the wall far enough for her to reach me with her mouth. I hear her groan as she comes within eye-level of my small triangular bush – the only hair remaining after a Brazilian. I can't believe how hungry I am for her touch, for the warm moisture of her mouth. She teases me with her hot breath expelling against my twat. I shove my hips forward, trying to reach her darting tongue.

Her hands clutch my ass again. I whimper and bounce my hips forward and back, returning her tease. At my next forward push, her tongue connects with my nether lips, and I freeze. She twitters her tongue up and down my wet creases. I whimper my delight and push lower into her mouth increasing the pressure. When she discovers my swollen clit, she curls her tongue around it, then flicks back and forth until I'm near delirium. My juices drip between my folds and fill her mouth. I hear her slurping as her tongue swirls and darts in and out.

She slips her middle finger inside me and steadily begins to wiggle it. 'You like that, Ava?'

I groan in response, too embarrassed to speak.

'You want me to finger-fuck you, Ava?'

Again, I moan.

'Talk to me, Ava. You've got to say that you want it.'

'Yes,' I mouth.

'Louder, Ava. I can't hear you.'

'Yes,' I pant.

'What?'

'Yes!' I shout.

She inserts a second finger and pumps me hard in rhythm with my rocking. Her mouth latches onto my clit, sucking and raking her tongue back and forth while she finger-fucks me. In my excitement, my arm flings to the side and knocks the jewelry and deodorant from the shelf. The commotion only exhilarates me more. The pace of my hips matches my ecstasy, building again and again to climax. Vibrations convulse the length of my body, all the way to the throb in my head. I look down and see Ginger's face covered in my slippery fluid. The sight is more than I can take and my knees give way. I slide to the floor in front of her, and then I reach for the support of the jeans hanging from the shelf hook.

Ginger sits forward, and I'm amazed by the tangy taste as I begin to lick her face. Tasting my own come for the first time, my appetite becomes insatiable as I slurp her cheeks, devouring every drop.

'Oh yes, baby. Eat it up. Clean me.'

I obey, sucking her face. I never thought I could kiss a woman, but now I'm overcome with desire to bond with her mouth. I grab her face with both hands and lock onto open, waiting lips. Her tongue wraps around mine; her arms embrace my back and pull me closer. My hands slide to encircle her narrow shoulders, her frame so tiny within my grip. She tastes and smells clean and fresh, like spring rain. My passion flames.

I grope at her waistline searching for the bottom of her tank top. Lifting it over her head, I gasp at my first glimpse of her naked bosom. Tiny triangles of white skin frame her nipples, creating the most seductive portrait. Touching her bare flesh, I tremble as I enclose my hands over her perky mounds. I can't believe the pleasure that pulses through my whole body. Leaning toward her, I draw her nipple into my mouth. I support her as she arches her back into my arms. I suck one taut peak to the other before moving to the crevice between her breasts and licking my way downward. I begin to pull down her shorts, and she rises to her knees. I think she's going to help me remove her pants, but instead she stands, puts her top on and backs away.

I shiver at the loss of her. Ravenous to taste her, I know disappointment shows in my eyes.

She adjusts her tank top, discreetly opens the door and slides through. Before pulling it shut, she pokes her head back inside. 'I think your back is covered now.'

Startled, I stare at my reflection – dejected and exposed. The red carpet casts its hue over me, magnifying my humiliation. I crumple over in shock. *What just happened?*

It takes me twenty minutes to get myself together and climb into the booth. I turn up the music but don't dance. I shudder. When the timer buzzes, I dress quickly. I can't wait to get away from here.

As I leave, I attempt a smile as I scurry past her counter.

'Bye, Ava,' she calls as I push open the front door, 'I'll look forward to your next visit. Can't wait to see the progression of your tan lines.'

I normally tan at least once a week. Two weeks pass, but I can't muster the nerve to return to Ginger. She consumes my daydreams and stars in my night dreams. I analyze every possible motive why she pulled away from me. *Was she teasing me? Toying with me? Wasn't she aroused too?*

Friday afternoon, I'm shocked when I answer the phone and hear her perky voice. 'Hey, Ava, where ya been?'

'Oh . . . h-hi, Ginger. Just been busy, I guess. I'm planning to come next week.' *Maybe I will . . . now.*

'Super. A group of us are going to LeRoy's Bar tonight. I thought maybe you'd join us.'

'Tonight? What time?'

'We'll probably get there about nine. There's a live band. Sure hope you can make it.'

'Yeah. I'll see,' I equivocate. *What if I'm subjecting myself to more embarrassment?*

It takes me two hours to decide what to wear. I try on every possible outfit in my closet. I've never done this for a man. What's wrong with me? But Rusty cared very little about fashion. He'd say I looked good no matter what I wore.

My nerves jitter throughout the drive to Leroy's. I arrive at 9:35, not wanting to appear too eager. Bodies jostle as I work my way through the crowd and scan faces for Ginger. The bass booms, vibrating my breastbone.

'Ava! Over here!'

I turn to see Ginger waving. Warmth permeates my body at the sight of her. I collide with a tall, lumberjack-type. 'Hello there, Beautiful. What sign were you born under?'

'Do Not Enter,' I retort and keep moving.

I bulldoze my way to Ginger and throw my arms around her in relief. *What am I thinking?* She reciprocates, her hands lingering on my back and her breasts crushing against me. I sigh in relief.

'It's great seeing you again, Ava,' she shouts over the music.

'You, too,' I yell.

She smiles. I smile. She pulls out a stool beside her for me to sit. Conversation is impossible, so we turn to watch the band and bop to the rhythm. When the next song begins, she grabs my hand and pulls me to the dance floor.

The band's fusion of jazz, blues, hip-hop and pop, makes their rendition of *Brick House* better than the Commodores. We continue to gyrate with the crowd more than with each other until the band announces a break. Ginger leads me back to her group of friends and introduces me. They welcome me with hugs and kisses, including two men who have joined her group of buoyant females.

'Come here often?' Troy, the tall, curly-haired blond asks.

'First time,' I offer.

'First time for what?' he quizzes with a sly smile.

What does he know? 'Damn, you've already figured out I'm a virgin.' I play his game.

He guffaws a hearty chuckle. 'I'd be honored to be your guide.'

I smile and peer over his shoulder at Ginger, who seems to be eyeing me.

'Ava's my favorite customer at the salon,' Ginger butts in.

'Ah, so that explains her luscious skin,' Troy compliments.

I blush and Ginger huffs. I enjoy her reaction – is it jealousy? – but decide to not risk pissing her off.

'Ginger takes very good care of me,' I brag, wrapping my arm around her waist and pulling her closer.

'I see . . .' Troy drops his chin and draws his head back, peering at both of us.

How well does he know Ginger? How well do I know her? Is she into chicks or men? Or both?

'I take care of all my customers.' Ginger smiles. 'I haven't seen you in a while, Troy. Whatcha' been up to?'

I loosen my hold and let my arm return to my lap. 'I was gone for a while on the herring runs,' Troy answers.

'Troy's a commercial fisherman,' Ginger says.

I'm not surprised; it's a common profession here in northwest Washington, and he possesses that rugged, tanned outdoorsman look.

The music starts up again, and Troy is first to ask me to dance. I glance back at Ginger who has turned her attention to the girl on the next stool.

Troy never takes his eyes from me; his virility draws me. I'm reassured that a man still finds me attractive and, strangely, also relieved that I'm attracted to him.

When we return to the group, I'm taken aback when I see Ginger flirting with a new man who has joined our crowd. 'Meet Tom,' Ginger introduces him to me.

'Hey, Tom.'

He tips his cap and Ginger races on, 'Tom and I have known one another since kindergarten. He's always been there for me.' She leans on his arm and gazes up at his face.

He looks down at her tenderly, and I experience my first pangs of jealousy. Ginger beams.

The evening continues – dancing, drinking, friends sparring back and forth. I'm careful not to hang with Troy exclusively. Ginger and I dance a couple of times, flirt with our eyes and find small ways to touch inconspicuously. When the band announces their last song, Troy takes my hand and leads me to the dance floor for the first slow song of the night. He pulls me tight against him, his hand sliding down to my ass. He applies pressure, pushes my front into his crotch, and I feel his boner swelling. My pussy engages, reacting to his heat and size. His mouth grazes my neck, and I feel the moisture of his lips.

Congregating in the parking lot, the gang decides on a late-night breakfast. My quandary intensifies as Ginger takes my hand and coaxes me to join them at the all-night diner. 'Okay,' I agree, part of me hoping Troy declines and the other part praying he doesn't.

Walking to my car, Troy catches up to me. 'I've got to beg off going to the diner. Leaving at dawn for Bristol Bay.'

'That's a long way. I'm guessing you won't be back for a while.'

'Probably a month. Depends . . .'

'Well, here's to good fishing,' I say, raising my hand for a high five.

'Thanks,' he smiles as our hands smack. 'Would you like to come back to my place while I finish packing?'

'Uh . . . sorry. I already told the others I'd see them at the diner.'

'That's no problem. They'll figure it out.'

That's what I'm afraid of. 'I know, but I just met you. Maybe we'll see one another when you get back.'

'Can I get your number?'

'Sure.' Jotting it down on the back of his card, I catch a glimpse of Ginger watching me.

'See you later.' I open my car door and plop into the seat before he can kiss me. *Not in front of Ginger.* I wave, as I back the car out. In my rearview mirror, I see him watching me drive away; his eyes bug and his mouth gapes.

Entering the diner, I spot Ginger and slide beside her while we wait for a table. She's warm and tequila flirty. Ginger sits between Tom and me, her hands groping both of us. 'What happened to Troy?' She suddenly seems to remember.

'He went home. He's leaving early in the morning for Alaska.'

'I'm surprised he didn't ask you to come home with him.'

'He did.'

She jerks her head and stares at me with questioning eyes before breaking into a smile.

When we rise to leave, Tom suggests he drive her home as she's had a few too many. *What else will he help her with?* Before getting into his car, she pulls me aside and pleads,

'Come to the salon tomorrow afternoon about four thirty. I close at five on Saturdays.'

I check the clock as each hour passes until it's time to go to the tanning salon. I teach three classes in the mornings, but Saturday afternoons are free. I try to read, watch episodes of *Grey's Anatomy* on my DVR, and clean house, but time still moves in reverse. *Did Tom spend the night with Ginger? Did they make love?* At four o'clock I get in my car and drive, even though Ginger is only ten minutes away. I tour the neighborhood, the shopping/restaurant district, stop to get a soda, then change my mind. *Don't want to have to pee in the middle of my session.*

Ginger is behind the counter when I enter. Her mouth spreads into a wide smile when she sees me walking through the door. 'Ava!'

'Hey, Ginger.' I struggle to control the vibrato in my voice. I've got the jitters . . . bad.

'I've got a treat for you today!'

'Really?' I didn't expect her to be so blatant.

'Just got a new steam shower delivered and set up. It's awesome! When you finish tanning, you can try it out . . . on me.'

'Cool.'

'I have the stand-up ready for you.'

In the booth, I yank off my shirt, pull on my bottoms and apply bronzer. I'm almost finished when I hear a knock at the door.

'Yes?' I open a crack.

'I came to get the middle of your back,' Ginger announces.

I open a few more inches and turn to face the wall, like last time.

Same as before, Ginger warms the bronzer in her hands and smoothes it over my back.

'There, I think I've got it. I'll get the steam unit ready.'

I shudder at the puff of air-conditioned air as she closes the door. *Now what?*

The twelve-minute tan seems like twenty-five before it shuts off. I remove my bikini bottom . . . *Dress? Wrap a towel? What?*

Another knock at the door. I crack it again and she slides a white, fluffy robe into my hand. 'Oh thanks, Ginger.'

The steam shower is as high-tech as *Star Trek*. In a businesslike tone, she explains the buttons, knobs and symbols on the LED display. She leaves and I let the robe slither down my body, step into the chamber and slide the doors closed. I touch a knob, pull away and touch another. *Which one does what?* The steam is fogging the sides, and I can't read the labels. I should have paid more attention to Ginger's instructions, but it was hard to concentrate with her standing so close.

The music, new-age xylophone, chimes around me. Orange essence from the diffuser permeates my senses. Colored light shifts from blue to green to gold. The music, the oils, and the steam drift me into the zone. I reach out and turn the middle knob far left. Six nozzles spray my torso at different angles. The upper jets hit my nipples. I squirm. I redirect the bottom spouts to my mons. My nipples are hard and tingly. I run my hands up my stomach, encircle my breasts, then down between my legs. I slide the middle finger of both hands inside my slit and spread the folds. Tilting my pelvis at just the right slant, the spray engages my clit. I use my thumbs to lift the labia and get the full force of the water. My head falls back, and I shudder as the squirts propel me into nirvana.

I'm so engrossed in the ecstasy I don't hear the double doors slide open and close. I don't sense the bodily presence behind me until I feel arms encircle my waist. 'I knew you'd know what to do with those jets,' Ginger says into my ear.

I collapse against her. She glides her hands over, around, up and down my stomach. She cups my breasts and squeezes my nipples with her thumbs and forefingers. I turn my head and nuzzle her neck. She tilts her head and latches onto my lips. I'm floating like those lopsided, billowy bubbles children blow through wands. She turns me around. I slide my arms behind her back and draw her close. I kiss her cheeks, down one side of her neck and up the other side to her mouth. Our lips lock, and I slide my hand up the back of her neck to hold her there. The automatic timer shuts down the unit.

I pull back and admire her perfect, petite body. I examine her pert tits and engulf one nipple, then another. I slide my hands down the sides of her hips and eye the previously *forbidden* territory. I brush my fingers through her bush, and she slides open the shower doors. *Again? She's going to abandon me again?*

She clutches my hand and draws me into the dressing room. I step onto a cushion of layered blankets, which she must have spread on the floor. Ginger guides me downward until we're sitting face to face on the blankets before she kisses me again. With our lips interlocked, she presses me onto my back landing on top of me. Our bodies fully engage – hands groping, legs entwining, knees pressing – as we roll from side to side. She wriggles down my body and tongues my slit, exaggerating the movement, as if she's licking a giant lollipop from bottom to top. Her tongue explores my crevices up and down, in and out of every fold, every crease. I draw up my knees, spreading wide to allow her total access. Her hands slip beneath my buttocks, lifting me as she suckles me into oblivion. I moan and writhe side to side, then grab her hair with both hands before collapsing against the blankets.

With both arms I reach upward, beckoning her to my mouth. Kissing her, I reach between her legs and insert a finger. My movements are swift and to the point, or, more accurately, clit. I leave no space for her to change her mind. I pinch her round nub and roll it between my fingers before strumming it back and forth. She groans and arches her pelvis. I grasp the opportunity, and shift my lips from mouth to pussy. So intent on completing this mission, I slurp and suck and eat in crazed frenzy. She moans fly-me-to-the-moon encouragements and spreads her legs. Her body begins to buck and she screams her ecstasy. Her body goes limp. I caress her full length as I crawl to her face and kiss her trembling lips.

We unwind, snuggled into one another's arms.

'Ginger?'

'Yes, baby.'

'Why did you pull away from me before?' *I have to know.*

'Anyone can enjoy oral sex, regardless of who's giving it,' she says, in an out-of-character tone. 'But to give it, that's crossing a line, a commitment, so to speak. I wasn't sure you were ready for that.'

'You mean you were trying to protect me?'

'Yes. I didn't want you to experience the angst, questioning what you'd done. I wanted you to be sure.'

'What makes you think I'm sure now?'

'You've had time to think about it. You weren't just caught up in the moment. And . . . you didn't go home with Troy last night.'

I hesitate with the next question, but I have to know. 'You think I'm a lesbian?'

She laughs. 'No. I think you're exploring the possibilities . . . like me. I could sense Troy had an effect on you. I watched you closely. But you were curious enough that you chose to be with me instead of him.'

I rest my head on her chest and sigh contentment. At that moment I think I love her. All this time when I thought she'd rejected me, she was just giving me time to know my own heart.

We stand, and she rubs a towel over and between my legs. Then she runs her fingers along my tan line. 'Mm, Ava. Look at that. Your lines are becoming more defined.'

Queen of Swords

by Inara LaVey

Sweat pours off me in rivulets, soaking the thin cotton beneath the bronze and boiled leather armor I wear during weapons practice. It's especially annoying under the breast-plate, and I can't wait to strip down and bathe. My helmet comes off first. Even with my hair braided and wrapped around the crown of my head to cushion my skull, repeated blows to the helmet leave me with a headache and ringing ears.

Unbuckling my scabbard, I toss it carelessly onto the rumpled silk sheets of the bed. The battered leather of the scabbard and tarnished bronze of the sword hilt look out of place against the cobalt blue silk. A study in contrasts, like much of my life.

I could take that train of thought further but choose not to. I want my bath, to lie back in hot scented water and drink spiced mead until I drift away to sleep, maybe even slip underneath the water and never wake up again –

'You look tired, my Queen.' My maidservant, Lyra, enters the bedchamber, a pile of freshly laundered garments in her arms. Her gentle voice interrupts my dark thoughts. She sets the laundry down and comes up beside me. 'Your bath water is drawn. Let me help you disrobe.'

'Thank you, Lyra.' I stand still as she deftly unbuckles the various pieces of armor, placing them with care on a massive wooden chest I use to store my weapons and other fighting accoutrement. The bronze must be wiped down, the leather oiled before they're put away. She retrieves my scabbard and sword from the bed, adding them to the pile on the chest as I stretch, feeling the aches and pains from practice lurking in my muscles, waiting to make themselves known the next day. But they would be minimal compared to the aftermath of previous combat. I no longer care enough to push myself.

Lyra starts to peel off the sweat-soaked cotton shift, but the sound of heavy footsteps makes us both freeze in place.

Ismet, ruler of the Kingdom of Swords, strides into the room, regal in robes of vibrant crimson silk. The fabric billows out and away from his body as he walks, displaying caramel-colored skin covering muscles toned to perfection. His eyes, framed with thick black lashes, are the same blue as the bedclothes; a blue so rich and vivid they seem unreal. Luxuriant black hair ripples down to his shoulders. He is magnificent, every woman's fantasy come to life.

He is my husband.

And I hate him.

Lyra fades silently into the background as Ismet approaches me, careful to do nothing to attract his attention. Catching Ismet's eye rarely results in a happy ending, so unobtrusiveness is considered a survival trait amongst servants and courtiers alike.

I stare straight ahead while Ismet moves behind me, hard body pressed up against mine as he runs rough hands over my shoulders, fingers catching in the flimsy cotton on either side.

'Your cuts were apathetic, your parries weak, and there was no fire in your belly.' One hand travels down to my stomach, fingers splayed against it. The other pulls the shift down over one shoulder, strong fingers idly caressing my skin.

'I was tired.'

'A day before the tournament and you're tired?' Ismet's laugh holds no humor. 'One would think you don't care about winning, my queen.'

'I haven't been feeling well.' I keep my tone even, knowing any hint of emotion will provoke him.

'Could there be something else in your belly?' His palm presses against the curve of my well-muscled abdomen. 'A child, perhaps?'

I can't help the hiss of indrawn breath. This is cruel, even for Ismet. My inability to bear a child is one of the reasons I am once again competing in the tournament for the crown. A queen is given thirteen months to prove herself able to bear the King's heir. If she fails in this most essential royal duty, the tournament is held to give other ambitious – and foolishly romantic – women the chance to compete for the privilege of proving themselves more fruitful. Such ambition and romantic dreams are why I am now standing before the King of Swords and wishing either he or I was dead.

He hears the catch in my breath and smiles. 'No child, then.' He caresses my skin. The deceptively gentle touch makes my flesh crawl. 'It is a pity, Adisa, for you are by far the most beautiful woman to wear the crown and share my bed thus far. Maybe you will win, and we'll have another thirteen months to try.'

I know what comes next, so I'm ready when he rends the shift from my body in one swift move and shoves me onto the bed. His teeth sink into the chafed flesh between neck and shoulder where my shoulder guard had rested as he lifts his robes so he can thrust himself into me.

Ismet is nothing if not predictable.

The first time I experienced Ismet's brand of sex, I cried and pleaded with him to be gentle. This only led to acts of greater cruelty. Then, as I learned to hate him, I fought. This pleased him as it gave him a challenge in bed. I finally learned the only way to guarantee a quick finish was to be impassive. That way Ismet would grow bored and finish quickly, taking his perverse pleasures on more responsive partners, both willing and not. He only lay with me these days to ensure no one could accuse him of not carrying out his royal duty to produce an heir with the greatest female warrior of our kingdom.

So now I lie here still and silent as he ravages me, his magnificent body used as a weapon to hurt and subdue. This is not an act of love; it's an act of war. By the time he's finished, I hurt inside and out, but I keep my pain hidden.

He rises off the bed, his robes falling back around his body as if they'd never been in disarray. Without a backwards glance, he strides to the door and leaves the room.

Within seconds Lyra is at my side, helping me to my feet and leading me to the adjacent chamber containing a huge marble bath sunk into the tiled floor. The scent of vanilla and cinnamon rises towards me as I lower myself into the tub, hissing slightly as the hot water hits the scrapes and cuts I sustained during practice. Lyra keeps a firm grip on my arm until I've seated myself on the submerged ledge. Her fingers brush my shoulder and neck before she busies herself removing the pins holding my braids in place.

I shut my eyes and listen to the tiny clink of pins landing in the copper dish Lyra uses to hold them. When she finishes taking out the pins, she nimbly unbraids my hair from three separate braids, fingers gently running through the copper strands to shake them free. I sigh as she massages soap into my hair and scalp, strong hands working wonders from scalp to neck. I feel the tension dissipating from my muscles and rub my head against her hands like a cat seeking to have just the right spot scratched by its owner. Lyra instantly responds with more pressure where I need it. Her hands are magic.

The downside to this release of tension is an inadvertent opening to a floodgate of emotions I've been holding back for days. Tears slip down my face and my body starts shaking as I try to force them back. But they won't be stopped. And neither will the cold fact of the matter.

'I am nothing,' I murmur without thinking.

'My queen?' Lyra's hands pause in their ministrations.

'What good is a queen who cannot bear her king a child?' My hands clench under the water, self-hatred flooding through me.

Lyra pours warm water over my head to rinse my hair,

taking care that the soapy water stays out of my eyes. Then she speaks. 'My queen, it is not your fault. King Ismet has taken three wives to his bed and lain with numerous servants and ladies of the court.' A pause as she draws her fingers across my forehead and down the back of my scalp. 'None of them has borne fruit.' She finishes rinsing my hair and wraps it in a towel to keep it out of the scented water. I keep my eyes shut as she slowly scrubs my shoulders and back with a rough sponge, careful to avoid the abrasions.

'How . . .' I swallow, unwilling to accept this easy dispensation for my guilt. 'How do you know this?'

'My lady, it is common knowledge throughout the palace in the servants' quarters. Very little happens here that we don't know about first.' The sponge dips down my back to my waist and around to my stomach, the gentle circular motion as soothing as Lyra's voice as she speaks again. 'Please don't give up, my queen.'

'What do you mean?'

'The tournament.' There's a soft splash as Lyra enters the bath, something she's never done before. 'Don't let him destroy you.' She kneels in front of me in the bath. 'Please. I beg you.'

I look at her, really look at her for the first time since I became queen and she my maidservant.

Like everyone in the royal palace, Lyra is beautiful; my husband requires everything around him to be aesthetically pleasing, be it furnishings, artwork, or servants. But I've never before this moment noticed just how truly lovely she is. Dark brown hair streams down her back in glossy waves, drawn back from her face in several intricate braids starting at her brow and connecting at the back of her head. Her eyes, now gazing at me with an intense pleading look, are the same chocolate brown as her hair, and lined with thick black lashes. Her nose is straight and fine and her lips, dark pink and shimmering with a faint gloss, are as full as my own. She wears a robe of white silk, a bronze belt around her tiny waist. The silk clings to her small, rounded breasts and full hips. Her arms and thighs, glistening with moisture, are beautifully toned, the skin like golden velvet over the muscles beneath. She is a work of art in her own right.

'Lyra, you must mind your clothes or you'll ruin them.' She freezes like a doe, her eyes wide with fear that she has displeased me.

'My Queen, I beg you, forgive me. I should not have presumed to enter the water with you – '

I raise a hand to calm her alarm. 'Hush, Lyra. It is not your company that troubles me. You belong here in the water. It is your lovely silks and belt that do not.'

Her cheeks grow flushed for a moment, and she lowers her gaze.

'You are right, of course, my queen.' She rises from the pool to stand before me, water sluicing down her legs. Demurely, she unclasps her belt, folding it daintily before setting it down on the tiles with a soft click. Then, with lowered gaze, she bends down to gather up the wet folds of silk and pulls them up, first past her knees and thighs, then swiftly up and over her head, silk robe and cotton undergarment alike. She stands there, diffident and silent:

her head down, her hands clasped before her in all modesty, even as her breasts stand proud. Then the moment passes, and she lowers herself into the water to take her place before me once more.

I close my eyes, numb with this blackness hollowing out my heart. Despair seems too small a word for the grinding emptiness it leaves behind. What flesh remains feels cold and stony, as though stricken by a medusa's baleful eye. A flicker of warmth stirs my skin: Lyra has returned to her ministrations. Her hands cradle my face as she rubs my temples and drives her fingers through my hair, easing my aching skull. I open my eyes to find hers intent on me.

'My lady?' Her face is that of a concerned mother leaned over the cradle.

'My life will almost surely end tomorrow, Lyra.' I silently curse the fresh upwelling of tears that I cannot stop. A queen does not cry before her subjects. But I can't stop them, or the words that rush out of me without volition on my part. 'I feel dead already, my life force running out of me like wine spilled from by a careless drunk at a feast – '

'You are wrong.' The intensity of Lyra's voice stops my self-pitying monologue. I'm shocked by her trespass, but even more by the penetrating gaze of her eyes. Somehow it is fierce, determined, imploring, sorrowful, and bright all at once. It overwhelms me. If I were Ismet I'd call for the guards to have her punished – but I'm not Ismet. And even if I were so inclined, I cannot move a muscle, not even speak.

She clasps my face close to hers with an iron grip, and

commands me with words like hammered steel. 'Hear me, my lady. Your life is *not* yet forfeit, and you will *never* surrender to death tomorrow, or any other day, until you are old and wise with hair as silver as your sword, in your bed surrounded by your children's children. Do you hear me?'

I nod, dumbstruck.

'You will do this, and you will do it for your subjects who love you.' Her tone alters almost imperceptibly. 'My lady . . . my queen . . . Adisa . . . you will do this for me, I who love you most of all.'

Her lips meet mine and conquer. I succumb completely to the strength of her desire. Her kiss awakens my heart; it roars to life like bellows on a forge. I reach for her, clasping her to me. Suddenly I want nothing in the world so much as I want the touch of her lips on mine and the press of her body against me. Cinnamon- and vanilla-scented water splashes over the marble lip of the tub as we wrestle together, but we pay it no heed, distracted by our kisses.

At length she slips an arm around my shoulders and hooks the other around my hip, lifting me so I float suspended in the water. I am a virgin maiden lying down beneath her princely suitor; I am a baby nestled in the crook of her mother's arm. And like a babe, I turn my mouth to her breast and suckle on its firmness. Lyra holds me tightly, groaning her pleasure while she strokes my cheek and ear. I cling to her, happy for the first time since I became Ismet's bride and had my romantic dreams destroyed in a night of sadistic rapine.

Lyra's free hand trails from my face to squeeze my breast before caressing me down the length of my body and settling on the curve of my bottom. Her nimble fingers make me feel as wanton as a tavern wench. My excitement builds; I have to pull her head down for more kissing, deeper this time, our mouths open and eager.

Never have I been so hungry for the kiss of another, not even in my youth – certainly never for my royal husband. My lips move of their own accord to the graceful curve of her neck, tracing the line with the tip of my tongue and enjoying the hiss of indrawn breath this elicits. Emboldened, I graze my teeth against her flesh, feeling her life pulse against my mouth as I bite and suck just hard enough to leave a mark. A tiny part of my mind cries out for caution as I do this. After all, adultery is considered high crime against the king and if caught in the act, the punishment is a slow death. I wonder, though, if the laws set down apply to another woman. And even if they do, the fear of pain and death cannot dissuade me. But still – no need to make it public. Reluctantly I stop nibbling on her delectable skin.

Lyra slips a hand between my thighs and plays with me there, stroking, rubbing, tickling me with an audacious, knowing touch. Under her nimble fingers and relentless kisses, my legs become weak and slippery like eels, but then the opposite occurs: my limbs stiffen and my whole body arches, seized by a tremor of sheer delight, the likes of which I scarcely even imagined possible. Again I feel like a newborn babe. I cry and shake, making wordless sounds to express feelings I hardly even understand.

Lyra is not finished with me. It pleases me, since now

I desperately want to return the pleasures she has so generously bestowed on me. She has me lean back against the side of the pool and extend my arms to grasp the marble rim for support. Then she swims up to me like a river nymph. Now I truly feel like a young princess about to be ravished by a bold knight. I cannot stop my legs from their trembling. She takes hold of my shoulders and pulls herself close, bringing her body to bear atop me.

I wonder for a moment what she could be planning – until her sex presses against mine, and I gasp at the tiny lightning bolts racing up and down my spine. She pulls us closer together still, and we grind our womanhood into one another. Our gazes lock together as well. I am stunned; I had no idea two people could yield such pleasure with each other, to say nothing of two women without the benefit of any manly parts.

When the raptures take her, she closes her eyes and moans and groans as if in a swoon. I can feel her shudders; they bring me along with her. Even after our delights fade to a sweet, gentle afterglow we hold each other, floating in the warm, scented water, lost in one another's arms before finally moving to the bed for the remainder of the night.

She holds me against her, my head cradled on her shoulder. Kissing my hair, she says fiercely, 'Promise me you will not die tomorrow, my queen.'

'I promise,' I whisper as I drift off to sleep.

I watch the tournament in the royal seating area, my chair butted up next to Ismet's, no chair arm between us so we can sit as close to each other as possible. I wonder if anyone else in the audience notices the irony of this arrangement, especially since I'm pressed against the far side of my chair to make as much space between us as possible. Luckily Ismet is too engrossed in the combat below to pay much attention to me. Once in a while his hand reaches out to caress my thigh or arm in a proprietary manner, just to remind anyone who might be watching that I belong to him – at least until one of the several dozen challengers in the arena below defeats me in battle.

Ismet drinks goblet after goblet of spiced wine, frowning at me when I refuse to drink with him. I eschew the heady brew for water, knowing I need a clear head if I am to live to see another day. This year's crop of challengers are fierce, each one determined to be the one to replace me at Ismet's side, and in his bed.

I might know some, if not all, of these women, but I have no way of recognizing them. Tradition decrees that boiled leather masks that stop right above the wearer's mouth cover the faces of all challengers. There are openings for the eyes and nostrils, but it's nearly impossible to identify individuals. Hair is pulled back into tight braids and tucked under simple metal helmets held on with leather straps buckled under the chin. Their bodies, on the other hand, are revealed clearly in short white gauze shifts with minimal armor covering their extremities. Breastplates and arm guards are allowed but otherwise it's all down to how well the combatants wield their short sword and shields.

This is a test of agility, skill, endurance, and pain. Bruises and welts are raised. Blood is spilled as sharp blades slice through unprotected flesh. But no one dies. Only one match is to the death.

Only I am allowed bronze armor, having earned the right by defeating the fully armored queen before me.

Only a true warrior can aspire to be queen of the Kingdom of Swords.

Ismet watches the bouts with a smile curving his full lips. He comments on the fighting skills of each combatant, as well as their physical attributes.

'That one,' he says, pointing to a particularly ferocious warrior who has won three consecutive matches. 'She reminds me of you when you first fought for the crown. She moves like a jungle cat.'

I watch the woman who has caught Ismet's attention. She's lithe and toned, skin kissed a smooth gold by the sun. She wears a boiled leather breastplate, and she wields a sword like she was born with one in her hand. She is a warrior to be reckoned with, and I know it is she who I'll be facing in the final bout.

I pity the ambitious bitch because I have something worth fighting for now.

The smell of sweat, blood, and sand blend together as the morning turns into afternoon and one by one the combatants are weeded out from the tournament. I eat a light meal of bread, fruit, and cheese, just enough to give me energy without weighing me down. My turn in the arena is drawing near, the last bout before the final challenge drawing to a predictable finish. The lithe warrior fights as though possessed and even though her opponent is skilled, she is no match for the other woman and concedes defeat.

There will be a short break to give the victorious fighter a chance to catch her breath. Not too long, of course, because stamina is one of the qualities the Queen of Swords must possess.

Ismet turns to me, eyes aglow with the anticipation of the bloodshed to come. 'I knew it would be that one. She is a worthy opponent for you, Adisa.' His smile is cruel as he adds, 'And perhaps a worthy replacement.' He lifts his goblet in a mock toast. I surprise him by taking it from his hand and downing the contents. It's only a quarter full, just enough to fire my blood without muddling my head. And if this is to be my last drink, let it be the best wine the land has to offer.

I toss the empty goblet back to Ismet and pick up my helmet, shield, and sword. Then, without a backwards glance at my husband, I go to meet my fate.

The crowd cheers as I take the field of battle. I wave to them with the confidence befitting my station. I am already wearing my armor and it is a matter of seconds to don my helmet. I limber up with stretches and lunges, then take a few practice swings with my sword to warm up my arms and shoulders.

My opponent returns to the sands and the crowd cheers her as well. I don't mind; she deserves their accolades. I admire the play of muscles under her golden skin as she walks towards me, the controlled grace with which she moves. Her death will be a waste, but it is the law. Life's blood must be shed at the end of this fight.

We face each other. I give a small nod of acknowledgment and salute her with my sword, pommel pressed to my left breast with the blade held high. She returns the salute and we both drop into fighting stances. I lead offensively, blade and right foot forward, shield held at the ready, while my opponent's stance is defensive, her shield in front. I find this surprising, as she has fought offensively in every other bout today.

We circle one another warily, looking for openings. I feint a cut to her left shoulder, then lunge with the point towards her stomach as she uses her shield to defend against the feint. She is quick to recover and parries the thrust with her blade, responding with a head cut that I deflect with my shield before launching a series of cuts and thrusts that cause her to retreat as she uses both sword and shield to keep my blade from reaching her flesh.

I press my advantage and ruthlessly launch another offensive, forcing her to retreat yet again. This time my sword catches her across a shoulder, then her thigh, drawing blood with each cut. The animal grace and confidence that marked her movements in previous fights seems diminished, as if I intimidate her. The audience hisses and catcalls its disapproval at such a one-sided fight and, indeed, I am disappointed to find her less worthy of an opponent than she had appeared. But I have no desire to draw the fight out any longer than necessary even though I know such an anticlimax to the tournament will disappoint the crowd and infuriate Ismet.

I charge, smashing her shield with mine, the impact sending her sprawling on her back on the hot sand. She raises her sword in an attempt at defense, but I sweep it aside with my blade, giving a flick of my wrist that wrests the hilt from her grasp. The sword flies through the air and lands a few feet away. I quickly kick her shield aside, pinning it and her left arm to the ground with one foot. Then I lean forward, sword point against her neck. The audience roars in the anticipation of the blood to come.

'I do not wish to kill you,' I say. 'I had not planned on seeing another sunrise. But I made a vow that I cannot and will not break.'

'I understand, my queen.' Her voice is muffled by the leather helm, but there is no anger that I can hear in her reply. She tilts her head to one side, baring her neck in preparation for the deathblow. The cords in the slender column of her neck stand out. I see her pulse beat.

And I see the faint bruise and what look like teeth marks at the juncture of neck and shoulder, and I know why my opponent has lost the fight so easily. 'Lyra?'

Her lips curve up into a smile under the helm, and I drop to my knees beside her, horrified by the realization that I'm responsible for the blood running from the cuts on her body. I unbuckle her helmet and toss it to one side, seeing my beloved's face covered in dirt, sweat, and yet more blood. 'I almost slew you,' I whisper.

'Better I should die at your hands than live after seeing you slain by another,' she says, her smile so full of naked adoration that my heart swells near to bursting.

'You shall not die today.' I stand and help Lyra to her feet, turning to face Ismet as the crowd continues to call for blood.

Ismet stands, swaying unsteadily from too much wine. 'What is this, Adisa?' he yells. 'Kill her now!'

The crowd echoes his sentiment. I stare them down, turning in a slow circle until I once again face my husband. 'I will not kill her.'

Unsheathing his sword, Ismet leaps over the balustrade of the royal box onto the sand of the arena, fury marking his every move.

'Life's blood must be shed in combat on this sand,' he shouts, his voice carrying across the arena to the highest rows. 'It is the law of the Kingdom of Swords!' He turns to us, sword raised. 'My queen, either you spill this blood or you forfeit your crown and your life.'

I step protectively in front of Lyra and say, 'I defy you, Ismet.' I do not yell the words, but my voice carries to the guards, the court, and the royal counselors, who all stare at me with varying degrees of shock.

Ismet's face turns purple with rage. 'You dare . . .' Speech fails him for a moment as he strides towards me, sword at the ready. 'Then you die, my queen.' He thrusts the point of the blade toward my stomach in a killing blow – that I deflect with my own sword, sidestepping as I do so. In one quick move I reverse my grip and drive my blade into Ismet's stomach, the bronze slicing through silk, flesh, and muscle with equal enthusiasm.

Ismet's face registers pain and disbelief in equal measure. He falls to his knees, and I pull the blade out, bracing one foot against his thigh as I do. I raise my sword again and decapitate Ismet with one well-placed blow. Wrapping my fingers in his hair, I heft Ismet's head into the air, holding it so all can see. 'Life's blood has been shed in combat!' I cry with the full force of my voice. 'The law of the Kingdom of Swords has been upheld!'

Guards and audience alike gape at me in shocked silence. I stare back at them defiantly as the Royal Counsel begins muttering amongst themselves. An order is shouted and the guards break free of their stunned immobility to surround us, swords drawn. Lyra slips her hand into mine and we wait to see if we will die together this day.

After what seems an eternity, Abad, the oldest and most revered of the advisors, steps carefully onto the sand and approaches us, four guards on his heels. I steel myself for what I hope is a swift and merciful death for both Lyra and myself.

Abad stops in front of me, his face impassive as he looks from me to the fallen body of his king. He gives a little nod, then turns to the crowd and raises his arms, immediately commanding the attention of all who are present. 'The Royal Counsel has ruled that the law has indeed been upheld. Queen Adisa, the rule of the Kingdom of Swords falls now upon your shoulders.' He puts a hand on my shoulder. 'May you rule with more wisdom and compassion than your predecessor.'

The crowd erupts in chaos, shouting and cheering as I pull Lyra to me, tasting the tang of blood and sweat on her lips. And the kiss is pure because it tastes of freedom – and hope.

Monkey Business

by Fifi Bernard

It's 2010. Twenty-ten – don't you like the sound of that? A decade of new beginnings. And thus begins a first in my lifetime experience – up in a tree house.

You'd think the rainy season would be perfect for the Rain Forest Aid concert on the Osa Peninsula of Costa Rica, but hardly anyone comes and those who could slip and slide their cars out of the parking lot have already gone home. All the better for us. The meager attendance dwindled by constant rain has raised our chances of winning the big raffle prize: a free weekend in a tree house resort, Finca Mono Verde.

At the finale, the rain pours down on the soccer field, splashing mud up to our asses. Barely audible through the pounding rain, I hear, 'And now, the big raffle prize! The ultimate tree house experience, a weekend stay at Finca Mono Verde goes to . . . Angelina White.'

I scream, 'Wow! I did it!'

After jumping up and down and clapping, my husband Joe's big laugh becomes a huge hug and kiss. 'Angie, you're my lucky star. What would I do without you?'

* * *

'I've got a real surprise for you this birthday,' says Joe, as he nuzzles my neck in the place that gives me goose bumps all over.

'You think I've forgotten about the tree house vacation?' I roll my eyes. 'My memory's not that bad.'

'No, there's something else.'

'Hint?'

'Okay. It'll include Mark and Claire.'

'Superb. We have such fun together.'

'You'll find out more about it tonight at dinner when you open your presents.'

It's the winter holiday season in Costa Rica, and there's excitement in the air. Our little pueblo on the beach is packed with snowbirds getting away from a white Christmas, and local families setting up their traditional camps near the water's edge during the holiday.

The night of my birthday we meet Mark and Claire at the open air seafood restaurant on the beach for our favorites: either *pescado entero,* whole red snapper fried to perfection right down to the crispy tail, or freshly caught lobster dripping in melted butter with all the local trimmings. We order two of each and share, licking our fingers in contentment. For dessert Claire produces her *piece de resistance*, a chocolate decadence cake, served with fresh strong Costa Rican coffee.

'Oh, Claire, what a wonderful, tasty gift. I don't know how you can make and eat these things without gaining a pound.' She's dark, willowy, gorgeous, and could pass for a *Tica,* the local diminutive for a Costa Rican. Mark, on the other hand looks totally gringo, a good-looking, blond-brushed-with-grey, surfer-type. We've built houses on the same mountain, and first became good neighbors, then best friends.

'The cake isn't the only gift,' Mark said, handing me an envelope that I immediately tear open.

On the front is a photo of one of the beautiful tree houses that are part of the Finca Mono Verde resort, high up in the canopy of jungle giants. Inside I read, *The more, the merrier! Let's swing like the monkeys!* And out falls a certificate: *Good for a three-on-one massage. Happy Birthday!*

'Is this luxury, or what?' I exclaim.

'It's planned for this weekend. There are two bedrooms and all the amenities. What a treat!' Joe rests his arm around my shoulders.

'This is the most exotic gift I've ever received. Swinging in the trees? I'll bet you were in on this, Joe?'

'Sure.' He shrugs and kisses me, his long grey curls bobbing as he nods and grins like a Cheshire cat. 'And I read they have ziplines to help us get around, since we don't have monkey tails. That is, if there's any reason to leave our little aerie. Heh, heh.'

The four of us are on our way to the resort with our directions in hand. It begins:

You won't find billboards or roadside signs that lead you to Finca Mono Verde. We are not a full-service spa, but we're pretty fancy. You won't find TVs in our solar-powered cabinas. What you will find is a fully comfortable, eco-friendly retreat from the outside world to explore and enjoy on your own.

As per directions, we follow the coastal highway south to the remote pueblo of Piedras Negras and turn left at the only restaurant in town. According to the pointer sheet, it serves the best fried chicken in this area, and since it's lunchtime we decide to stop. We eat, have a few beers, and get into the vacation mode. Joe plays footsie with me under the table. We've already started celebrating my birthday by reviving our latent sexual desires. A once-in-a-lifetime concurrent lunar eclipse, winter solstice, and Mercury coming out of retrograde has lifted us to new heights in several areas of our lives.

'My horoscope this week said I'd be experiencing something new and very delightful, and it's already happening.' I laugh.

It looks like Mark and Claire are feeling the same vibes as they laugh at something he's whispered in her ear. They both look good, Claire especially.

Back in the car we finally see the obscure sign for Finca Mono Verde. We follow the dirt road a few miles to the base camp and pull into the only parking area. The community center, kitchen, and dining room are surrounded by well-kept gardens and trails through twenty acres of primary forest. Co-owner Sue greets us, shows us around, then leads us through the jungle to our tree house. The trail is long, steep, and slippery. As the luggage gets heavier Joe asks, 'Where are the ziplines?'

'We use those mostly for bringing in supplies to each tree house. If you're interested in trying them, my husband Paul would be happy to show you.'

Thank goodness we're in good physical health, but the destination is worth every step. A handmade sign, 'Mis Brasas Treehouse,' points to a two-story wooden structure set high in the canopy of four giant rainforest trees with one more steep ladder-like staircase to our heaven.

After showing us around and giving last-minute advice, Sue leaves us with, 'Will you be coming for dinner at seven back at base camp?'

Mark opens the fridge. 'Hey, all the food we ordered is here.' It's stocked with fancy olives, gourmet cheeses, pate, assorted wines, and beer. On the counter are fresh-baked bread and croissants for breakfast. 'We don't have to go anywhere.'

We all agree and thank Sue.

'Okay. See you all tomorrow. Enjoy.'

We sit on the balcony and soak in the exciting new adventure of being an integral part of the majestic jungle hundreds of feet below and above us. 'We're so lucky . . . because you are,' says Joe, winking at me. 'You win stuff all the time.'

But luck isn't all of it. Whether you believe in horoscopes or not, taking risks and making changes is what makes our lives rich and exciting. And now here we are in the treetops of the Costa Rican jungle drinking Cuba Libres, nibbling gourmet snacks and cookies. In our faces, the insistent sound and sight of the waterfall intertwines with sweet and raucous birdsongs and fluttering blue iridescent flashes of morpho butterflies. We relax and slowly melt into the scenery.

After naps and showers Claire sets up the spa. She and Mark have done their share by contracting with the owners to supply the fancy food and drink, and a mini spa with all the trimmings. The afternoon sunset is infusing the room and its occupants in a golden glow.

'Strip and lie face down on the table. Are you ready for the luxury of a lifetime?' Claire pats me on the ass. As the professional masseuse of the group, she chooses my torso. Joe positions himself at my head and Mark at my feet. We've all enjoyed her hands and learned a lot by reciprocating. Flickering candles and tinkling music complete the scene.

Three sets of hands in different places on my body – sliding, kneading, pressing, tingling – soon become one swirling vibrating rainbow. First it's butterflies, then snakes. Utter relaxation turns to electricity as light fingers drift under my armpits and follow the line of my breasts. More hands are following all the lines, cracks, and crevices of my body: backs of knees, between fingers and toes, over the curves of my hips and ass. I inadvertently groan in ecstasy, my body pulsating with energy.

'Okay, turn over.'

I open my eyes. It's dark now except for the candles' glow. Everyone's face looks as dazed as mine. They're enjoying this almost as much as I am. A cool scented towel is placed over my eyes. Gentle strong fingers massage the muscles of my breasts until I can feel my nipples turn to ripe firm blueberries. It's got to be Claire. She can feel it too. A woman knows exactly the pressure needed. Other hands slowly encircle my navel in ever-widening rings to the edges of my pubic hair. I begin to slither, my head flinging back as my chest rises and my hips begin to gyrate. The hands follow and match my movements. Fingers are placed in my mouth to suck and tongue, and in other orifices, like busy bees, to find sweet nectar spreading over and through me. Tremors radiate out from my breasts into earthquakes felt through my whole body with waves of such intensity it surprises us all. They cover me in warm towels and slowly drift away to let me recover in solitude.

None of us knew the massage would end like this. Or – am I the only one who didn't know? Joe has always had an interest in a threesome – which we tried once, two guys one girl – but three on one? I'd read that back in the early 1900s, 'hysterical' women were prescribed orgasmic massages to give them release from their stress. Often the prescribing doctors gave the treatment.

I smile; it works.

Is this the prelude to our foursome? It was Claire who really turned me on. Why have I never tried a woman's sexual touch? I drift off, remembering the tornado of communal pleasure.

I'm awakened by Joe and led to a bed under a dark bruising sky pelting rain onto the thatched roof. He enfolds me in his arms and feeling his insistence evokes an immediate reaction to the incredible past experience. We're all over each other, both of us hyped like never before: sharing kisses and fluids, licking and biting, moaning and laughing. Reaching ecstasy together makes us laugh out loud.

At dawn's first light, still wrapped in each other's arms, we awake to the booming calls of the howler monkeys marking their breakfast territories. We take ours on the balcony as the sun glitters diamonds through the billowing mist above the falls. The birds call good morning, flying through the shocking blue iridescence of dozens of morpho butterflies. Claire and Mark join us, arms wrapped around each other and smiling a bit guiltily. We smile back as I put us all at ease. 'I just want to thank you all for the most unusual and pleasurable experience of a lifetime. I don't think any of us thought it would end the way it did, but let's just chalk it up to getting lost in the moment. Again, I was the lucky one. I hope you guys had as much fun as I did, and later, we did.' They nod and look relieved.

'We definitely all got carried away, didn't we?' Mark laughs.

We're startled from our conversation by something huge flying through the air. Is it a bird, a plane? No, it's SuperPaul on his zipline. 'Hey, good morning!' he yells, landing on a platform nearby. 'Just on my morning rounds. Do you all need anything?'

'Well, I'm interested in flying through the air,' says Joe. 'Any chance we could try the zipline?'

Mark nods. 'I'd like to try it, too.'

'Sure. Meet me at the zip platform just below your tree house. Girls?'

'I don't want to leave this paradise. You guys go.' I answer.

Paul advises, 'Well, there's a short trail to that beautiful waterfall you can see from your balcony, with a bathing pool beneath it.'

'I'd love to get in the water,' replies Claire. 'Let's hike to the waterfall while the guys act like monkeys.'

After watching the animal life in the canopy, we decide to join it. The first trail, though short, is a steep heart-pounder. It takes us up to the edge of the waterfall that has been the backdrop to our treetop aerie. Standing atop the massive surge of water is exhilarating yet frightening. 'It feels like it's sucking me over!' Claire yells over the deafening roar.

'Yeah, it's too daring for me. Let's find calmer water for a dip.' We follow the trail in sinewy curves down and along the crystal-clear Rio Mono Verde rippling over smooth rocks. Eden calls. Stripping off our sweaty clothes, we frolic like otters in the cool water, then slither onto the flat hot rocks to bask in the sun.

Claire raises the subject of the previous night's passion. 'Angie, I had no idea things would progress the way they did either, but everyone was carried away with pleasure.'

'Well, I obviously was, and it was your touch that started it all. I've always known women's bodies could turn me on as much as men's, but I'd never tried it. My breasts have always been the key to my sexuality and you sure knew how to unlock the door.' Just thinking about it makes my nipples harden to that ripe berry stage, and Claire notices.

'I have tried it and learned a lot in the process. Being a masseuse had something to do with it.' Facing me, she gently puts both hands on my shoulders and begins a slow massage down my chest and around the slight mounds of my breasts. Then, opening her hands, she begins circling her palms on my already erect nipples. The effect is breathtaking as my back arches and my chest unconsciously strains towards her mouth. Her lips take in the nipple as her tongue laps the areola. My knees draw in and spread, revealing a blossom ready to burst, demanding touch. First her fingers caress each fold with life-giving nectar until I ache for her tongue. When it comes I move with it faster and harder until I split open, moaning, then laughing in bliss – thinking not of the past or the future, but of the momentous now.

When I recover, I take her in my arms. 'Tenderness of touch, that's what I love, miss, need. It's my turn.'

Claire's laugh is delightful. 'Can't wait.'

'Perfect. Let me love you from tip to toe.'

I start slowly, recalling my pleasure, following my instinct to kiss her – the perfect beginning. I gently rub my lips over hers until our tongues can no longer stay still. They tentatively touch and retract like little chameleons, then intertwine and explore inside and out. I continue down over the fast pulse in her throat, across her chest, over her full breasts to her dark, rich nipples, sweet as chocolate drops – so different from mine.

She sighs and sings and gently leads me lower. I savor her smooth curves and deliciously soft skin, so different than Joe's, leaving snail tracks on her stomach, around her navel. My hands precede my mouth as I part her thick dark bush and savor the mysterious loveliness of another woman's sexual flowering. My tongue draws into this bud, each emerging petal sticky with her sweet mead covering us both in love. Claire trembles all over in visible elation. 'You're *so* good.'

'You're a great teacher!'

Replete in the moment, we hold each other until our passion ebbs and the future dribbles back in. Will this be our secret? Will we draw our husbands into the melee? Will we do nothing? It's not the time to answer these questions. I sigh and quote, 'Our flesh surrounds us with its own decisions.'

Humuhumunukunukuapua'a

by Kilt Kilpatrick

'C'mon, Mila, just try it,' Mina says. She's so gorgeous it makes my teeth ache, but I can't just jump right in with her. I have to drag out the fun a little longer.

'No.' I pout. 'I can't . . .' I'm such a tease.

'Here, just let me show you.' She leans in a little closer, adjusts her top. I pause as if considering it, but I don't overplay the shy act.

'Mm . . . okay.' That makes her eyes light up.

'Thatta girl . . . all right, we'll take it real slow and easy, okay?'

I nod again, delighted. She sits up straight, all business, like a dedicated schoolteacher who really loves her subject. It's irresistible.

'Now see what I do, then you try it. Ready?' She licks her lips. I nod, and she begins.

'Humu . . .'

'Humu . . .' I repeat.

'Un-huh. Now another humu . . .'

'Humu . . .'

'Nuku . . .'

'Nuku . . .'

'Nuku . . .'

'Nuku . . .'

'Apu . . .'

'Like the Kwik-E-Mart guy on the Simpsons?'

'Yep. Just like.'

'Apu . . .'

'A'a . . .'

'Ah-ah . . .'

'Close enough. Now start to put them together. Humuhumu . . .'

'Humu-humu . . .'

'Nuku-nuku . . .'

'Nuku-nuku . . .'

'Yeah! You're doing it. Okay, let's bring it home. Humuhumunukunuku'

'Humuhumu . . . nukunuku'

'Altogether now.' I take a deep breath.

'Humuhumununu-noo-noo . . . ' I blow it and start giggling. She laughs too, but slaps my arm.

'No! So close! C'mon, get it together, girl!' But now I can't stop the gigglefest. She's smiling, but I know inside she's exasperated. She takes her native culture *very* seriously. She soldiers on.

'Hey, it's shorter than supercalifragilisticexpialidocious, and you can say that.'

Just between you and me, I *do* totally know how to say it, but I can't help it – learning how to say the ridiculously long name of the Hawaiian state fish is practically a rite of passage here. I just love the way Mina looks when she says the word. Every syllable looks like the beginning of a kiss.

God, that *did* sound totally lesboid, didn't it? I don't know what's gotten into me. I guess Hawaii makes me gay for everyone: the surfer boys with their perfect tans on their perfect bodies; hair spiky short likc hedgehogs or long straggly sun-bleached strands; their arms black with dense, intricate Polynesian tattoos; shark-tooth necklaces and cocky grins. And not just them, the girls too: blond mainland tourist girls shopping in sarongs; chic Japanese schoolgirls dressed for strolling Manhattan or decked out in crazy *Harajuku* street fashions; the knockout native *waihine* surfer babes striding across the beaches with their boards under their arms. I mean, just look at them. Hey, gorgeous is gorgeous.

And Mina is definitely gorgeous. The first thing I noticed about her was how perfectly *red* she was. Her cute pixie-cut hair is the exact same color as her soft tropical skin. Both are this striking shade of deep red, like schoolhouse bricks or maybe the surface of Mars, except that makes her sound ugly, and she's the most beautiful girl I've ever seen. Let's say she's the same color as cinnamon or paprika or saffron. Saffron's red, isn't it? Anyway, I'm sure if we went down to one of the little Asian markets I could find a bin of some exotic precious spice in just her color.

Her Apache red skin is offset by the most perfect Polynesian smile of dazzling flawless white teeth and bright almond eyes, a djinni's eyes. She says she's a mutt, a mix of native Hawaiian, Filipino, Vietnamese, Portuguese, and God knows what else. It all comes together so beautifully to make her one hundred percent *kama'aina*.

I had only just arrived on Oahu from upstate New York with my mom, a newly transferred flight surgeon. Me? An army brat in a new place where I knew nobody and nothing, out of my element as usual. I couldn't even get my bearings straight. On Hawaii, there's really no such thing as north, south, east or west. Everything is either *mauka,* toward the mountains; *makai,* toward the sea; and either toward Waikiki or toward Ewa. So you ask somebody for directions to somewhere, and they might say 'Kapaolono Park? Dat on the *mauka* side of Kilauea, *waikiki* of Pokole.' I tell you, Hawaii is a different planet.

One happy surprise was discovering I had a particular advantage here. I'm half Canadian French-Indian and half Russian, and even though I was a total east-coast girl with genes from the frostiest parts of the world, somehow my brunette hair and Iroquois eyes made most island folk assume I was a native. At least until they asked me something in Pidgin.

The plan was I would start college next semester. Until then, I was free to get a summer job and take advantage of living in paradise. I resolved to thwart my natural tendency toward shyness. So when I stumbled onto a flier for a Zumba class at a neighborhood gym, on a whim I went in and signed up. But when I walked into the studio on that first day, I got self-conscious again and stuck to the back of class, intimidated by the competence of the other students. Everybody had clearly done this before. They breezed through the choreography, segueing effortlessly from spicy salsa jiggles to reggaeton gyrations to undulating belly dance moves. I struggled to follow along, always a beat behind the rest of the class. My frustration grew. One girl took pity on me.

'Don't sweat it,' she said with a kind smile. 'You're doing great. Lemme show you. It's easier if you forget about the arms and just worry about the footwork.' It was Mina, of course, shaking it in tight black workout pants and a bright floral-print tank top. Ignoring the rest of class, she walked me through the steps. I watched her swaying hips carefully, grateful for her help. She was right; it *was* easier to get the footwork down first. Soon, I had it.

'Hey! Look at you – you've got it!' Her spirit was infectious.

Then the next number changed tempo again, and I had to start all over, but I had definitely turned the corner in my attitude, if not my aptitude, for dance.

Toward the end, our perky instructor called out, 'Freestyle,' and encouraged us to do any steps we wanted to the music. I went for samba moves, the style that was giving me the least trouble. Mina, meanwhile, shifted into a hula routine: She did a gentle bow, swept out her arms as if gathering flowers, brought her hands to her heart, brought them up again in exquisite gestures for birds, for fragrant blossoms and ocean waves. All the while she swiveled her hips and moved in graceful little orbits. I was enraptured.

As class wrapped up, she flashed me a last smile and a little wave before she left. I watched her go and followed her from a safe distance. In the locker room I hesitated for a few anxious moments of nail biting, but finally screwed up my courage and came over to her.

'Hey, um, I just wanted to say thanks again for rescuing me back there. You're so good at this.' She looked up from untying her shoes.

'Oh, hi! Hey, no worries. I thought you moved your *okole* great once you got the hang of it.' She dropped her sneaker and stood up. 'I'm Mina.' She leaned in and whispered, 'It's short for Wilhelmina, but I don't like that so much. I don't even know why I just said that.' She laughed. I was touched by her disclosure.

'My name's Mila,' I said, and lowered my voice too. 'It's short for Ludmila, which I've never told anyone in my whole life, *ever*.'

'We're both bound to secrecy, then,' she said conspiratorially. We laughed and shook on it.

We were inseparable after that: Mila and Mina. Since we were both between boyfriends, it was easy to spend long hours together just hanging around the neighborhood in Kaimuk or heading off to the windward side beaches. We would bop down Kapahulu Avenue hitting the thrift stores or browsing the Goodwill or checking Peggy's Picks for irresistible bargains on jewelry. If we were feeling flush from our part-time jobs, we'd go shop for bikinis at the funky little boutiques. When we grabbed a bag of M&Ms from the cramped little corner market, we would tell each other that they were made especially for us, and somehow the joke never got old.

Grabbing a lunch of native grub at Ono's became part of the ritual. She got me hooked on oodles of varieties of meat, usually pig and usually wrapped in taro and ti leaves: *pipikaula* pork jerky, shredded steamed *kalua* pig, *laulau* (sort of a Hawaiian dim sum) and *na'au pua'a* (don't ask). Even Spam tasted good Hawaiian style, though I still haven't quite warmed up to poi yet. Most of the time we'd finish with jiggly blocks of *haupia*, coconut milk pudding.

Once Mina inherited her cousin's beat-up Jeep, we really started going places. We drove up to Kuli'ou'ou and hiked up the ridge trail all the way to the top. We felt like Indiana Jones in the jungle, especially the higher we got, when the muddy, slippery trail became so razor narrow you could see the mountain dropping off sharply on either side. Thick flood rivers of mist filled the valleys between the curdle of tropic green mountains, except when the occasional break would surprise you with a queasy reminder of just how high up you were. On the steepest portion of the trail, we pulled ourselves to the top with ropes. At the ragged little summit of bare, packed earth, we shivered with cold and fear of heights, but the view was spectacular.

Other days we would drive up to the North Shore to see the sea turtles nesting at Laniakea beach, and freeze our mouths polishing off a delish shave ice at one of the venerable little roadside places up Hale'iwa way. Because Mina was a native, she knew all the secret breaks on the leeward side, and we could go surf there without getting hassled by the fiercely territorial island boys. At the end of the day we would find a public park at the top of the rises and listen to the cicadas while watching the sunset transform the baby-blue sky over Honolulu to a swirl of fire, sherbet pink and golden butter. We would joke about what a waste all this romance was on the two of us girls with no guys to take advantage of it. But secretly, I thought everything was just perfect the way it was.

I never uttered the word *lesbian*, not even in my own head. I just had the biggest crush on my friend and loved spending as much time with her as I could. She was just so easy to hang out with, and we always had such fun together. Though gradually, I realized I was developing a kind of itch I couldn't quite scratch. I surprised myself with how badly I wanted to touch her. I didn't want to, you know, *do things* to her. I just wondered what it would be like to kiss her, and sometimes when I was alone and sure no one could catch me, I would kiss my hand and pretend it was her lips.

I kept an eye out for any sign that Mina might feel the same way and treasured every tiniest little positive clue, analyzing its significance for hours while I thought of her late at night in my bed: the smile she would shoot me when we'd meet, the way she would grab my arm when we made jokes, the little bone-hook necklace she bought me at a roadside stand. I'll never forget the sensation when she helped me put it on, the touch of her fingers against the back of my neck when I pulled up my hair so she could get the tiny little clasp closed. It sent a tingle from the base of my skull all the way down.

But mostly I kept the feelings to myself. For every hopeful indication floating like a flower on the sea, there was a crushing wave of anxiety. What if I was wrong? What if I tried something and she freaked out? I couldn't stand to lose her – better if I kept it all to myself and let things stay the way they were. If only I could –

The day I blew it started out so nice, too. I ran out, happy as a songbird, as soon as I could hear Mina's battered old Jeep coming down the street. She was adorable as usual in sunglasses, a raspberry-colored bikini, Daisy Duke cutoffs, and an island cowgirl hat, woven from straw with a thin leather band of cowrie shells.

'Hey, cowgirl, cool hat!' I called out as I hopped in next to her.

'Yeah, you like it? Good, 'cause I got one for you too.' She pulled out a matching one from behind her seat with a flourish, like a magician presto-change-o'ing a bouquet from out of thin air.

'Really?' I said with a little squeal of glee. I grabbed my present and without even thinking gave her a tight hug of thanks and a peck on the cheek. A split second later I realized I was squeezing the side of her boob and let go, a little too quickly. The shock must have registered on my face, and I scanned hers for her reaction. But no disaster yet; she wasn't freaking out. I added that to my mental collection of hopeful signs.

We drove up the Pali highway to Lanikai. According to Mina, the beach there had become overdeveloped, like so much of the island, but she thought there was still a secret place she could find for us. I liked the sound of that. She parked the Jeep in an alley behind a row of houses, and we walked down to a little unmarked beach access, guarded only by a trio of chickens. It's surprising how much poultry seems to roam the island freely, afraid of nothing except the occasional mongoose, which also wanders freely.

A few footsteps later I had to catch my breath. The nondescript suburban walk suddenly opened up onto a bright, sunny vista of surf and sand, postcard-perfect. Crystal-clear water the color of blue topaz and emeralds lapped at a beach that seemed to be made entirely of miles and miles of golden brown sugar. Just a little ways off the coast lay a pair of hilly islands, like a couple of great green dromedary humps floating in the ocean. 'It's perfect,' I sighed.

We strode barefoot for maybe a mile or two until we came to a nice secluded spot – just us and tiny brown lizards sunning themselves on the outcroppings of sharp, spongy black lava rock. After staking out a place for our stuff, we stripped to our bikinis and spent an hour or so snorkeling through the coral reef beds along with a colorful menagerie of tropical fish. When our fingers were pruning, we came out again and rolled out our beach towels. We helped each other put on suntan lotion. No, nothing like what you're thinking – it was perfectly innocent. While we helped each other touch up our cheekbones and the sensitive areas under our eyes, she started up our Hawaiian language lesson for the day – with mixed success, you'll remember. Like I was saying before, she finally grumbles, 'Hey, it's shorter than supercalifragilisticexpialidocious and you can say that.'

I hated for Mina to think I was some kind of feeb, but a perverse part of me wanted to torment her longer, so I begged off the lesson and stretched out on my towel to catch some warm sun on my backside. She lay down next to me, but I could tell she was still miffed. She rested her chin on her folded arms and hid beneath her cowgirl hat. The two of us lay like that for a few prickly minutes. I took advantage of the lag time to sneak a peek at her through half-closed eyes. Her bikini bottom was so cutc; it had little ties on the sides and the dusting of golden sand on the wet material caught my eye. I decided I had better make nice. I rolled over, facing her, and on a whim, reached over and gently poked her in the ribs.

'Quit it,' she growled from under her hat. I didn't. Instead, I began writing on her back with my finger in one long string of ornate cursive letters.

'What are you doing back there?' she muttered, all Miss Grumpy.

'I'm writing. Here, I'll do it again.' This time I printed, and went extra slow for good measure: I M S O R R Y

She got it this time, but her highness still wasn't fully appeased.

'You're really bugging me today. You'll need to do better than that.'

My heart skipped a beat at that last part. Was she giving me a signal? Or was it just wishful thinking? I proceeded with caution – or so I thought. I got up on one elbow and leaned over her in order to draw a picture on her back. First I wiped the tiny droplets of seawater off her skin to clear the canvas. With my finger, I encircled a big ball over one shoulder blade for the sun, and drew rays coming off it.

'What are you doing now?' she asked, a bit softer now, genuinely curious.

'I'm drawing you a picture. That was the sun.' I moved on to the ocean. I dragged four fingers down the curve of her back, tracing a line of gentle waves from her shoulders all the way to the hem of her bikini bottom. She gave her approval with a wordless groan of *mmm.* I added curvy v-shapes for birds in the sky, tickled her with little fish in the sea, drew a stick figure *us* on our blankets.

'That feels good,' she murmured.

I got bolder, a little drunk on her smooth skin and encouragement. I let my fingers drift, not drawing, just running the back of my hand up and down her beautiful sun-drenched back. I watched carefully for a reaction, but she remained still and let me do as I pleased. I slipped my hand under the string of her bikini top and idly rubbed between her shoulder blades. She was very quiet. I bit my lip and ran my palm down, settling into the indentation of her lower back, and let it creep slowly further, to the edge of her raspberry bikini bottom – then past that, to softly caress her butt.

The sight hypnotized me. It felt like I was watching someone else doing it, or that my hand had a mind of its own. Then I felt her stir, and shot my hand back again. Mina lifted her head, agitated. She didn't say a word, but sat up, her gaze locked on me. Oh God.

'Mila? What did you do that for?' She looked baffled, like she was trying to solve a particularly thorny puzzle. *Oh God. Oh God. Oh my God.* I didn't have anywhere near the nerve to play it cool and shrug it off as an accident. I just lost it. Deep inside, my heart began crashing around like a bird in a cage trying to fly away. Pinned by the look in her eyes, I started to cry and my voice went all high pitched and weepy.

'Oh God, Mina, I'm so sorry. I'm so, so sorry. I didn't mean to – '

'Mila . . . are . . . are you gay?'

My breath started tripping over itself in my throat. I was sure I was going to pass out. 'Omigod, no, I swear.'

'Then why . . . ?'

'I didn't mean to! It was just an accident, oh God, Mina, I would never do anything like that to you!' I kept babbling hysterically, and Mina kept staring at me. Finally she'd had enough.

'Mila! *Mila!* Shut up! Just shut up and listen to me!'

I choked off my apology in mid-sentence. She continued, in a cool slow voice.

'I'm not a lesbian, understand?' she said. My heart slipped off its precarious hold and tumbled down to hell. I couldn't bear it for another second. I had to get out of there. I tried to get up and run away, run anywhere, run off a cliff on to the rocks, but Mina grabbed my arms, furious, unwilling to let me escape.

'Hey! Look at me!' She shook me until I did. Her voice was cool and collected. 'Listen to me.Look, I'm not gay. I'm just not into girls.'

I stared at her, my eyes streaming, miserable. Her voice softened, and she pulled tear-slick strands of hair away from my face, resting her forehead against mine so we were eye to eye.

'But Mila . . . Mila, baby . . . I'm so, *so* into *you*.'

What? What did she just say? I couldn't process a response. I could barely string together her words, let alone believe she had really said them. I stared at her beautiful, so-serious face until a tear came down her cheek, and she broke into a smile.

'I wouldn't even mind if you wanted to kiss me. That's what you want to do, isn't it?' she asked in a soft voice, her eyes wide and earnest. I kept staring, then sniffled, bit my lip, and nodded, numb and mute with overwhelming emotions rising up in me. Her response was barely audible.

'Then come here.' She took my face in her hands and pulled me into her. My lips parted just a bit before they met hers. Oh my God! Her lips tasted so good – so soft, so warm, just as delicious as I had imagined. Our kiss went on and on like a dream. I suddenly went all lightheaded, feeling like we were spinning on a carousel. I held on to her to ride out the dizziness. She wrapped protective arms around me and squeezed me tight.

I know I said I only wanted to kiss her, just a sweet little innocent kiss on the lips, no more than that. And it really did start out so warm and tender, but the longer it lasted, the more urgent it became. Our tongues met, and our breathing came in ragged bursts as our sweet, gentle little kiss turned into a hard, deep lip lock. I felt our excitement build, growing hotter and hotter. I wanted more. She did too. I felt her hand slide around and start to knead my breast. Her touch made me gasp, mouth wide open. She took the rising nipple in her hand and gave it a squeeze.

'God, your tits are so nice, Mila. I'm so jealous,' she panted. Her hand slipped back behind me again. I could feel her untying the string to my top, and then it was gone.

'Mmm ... I want them,' she purred in my ear. I leaned back, starting to shake a little as she kissed her way down my neck toward my breast until she reached her target. As she wrapped her mouth around my areola, I groaned and dug my fingers into her hair, clasping her head to my chest while she kissed and suckled on my hard nipple. I shuddered under the touch of her insistent tongue and lips, and she took advantage of my vulnerable state to gently but firmly ease me back on my beach towel.

I hugged her to me with both arms, trapping her head while she kept going back and forth between my breasts, teasing them with her mouth. She straddled me. I felt both her thighs clasping mine. I let her go, but only so I could feel her up. I ran my greedy hands over her bikini top. Her breasts were a little smaller than mine but nothing to be ashamed of: round and wonderful, fitting her frame just right. I couldn't wait for my turn. I pushed her off, just enough for her to sit up so I could better grope her. She laughed as I undid the knot in back and pulled off her top. Her tan lines were coppery compared to her tropical scarlet skin.

'Hi there,' I said to the twin sunbursts of her sweet little nips. I made Mina squeal when I tweaked them, which amused me greatly. Before she could recover I craned my neck to lick them. She closed her eyes and grinned while I nuzzled her happily. Her nipples were small and sensitive. I had to be careful to keep from tickling her. I could feel her legs tensing too, and with a twinge of surprise I realized she was riding me, humping my thigh with her pussy. The realization lit me up from the inside like a line of fireworks going off. I reached down and grabbed her butt. With a jerk that made her whoop like a cowgirl on a bucking bronco, I pulled her closer so that her knee was right up tight in between my legs, turning her whole leg into my sex toy. She took the hint and leaned forward again, supporting herself on her outstretched arms so that we could grind our laps into each other. What a rush! I shuddered out another one as she stared down at me, her eyes smoldering with a look I had never seen from her. I could feel her trembling, too. I held onto her sweet butt and kept pulling her into me.

'I want you,' I told her in between sharp intakes of breath.

'I want you too, *Ipo*.'

Time to take it up a notch. A delayed flash of paranoia pinged in my head. I quickly scanned the beach to see if any innocent bystanders or axe murderers had wandered up. All clear. The nearest people were tiny specks a mile or so down the beach, or cavorting in the surf on the twin islands across the water. I locked eyes with her and started to undo the little ties on her bikini bottoms. Her eyes grew large again, but she gave me a little nod, and held still while I undressed her. She never looked so beautiful.

'Now you have to get naked too,' she breathed. I smiled and reached down for my bikini bottoms, but she stopped me before I could shimmy out of them.

'No, wait. I want to do it.' She snaked her hands under me, as I lifted my ass to let her peel them down past my hips. Once she had the loop of swimsuit bottom untangled from my ankles and tossed them to the side, she came back to me, straddling me again, but this time so that our torsos were locked V to V. We were both so wet, our juices were mingling as we ground into each other. It felt incredible, so utterly intimate. I had never been so turned on, but again, inventive Mina surprised me further. From behind her back, she slipped her hand between her own legs to work over my poor love-starved pussy. Oh. My. *God!*

She was feeling it too. My clever girl was thumbing her own clit while her fingers strummed me. I held on to her for dear life while my body stiffened and shook and came so hard as she finger-fucked me over and over, until I couldn't take anymore and begged her to stop. She was having way too much fun.

When she finally relented I sat up, panting hard, and gave her the evil eye. She grinned back and tried to play innocent, but she was giggling too much to pull off her *who, me?* I raised an eyebrow in determination and with a sly smile pushed her down on her back. My turn to torture her. I played nice at first, pinning her arms down and giving her a big fat kiss. She squirmed a little underneath me, rubbing hers against mine, which was pretty effing awesome, actually. But I had a plan, so after a few minutes of her yummy distraction, I had to leave her warm delicious lips and pull away from her lap dance-from-below. I started laying a trail of kisses from her clavicle down to her breastbone, to her belly button, and headed further south – further *mukai*, I mean.

I spread her thighs apart and gave her one last bit of direct eye contact as I lowered my face down to her waiting folds. I was a little freaked out by my own boldness and wasn't quite sure what I was supposed to do, but I was ready to surf that wave and figure it out. Acting on instinct, I made a beeline for her clitoris. I touched it daintily with my tongue first. *Whoa, look at me. I'm going to eat her out.* Then I dove in and sucked it hard. Too hard. Mina's whole body wrenched and she let out a weird little squeak.

'Oh, oh, oh . . . too much, too much! Sorry, hon. My clit is way too sensitive for that.'

I backed off and rubbed her mound with my fingers for a minute to bring her down again, then gently spread the downy outer halves out of the way so I could give her wet inner lips a nice long tongue-lashing. That got her moaning and rolling her head back. She reached her fingers out to grasp my head and groaned out semi-intelligible bursts of encouragement. I went back to her love pearl and gave it gentle love licks around its little hood instead. Ah, better. She made a soft burbling noise like a happy baby and grabbed her legs to spread them further open. A flash of inspiration came to me. I spread her folds again, kissed her lips and whispered into her. She laughed.

'Ohh . . . you *can* say it . . . sneaky bitch . . .' She sighed, then got louder, yelling, 'Oh God, *Ipo*, say it! *Say it*! Yeah . . .' Words failed her and washed out with the tide into a sea of groans and sighs. While she writhed under my tongue, I kept a firm grasp on her thighs and continued chanting my magic word, over and over again.

Humuhumunukunukuapua'a.

Needs

by Farrah J. Phoenix

A vacation is long overdue. After all the drama from my divorce and the insanity at work, all I want is to fly south like the geese in winter. Too long has been spent living for others, taking care of others, and ignoring my own needs. I need complete seclusion: time to reconnect with myself, touch my roots and all that spiritual mumbo-jumbo they always talk about when something drastic changes in your life.

As I get off the airplane in Miami, the stale, warm terminal air seems to melt over me. I feel the tension in my body begin to release as a light glistening of sweat develops over my skin. Tingling energy flows through me in anticipation of the well-deserved retreat. It's been six years since I have felt like myself. Beaches, spas, shopping, and yoga classes will be the perfect way to relax and rejuvenate my trampled spirit.

I breeze through the airport without much notice of the people around me. A blast of Florida heat greets me at the door as I drag my luggage out of the baggage claim to meet my shuttle. Palm trees sway against the beautiful blue sky and the sun caresses my face and exposed shoulders to welcome me.

Bumping along through the streets of Miami and South Beach, I can feel my body respond to my new independent freedom. I feel like a teenager again with my heart racing, my face flushing, and my tummy dancing gracefully. I am free.

After I check in at the resort, I take a moment to enjoy the quiet of my modern suite. The view is stunning! I watch the waves lap against the beach below. The sun is beginning to descend, casting orange, yellow, and purple hues across the skyline. I close my eyes, take a deep breath and feel a new energy surge through the tips of my fingers and toes. I hear the waves outside – feel them penetrate my soul. The waves are calling me, welcoming me, enticing me.

Not wanting to waste the evening, I quickly slip into a pair of shorts and form-fitting tank and grab a sweater. I smile into the mirror on my way out the door, taking a moment to adjust my long, wavy brown hair. I look good. I feel good!

I walk along the vacant beach, watching the sun set. Everything is quiet except for the sound of the waves. I feel my body submit with each step – as though the sand at my feet and the sun against my skin are working to gently massage away the years of tension. Together they embrace me like a long-lost lover. I shudder. Everything feels new. I am being reborn.

The sun has almost vanished completely beyond the horizon. As I turn around and head back I hear the sound of a branch snap. Startled, I turn my head towards the sound, heart racing.

Against the glow of the setting sun stands the silhouette of a woman. I blush as my eyes capture the orange reflection of the sun on her skin. Each curve of her body is bare. My breath catches in my throat, but I can't look away. The curvature of her breasts, her back, and bottom look as though they have been molded by the hands of a master sculptor.

I watch as she stretches her long form against the colors of twilight and my heart races. I have never looked at a woman this way before. I can't understand the sudden rush of blood, the beating heart or the clammy hands. I breathe deeply, trying to control myself. I'm afraid of my feelings – afraid of my response to this woman's appeal.

As she reaches the peak of her stretch, she turns her face towards me. Everything stops: my heart, my breathing, and my self control. I feel perverse standing here watching her. To my surprise, the look on her face is not one of disapproval. It's almost flirtatious. She seems pleased.

Her smile is subtle and sweet. Her lips open a bit, showing off a small portion of her teeth. Her eyes are deep and sultry. I'm afraid she can see right through me. I freeze in place, mesmerized. I can't take my eyes off her.

Bending over she grabs her towel and loosely ties it around her chest. She starts walking towards me – no, not walking, but floating. Even if I wanted to, I can't move – immobilized by the allure of the enchanting creature in front of me.

All of my blood is rushing to my face. I can feel it burn against the cooling twilight air. I can feel a familiar, warm pulsation between my legs.

As she approaches, her eyes lock on mine as though in a deep, sensual embrace. My hands tremble.

She slows as she passes by me. She is so close. The scent of coconut oil twirls around us. It's intoxicating. Arousing.

Without a word, the beautiful sun goddess stretches her hand towards me running her fingertips down my side. Her touch is electric! As her hand moves over the curvature of my breast and along the sides of my tummy, my body trembles. I close my eyes and take deep breaths. The warmth between my legs increases. I am so aroused.

Then she is gone.

I stand trembling in the sand while the sun takes its final dip below the horizon. My brain strains to understand what has occurred. My body, however, is aware and longing for more.

The next few days go by like any other vacation. I relax on the beach with a good book with the sun casting its glow over my exposed skin followed by a refreshing dip in the resort pool. I enjoy the company of some new friends during a snorkel excursion and shop until my credit cards groan in protest. The spa and yoga classes are daily events to stretch and de-stress my tightly wound muscles. Vacation is bliss.

My naked sun goddess, however, is never too far from my mind. I think of her during quiet moments, wondering if she has been thinking the same things I had been during our brief encounter. When I hear feminine giggles pass by on the beach, my heart starts racing again, and I instinctively look to see if it is her. Hoping it's her.

Not that I'd know what to do if she does reappear. My body wants her, but my logical brain fights the desire. After all, I am a straight woman who has only been with men. I was married, for crying out loud. What is happening?

In the privacy of my suite I bring my favorite vibrating bullet out to play, but it's not a man that's on my mind. A throbbing cock thrusting mindlessly is the last thing my body longs for. I'm imagining *her*. Wanting her.

As I run the silver vibrating joy over my clitoris and rub my hand over my breasts, I picture her sampling me, touching me, loving me. At the height of my orgasms I see her sultry eyes boring into me and smell the coconut oil on her skin. The thought of her brings about the best release I've ever experienced. I spend hours thinking of her, enjoying the fantasy.

The end of my vacation draws near without a glimpse of my sultry mistress.

On my last night in Florida I decide to join some new friends at a local club for a fun night of drinks and dancing. The girls I accompany are a bunch of sorority sisters whom I met while snorkeling. They are a lot of fun, bouncy and beautiful. Their smiles are our ticket past the doormen at the club and without waiting a minute in line, we are inside, where the music is booming and the walls seem to vibrate from the insane number of people dancing and exalting the joys of life.

It takes precisely placed elbows at the bar to get some drinks, but after downing a Singapore Sling and a few tequila shots, the girls and I are buzzing enough to hit the dance floor.

Spinning and dancing, I feel the power of my freedom wash over me. I can't remember the last time I felt so good, so free, so much like *me*. This vacation has been everything I had been hoping for, everything I needed.

I continue to dance like it's my sole purpose on Earth. I am so busy enjoying myself that I don't notice the sorority sisters disappear into the dark corners of the club with random men. It is all good, though. I am finally comfortable just being me.

Like a scene out of a movie, the dance floor opens up out of the blue. Through the human red sea I recognize my fantasy woman. My stomach flutters.

She drifts gracefully towards me, her eyes never leaving mine. Once again I am rendered immobile, like my limbs have been filled with lead. Even the influence of alcohol cannot entice me to move.

My golden beauty approaches me head on, her intention evident. She cups the back of my head with her hands. My heart stops. *Is she going to kiss me?* Her face slowly leans towards mine.

The sweet aroma of her breath and the flowery scent of her perfume fill my nostrils. It is intoxicating. My brain admits defeat to my body, which is now vibrating less from the music and more from this woman's presence. My body wants this, needs this.

I brace myself in preparation for new sensations to meet my tingling lips, but to my surprise she doesn't kiss me. Her soft lips graze my cheek as she leans in to whisper,

'I've been watching you all week. I can see you've been thinking about me. I've been thinking about you too.'

I stand in stunned silence. She's been thinking about *me*? If she only knew the way I have thought about her, and the things I was doing when I was thinking of her. Is it possible she's been doing the same?

'Come with me, precious,' she whispers. 'I want to give you what you've been longing for.' I feel her tongue over my earlobe and across my jaw bone. My breath catches in my throat. A shiver runs down my spine and sensual juices flow freely.

Grabbing my hand, she escorts me out of the club and down the street to my awaiting suite. Inside, I am overcome by a wave of fear. Instincts try to override desires. I cower across the room like a virgin on her wedding night, breathing erratically.

With a girlish giggle she places her soft hands on my petrified face and kisses me uninhibited. Her lips are cherry delicious, her tongue deliberate. Instantly, my panties are soaked with pleasure. Having her hands on me is better than I ever imagined in my fantasies. I am scared and excited all at once. Closing my eyes, I kiss her back. Our skin melts together as our hands work to release each article of clothing. Her skin is soft and smooth under her T-shirt. Her breasts peak when I run my hands over them. The curvature of her body and the texture of her skin feel natural under my touch. I want to please her.

Bare as the day we were born, we fall together to the floor, bodies rubbing against each other, hands exploring, lips indulging. I kiss her intently along her jaw, down her neck, and between her beautiful breasts. She moans loudly as I trace my tongue around the large, soft mounds and tease each of her nipples. Thc movements are oddly natural to me. I've never been this turned on in my life.

'I want you!' she moans, grabbing one of my hands and guiding it between her legs.

I can feel her excitement dripping over my fingertips. At first, I'm not sure what to do so I choose to explore her slowly. The intense heat makes me quiver as I slip my fingers between the petals of her pleasure. Delicately, I remove my fingers from inside of her.

She moans, encouraging me to explore a little deeper. I feel her thighs twitch with excitement and anticipation.

Once again I stick my fingers in and pull them out, allowing my fingertips to graze her engorged g-spot. I look her in the eyes as I bring my fingers slowly to my lips. The expression on her face and the way she lightly bites her bottom lip tells me that this excites her. I have never tasted a woman before. Her sweetness is delectable. I want more. I let my fingers slowly move over my lips and the tip of my tongue so I can indulge in this exciting new sensation.

I can tell she is pleasantly surprised as she gently writhes beneath me. Reaching out, she grabs my head, wrapping her legs around me as I fall on top of her. We kiss again, licking each other's lips and embracing each other's bodies.

I didn't know I could feel this comfortable with a woman. I am no longer scared. All I want to do is bring her pleasure, and I know that's what she offers as well. For hours we toss about the suite: holding each other, exploring each other, tasting each other. Our skin sparkles with sweat. Blood rushes through me as I place my lips to the delicate, pink petals between her legs and hers to mine. Our hips rock as our tongues work at each other's engorged clitoris. I slip my fingers back inside her to overwhelm her g-spot as I suck, lick and kiss her sweetness.

The touch of her lips on my goodness is gentle and knowing. She knows how to please me as though we've been together for years. I can't remember the last time this felt so natural, so good, so real.

Upon release, her intense eruption covers my fingers and drips sweetly into my mouth. I lap up every last drop of ecstatic elixir.

Tasting her and feeling her body react induces my own release. Her tongue continues to move through my slit as euphoric waves of ecstasy crash through my body over and over again. As the waves subside, she rolls me to my back, pinning me beneath her with a playful giggle.

With her mouth still making love to me, she slips her fingers inside. The sensation is almost unbearable. I groan loudly, desperately gripping at anything I can find. My body writhes and sways uncontrollably. Her free hand moves over my breasts, tummy, and thighs as she continues to love me. Each rush of pleasure is almost painful as my arousal increases after each orgasm. My body can't take it anymore. An explosion rocks me from the inside out.

I grab my lover's head and wrap my legs tightly around her as my hips convulse under the immense power. In that moment I release every last hang-up I have about my past, and everything I have believed about love.

All that matters is this moment.

When morning dawns it all seems like a dream. The only evidence remaining of the woman from the beach is a little note on my bedside table. There are no words on the note, simply a lipstick mark and 'xo' written in delicate handwriting. That is all I need.

Buried Desire

by Jen Bluekissed

Sure, my divorce was final, but my life was far from beginning its next chapter. Until the house sold, how could I move on with everything? Ken and I weren't much for saving money, and my share of the joint assets was tied up as equity in the house. What I wanted more than anything was to get out of town to start my life over again. Scrambling to make a deposit and first month's rent on an apartment would be hard enough, but since Ken did everything in his power to wreck my credit before our divorce was finalized, even renting my own place wasn't happening any time soon.

I unfolded the crumpled-up wad of paper that had been burning a hole in my pocket like unspent birthday money from Grandma. Even though I'd read the want ad at least ten times already, I couldn't resist reading it again. There were so many pros and not so many cons to trying for this job. A roof over my head, three meals served daily, and a change of scenery were just what I needed.

The logical, grown-up part of me screamed, *you can't just quit your stable job with medical benefits to take this gig. You can't. You just can't.*

The adventure-seeking newly divorced woman inside

me whispered back defiantly, *health insurance and stability be damned. Look what stable has gotten me these past seven years. A whole basket full of nothing.*

I called the phone number listed on the help-wanted ad and held my breath as I waited for someone to pick up. The way my heart was beating in my ears made me think I should start breathing again.

'No, we haven't filled the position yet. You interested?' a nasal male voice asked.

'Yes, I'd like to interview.'

'No need. We need someone *asap* because the tour leaves tomorrow. Drop by with your Social Security card or birth certificate as well as your driver's license so we can complete the I-9 paperwork. Dress casually, and when you pack for the trip, bring lots of comfortable clothes and shoes. Our people are dressed to the hilt, but we need you to be able to move quickly, quietly, and with a full range of motion. Bedroom slippers. Pack bedroom slippers.'

'I beg your pardon?' I said as I steadied my shaking hand while holding my cell phone to my ear. I didn't even have a pen and paper handy since I thought I was going to chicken out and hang up before someone answered the phone.

'Bring bedroom slippers. We need you quiet as a church mouse.'

I hung up the phone and cursed under my breath. Not even something simple like a pair of slippers was easily within my grasp. I owned three pairs of them, but I'd have to run by the mall to buy yet another pair because even they were tied to the house. My ex-husband had a restraining order against me, so I couldn't show up to collect them without getting my attorney involved. A quick trip to the mall would be less expensive than getting my lawyer involved just so I could gather more of my belongings from the house.

When I arrived at the studio, there was a flurry of activity to get me ready for the job. I wondered why the theatre improv troupe was so quick to hire me without so much as a formal interview, but I didn't have a whole lot of time to wonder. As soon as my paperwork was signed and I had a chance to see the trailer I'd be calling home for the next few months, I was told to go home to pack up any belongings I wanted to take with me.

'Be back for the dress rehearsal at five,' Larry, my new boss, said. 'We leave tomorrow for our first stop on the comedy tour.'

'Can I at least meet everyone first?' I asked as I finished shaking his hand.

'Nope. No time. The ladies and gents are too busy packing up and saying their own goodbyes.'

A few hours later, I returned for the dress rehearsal. The traveling comedy troupe was an improv group who does half audience suggestion, half pre-arranged skits. Every scene involved different costuming and set changes. My new job was to be the attendant to Darla Rae, one of the country's most well-known comediennes. I learned that her stage make-up would remain relatively unchanged, but between scenes I'd have to help her change from one costume to the next. She wore everything from bib overalls as part of a farmer's daughter scene to an elaborate Elizabethan-style gown. Most of the costume changes had to happen in less than ten minutes during the live show.

The stage manager explained all this to me while we waited for Darla Rae to return from saying goodbye to her own friends and family. I'd begun to wonder if I'd gotten in above my head. After all, I'd never worn a corset or handled period-specific clothing before. How on earth would I be able to help this woman get into and out of ten changes of clothing for a three-hour performance? My idea of fashion was a baggy T-shirt or sweatshirt with jeans and sneakers. I stared at the signed poster of Darla Rae, which had been taped to the hallway. The stage manager walked away, busy with a last-minute prop problem. Before he was out of earshot, he pointed to the door on my right.

'Lucy, go ahead and wait for Darla Rae in her dressing room. It's unlocked. All the clothes she'll need are hanging on the rack. She's almost always late, so don't be surprised if bras are flying before you have a chance to properly introduce yourself.'

I let myself into Darla Rae's makeshift dressing room and flipped the light switch. The room was sparsely furnished with two folding chairs, a rack of costumes, a sink, and a mirror. There was a folding table in the corner of the room. It was completely covered with brushes, stage make-up, and Styrofoam heads wearing wigs. None of the hairstyles was contemporary. Not even close. Well, if you didn't count the mullet. A lot of things had come back from the eighties, like leggings and crimpers, but I doubted mullets would make the grade.

I had always worn my hair in a pixie cut. I fingered the wigs cautiously and toyed with the idea of trying one on. What could it hurt? Darla Rae probably wouldn't show up for another half hour or so. I quickly plopped the white-blond mullet atop my head, then caught my reflection in the mirror. Unfortunately, I also caught the reflection of Darla Rae standing in the doorway behind me.

'Don't you look cute?' she said.

'Sorry – '

'Don't apologize. It looks better on you than it does on me.'

I turned, the movement knocking the mullet slightly off-center on my head. Sure that my cheeks were red, I extended my right hand for a handshake while removing the wig with my left.

'I'm Lucy. I love the wigs. Just couldn't resist, ya know?'

Rather than shaking my hand, Darla Rae took the mullet from my left hand before gingerly placing it back atop my head like it had been when she stood in the doorway. Her smirk was cute. Dangerously cute. She had long, curly red hair that cascaded perfectly down her back. I hated the thought of covering her perfect hair with these awful wigs during the show. Her green eyes twinkled, setting off her light freckled skin. Darla's accent said Southern, but her looks said Irish.

She walked to the rack of clothing, her full hips swaying with the stride of a woman who knew how to work an audience, albeit my audience of one. As she lifted her

V-neck shirt over her head, she spoke into the cotton fabric. I didn't quite make out what she was saying. While I asked her to repeat herself, she had the shirt off and was already unclasping her bra.

'Keep the mullet on. Seriously. We scrapped the eighties rocker scene at the last minute. It doesn't fit with the rest of the sketches we have planned.' She sighed after her bra dropped to the floor, as if she felt relief from having it off of her body. They didn't call them over-the-shoulder-boulder-holders for nothing. Her breasts were just as freckled as her face, and her nipples hardened in the chill of the room.

'Hand me that corset, will you?'

Her jeans were already around her ankles by the time I realized I wouldn't just be handing her the corset. There was no way she could lace it up unaided. Darla Rae didn't seem the least bit embarrassed by her nakedness around me. The mullet-induced shame I felt subsided as I breathed in her fruity scent. Her shampoo smelled like peach blossoms. I made a mental note to ask her the brand. During the last chapter of my life, I wasn't able to wear anything scented because Ken was allergic. The urge to buy a whole drawer full of scented lotions, soaps, shampoos, and body sprays made me lose focus on the corset momentarily.

'Dress, please.'

'Oh, yeah. Sorry.' *Concentrate on Darla Rae*. 'Which dress?'

'The one on the end.'

I finished lacing up the corset, reached for the dress, then met Darla Rae's gaze. The look was one of utter desire. She stood before me in the corset and panties, but she might as well have been nude. I lifted the impossibly heavy gown over her head, messing up her hair, but when she resumed eye contact after the gown was in place, her lips were moist and her eyes shifted to my breasts.

I had never been on the receiving end of another woman's desire before, at least not that I was aware of. Little electric jolts raced down my spine as Darla Rae touched my jaw. I leaned toward her expectantly, unsure of what I wanted to happen next. Did I really want her to kiss me? I needed a job, not anything to mess with my emotions after the divorce from Ken.

'This is the first time Larry has ever given me an assistant who was a dyke like me,' Darla Rae said in a half whisper.

Then she kissed me.

My body processed the gentle caress of her lips much more quickly than my mind processed her words. Fluffy feathers of excitement rose in my stomach as I breathed in her scent before returning Darla Rae's kiss. Her tongue slid between my lips momentarily while her hands fumbled with the zipper of my jeans.

The loud knocking at the door startled me so badly that the mullet fell off my head when I jumped. My real hair, the light brown pixie cut, would have to suffice. Larry kept knocking even though Darla Rae and I were both laughing deep belly laughs at the mullet. It looked like a small animal on the floor.

Larry's voice suddenly got louder. 'Darla, get your ass on stage. We have press here tonight, you know.'

'Shit.'

'What?' I asked.

'Nobody brought my shoes down from storage. I can't wear this Elizabethan gown with sneakers.'

'Why not? The gown goes down to the floor.'

She shrugged. 'I suppose you're right.'

Darla Rae left the dressing room for the improv sketch. I was left alone for twenty minutes or so, her words finally registering. She had called me a dyke and kissed me. I had kissed her back. Up until that kiss, I had been denying a helluva lot about my life. Denying things to my family, to my friends, and to myself. I wasn't sure I was ready to actually think about myself as bisexual or maybe even a lesbian, but I knew that what I'd had with Ken hadn't worked. It hadn't worked from the beginning.

Neither had the other guys I'd dated before Ken.

Neither had senior prom or any of the other supposedly *best time of your life* type of experiences I'd had romantically. As I sat on the metal folding chair, my head swam with memories of shoving round pegs into square holes. Darla Rae's pronouncement and her kiss had been the first time I'd experienced anything resembling a fit.

The door opened with a loud squeak. 'I'm back,' Darla Rae said.

'That was a fast twenty minutes.'

'Always is. Here. Help me out of this dress. It weighs as much as I do.'

Once I had the dress back on the hanger, Darla Rae stripped out of her panties and pointed toward the corset. I helped her out of it while wondering why she had taken her panties off. She must have been able to read my mind because she said, 'Beach scene's next. Hand me the bikini, will you?'

My eyes should have followed the projection of her finger to the clothing rack, but instead I stared at her red, curly pubic hair. It was neatly trimmed. I sighed softly as I thought about her covering it back up with the two-piece bathing suit. I removed the bright blue bikini from the plastic hanger and then tried handing it to Darla Rae.

'I think you want to put it on me.' She bit her bottom lip and shivered as she stood before me, naked and vulnerable.

'We only have a minute,' I said over the drumming of my heartbeat in my ears.

'Just because we only have a minute doesn't mean you don't want to be the one to put my bikini top and bottom on me.' Her grin was infectious.

She was right, of course. My words caught in my throat as I tried to reply, so I didn't verbalize my response. Instead, I helped her step into the bikini bottom. As I pulled them up her lush thighs and over her hips, Darla Rae reached for my hand. She guided my pinkie inside the crotch of the bikini bottom so that I felt her red pubic curls, then her flesh as she widened her stance then her slickness in response to my touch. My other hand was already fondling her full breast. Her hands were under my T-shirt and fumbling with my bra as her mouth again brushed against mine.

'Kiss me there,' she said as she guided me onto my knees and ran her fingers through my pixie cut.

Rolling the bikini bottom down so it was around her knees, I kissed the inside of her thigh, then I parted her, my lips finding her clit. If we would have had more time, I would have licked it, sucked on it, made love to it with my mouth. I wanted to fill her with my fingers and press my face deeper between her sensitive lips. Instead, I had to be content with the simple caress of a kiss to her clit.

This was nothing like round pegs with square holes. This was more like the first time I tasted Gremlin cheese-cake. Decadent. Sweet. Moist.

Larry's fists pounded on the door again. 'Darla Rae, you'd better be ready,' he said through the cheap wood.

I groaned as the pad of her fingertip brushed against my nipple.

'Whatever you say, Boss,' Darla Rae said loudly enough to be heard through the door before ending the kiss I had placed between her legs. To me, 'I'll put the bikini top on myself.'

She winked as I handed it to her.

With every clothing change, Darla Rae teased me. My arousal went in a cycle of heightening and lowering until we reached the last costume change. She entered the dressing room wearing the French maid costume I'd helped her into. By the time she locked the door behind her, my hands trembled.

She removed the black wig, which was cut into a straight bob, placing it atop the Styrofoam head. Wiggling out of the French maid uniform, she shook her ass with a grace I'd never have been able to master in a hundred years. I still sat on the metal folding chair in my jeans, T-shirt, and slippers. My bra had long since disappeared into the depths of my purse. I desperately wanted her to sit on my lap but was afraid to ask her to do so because she outweighed me by probably thirty or forty pounds. Darla Rae wasn't exactly full figured enough to shop in a different section of a department store, but she was all curves and had a few inches of height on me. I, on the other hand, was built like a female gymnast but without any athletic skill.

Darla Rae grinned at me while stepping back into the original clothes she wore upon entering the dressing room when we'd first met. By now the room no longer smelled fruity, and I wasn't sure if I was inhaling the scent of her desire or mine. All I knew was I wanted her. She was once again fully clothed, and I wanted her.

'Larry told me to give you this,' she said as she handed me a key. 'It's to your trailer.'

'Oh.'

'Don't look so sad.'

'It's just that I thought – '

'That doesn't mean you're not invited to my trailer, silly. It just means you have one to call your own while we travel. Meet me tomorrow morning for a cup of coffee. Tonight I have to go and give some quotes to the press before we start the tour and pack up the rest of my stuff. Actually, my mother showed up at the dress rehearsal and will be expecting to help me pack my suitcases. She has always been a little bit of a micromanager. My trailer is the one at the end of the row next to the gate.'

She dropped a second key into my outstretched palm. It was the spare to *her* trailer. Darla Rae kissed me slowly on the lips before backing away toward the door. The woman was a tease, but I didn't care. It wasn't as if I needed to go and get myself involved in a heavy-duty relationship right after my divorce. I was content with the promise of brighter days ahead with a job, a roof over my head, and a woman to teach me about my *buried desire*.

Tight Lacing

by K. Ann Karlsson

'After all these years, I see that I was mistaken about Eve in the beginning; it is better to live outside the Garden with her than inside it without her.'

Mark Twain, *Adam's Diary*

Rome, 1898

'And over here, if I may direct your attention, is the site of the tomb of Julius Caesar, the first emperor of Rome, who . . .'

I ignored the drone of the Forum guide, a mustachioed Italian man with a dreadful comb-over and a greasy bowler hat, in order to concentrate on breathing in and out. I trailed behind the group that contained Mother; Edward Mainwaring, my fiancé; and Mrs. Mainwaring, my future mother-in-law. I had waved Edward off earlier when he had politely suggested the tour might be too much for us ladies. Now, however, I regretted that moment of careless insouciance.

I'd begged Elise not to lace my corset so tightly this morning because I knew we'd be tramping through the dusty Roman Forum in the hot summer sun, but Mother had insisted. And, of course, what Mother insists on, no one had better gainsay.

'Nonsense. Pull her laces as tight as possible, Elise,' Mother had said to my maid.

Then to me she'd hissed, 'Really, Miranda, one would think you had no idea how to go on. You'll wear the dark grey walking dress with the Alençon lace at the throat, and the matching picture hat. You owe it to your fiancé to dress appropriately.'

It was bad enough I possessed an overabundance of thick red hair, but I also had to contend with a body whose various parts were not all fashionably slim. Years ago, at a trip to the zoo in Central Park, I'd been present for the feeding of an anaconda. I'd felt deep sympathy for the rat the zookeeper had flung into the serpent's cage. The coils of the snake's body had tightened with every breath the frightened rodent had expelled. Constricting, squeezing –

I looked ahead to see that Edward had ventured deep into Rome's rubble, straw hat perched jauntily on his blond head, to examine some first-century bas-reliefs. The other ladies, perhaps owing less to other people and thus not as tightly laced, seemed fine with the sedate pace, while I had to concentrate just to keep from panting like a dog. My eyes scanned the Palatine hill above the Forum with longing. I could readily picture the patrician families of Rome wanting to escape the airless heat, dust, and bustle down here for the cool breezes up there. My hand crept up under my hat, and I surreptitiously loosened the top button of my blouse at the nape of my neck.

'Miranda.'

I dropped my hand guiltily at my mother's sharp voice, but she wasn't paying any attention to me. She had her eye on a fashionable young gentleman on the periphery of our group, who was leaning indolently against a marble pillar at the Temple of Vesta. In the shade, I might add. When I realized he was looking straight at me, my stomach dropped and my eyes skittered away from his sultry expression.

'Do you know who that man is?' Mother spoke in a stage whisper that I was sure could be heard in Sicily.

I gripped the stem of my parasol. 'No, Mother.'

'Mrs. Mainwaring just told me that it's Alex du Plessis, the Duc du Moncrécy.'

Ah, now I understood Mother's prurient fascination with a stranger. Alex du Plessis was the talk of the fashionable world this summer: a fabulously wealthy French duke who had been caught in a scandalous dalliance with Miss Elsie Porter, daughter of the American ambassador to Paris. Miss Porter's upright New York family had discreetly packed her off to Switzerland, but apparently the Duc had ventured to Rome to escape the gossip.

Mrs. Mainwaring came over to trade further tidbits on the Duc with Mother, to which I only half-paid attention, 'His mother . . . a show dancer . . . American . . . so handsome and rich as Croesus, you know.'

My mother nodded as if she did know, then cast a stern glance at me, the one that warned *and* threatened. As if I was going to run over and invite the man to my boudoir right this moment. As if I'd ever done anything so rebellious.

'Oh, well. He's gone now,' Mrs. Mainwaring chirped, nodding her head so she and my mother looked like a couple of bobbing birds.

The guide fortunately chose that moment to direct our little group down into the ruins, and I took the opportunity to lag even farther behind. When I noted Mother fully engaged in gossip, I seated myself gingerly on a fallen column, and pressed a hand to the front of my bodice. Beads of sweat had collected at the small of my back and between my breasts, but the thickness of my gown and corset prevented any cooling air from reaching my skin.

Young ladies, I knew, did not sweat. I wondered if anyone would notice if I took out my handkerchief to dab at my upper lip. Lord, I was so hot, I just wanted to rip off my clothes and douse myself in one of the many fountains we'd seen on our way here.

'Forgive me, Mademoiselle.'

A light, husky voice cut into my thoughts, and I looked up into the boyish, captivating face of the Duc du Moncrécy. It took me a moment to realize he was holding out a glass.

'I have taken the liberty of procuring some sparkling water with lemon from a nearby café. You appeared in need of refreshment.' His English was perfect, but held the slightest accent.

He was not tall – then again, I measured five feet nine in my stocking feet – but his build was slender and his presence such that he seemed taller. And there was something about him – maybe his dark eyes, maybe his unusual voice – that scrambled my wits entirely.

'Was I wrong?' His tone held a hint of amusement.

'What? Oh, no. That is . . . thank you.' I reached for the glass, my need overcoming my scruples in accepting such an offering from a stranger. I was unable to avoid touching his hand as I took the drink from him. Ignoring the jolt of electricity that shot up my arm, I tipped the glass to my lips. The cool, tart liquid felt so wonderful to my throat, I downed the entire contents in a few large, unladylike gulps. I finished with a sigh, refreshed, but an unfortunate belch escaped me before I could stop it. I covered my mouth and cast an embarrassed glance at the Duc.

He laughed.

'Oh, I do beg your pardon, Monsieur,' I said, wishing the earth would swallow me.

Still grinning, he gestured to the fallen pillar. 'May I?'

I nodded to indicate he could sit down beside me. I had a fairly clear idea what Mother would say about this situation, but for various reasons, I was finding it difficult to care.

'Th-thank you, Monsieur. I just felt a little unwell for a moment. The heat – '

'*Tiens*. Please, you must call me Alex. And you are the famous heiress, Miss Miranda Van Heuysen, *hein*?'

I stared at him. 'Yes, how did you – '

'Forgive me, *chérie*, for interrupting once again, but we haven't much time before your *Maman* returns. Now, I have a plan to extract you from your uncomfortable cloth

– ah, that is, this most uncomfortable situation.' My eyes widened at that pronouncement, but he continued, 'I have a lovely palazzo nearby where it is cool and quiet. We can be there in a matter of minutes. But you must trust me.'

My mouth dropped open. I hardly knew what to focus on first from his stunning speech. The palazzo sounded lovely indeed, but how did this gentleman know I was uncomfortable? Had he been studying me for that long? And why did he think I would do what he asked? I felt a hot blush rush to my cheeks to add to my general discomfort. His sparkling eyes were steady on my face as he waited for my answer. His mouth quirked up in a small half smile, and he raised one of his fine, dark eyebrows.

'All right,' I said slowly. 'I trust you.' As soon as the words left my mouth, my stomach plunged in terror, but I realized what I had said was true. I did trust this stranger.

His half-smile became a wide grin. '*Bien*. You won't regret it, I promise. *Alors*.' He made a circling motion with his hand. 'Turn your back to me.'

I raised my eyebrows but quickly did as he asked. Even through my thick clothes I felt the pressure of his finger along my spine as he swept it down the row of buttons that fastened me into my gown.

'*C est diabolique, ça*.' He muttered a few more imprecations in French. Then my mind froze entirely as I realized he was unbuttoning my dress in order to loosen my stays! I would have squawked in protest, but the relief of being able to breathe was too intense for me to form any objection at all. I looked up to see my mother, Mrs. Mainwaring, and Edward barreling down on the fallen pillar where I sat with *le Duc*.

'Now, *chérie*, you must pretend to faint.'

Lord, that wouldn't be difficult. I felt near enough to actually fainting, but how would I –

'Relax back into my arms, *chérie*, I'll do the rest.' His voice was close to my ear, and his warm breath sent electric tingles down my neck and arms. And as if I weren't embarrassed enough about my body's recent betrayals, my breasts tightened, the tips rising solidly against the edge of my corset.

That, finally, was too much. The world receded, narrowing to a pinpoint. I heard Alex say, 'Here, help me. I am afraid the young lady has fainted in this heat.'

Then, nothing.

I recovered from my embarrassing swoon in one of the coolly lavish bedrooms at the Duc's palazzo, just as Alex had promised. I lay on the tester bed, looking up at the silk-draped canopy and blushing furiously as I relived every moment of our encounter. Later, I returned with Mother and Edward to our hotel without seeing the Duc.

One would think after that scandalous introduction, coupled with the Duc's mildly unsavory reputation, Mother would have had nothing further to do with the man. But that was far from the case. In fact, we began visiting his palazzo nearly every day. Mother greatly enjoyed the up-tick in social status that being known as a friend of the Duc's gained for her. For myself, I began to treasure the quiet moments when Alex would draw me aside and ask me about my interests, my preferences, and my dreams. I'd never had a man pay such close attention to my actual thoughts. It was, frankly, intoxicating to be so consulted, and I could see why Miss Porter had been tempted.

My fiancé, Edward, rarely accompanied Mother and me on these visits, preferring to poke around by himself in the dusty antique shops on the Via Baullari. I was glad. Edward's presence had become a mild irritant, and though we had never been particularly demonstrative in our relationship, I now avoided even his polite goodnight kisses. His cold-fish lips repulsed me.

It was during a late-afternoon call at Alex's palazzo when we were on the terrace enjoying coffee served with light-as-air pastries that the Duc invited us to stay with him.

'Oh . . . well,' Mother said, 'I'm not sure that we – '

'My dear lady, I insist,' the Duc responded. 'The truth is you will be doing me a favor. My aunt, *la Contesse* du Roche, arrives tomorrow from Paris and she would be so grateful to have the company of you ladies, rather than just my bachelor self for entertainment. She is a recent widow, you know.'

Mother commenced nodding again. Her eyes shone like stars at the thought of being in the rarified company of the *Contesse*, and the presence of the Duc's aunt made his invitation respectable, indeed. 'Well, in that case, thank you, Monsieur. We would be happy to stay.'

'And Edward?' I asked in a soft voice.

Alex's eyes flicked to mine, and I caught an expression of – bitterness, was it? Before he said smoothly, 'Of course, he must come too, and Mrs. Mainwaring as well.'

A servant arrived to announce a group of my mother's contemporaries. Alex greeted the newcomers, but when they were all settled into picking apart the latest scandals, he offered to take me on a stroll in the garden below the terrace.

I looked over at Mother. She absently nodded her assent, and my heart beat painfully in my chest.

Alex and I were both quiet as we trailed through the paths of flowers and shrubbery. Thrilled and terrified at this opportunity for a private chat, I couldn't help casting sidelong glances at my friend. Alex's beige linen summer suit outlined his slender form, particularly when he drew back the jacket and shoved his hands in his pockets. He always wore a high collar, but rarely a hat, I'd noticed, even in the hot summer sun.

We were out of sight of the terrace when he turned to me rather abruptly. 'Miranda.'

I met his eyes directly. I'd discovered we were exactly the same height, and there was a particular thrill in being able to look a man right in the face. 'Yes?'

His eyes lifted to my hair and then dropped to my mouth. '*Je dois* – that is, I would like to kiss you. May I?'

I swallowed. 'Yes.'

His slender, elegant hands came up to graze over my jaw line. 'So beautiful,' he whispered, then cupped my cheeks and set his lips on mine.

He was delicious and exotic, tasting of coffee and sugar

as his mouth and tongue nipped and shaped my lips. There was an instant of perfect stillness as I breathed him in – sandalwood and summer – and then a tidal wave of desire broke over me. My hands locked on his wrists, and my breasts swelled against my underclothes. I moaned into his mouth, which caused him to mutter in French and draw me closer. One of his hands slid to the back of my head, while the other pressed my waist. My fingers threaded into his warm silky hair as our mouths slanted and our tongues delved deeply. The movement of his soft, firm lips built a hot tension inside me, and I squirmed with the delicious discomfort. I noticed the hard heat of his body pressed against mine, and the smooth texture of his skin. *He must shave often,* I mused vaguely, but then all thought fled when his palm came up to cup my breast over my clothes.

A fine tremor took hold of me. I whimpered at the restrictions of our dress. Abruptly, I wanted to feel him, feel the skin of his body, press it close to mine, but when I gripped his shirt to yank it out of his trousers, he pulled away, grasping my hands in his. '*Assez*, enough, *chérie*. We grow too, ah, heated.'

A hot blush poured into my cheeks, and I looked away from him in embarrassment.

He gently pulled my gaze back to his with a hand on my chin. 'It is my fault. You are not ready for this.'

I shook my head slightly, and caught a flare of regret in his gaze. Then he took my hand, kissed the palm, and placed it on his arm so we could continue our stroll. He'd obviously interpreted the shake of my head as agreement but, in fact, I *was* ready for him. The blood surging through my veins and the heavy dampness between my legs proved it. I would just have to show him, I decided.

And soon.

About a week after our encounter in the garden, I cornered Alex in the drawing room. We'd just returned from a formal reception for the sad, lovely Queen Margherita at her palazzo on the Via Vittorio Veneto. The crush had been 'exhausting,' so Mother had retreated immediately to her rooms with the announced intention of sleeping late the next morning. I knew she would dose herself with her personal 'restorative,' which contained mostly laudanum. She would be out cold in a matter of minutes. The other members of our party likewise decided to call an early night, so I seized my opportunity.

Upon finding Alex alone in the drawing room, sorting through some mail, I shut the doors and skipped over to him. I immediately grabbed for his collar and began unbuttoning the front of his shirt.

His hands came up at once and closed over mine. 'Miranda, *chérie*, what are you doing?'

I looked up into his dark gaze, my heart catching on a splinter of fear that I'd gone wrong somehow. 'I want to know, Alex. Our kisses are so passionate, your touch . . .' A rush of blood heated my cheeks, but I forged on, 'I . . . I want to know what . . . lovemaking . . . would be like.' I bent down until my forehead rested on our clasped hands. 'With you.'

The stillness of his body, and the utter silence in the

room, told me everything. My stomach roiled in distress. I'd shocked him. He thought I was a wanton, an adventuress. More importantly, he didn't want me in the same way I wanted him. I pulled my hands away from his and covered my face. 'Oh, God. I'm sorry. You don't . . . you're not . . .' I shook my head, tightening my lips against the nauseating pain and embarrassment.

When he still didn't respond, however, I looked up. His mouth was twisted as if holding back an oath, and his eyes were wide with unreadable emotion, but he made no move to touch me.

I cleared my throat and stiffened my spine. 'I do beg your pardon, *Monsieur le Duc*. I have clearly misunderstood your intentions.'

To my shock he whirled away and banged his fist against the wall, letting out a howl of anguish. I lifted a hand towards him and took a tentative step in his direction.

'No, *chérie*.' He turned around, and my heart leapt at the blaze of desire in his eyes. But when I reached for him again, he stepped past my arms and began to pace. 'No, you have not misunderstood. I long for you above all others. I just didn't think you would ever . . . that is . . .' He stopped, his glance toward me was direct, yet pleading. 'I didn't foresee that you could ever return my passion.'

'But Alex – '

He held up a hand. '*Non, chérie*. You must let me speak. I have a terrible confession, *et le bon Dieu m'aide*, I don't want to tell you because I know you will turn away from me.' His voice was hoarse, his eyes tear-filled.

My heart felt wrung dry, but I couldn't stand it. 'You're not really the Duc de Moncrécy.'

'*Mais si*, I am indeed. That is – '

'Then you're dying of the pox.'

His bark of laughter was denial enough. I frowned. 'Well, if you are the man you say you are, and you're not dying, how terrible can this confession be?'

His face sobered instantly, and his voice softened. 'Because, *chérie*, even though I am *le Duc*, I am not man at all. The truth is: I am a woman.'

The bottom dropped out of my stomach, and I took an involuntary step back. I shook my head, but inside me some last piece of a deep, unknown puzzle clicked into place. A woman. I *knew* his – her – words to be true, but in my confusion I lashed out, trying to hold off the wave of pain that was surely coming to crush me.

'No. No. I don't believe it. How can the Duc de Moncrécy be a woman? That would be an . . .'

'Abomination?'

I tossed my hair wildly, on the verge of hysteria, and jabbed an accusing finger at him. 'I was going to say an impossibility, because that would make you a woman who loves . . .' My hand came up to my mouth and my eyes widened.

'Women,' he whispered.

I stared at the man – *woman* – I'd come to cherish. Alex's dark eyes searched my expression, but I fear he – *she* – didn't find what he was looking for because he gripped a handful of his hair and squeezed his eyes shut. My heart beat cruelly, painfully. Dear God, what had I said to cause such a look? Then he blew out a small puff of air and seemed to gather himself.

He made an elegant gesture of dismissal, in control once again. 'It is a long story, one I am not willing to share at this moment because I see now you are not ready to hear it. But I will tell you this: if you have any regard remaining for me at all, you will keep this information to yourself.'

I nodded automatically. Lord, who would believe me anyway?

His gaze grew fierce. 'Tell no one, Miranda, even, or maybe especially, your mother. If you value my life, tell no one.' He turned towards the door.

'Alex!' I had no idea what to say when he faced me, clearly impatient to be gone. 'Is that your real name? Alex?'

He looked down at his boots, and suddenly I could see *her*. The woman in man's clothing. She looked up, her eyes soft. 'When I was very small, they called me Alice,' she said. Then her face twisted into a bitter smile and she shrugged. "Alex' is close enough, *n'est-ce pas*?' Then she left.

Overwhelmed, I collapsed heavily onto the burgundy settee in the middle of the room. The fast beat of my heart and the emotional upheaval of the past few minutes should have incited a swoon, but I was made of sterner stuff. Alex had taught me that.

I contemplated my shock, searched it for signs of disgust or betrayal, but found only extreme curiosity and compassion. Something about Alex's 'confession' jarred me, however. Determined to find some answers, I got up and followed her. I trailed her to her bedroom, where I found her in the process of pouring a glass of brandy.

I closed the door behind me, turned the key in the lock, and faced her. 'Alex.'

'*Mon dieu*, woman. Will you never just give up?'

I gasped in outraged hurt, but then I narrowed my eyes. 'No, I will not give up. If you think I will, you have seriously underestimated me. You must tell me about, well, about you. Then we will decide what to do. Together.'

She hesitated, and then her arms opened wide. I ran to her, and she caught me up. 'I've been so afraid,' she whispered in my hair. 'I couldn't lose you, *chérie*, but to deceive you . . .'

I pulled away to look into her face. 'Alex, I – '

She placed her thumb gently on my lips, 'I will tell you all. But first . . . first, I must . . .' Her eyes dropped to my mouth and I understood. The surge of heat in my body made it crystal clear that man or woman, I wanted Alex du Plessis. Badly. And now.

Desperate to finally press my skin to Alex's, my hands first flew to my throat, clawing slightly to get the hated ornate necklace known as a 'dog collar' off my neck.

Alex made a clucking sound. 'Here, *chérie*, you will damage it, or hurt yourself. Let me.' Her elegant fingers brushed mine away, and she began working on undoing the necklace.

Our mutual seduction began then, with a careful disrobing as we were both still wearing our elaborate court dress. For me, that consisted of a tightly fitted emerald satin gown with a court-length train, and a king's ransom in jewelry. Thirteen pearl strands marched up my neck, secured by diamond fasteners that matched the sparkling butterfly clips in my hair. A diamond-and-pearl-encrusted belt circled my waist to complement the bracelets on each wrist. The American wealth of the Van Heuysen's had been on ostentatious display tonight.

Alex's touch was warm and gentle, and it calmed me in a way my maid's businesslike ministrations never had. She proceeded slowly and carefully. Each piece of jewelry went into a pile on the dresser, then she gently turned me so I was looking into the cheval mirror that stood against one wall of the cavernous bedroom.

I could see myself clearly, a splash of color against the dark hue of her formal suit. In a familiar gesture, she began to loosen my gown.

'How did you get so good at disrobing ladies?' I asked, then cringed at the inelegance of the question.

But Alex chuckled warmly. 'My Aunt du Roche insisted on a thorough education.'

I raised my eyebrows, but only said, 'Lucky me.'

My gown sagged and then dropped to pool at my feet. The mirror's reflection revealed me in my corset, shift, bloomers, and stockings. The candlelight picked out the sheen of the satin corset cover and the sparkle of gold thread embroidery on my garters. The corset boning had pushed my breasts up and forward, and without the dress bodice to hold them in, their generous proportions threatened to spill over. But Alex was not satisfied with this partial disrobing. She made quick work of my corset ties, and pulled my shift up and my bloomers down, flinging the garments aside in a move that was the antithesis of her earlier care with the jewelry.

Now I was naked, except for my shoes and stockings, while she was still fully clothed.

'*Mon Dieu*, Miranda,' she murmured, her eyes glittering in the reflected light in the mirror, 'you take my breath away.'

My hair provided a bit of modesty, spilling over my shoulders and curling around my breasts. Alex groaned behind me and slid her hand around my waist, pulling me hard against her body. She raked my hair aside and pressed wet kisses on my neck and shoulder until I sagged against her supporting arm.

'But this isn't fair.' My voice came out breathy and slightly plaintive. 'I want to see you too.'

Again she hesitated, but I refused to be the only one so exposed. I turned in her arms and started with the outer layers: coat, stock, tie, sash displaying the Royal Order of Something-or-Other, waistcoat. She was not still as I took off her clothes. Her hands ranged over my body, shaping my full breasts, stroking down my arms, patting my round behind. But even with such distraction in front of her, she stopped me when my hands went to the buttons of her shirt.

I stared into her eyes. 'Here is where *you* have to trust *me*, Alex.'

She bit her lip, then touched my cheek lightly with her clever fingers. 'All right, *chérie*,' she spread her arms wide, 'I am yours.'

Now my hands shook as I unbuttoned her shirt and pulled it out of her trousers. She helped by shrugging the shirt off her shoulders and stepping out of her pants. Men's drawers covered her lower body, and her feet were encased in men's socks. She reached down and stripped her knit undershirt over her head, revealing a stark white binding garment. I didn't know what else to call it. It wasn't quite a corset; it was too plain and straight-bodied for that, but it covered her from just under her collarbones to below her waist. It didn't follow the natural – or exaggerated, for that matter – curves of a woman's body. Instead, this garment was for concealment, to disguise her and turn her into a man. Suddenly I understood Alex's sympathy with my predicament in the Roman Forum. She must have often felt the constriction of such a piece of clothing.

I set my hands on her sides. 'How do I . . . ?'

She lifted an arm to indicate the laces at the side, cleverly situated so she could tie the garment tightly herself. I pulled the knotted lace and the 'corset' loosened instantly.

Alex took a deep breath and let out a shy chuckle. 'Well, now, that's better, *hein*?' The binding garment slipped to the floor, and she stepped out of it, but I still wasn't down to her skin.

I raised my eyebrow at the cloth that wound tightly around her breasts, smashing them close to her body. 'Is this the last bit?'

Her chuckle was a gasp. I looked into her face and saw tears standing on the tips of her long eyelashes. My heart clenched, and sympathetic emotion pricked at my own lids. 'Oh, my dear – '

'*Alors*,' she interrupted. 'It's all right. Just . . . a relief.'

I nodded, speechless.

She handed me the end of the cloth that bound her

breasts, and I circled her slowly, unwinding the last element of her deception. I noticed a small tremor in her hands and body as she slipped off her drawers and socks. Then finally we were naked, together. She was beautiful, stunning really. I could have studied her for hours. Her body was slim and strong, the muscles defined like a man's, but her breasts were round and feminine, and her skin was flawless.

'Sh-shall we g-get in bed?' Her teeth chattered, even though the room was relatively warm. I quickly pulled back the duvet on her tester bed and climbed under the sheets with her. We embraced each other tightly, and slowly her shivering quieted.

'I am lost, *chérie*,' she whispered. 'Without my disguise I don't know who to be.'

I stroked her hair, enjoying the cocoon of warmth our bodies made in the soft bed. 'Ah, my love. It is only me, your little Miranda. You can be yourself, of course.'

Even as we lay there quietly, I could feel every beat of my heart as an insistent ache in tips of my breasts, and a throb between my legs. Heat began to gather between us almost tangibly. Alex stirred and lifted her head. Her eyes were fathomless, the centers dark and wide, her skin flushed and moist. She bent down and kissed me, and my mind went white. Alex! My garden lover and my lovely lady Duc – the combination, for me, was potent indeed. We rolled and writhed together on the bed, entwining our legs, touching every part of each other we could reach.

Finally capturing my hands, she straddled my hips and

sat up, laughing. 'Let me see you,' she said. 'You didn't let me get a proper look earlier.'

I laughed up at her. 'That's because I wanted to see you too.'

She trailed her fingers down the center of my chest, then took my breasts in her hands. 'So big,' she murmured.

I blushed hotly. 'Too big.'

'No.' She shook her head sharply. '*Non*, generous maybe, but so feminine and soft.' She massaged the twin mounds, shaping them in her long fingers. I felt the pull deep in my core. 'You are the Earth goddess come to life, *chérie*. Eve herself before the fall.' She bent down and set her lips to one hard peak.

'Ah,' I moaned, 'Do I . . . do I tempt you?' The suction of her mouth on my nipple made me tighten my hands in her hair.

'Yes, *mon Dieu*. Yes.' Her tongue swept between my breasts to the other peak, and my lower body bucked against hers. She sat up then and reached one of her hands behind her. Her fingers stroked up my thigh, then delved into my nether lips.

I clenched my back teeth at the spear of pleasure that centered on her clever hand. 'Oh-my-oh-my-oh-my . . .' I hardly knew what I was saying as my hips rocked in rhythm with the plunge of her fingers. My legs and arms spread wide on the bed and my head thrashed back against the pillows. I was reaching for something, something close and sweet and violent, but I couldn't quite find it. Then Alex took my hand from the bed and placed it on her breast. Her nipple rose hard against my palm, and the sweet edge of that unknown explosion gathered speed. I pulled her down with my arm around her neck and lavished kisses and licks on her hot, soft mouth. She began to rock her hips on me, moving the hot wet center of her labia over my pubic bush.

She sat up again, and her two fingers plunged deep into my vagina. My hips pistoned against her hand, my body knowing instinctively how to move. I swept my hand down her front, and pressed my own fingers to her soft, wet core, to the little pleasure pearl I knew lurked there. She cried out, and I looked up at her: Alex du Plessis, le Duc du Moncrécy, beautiful, flushed, and drenched in her passion and strength.

'Alex! Oh, my God. Alex, I think I'm' – the pleasure crashed through me drawing out a shriek of completion as my mind shattered into tiny fragments – 'dying.'

'Yes, *chérie*, yes,' she cried. 'Die with me.' Her back arched and her sleek stomach muscles rippled with the violence of her climax. She hovered there for a moment, taut and lovely, then she collapsed boneless onto my chest. My arms went around her, and I held on tightly as aftershocks jolted us both.

A little while later she moved off me, and we rolled to our sides, face to face. She reached up to tuck a dark red curl behind my ear. '*Alors, ma petite* – no, let me say this in English: I love you, Miranda Van Heuysen. You are my soul.'

I reached up and took her hand in mine, threading my fingers through hers. 'And I love you, Alex du Plessis. You are my . . . duke.'

We laughed in sheer, free, naked delight.

* * *

A little later, as I traced the marks on her fine skin left by the binding of her disguise, she told me about her family and her brother, Alex.

'We were twins,' she said, her voice soft and distant. 'I was born first, a strong, healthy girl, and Alex came second, small and sickly, but the son and heir. Our mother was the American opera singer, Julie Hampton. Apparently, she'd entranced my father when he'd seen her perform at La Scala in Milan. Their marriage had been the scandal of Paris in 1868.'

She picked up my hand and kissed the palm, then threaded her fingers through mine as she told me the rest. 'Perhaps things would have been different if my mother had lived. But she died of complications from the difficult birth when Alex and I were barely a month old. My father, grief stricken, went off to war. He was killed soon after, fighting the Prussians in Alsace. My Aunt du Roche was named our guardian. When Alex and I were about three years old, we both contracted a fever.'

She gripped my hand tightly, and I made a small sound of comfort, but she shook her head and met my gaze steadily. 'As you see, I survived and poor Alex did not. But my Aunt, in order to preserve the Moncrécy estate, made the decision to tell everyone that Alice had died instead, and then she trained me to keep our terrible secret. In fact, I have never told anyone. Until you.'

'Oh, my dear . . .' I put my hand on her cheek.

She closed her eyes. 'You now hold my life in your hands, Miranda.'

I leaned forward to kiss her. Her arms came around me,

holding me tightly. 'I will guard your secret with *my* life,' I whispered.

She pulled back after a few moments, and I caught a familiar sparkle in her eye when she asked, 'Will you marry me then, Miranda? Cast off Edward, and run away with me now that I've had my wicked way with you?'

My heart soared as I gave the only answer possible at that moment. 'Yes, my love. Oh, very much yes.'

Nimble Fingers

by Lucy Felthouse

It was the guitarist that did it for me: tall and athletic-looking with a mop of dark hair. And oh, those fingers. Long, slim, and nimble with tidy nails, that manipulated the instrument into making the most intoxicating sounds I'd ever heard. The floor vibrated; the atmosphere was electric. I was hooked.

The place was packed. I listened to the band play with people singing and dancing all around me. They waved their arms, sloshing drinks everywhere and good-naturedly jostling one another. Despite all that, I felt like the only people in the room were the guitarist and me.

I watched those fingers glide up and down the fret board and wondered how they'd feel against my skin. Would there be calluses, dry skin perhaps, to chafe my most delicate parts? I didn't care. I was deeply in lust and wanted those hands touching me, pleasuring me, delighting me.

I was quite surprised by the intensity of my feelings – after all, we'd never even met. I'd simply observed her from the floor. Yes. Her. I'd shocked myself by developing a crush on a woman. It'd never happened before, and it's never happened since. But she was special, different somehow.

I watched her, fascinated and in awe. I was like a rabbit caught in headlights. I couldn't take my eyes off her. She captivated me, almost as if she'd cast a spell to make me hers. But of course, she didn't know I was alive.

Towards the end of the first set, the lead singer announced they were taking a break after their next song. As the music died down, so did the audience. They began to make moves towards the bar and restrooms, in anticipation of huge queues at both. I stayed put. I watched her play the final notes of the piece, fingers a blur and her wild hair swaying as she tossed her head with abandon in time to the music. Beautiful.

I stood glued to the spot as the rest of the group put down microphones and drumsticks. I watched as she bent her neck forward to pull the guitar's strap over her head and place the instrument on a nearby stand. Then she looked up. A spark of energy pulsed through me as we made eye contact. She smiled, and I was in heaven. Then she left the stage and headed where any sane person would: the bar.

She'd smiled at me. I felt warmth spread throughout my body, culminating between my legs. Then I berated myself for being such an idiot. She was just being polite, like anyone would. There was no point reading anything into it. As I was busy having this internal argument, standing in the same spot I'd been all night, I was receiving odd looks from people who were milling around, getting drinks, chatting to friends, going for a smoke.

Suddenly, those odd looks changed to ones of interest, and in some cases, jealousy. I sensed a presence by my side and turned. There she was, standing next to me as if it was the most natural thing in the world. She smiled again and handed me one of the two bottles she was carrying. I took it from her, raising an eyebrow questioningly.

'You looked as though you needed one. I'm Samantha, but most people call me Sam.'

'T-thanks.' My brain stumbled to catch up with events. 'I'm Jessica.'

'Good to meet you.' Sam stuck out her hand, and we shook. It was all I could do not to stare down at her hand, imagining once again what I'd like to have it and its duplicate do to me. I kept my eyes firmly focused on hers.

Up close, she was even more awe-inspiring. Her chestnut hair hung in wild curls around her face, striking against her alabaster skin. Her eyes were beautiful, a dark shade of blue, like deep lagoons. I felt like I could stare into them forever and still not reach the bottom. At a loss for words, I took a swig from the bottle. Processing the unfamiliar taste seemed to focus my brain and calm me down. I swallowed, then took another hit for courage.

'You're a fabulous musician,' I said, fumbling around for a conversation starter. 'I really enjoyed that set.'

'Thanks. That last song is one of my favorites. I was heavily involved in the writing and composition of it.'

'It was very soulful. I felt like closing my eyes and drifting away.'

'You didn't, though. Close your eyes, I mean. You were watching me.'

That caught me completely off guard. There were no excuses, and the heat rushing to my face must have given me away. What she said next made the blood rush from my face to other parts of my body.

'I didn't mind you watching me. I liked it. You looked like you were imagining me naked.'

I opened my mouth, no doubt to spout some incomprehensive gibberish, which I hadn't yet thought about, when she continued.

'Would you like to undress me for real?'

I looked down at the drink in my hand, wondering if I'd downed the lot, was drunk out of my mind, and hallucinating the whole conversation. That wasn't the case. I put the bottle to my lips once more and began to gulp down the amber liquid like it was going out of fashion. I drained the bottle, felt the alcohol begin to buzz through me, and said, 'Do you want me to?'

'Yes. I want you to tell me what you were thinking about when you were watching me play. What you were imagining. I want to talk about it, then I want to do it. Come back to my place after the gig.'

'Um . . . okay.' I surprised myself. Up until that evening I'd considered myself completely straight, and here I was agreeing to go back to a total stranger's flat for some girl fun. Suddenly, the amount of alcohol I'd knocked back hit my bladder.

'Will you excuse me? I need to use the toilet and don't want to miss the beginning of the next set.'

'I'll come with you. After all, they can't exactly start without me, can they?'

We headed to the ladies', and it occurred to me just how odd this situation was. I'd just about come to terms with finding out I wasn't one-hundred-percent hetero-sexual, and now I was heading to the toilet with my lesbian squeeze.

Once in the line, I felt completely self-conscious. As a teenager, I'd often sneaked boys into the women's toilets for a bit of a grope in the relative safety of a locked cubicle. Somehow, though, it would be so much naughtier with a woman.

I told myself I was overreacting. She probably wouldn't even come into the cubicle with me. Not that it would really matter. In the space of a couple of hours we'd be alone together at her flat doing heaven knows what, so what did it matter if we indulged in a little light foreplay now?

Sam grabbed my wrist and, pulling me to a just-vacated cubicle, suddenly shook me from my thoughts. We crammed into the tiny space, and she reached over me to lock the door. Just as I thought she was about to pounce, she unbuttoned her jeans before wriggling them and her panties down and crouching over the porcelain. Then I heard the unmistakable sound of peeing. She looked up at me and my face must have been a picture because she laughed.

'What's the matter? Haven't you ever seen another woman pee before?'

'Of course I have, I just . . .' I didn't know what to say. I couldn't very well admit I was thinking she'd been about to seduce me. How arrogant would that have sounded?

She stood up, completely unabashed, and grabbed some paper to wipe herself before pulling up her jeans and fastening them. She shuffled around to let me use the facilities and she watched me as I went. By this point, I was pretty confused. Did she want me or not? Or was she just teasing?

I didn't have to wonder much longer. When I was all buttoned up and ready to go, Sam pushed me against the cold tiled wall of the cubicle and kissed me. Her body felt alien against mine, breasts pushing against my breasts, long hair tickling my collarbones and no hard lump in the groin. It felt different, but incredible. I relaxed into the embrace and opened my mouth to admit her tongue. Her lips were soft, as was her approach. It was passionate and intimate rather than rough. Her hand cupped my face and pulled me more tightly to her as she explored my mouth.

I felt my pussy getting hotter, and my juices starting to flow. Then, just as I was starting to get used to the feeling of kissing another woman and being ready to reciprocate more fully, she pulled away.

'Come on,' she said, 'before the guys send out a search party. We'll finish this later.'

She slid the lock across and left the cubicle with me in tow. I looked around, expecting to see shocked faces staring at us because of what we'd just done. But of course, no one looked twice. Girls go into toilet cubicles together all the time. They had no idea we'd just been kissing. The whole experience felt surreal. I washed my hands, splashed cold water onto my face, then ruffled my hands through my hair to make me look a little more presentable. My face was red, but I guess people would think that was due to the atmosphere of the place and too much alcohol. Truth was, I was damn horny.

I'd been horny ever since I'd laid eyes on her, and the prolonged teasing and foreplay was adding to it. It was going to be complete torture to watch her play the second half of the gig when all I really wanted to do was see her naked and have her hands on my body.

It wasn't that bad, actually. In some ways, it was easier. During the first half of the band's gig she was just a girl I thought was hot and wanted to take to bed. Whereas in the second half, she was Sam – who felt the same about me.

Later, when it was all over and the band took their bows and did their crowd-pleasing bit, I made my way towards the door. I waited until she stood facing the crowd. I saw her eyes scanning the crowd, confused because I wasn't where she'd last seen me standing. Finally, she saw me. I inclined my head, gesturing outside. A nod, imperceptible to everyone else, meant everything to me.

I stood on the pavement, waiting for a taxi. They always passed up and down that particular road, hoping to pick up drunken revelers and relieve them of their remaining cash for the evening. Soon I was able to flag one down and was just about to ask him if he minded waiting for my friend – with the meter running, of course – when Sam came jogging out of the club. I hadn't been expecting her so soon, thinking she'd have to pack up, so immediately I thought she was going to cancel our liaison. But then she hopped into the taxi beside me.

'That was quick,' I said, unable to suppress the surprise

in my voice. 'I thought you'd be a while sorting all your gear.'

'I called in a favor with the guys. I always help them out when they meet girls and want to carry on partying. This time it's my turn.'

'Fair enough.'

Sam gave the driver directions to where she lived, and off we went. Her hand crept across my lap and grasped mine. Hand in hand, we said nothing. There was nothing much left to say. Not that could be said in front of the driver, anyway. Luckily, he broke the silence with a bit of taxi-driver banter, asking us if we'd had a good night and all that. We indulged him with all the niceties, but I was relieved when Sam spoke.

'This is my road. Could you just pull in by that wall? Thanks.'

We paid, and as we got out and he drove off, it was as if a spell had been broken. She grabbed my hand, and we ran up the path, giggling.

'Take your shoes off,' Sam whispered. 'It's quieter and safer. These stairs are a nightmare.'

I could see her point. Said staircase was uncarpeted and two girls in heels would no doubt wake the dead climbing it. I did as she asked and within seconds we were at the door. Sam made short work of unlocking it, pulling me in, and closing it behind us. She relieved me of my shoes and bag and dumped them in a recess by the door.

She kissed me again. This time it felt different, more urgent. I kissed her back, my tongue slipping between her lips and my arms reaching around her neck. Again, I noticed how much more pliant her body was than a man's. Despite her obvious passion, she never felt overbearing, just incredibly erotic. She pulled away, only to walk towards a door. It was closed, so I could only guess it was her bedroom. She threw a glance at me over her shoulder and wordlessly I followed.

She opened the door, and beyond her I could see a bedroom with an enormous, immaculate-looking bed. Sam entered, then turned back to me and sat on the corner of the bed. She patted the space next to her. Once more, I was like a rabbit caught in headlights. She beckoned. Finally, I moved. Despite the flat being empty, for some reason I shut the door behind me.

I joined Sam on the bed. She reached for me and tenderly tucked my hair behind my ears.

'You've never done this before, have you?'

Somehow I knew she meant with a woman, and I shook my head.

'Don't worry, I'll look after you.'

She pushed me down on the bed and crawled up beside me. She cupped my face, and leaned in for a kiss. She was slow, gentle, and it was incredibly erotic. As our tongues intertwined and the kiss became more heated, her hand slid from my cheek and crept down my body. It found its way to my left breast, which she squeezed. I felt a jolt radiate from beneath her hand right down to my pussy.

I grabbed her face with both hands and pulled her tightly to me. Our mouths mashed together more violently now. Sam swung a leg over me so she was straddling me, our crotches grinding together through our clothes. The seam of my denim jeans rubbed against my vulva and gave my clit some much-needed friction.

Suddenly, Sam pulled away from our kiss and sat upright. Reaching down, she grabbed the hem of her skinny tee and pulled it over her head, barely breaking eye contact with me as she flung it across the room. Neither of us knew, or cared, where it landed, because next she undid her bra. That, too, ended up discarded on the floor.

Shuffling up my body slightly, Sam bent down to feed a nipple into my mouth. Instinctively, I sucked it in. I flicked my tongue around and across the nub and areole, smiling inwardly as I heard Sam moan at my ministrations. I reached up to pinch and pull at the other breast, feeling the tip grow hard beneath my hand. Popping her nipple out of my mouth, I cupped both soft mounds and pushed them together roughly so I could lick and suck both in rapid alternation. By now, I could feel that beneath my jeans and panties, my pussy was saturated, and I suspected Sam's was too.

Sitting up, I pushed Sam off of me and onto her back. I started removing my clothes and she did the same, all the while watching each other hungrily. Once naked, we paused momentarily. I took the opportunity to drink her in, her hair tousled, cheeks colored, and eyes sparkling. Her body was incredible. Her ample breasts were blushed from my touch, her body curvy in all the right places, and a triangle of short dark hair pointed south from her pubis. I desperately wanted to follow that arrow.

Our eyes met and we moved toward one another once more. Kissing with complete abandon, I stroked her hair, her face, her neck, breasts, ass, thighs, anywhere I could reach. Soon, I grew bolder and slipped my hand between her legs and sought her pussy. Naturally, I didn't have to search for long. I simply followed the heat and damp emanating from her core.

Sam parted her thighs to let my hand wander. I brushed my fingers against her outer folds of flesh, marveling at the heat and how sodden she was. I was pleased and flattered that she appeared to be just as horny as I was. Pushing onward, I slid two fingers slowly inside her, growing more aroused myself as I felt her tight cunt clenching. I longed to lick her pussy, but was paranoid I wouldn't know what to do. Instead I removed my fingers and slid them between my lips, licking and sucking her sweet juices.

Taking advantage of my momentary distraction, Sam decided to return the favor, pushing me onto my back once more and parting my thighs. Her hand dipped into my copious fluids and she spread them across my aching clit, lubricating it. Then she pushed two fingers into me, maneuvering her hand so her thumb nestled tightly against my clit. She began to thrust gently in and out of me, bumping and rubbing my sweet spot expertly until I felt my orgasm begin to build.

'So,' Sam said, interrupting my race towards climax, 'are you going to tell me what you were thinking about me? What you were imagining?'

She'd slowed her fingers, meaning I could claw back some of my brain's functions and stutter out a reply.

'Th-this.' Her thumb was tracing lazy circles across my clit, and I was so close to coming that it almost hurt. 'I was watching your hands on the guitar, imagining them on me, in me.'

'Really? What happened next?'

I wasn't stupid. I knew what game she was playing and luckily I had my wits about me enough to be a valid contender for the prize.

'You made me come all over your hand. In my head, it was the most incredible orgasm of my life.'

Of course she obliged. She rubbed and stroked at my clit until I was writhing on the bed. Then my climax hit. I arched my back as the intense tingling throughout my body headed between my legs. My pussy spasmed wildly around Sam's fingers, leaking juices all over her hand. She didn't seem to mind. In fact, when I looked at her face, she was gazing down at me in wonder, a smile on her face and her eyes gleaming.

When I had enough presence of mind and energy in my limbs, I sat up. Our mouths met: hers sticky and sweet with the juices she'd sucked from her fingers, mine hungry for more. I pushed Sam onto her back and crawled between her legs, aching to taste her pussy. I tentatively poked out my tongue. As it came into contact with her skin, I figured if I just did what I like having done to me, I couldn't go wrong.

Judging by Sam's reactions, it was a good strategy. As I explored her folds and teased her clit, she moaned and wriggled beneath me, her hands grasping at the bed sheets. The more aroused she became, the hornier I got. I really wanted to make her come. I didn't have to want for long. I pulled her swollen nub between my lips and sucked it while thrusting two fingers in and out of her molten core.

Feeling Sam's body tense, I upped my pace on her clit. Seconds later, her cunt clamped down on my fingers and she cried out, the contractions of orgasm following rapidly. I stopped sucking her, knowing she'd be sensitive, and watched in wonder as she bucked and thrashed. I'd done that.

I smiled and snuggled up beside her as her breathing and heart rate returned to normal. Grasping my hand, we lay in a companionable silence.

We didn't sleep much that night. We made love a number of times, each time better than the last.

Her nimble fingers made me wish I were a guitar.

Things That Go Hump in the Night

by Elizabeth Black

Bridget gunned her Toyota's accelerator as the car jumped from sixty to eighty miles per hour. *If I keep this up, I'll crash into a bridge embankment.* So angry she white-knuckled the steering wheel, she drove aimlessly along the deserted rural Highway 14, fuming about her boyfriend, Mike, and that sharp-kneed whore who Bridget had caught him fucking – on her birthday, no less.

Mike and Boobs-on-a-Stick didn't expect Bridget to come home early to celebrate her twenty-fourth. Instead of finding a birthday cake and scrumptious dinner waiting for her, she found Can't-Keep-His-Dick-in-His-Pants and that horse-faced skank doing the mattress mambo – in Bridget's bed. Pissed enough to spit drywall screws at them, she'd fled her bedroom, grabbed the two bottles of expensive pinot on the kitchen table, which Mike had bought her as gifts, and ran from the house. So now she found herself speeding along the road as the sun set in the autumn sky, not knowing where her flight would take her.

Towns so small you'd miss them if you blinked gave way to expansive fields of corn and soy as she drove. Her anger raged until tears took over, a gamut of emotions that exhausted her after a half hour. She spied a sign in the distance, and through her tears and the glowing pink of sunset she read the lettering: *Mountain View Inn: Vacancy*.

She couldn't go home, not with those murderous feelings boiling to the surface. Her cell phone beeped, and Bridget knew Mike left yet another string of text messages, trying to make up for his big mistake. She refused to hear any of it. She needed an escape – a breather from the harsh reality of Mike's latest indiscretion. *Why do I stay with him? This is the third time he's cheated on me. I really need to break it off.*

She pulled into the Mountain View Inn's parking lot, grabbed her purse, the wine, the overnight bag she always kept in her car for traveling purposes, and walked to the main entrance. She liked the look of the place. The Mountain View Inn was one of those Scandinavian-styled wooden A-frame chalets she had often seen in the mountains near where she lived. A sign on the main entrance door said, *Rooms to Let*. An idea percolated in Bridget's head. Maybe it was time to start working on her life. She liked the inn. It was an old house, and she liked old houses. It was also in the country, and she longed to get away from the main part of town where she lived with Mike, where it was far too noisy. A nice apartment in the inn in the quiet countryside might work out well for her. It wasn't far from the center of town so she'd add only an extra twenty minutes to her commute in the morning. She decided to wait until morning to ask the desk clerk about monthly rates and which rooms were available.

She was pleased that her suite had its own private bath and kitchen. Most Inns had communal bathrooms. Normally she wouldn't have minded, but she was not in the mood to deal with people in her current state of distress. The desk clerk gave her a key to room 1097. It was on the third floor, overlooking a pond. She'd requested a view, and she was blessed with a beautiful one.

Once inside her room, Bridget was amazed at its size and cozy appearance. Rather than seeing two beds like she expected the moment she opened the door, she found herself in a snug living area complete with couch, armchairs, a hand-carved wooden coffee table, and an entertainment center in an armoire. The red Navajo rug offset the warmth of the wooden floor and walls. A fireplace sat kitty-corner to the couch. She felt as if she'd walked into someone's living room rather than a hotel room.

She double-checked her receipt to make sure there wasn't an extra zero on the price. This amazing suite came very cheap! Must be because it was off-season.

She walked past the living room into a small dining area and dropped her wine, purse, and overnight bag on the table. A spacious kitchen sat opposite the dining area. *Oh, is that a gas stove? Be still, my beating heart!* Bridget had always wanted a gas stove but the apartment complex in which she lived was not set up for one.

This place looks more like an apartment suite than a hotel room. She opened the sliding glass doors leading to the balcony to let in the cool autumn air, which helped to lift her mood. Ducks swam in the pond outside her balcony, and she heard the sound of a breeze blowing through the pine trees.

Where was the bedroom? Doors opened to closets, but she couldn't find a bedroom until she faced a spiral staircase that led to a loft, where she found a sleigh bed and a bathroom with a shower and sunken tub.

This room obviously was at one time an apartment that had been converted to a hotel suite when the Mountain View Inn first took paying customers. The luxurious setting eased her pain somewhat, helping her momentarily forget about Mike and his dalliances. But not for long.

She returned to the first floor where she opened her overnight bag and removed her toiletries. She pulled out a pair of black stretch pants, a T-shirt, and underwear. *Good, I have clothes for tomorrow.* As she unfolded her pants, a strip of celluloid fell out.

It was an old picture of Bridget and Mike taken at one of those photo booths at a carnival they'd attended several years ago. She stared at the smiling faces in the photos, tongues sticking out playfully, arms wrapped around each other. Happier times. Tears welled up in her eyes again. Too tired to resist, she bawled once again, dropping her pants on the table and retreating to the safety and comfort of the couch, where she cried until she exhausted herself and drifted off to sleep.

'So pretty . . . I haven't seen a woman in my room in a long time.'

Bridget stirred in her sleep, her brain confused over the

identity of the soft, feminine voice but not awake enough to make identification. Fingers fluffed her hair like a gentle breeze. Bridget brushed her hand around her face, as if to swat away a fly, and opened her eyes.

She lay on the couch, alone in the dim room. The full moon shone through the sliding glass doors, illuminating the entire floor with a soft glow. Her eyes had not yet adjusted to the dark. Her teeth chattered, body shivering in the chill that covered her like a blanket. The hair on her neck stood on end. Alert and nervous, she wondered why she felt such alarm when she knew she was safe. Wide awake, she scanned the room, feeling as if someone was in the room with her, but she could not see who had touched her. She hadn't imagined the tender caress through her hair; maybe it was a dream.

'Who is it?'

Bridget bolted upright. 'Who's there?' She turned on the lamp, flooding the living room with light.

'Turn off the light.'

'*Who* are you?' She whirled around, looking for the source of the voice but finding nothing.

The voice sounded young, like a woman barely out of her twenties, and it sounded like chimes singing in the wind. The young invisible woman spoke with a plea in her voice, as if she was afraid Bridget would flee, and fleeing was first and foremost on Bridget's mind as her heart pounded in her throat. She fought an urge to bolt from the room and run downstairs to surround herself with living, breathing people.

'I'm not going to hurt you. Please turn off the light.'

'I'm not turning off the light. Who are you?'

Silence.

Bridget stood in front of the couch, frozen. Her teeth chattered, and she clenched her jaw to make them stop. A chill descended over the room, making her shiver. She wished she had a blanket so she could stay warm – and hide.

'C'mon, tell me. What's his name?' the voice said.

'Who are you talking about?'

'The guy you're mad at. No woman comes to a hotel room alone with two unopened bottles of wine unless she has man trouble.'

'He's my boyfriend . . . er, *ex*-boyfriend . . . and what's it to you?'

'I saw you crying earlier, and it made me sad. What did he do to you?'

Why am I talking to someone I can't see? This is insane. Bridget looked around the room, trying to make sense of her predicament. Even in the dim light she could see she was alone. Her breath burst from her lips in a cloud in front of her mouth. Her body shivered and was covered with goose bumps. Afraid, she froze where she sat, wondering what lay in store for her.

'Well? What did he do to you?'

The bizarre nature of her position blew Bridget's mind but she couldn't help but answer. Her unseen roommate's gentle tone of voice lured her out. Bridget had felt a strong urge to dump all her sorrows on anyone who would listen, and her invisible guest made herself available. So what if she was a ghost? She was an eager and attentive audience.

'He cheated on me. And today's my birthday. I'm pissed,' Bridget said as she stood up to stretch. Lying on the couch had given her a body cramp. 'I can't believe he did that again, after he'd promised he wouldn't bed anyone else after the last time.'

'You mean he has a history of cheating on you?'

'Yes. This is his third time.'

'And you stayed with him? What a poor choice! You deserve some punishment.'

Thwack! Without warning, pain gripped her left butt cheek. Bridget whirled around, looking for her unseen confidante but seeing no one. It was one thing to talk to someone you couldn't see, but there was something exciting about being touched by an invisible entity. The hand that spanked her was small but strong. Bridget wondered what else her ghostly roommate could do with that hand.

'What was *that* for?'

'You need to be spanked, and badly. Making such poor choices. Did you toss him out yet?'

'No, but – '

Thwack! The painful smack that traveled from her butt cheek to slam into her pussy, making her feel strangely aroused.

'Stop that!'

'You don't need him, someone who cheats on you and treats you like dirt. On your birthday, no less. I know exactly what you need.'

'And what might that be?'

'You need me.'

The playfulness went out of her voice, and she sounded

gentle and tender. It was such a simple statement: *You need me.* Maybe Bridget did need a new lover, someone who would tend to her needs rather than act in Mike's selfish manner. Her ghostly roommate was right about one thing: she should have left Mike years ago, after he'd cheated on her the first time. But she was afraid of being alone, so she stayed and put up with his horrid ways.

No more.

'Please turn off the light. It's too glaring for what I want to do with you.'

Bridget turned off the light. Spectral fingers alighted on her hair as her eyes adjusted to the dark, and they stroked her tresses with a tenderness Bridget hadn't felt in many years. She curled her neck until her head rested in the unseen palm, closing her eyes and enjoying the gentle caress. She had never touched a woman's body before. Now was her chance.

'I won't hurt you. Can't you sense that? Let me take care of you tonight. I've been so alone here with no one to keep me company. Please let me touch you.'

'I've never been with a woman before.'

A delightful, feminine giggle tinkled in her ear. 'I suspect you've never been with a phantom before either. Two birds with one stone.' Soft lips brushed her cheek, running along her jaw and stopping just before her lips. 'I'll make you feel good. Take your mind off him.'

Bridget felt fingers tugging her blouse, and she reached up and unbuttoned slowly. After removing her blouse she slipped out of her black jeans and sat them on top of the blouse on the floor. Dressed only in her purple lace bra, panties, and black ankle socks, she stretched out on the couch, allowing her ghostly visitor to have her way.

She closed her eyes, helping her enjoy her new lover's touch. *Is she my new lover? What if I never see her again?* Unwilling to allow such a depressing thought to ruin her aroused mood, Bridget concentrated on the light dusting of fingers that grazed her sensitive skin. This woman's touch was much lighter than Mike's groping. *I don't even know her name –*

'Bridget.'

'Pardon?' the ghost asked.

'My name is Bridget.'

Silence greeted her for a few moments. Bridget listened to the breeze blow through the trees, and she heard the sound of night peepers in the forest not far from her balcony.

'Gillian.'

Such a sweet name for a tender lover. Rather than speak, Bridget felt Gillian's lips brush along her collarbone. Fingers fumbled with the clasp on the front of her bra until it snapped open. Gillian's soft lips found a nipple and suckled it until it stood on end. Her touch was much more gentle than Mike's, who liked to roughhouse with her to please himself more than her. She liked the rough play but such a gentle touch brought forth more erotic feelings than being jerked around and toyed with.

What will it be like to be with a woman? Bridget had never before taken a woman as a lover. She'd sometimes wondered what a woman's body would feel like but the opportunity never before presented itself.

It has now, and I should take advantage of it. She felt Gillian's mouth and fingers on her breasts, but she couldn't see her. Being unable to see her lover made the lovemaking much more exciting. What would Gillian do next? Bridget couldn't anticipate Gillian's moves. Curious for an idea of how her lover looked, she reached out one hand and felt around in the air until her palm alighted on Gillian's hair. Bridget ran her fingers through her short, wavy hair as her phantom lover kneaded her breasts and flicked her tongue over a nipple. She squirmed on the couch, feeling warmth growing in her core that needed attention. As if reading her mind, she felt a small hand slip beneath her panties, fingers sliding between her folds, seeking her sex. Gillian's touch was soft and sweet, staying off her clit so that she wouldn't feel overly sensitive. *I could get used to this.* Every man she'd been with ground his rough fingers against her clit, which made her feel uncomfortable. She preferred Gillian's lighter touch.

Gillian lifted her head, and Bridget ran her palms over her cheeks. A heart-shaped face with wide-set eyes and full lips revealed themselves beneath her fingertips. She lowered her arms until her hands touched delicate shoulders and firm, full breasts.

As Bridget's hand roamed her phantom lover's naked body, she felt a familiar stirring in her groin. Bridget caressed her soft skin and lithe form, wanting so much more. Gillian's body was lean and sweet, skin soft and pliant, possibly about twenty-five years old. When Gillian pulled away from her breasts Bridget let out a little mewl of disappointment, but her distress didn't last long. Within seconds, she felt soft lips against her pussy.

Gillian's tongue lapped at her folds with a gentleness that belied her own passion. Bridget heard Gillian's fevered gasps for breath as her lover's arousal overtook her technique. Hands gripped her thighs, pulling them farther apart. Gillian's tongue lapped at her sex, finding her clit and flicking around it in quick, excited motions. Bridget pulled on her nipples as Gillian worked her into an erotic frenzy. She felt two fingers slip inside her, more slender than what she was used to. A thumb flicked her clit like a lute.

Bridget felt light smacks on her ass that brought the blood to the surface. Before tonight, she'd never been spanked before, and she loved it. She arched her back at each smack, relishing the arousal she felt. When Gillian brought down her hand in a loud and painful *thwack,* Bridget groaned with unabashed delight.

Bridget felt an overwhelming urge to explore her lover's body. 'May I touch you? I've never been with a woman before. I want to feel you.'

'Of course. I'll lie next to you. Enjoy yourself.'

'May I see you?'

'I'm afraid that's out of the question. If I allow you to see me I won't have energy left to ravish you.' She giggled her delightful laugh once again. 'Besides, I think you already know what I look like. You felt my face.'

'I want to feel your body.' Bridget fished around in the dark until her hand smacked into Gillian's hip. Her phantom lover lay on her back on the Navajo rug. Bridget grabbed a few floor pillows and cushioned herself next to Gillian. Hands roaming over her lover's body, she felt broad hips and a slight belly. Full, pendulum-shaped breasts begged for touch. Being unable to see Gillian made her explorations of the woman's body all the more enticing. She could not rely on sight, only touch and smell. Gillian smelled of the forest: juniper and rosemary. Bridget lost herself in the heady scent that reminded her so much of fall.

She closed her eyes and allowed her hands to explore the soft flesh. When her fingers alighted on Gillian's belly the woman let out a snort, belly jiggling as she squirmed. *She's ticklish! How sweet!* Bridget found her breasts and kneaded them with both hands. Gillian twisted her body to accommodate the explorations. Bridget always wondered what someone else's breasts felt like. She had fantasized about fondling and sucking on a woman's breasts, but the opportunity had never presented itself.

Until now.

She lowered her head and took Gillian's nipple into her mouth. It puckered quickly, growing hard the more she sucked. She kneaded her lover's breasts, feeling how firm yet soft they were. The longer she kneaded and sucked, the more urgent her own arousal grew. She lost herself in Gillian's supple breasts, as if nursing like a young child. Her hands traveled down Gillian's body, feeling her curves and soft skin, so unlike the men she had bedded. A woman's body felt so much more alluring than the roughness of a man's body. Full of curves and tantalizing, delicate flesh, her first woman lured her into seduction like no other lover.

Bridget knew how a pussy felt since she had one herself and explored it often enough, but how would another woman's feel? She slid her fingers down Gillian's belly and was surprised to find a bush blocking her way. *So, my ghost had not shaved when she was alive.* Most women Bridget knew had Brazilian waxes, especially during skimpy swimsuit season. Mike had urged her several times to get waxed. She'd refused.

So here she lay with a lovely woman whom she could not see who sported a full head of hair. Curious to experience the total sensation of Gillian's sex, she shifted her body until her face was inches from Gillian's pussy. She buried her nose in her hair, feeling it tickle her face. She smelled of woodland fog and musk, a strong feminine scent Bridget recognized from her own private fondling. What would it be like to lick a woman down there? She had been taught from a young age that women's sex was dirty, and now she knew that was far from true.

She spread Gillian's lips with her fingers and buried her face in her sweet pussy. Not sure what to do, she decided to taste her first. Her tongue flicked out and slid over the soft folds, and Bridget tasted salt and warm fluid that tasted a bit like yogurt. It was a very pleasant taste, not too strong or overwhelming, which was what she'd feared. Gillian's sex tasted pungent and alluring. Bridget lapped her up, eager to take in as much of Gillian's aroma and taste as possible. Her tongue flicked against Gillian's erect clit and her ghostly lover moaned in ecstasy. Knowing what she preferred, Bridget ran her tongue in circles alongside Gillian's clit but not directly touching it. Her lover groaned and squirmed beneath her virgin touch. Bridget tentatively made love to Gillian, unsure of what she was doing but using what aroused her as her guide.

Gillian had shifted on the rug, pulling a pillow under her body as a cushion. She and Bridget lay next to each other, faces buried in each other's sultry sex. As Bridget kissed Gillian's thighs, Gillian's mouth found her pussy, and her tongue lapped her sex in long, languorous strokes. No man had ever been so gentle with her, nor had he aroused such intense amorous feelings. Mike had gone down on her as if he was in a pie-eating contest at the State Fair. No decorum whatsoever. Gillian, on the other hand, relished her taste and feel, taking time to explore and allowing Bridget to become even wetter with desire. Her hand came down once again in a resounding *smack* against her bare ass, making her shiver and crave more punishment.

Bridget followed Gillian's lead and flicked her tongue along her clit, at the sides but not directly on it. Her phantom lover moaned in ecstasy, squirming beneath her as she became more aroused. She synchronized her movements to the rhythm of Gillian's tongue and lips against her clit and folds. As she rocked in time to Gillian's movements, she slid two fingers into the woman's cave. Immediately, Gillian tightened around her fingers, pulling them in even further. Bridget took a chance and took Gillian's clit between her lips and sucked hard. She enjoyed the feel of her lover's soft skin in her mouth. Such silky smoothness! As she sucked she writhed beneath Gillian's talented mouth, feeling that familiar rise of passion as her orgasm overcame her. She bucked Gillian's face so hard she felt the phantom's teeth. Coming harder than ever before, she sucked on Gillian's clit until she came in her mouth, fluid gushing forth like a fountain of ambrosia.

After they'd come, Bridget crawled onto the couch to relax. She felt Gillian's arms embrace her, her head resting on her chest. Gillian's mouth brushed against Bridget's head and as she turned towards her ghostly lover, their lips met in a kiss. Soft lips pillowed her own, spreading them apart to make room for a small tongue that slid into her mouth. Gillian tasted of sunlight and mountain breezes. Her kiss was tentative and gentle, bringing their lovemaking to an end for the night.

'Happy birthday,' Gillian whispered in her ear, her tongue licking her earlobe in a playful manner. Never before had Bridget felt such a tender and loving kiss. As Bridget stroked Gillian's hair and caressed her body, she drifted off to sleep.

Bridget awakened at dawn. The room had warmed up. She was alone.

After showering and putting on some clothes, Bridget walked to the front desk. She requested room rates for a long-term stay. As she waited for the clerk to return with a room-rate brochure, she browsed the pamphlets off to the side. She saw fliers for skiing in the mountains, cabins at Crystal Lake, and one flier that caught her attention the most: the one about the haunted room at the Mountain View Inn.

She grabbed the flier as her heart raced in anticipation

of what she would learn. According to the flier, in 1996 a young woman lived in the apartment that would later become room 1097. A man who had met her and another woman at a bar on ladies' night had knifed her to death in the room. Police reports stated that he grew enraged when neither woman would pay attention to his amorous advances. Sensing they were lesbians, he followed one to her home, where he murdered her.

Her name was Gillian Michaels.

A photo of Gillian was on the right side of the flier. As pretty as Bridget expected, Gillian sported short, wavy auburn hair, large moss-green eyes, and a sweet face with a dazzling smile. In life, Gillian had owned a sex toy shop downtown that enjoyed many customers. After death, the shop closed but a plaque was erected in her honor, since she had been well respected in the town.

The clerk returned with her room-rate sheet. Bridget told him she wanted to rent the room she was in now. It was time to rid herself of Mike and get on with her life with someone who attended to her needs. Someone like Gillian. The owner was surprised since no one stayed in that room for long. Most people left it before the night was over, requesting another room. The owner gave it to Bridget at a reduced rate. Bridget knew it was because the owner didn't believe she would last in there for more than a week, if that long.

Bridget decided it was payback time for her invisible lover.

She walked back to the room. It felt a little chilly, but no phantom hands smacked her on her bum. If her little ghost was in the room, she was playing hide and seek. Bridget smiled as she opened her overnight bag, and retrieved the stash of goodies she kept in her car in case of emergency nights out with Mike. Now she'd share them with Gillian. She pulled out four silk scarves and a Hitachi wand. Now, it was her lover's turn to have some fun.

'Come out, come out, wherever you are,' Bridget called. 'I have a surprise for you!' When the room chilled even more, she knew she was in for a morning of sexual bliss with her new lover and roommate.

Girl on a Thursday

by Angela Mazzone

'The soul should always stand you ready to welcome the ecstatic experience.'

Emily Dickinson

As I reached to hug, she twisted. I held a breast. More than a handful. No bra. I was embarrassed, but she simply said something like, 'That was nice.' No sarcasm.

I probably said, 'Sweet dreams,' or something like that. I was dropping her off at her new Melbourne flat. Still embarrassed, I drove off.

That moment could have easily been forgotten, except Brindi telephoned an hour later. She offered another, 'Thank you for the ride,' and while asking if I might visit one evening, said, 'Just us.'

She'd recently broke off a yearlong relationship with an older married man from Sydney, leaving her more time for friends her age – twenty-three. Although she had some butch qualities, I never thought of her in a lesbian way.

We were both free on a Thursday. Ten days to wait.

A sort of a relative through divorce and re-marriage, I'm ten years older and had known Brindi since her teen years. At family events we would sit and talk like older and younger cousins. She radiated health in a milk-eggs-lamb diet, Australian country-town way. If she paid more attention to her appearance, with blue eyes and naturally curly, short blond hair, she would have been considered attractive, even beautiful.

Since finishing university studies she'd been writing programs for computers. She was a bit shy and geeky but, at the same time, bright and confident in a knowing-what-she-wants way.

Never having had a lesbian experience, I hadn't considered the possibility until after she'd called. I became more apprehensive with each passing day. Defying my Catholic heritage, a warped parable entered my thoughts: *two Eves* eating the forbidden fruit.

The next time seeing her we were with five mutual friends, blokes and sheilas, at a casual, come-if-you-can Chinese dinner on a Monday. Arriving late, I was not surprised to see her. Tangentially, we have the same friends. I seated myself across the round table, too far to converse. Instead, we did a heap of smiling – sort of secret-sharing smiles.

Afterward, outside the restaurant, hugs and cheek kisses were exchanged as we went our separate ways. On our parting, her hug seemed a bit more clinging, sort of confirming my relentless imagining.

On Wednesday, Brindi called, 'I'm taking Friday off work. Time to relax. Wear something informal . . . Yes, a white wine . . . I have new music . . . well, really from years ago . . . so sexy . . . you'll love it.'

She didn't say, 'Plan to sleep over,' like a girl's night in. That added anxiety. I wondered what old-new music she had that was so sexy.

Thursday, I bathed and slipped into my best come-fuck-me jeans. On the frilly-side, a white, open at the neck, front-button shirt and – matching my hair – a black agate pendant necklace. Open-toed, low-heeled wedge sandals. No bra. No earrings.

Following a slow tram on Route 16 toward St. Kilda, I had a slightly queasy feeling, like a teenager when eating an entire bag of sickly sweet candy. Something short of panic. I parked across from the entrance. Leaving my cell phone in the glove compartment, I crossed the street. Climbing three flights to her level resulted in a bout of breathlessness.

I was greeted with a hug and kisses to cheeks. Brindi seemed nervous too. All she said was, 'Nice jeans.' I was glad she took note.

I shouldn't have been surprised at how she appeared. I knew she was a biking enthusiast. She looked quite fetching in loose-fitting biking shorts: dark blue, darts in front, button fly, pockets front and back. Nice buns. Muscle-toned, lean, attractive legs.

Gold clip-on hoop earrings were a surprise too; they, however, went well with her white blouse. Her blouse stretched the fabric in the right places. A single strand of pinkish pearls looked too formal. Maybe, I thought, gifts from the older man. A warm, spring day so, like me, she was in sandals.

To cover my speechlessness, I offered a second hug and presented the wine, flowers and chocolates. Thanking me, she took my hand, saying, 'I know just the place for the flowers,' adding, 'Let me show you around.'

Brindi had anticipated the flowers. A vase with water waited in the middle of a table for two below a small kitchen window. Both the chocolates and wine were left on the table as she showed me about.

A guest room was turned into a hobby room with a work table for collages of textiles. I also saw a leather office chair and built-in-the-wall desk with her computer. She parked her bicycle behind the door. Ah, I concluded, explaining why no suggestion to stay in the *guest room* overnight.

Her bed-cover was turned back. She looked to see if I'd noticed. Playing it cool, I complimented her choice of the Monet print – the usual, restful, blue-toned water lilies – that hung over the queen-size bed. A vase of yellow tulips was bedside.

As there was a second place to dine – another table with a view outside in the living room – Brindi, after reminding me it was Chinese take-out, asked, 'Where do you prefer?'

To keep with the informality, I said, 'Easy at the kitchen table.'

My mind raced again to thoughts of how I needed to tell Brindi this was a first time. Better in the living room, I concluded. Later.

I also noticed a sound system and inlaid coffee table. After suggesting the kitchen, I added, 'Maybe in here for dessert, cordials, tea. What do *you* prefer?'

'I like that,' she said, then added, 'I'll save the special music until later. I only recently discovered the French lovers Gainsbourg and Birkin.' She turned to face me. 'Do you know them?'

Years ago, I saw one of their art-house films, something about *Jane*. Birkin is not French, as Brindi said. I knew her to be an English girl and the years-long lover of French filmmaker Serge Gainsbourg. Jane Birkin's look on screen was sensationally seductive. She was much younger than Serge Gainsbourg. I wondered if Brindi saw some connection to her recently ended, older-man relationship.

'Yes, I know something about them,' I answered. 'Let's talk over wine.'

Actually, when we got to the kitchen, nothing more was said about Gainsbourg and his relationship with that beautiful girl. *Later. Maybe something to talk about after eating.*

Brindi had a choice of wines including a French pinot gris. I'd brought an Italian pinot grigo. The wines had French and Italian spelling, but all were from New Zealand. Despite the sweet and low flute melodic tones, candles, wine, and a background of fleecy music, I wasn't actually enjoying the moment. My thoughts left me tense. I was too alert to everything new and to whatever Brindi says.

I couldn't say, as we moved about the small kitchen, anything sensual happens. We were, however, growing more and more comfortable sipping and making comments about the wines, about our new prime minister, Julia Gillard, and about the female premiers heading two of six Australian states.

I laughed when Brindi told me she had a made-up word for the new era of women in Aussie politics: Vagina-mite. Vegemite is an Australian breakfast toast spread – the first item packed when going overseas.

Finished with the meal, we left the table as it was. I carried our glasses, chocolates, and wine. Brindi carried two candles into the living room.

A soft-tan leather sofa and chairs with matching cushions were arranged around her coffee table. I noticed that two large mirrors and three paintings of River Gum trees made the room appear larger. A wide rectangular window looked west.

Usually, when with blokes, this would've been time to offer a neck rub or a shoulder massage. Get things started. Instead, after placing the candles on the coffee table, Brindi slid the kitchen door closed, reached to dim the overhead light, and, turning toward me, asked, 'Ready for something really sexy?'

Having just become emotionally calmer, I was now on full alert again. I took a deep breath and looked around.

With the overhead light dimmed, embers of the already-set sun hinted at a skyline. Her west-facing view was a beachfront, seen over the top of a Victorian house and extensive gardens. Palm trees marked the shore. I imagined waves brushing, stones hissing as the water receded.

My back to her, I was looking out as I answered, maybe provocatively, 'Anything you are ready for.' As soon as I said it, I wished I hadn't. I felt my neck muscles tighten. I turned.

She had slipped on reading glasses. Head lowered, looking over the top of the lenses, she offered a smile and quizzical look. Eyes widening, she replied, 'How about if . . . letting . . . ah . . . me . . . ah, massage your shoulders?' She straightened up, adding, 'I think we are both too nervous.'

Hearing her also admit to being nervous, made me feel easier. A bit cheeky now, in the spirit of fun, I answered, 'No drama.'

Seeing her mind occupied, bending, needing the glasses to read the buttons on her CD player, I added, 'If you like. Maybe later, when listening?'

Less nervous now, she replied easily, 'Yes, I'd like that.'

I continued standing as she inserted the disc. She then pointed to the sofa, shrugged her shoulders and raised her eyes in a *shall-we?* gesture.

More tense now, I said, 'Go ahead. You first.'

She sat, setting out one wineglass for me, the other for herself. Before reaching for the pinot grigo she looked up, perhaps wondering why I had not yet joined her.

Needing to tell her in a non-complicating way I had never before – I pulled an easy chair in front of the sofa and sat facing her.

Sensing something was on my mind, Brindi, without expression, said, 'Yes?'

I know I was fiddling with the pendent as I leaned forward.

She sat forward, too.

That made it easier, almost a whisper, as I said, 'Brindi, sweetheart, you are, er, since that night when I gave you a ride, and you invited me here? Ah, well, I have had thoughts of us . . . as lovers.'

It helped. It helped *so very much*, when she answered, 'Me too.'

'Really? Wasn't just me imagining?'

I saw a not-just-you shake of her head. Then she bit her lower lip. I waited, thinking she wanted to say something. Then she puckered her lips, again suggesting she wanted to say something. I waited.

Brindi looked thoughtful. I looked at her eyes for a message. She squirmed a bit, and I saw she chewed on a lower lip like a child does when they don't want to tell a parent something. I reached placing my hands on her bare knees. I stroked with my fingers. I was beginning to feel more confident – yes, like an older cousin.

Since she didn't say anything, I told her how I'd never had sex with a girl. I admitted being anxious, then asked. 'How about you? In college? Other girls, maybe?'

Before she answered, she placed her hands on mine and squeezed. There was a long pause as flying bats – or 'flying foxes' as the Tourist Commission re-named the winged mammals – passed overhead in noisy waves.

With the screeching from above receding, she tipped her head to one side with a smug grin and said, 'Maybe a little playing.' She looked into my eyes. Seeing acceptance in my expression, she went on, 'We got lonesome among ourselves. You know, bikini parties and sleepovers.' She paused before adding with a mind-casting-back expression, 'Even at boarding school.'

When she said, 'at boarding school,' I thought, *that*

means since she was a teenager. Now, at a complete loss for words myself, I was relieved when, dropping the topic, she said, 'Let's listen.'

Pointing the remote and clicking, she ushered me to sit by her. Leaving my chair and slipping my sandals off, I slid next to her. Facing the CD player as the voices began, I leaned back, half on her, half on the sofa. Brindi and the sofa felt equally soft.

She adjusted the sound. Placing the remote on the coffee table, her left hand came to rest on my upper leg at the edge of my pelvic bone.

Brindi whispered in my ear, 'Close your eyes. Listen.'

As the duet with background music soothed, barely audible then more clearly, the female lead, Jane Birkin, whispered – experiencing an orgasm. Not sharp-clawed gasps, but serene, gentle. The more the moments passed, the more arousing the effect.

Perhaps two or three minutes into the vocalist's whispering, Brindi, without pause, without subtle intent, reached her left hand forward, pressing her fingers between my legs. I laid a hand on hers. I held her hand still. I wanted to absorb the duet, the music, the moment. I tried not to give in to impulse.

Brindi whispered, 'Do you like that?' Hearing *that* told me she was not asking about the sensual duet.

I answered, 'Uh huh.' I pressed her hand down. I was weakening.

In unison we began to rock back and forth, timed to the slow beat emerging from the speakers.

As the tune faded, Brindi took her hand from between

my legs. Picking up the remote, she clicked replay. Then, as her right arm slipped under my right arm, she asked, 'May I?'

Before I knew her intent, before I said anything, I felt her fingers opening buttons. She started at my collar, working down skillfully, as easily as opening her own blouse. There was no sense of hurry.

This was *not* how I'd imagined us progressing.

I sat up and turned as, with both hands, she pulled the shirt from my jeans. I let her lift and push it back. Shrugging my shoulders, it easily slipped off behind, out of sight. Embarrassed about my tiny breasts, I covered them.

Again, a polite, 'May I?' as she leaned, lowering my hands, and kissed a nipple. As her fingers offered gentle finger-squeezes to each tiny breast, I wanted to apologize about being so little, but I didn't say it. She knew I was okay when I pressed her head to my chest.

Minutes later, as her tongue licked, I thought enough for now. I said, lightly, 'My turn.'

She sat upright as I lifted her blouse. Removing it, I leaned forward, grasped her head, and kissed her.

With our lips together, a little tongue, and eyes closed, I was still holding her head when I felt her movements reaching behind to unsnap her bra. I sensed her lowering straps, getting bare for me – for us.

Her hands now returned to my chest. Her palms slid across ribs to my back. She drew me to her. Her breasts pressed to my chest.

I felt the need to see her breasts. I wanted to hold and kiss. I wanted to suck her nipples. With a final, generous, wet sharing of lips, my voice hushed, I asked, 'May I?'

Of course, she knew. Brindi released her hold and leaned back. She was so lovely, so beautifully smooth, so fit.

As I took my pleasure, she – with nonchalance – removed her earrings. I sensed her confidence. Her experience shone as she again reached between my legs, pressing.

Then I had this idea. My grandfather was Italian. I remembered how he said, 'Never to do anything important without the taste of wine on the lips.' So I said, 'Let's sip a little wine,' and I told her about my grandfather.

So to toast Grandpa, and us, we put a little more wine in our glasses and sipped. Grinning, we looked at each other. It was a light moment. Still seated on the sofa, eyes wide, broad smiles expressed our delight. We rolled our eyes. We stared. We were actresses.

Then Brindi stood and put on a new CD. It was a tune I did not know, but it was perfect for dancing, so she danced and twirled and made sexy moves with her shoulders. As when jogging, her breasts were lively.

Provocatively placing her hand at her waist with fingers out like a model, she gave the come-to-me look. I noticed her lean biceps. Strong shoulders, too. I went.

We danced. Rubbed chests. She lifted and kissed my black pendant. I drew her beads across my lips. I was in my jeans, she in her bike shorts. Maybe we'd stop here, I thought. Maybe we'd just touch and see and kiss nipples. But she had already pressed her fingers between my legs, so I was thinking she would want to go the distance.

She changed the CD. I heard Janet Jackson belt out, *All Night Long*.

As we continued dancing she led me toward the open bedroom door. Inside we took our own jeans and shorts off. My jeans were tight, so while I stood, she helped me shimmy out and felt where I was wet. I felt where she was moist, too. We got into her bed. The covers were pushed off. The sheets smelled fresh.

Except for the vase of yellow tulips knocked over during gyrations – like puppies tumbling – nothing was left unloved, un-kissed.

'May I' and 'My turn' continued joyfully, as if tennis serves, in slow motion, into Friday's early morning.

As the sun rose like a morning bonfire, slivers of light beamed past an ajar door. The voyeur would have seen yesterday's fresh-laundered sheets now crumpled, the plush blue carpet divoted by knees. The slender girl was remembering the taste and fragrance of green tea at the quivering temperature of slippery-wet lips; the caressing of Janet Jackson's *All Night* and the intensity of Jimi Hendrix's *Freedom* both wafting in memory; shades, textures, tastes, colors balanced in comfortable intimacy; bedside clock ticks. Yellow spring tulips remained spread, and morning light falling on pink pearls and black pendant would draw eyes to waking girls hearing flying foxes screeching a new day, before delicate cuddles, then mutual washing in the spray of warmed water.

I felt oddly exhilarated, even if tired, as I left the main entrance of her apartment building. It was late Friday morning.

Returning to the quiet of my writing studio, I made notes. Through the fog of memory, I pieced together mosaic images from our Thursday dancing to our Friday morning shower.

Saturday, I rested.

We met at noon, Sunday, and walked the shore. Comfortable and casual, nothing was said about Thursday until Brindi offered, 'I suppose because, story-writer that you are, I'll soon be a celeb?'

I answered cheerily, 'I have a few notes.' With a grin, 'You want me to change names?'

'Seems it's up to the author.' Then, with an equally cheery tone, she said, 'That's how Jane Birkin got famous.' She grinned.

My cousin is not Italian, but offering the traditional, warm farewell, Brindi kissed her fingertips, then reached and pressed her fingers to my right cheek.

Jack's Ex

by Lara Zielinsky

Kelly

Late Friday afternoon I stormed into the home I shared with my boyfriend, Jack, and his kids, my goal the alcohol bar. I'd just lost my third client in three days. There was a missed call from the firm on my cell phone, and I intended to forget it was there.

I had a double vodka with lime twist in my hand when Leigh, Jack's ex-wife, came strolling down the main staircase. I grimaced, though this was nothing new. She hung around constantly, and it drove me crazy.

At first I was, like, fine. His kids, Jack Jr., ten, and Sara, sixteen, are her kids, too. I get that. Jack and I don't have any kids together. I want some, maybe two. Eventually. But co-parenting with an ex is not my idea of *having kids together*. I did resent some of the time Jack had to spend with Leigh when dealing with their kids, especially if I couldn't be a third wheel.

Leigh is gorgeous: tall with long legs, a pin-up quality blonde with just enough natural highlights of honey and brown mixed in not to be brassy. I'm not jealous. Jack had divorced Leigh long before he met me, so I never viewed her as competition. I consider myself good looking with dark brown hair and eyes to match. Jack is dark, too, so we make a striking couple, if I do say so myself.

'What're you doing here?' I demanded.

In my defense I had thought I'd be alone. Jack was out of town on business and wouldn't be back until Monday night. Leigh had said three days ago that she'd take the kids, picking them up directly from their schools. I wouldn't have been going for drunk if the kids were in the house.

Apparently deciding to ignore my tone, Leigh smiled and said, 'Hey, Kelly.'

'I thought you took the kids this weekend,' I said, desperate for my drink but wanting to be sure I wouldn't be irresponsible in front of the kids.

'I did. Jack forgot something.'

'Where are Jack and Sara?'

'Swimming at Grandma's.'

'Great.' Thus relieved of the sole obstacle, I drained the contents of my glass in one long swallow. The burn brought tears to my eyes. I wiped my mouth with the back of my hand still holding the glass. The liquid hit my stomach and spread blessed warmth.

'Why are you drinking?'

'Why are you still here?' I countered. She gave me a look that immediately made me feel like the heel in a fight. 'Fine. I lost another client.' I refilled my glass with vodka and lime, appreciating the ice clinking sound with a smile.

'You drink every time you lose?'

I waved the glass to punctuate my response. 'Three clients in a row, I do.' I sipped at my second drink and settled on the nearby couch. I braced both elbows on my knees, leaning forward as I swished a thumb through the drink's surface, making the ice clink again.

I was lifting the glass to my lips when her hands closed over mine. 'Hey!' I glared up at Leigh through a curtain of hair. 'You want a drink, get your own.'

'It's not good to drown your troubles.'

'Don't lecture me. I'd never drink in front of Jack or Sara. And I'd be *alone* now if you'd just get out.'

Damn woman pulled the glass from my hands and set it out of reach on the glass coffee table. Both her hands wrapped around mine and, despite the tingles as she brushed her thumbs over my knuckles, I continued to glare at her.

My brow furrowed, trying to decipher the unreadable expression in her green eyes. Her brow also creased. 'I don't want to get into this with you, Leigh,' I said. 'I'm an adult. I'm not going to endanger myself or anyone else. I'm just going to get drunk.'

'C'mon, Kelly, you're smarter than this. Getting drunk isn't going to solve anything.'

'Maybe not, but I'll feel pretty good for a few hours.' I laughed and even to my ears it sounded forced.

'And what happens after that?'

Now anger gorged in my throat. 'Don't tell me you care.'

She pulled away from me, eyes wide, seemingly taken aback. 'I . . . do care.'

I shot to my feet. If she wasn't going to let me at the drink I'd already poured, I'd pour another. She intercepted me halfway back to the bar.

'Oh, for God's sake, Leigh! Get out!'

'You're not one for letting go, Kelly. Is something else going on?'

'Well, we all can't be perfect like you, Leigh.' My tone was snappish, and she flinched. I didn't care.

I thought she disliked me on principle. Oh, she never called me names or bad-mouthed me in front of the kids. But alone, alone was another story. We'd come to near blows more than a few times. After all, I was my father's daughter and not very well versed in using my mouth to solve my problems.

'I'm far from perfect, Kelly.'

Our differences were never more apparent to me than at that moment. Leigh came from a tight-knit family of privilege and wealth. My background is considerably more working class. She had her work with a charity of underprivileged kids. Me? I threw up my hand toward her.

'Nothing ever fazes you,' I snapped. 'I lost three clients. In a *row*. I probably won't have a job Monday morning. Headhunting firms don't keep losers, you know.'

She stepped toward me again; I took a step back. 'Kelly,' she said. 'Were these people really place-able in this economy?'

I rubbed my temples to stave off the headache I felt coming on. 'I don't know. Maybe. Maybe not.'

'Then aren't you being too hard on yourself?'

'*All* I have is my job, Leigh.'

'You've got Jack.'

She said it without rancor, but the implication made me snap, 'Well, he isn't here.' My own voice made my head hurt. I cupped my forehead in my hands and turned away from her.

'Kelly,' she said. Her fingers barely touched my shoulder.

I turned fast, angry she was still here, angrier that I couldn't be alone with my failure. As a result I tripped over my own feet.

Falling backward I registered her surprised face, then I saw the ceiling fan slowly circling. Stars filled my vision as pain exploded in my head and back.

I squeezed my eyes shut against the pain and gingerly sought out the most painful spot on my skull with my fingertips. 'Son of a bitch,' I groaned.

'Kelly?' I felt Leigh's presence shift above me, crowding me, just as she grabbed my forearms. 'How many drinks did you have before I got down here?'

'Just the one. You wouldn't let me have my second!'

'Why on God's green Earth would you drink if you can't hold your liquor?' She laughed. I snarled, pushing away from her as I tried to push myself to my feet.

She laughed again, then helped me to a sitting position on the floor, still crouched over me. I had a view down her blouse as she examined my head. Closing my eyes against the sight of her naked breasts only made me dizzy though. I pushed her away. 'I'm fine. Fine. Shit. Leigh, I don't need you hovering.'

'You obviously need somebody.' Ignoring my protest, she continued to rub around on my head until she found the knot from my head striking the frame of the couch on my way down. That it was padded was the only reason I was conscious. It still hurt like hell.

'Hey!' I snatched her hand away from the tender spot. She lifted my chin, her gaze searching mine. I was so befuddled, I couldn't think of anything to say. Her thumb moved against the skin of my cheek and my stomach twisted. I turned away, embarrassed I might throw up after one stupid drink.

I squeezed my eyes shut and tears leaked out. Her arms slipped around my shoulders, and I tried to pull away. Her arms simply tightened, and I felt her body moving against my back.

'God, you're pushy.' I pushed back at her as I spoke, trying to dislodge her hold.

I turned my head to gauge my efforts, only to find her face mere inches from mine. Her warm breath ghosted across my nose and lips as I noticed the very deep green of her eyes.

Then my lips were swallowing her breath, skimming over her mouth. She made a sound – startled, but not angry. The pressure of her lips against my mouth softened. I thrust my fingers into her hair, gripping her head, holding it in place.

I nibbled at the softest lips I'd ever felt against my own. With a deep inhale, I caught the scent of perfume. It was something heady, not floral, and all I could think was I'd never been this close to Leigh to smell her scent before.

I wanted to get closer, much closer.

I twisted and pushed and pulled. Abruptly I was fully supine beneath her, my thigh rising between hers against the most incredible heat. Leigh moaned as I recaptured her lips over and over again with mine.

The fine strands of her hair slipped through my fingers, and I clasped her shoulders, arching my back so my body melded into hers.

Her lips left mine. I cried out, bereft. I felt her mouth again – hot kisses trailing across my cheek and down my throat. Her hand pulled at my shirt. I heard buttons pop. Hot breath seared the swell of my breast, followed by the soft sweep of her lips. The pit of my stomach tightened in expectation.

My hands left her head and trailed down her cheeks to her shoulders.

Which one of us was supposedly drunk here? I couldn't voice my thoughts.

She suddenly drew back. I sat up. She glanced under her lashes toward me, then turned her head away. I pulled my shirt closed with one hand and pushed the fingers of my other hand through my hair, setting it to rights. I inhaled deeply, then exhaled slowly.

I cleared my throat, though what could I say?

From beneath my own struggle for thought and words, I kept stealing glances at Leigh. She'd pulled herself into a seated position on the floor, one knee under her chin, her gaze fixed middle-distant, and left fingers lightly spread over her lips.

Her eyes slowly crinkled at the corners and her lips turned up in clear amusement.

'I've never kissed a girl,' she said slowly, as if she taste-tested each word before letting it out of her mouth.

The expression she shot me then was so clearly one of pleasure, I was stunned and remained silent.

'I liked it,' she said.

Her gaze finally focused on me – more precisely, on my lips – and I felt my stomach flip-flop again as I recalled in intimate detail the sensations of our kiss. How her body had felt sliding against mine, the taste of her breath on my tongue, the feel of it elsewhere, and the moans of pleasure – her pleasure – filling my ears.

'I . . .' My voice cracked. I cleared my throat. 'I liked it, too.'

As soon as the words left my mouth, I wanted to take them back – snatch them from the air and silence them. What the hell did I mean *I liked it*?

I'd never thought of kissing a woman in my life.

I liked it? I had liked it. I felt myself nodding.

Then I vigorously shook my head. No. No! What about men? What about *Jack*?

Leigh had gotten to her feet when I next looked toward her. Her back was to me, and I found myself studying the way her muscles moved, admiring the woman's visible skin in the bare shouldered style.

She stopped at the bar and mixed herself a drink.

Using the couch as leverage, I pulled myself to my feet and grabbed my vodka twist off the coffee table. Our eyes met past the rims of our glasses.

Leigh turned abruptly away. I heard a thunk as the glass she had been using fell heavily onto the bar.

'I gotta go,' she said. Still avoiding my gaze, she turned around. I moved quickly to stand between her and the door.

Leigh leaving was the last thing I wanted. My gaze zeroed in on her mouth.

She kept talking, babbling really. She mentioned 'the kids' and a business call she 'desperately' needed to make.

I crossed the space separating us in four quick strides, grabbed her face between my palms, rubbing my thumbs over her cheekbones, and at the same time I shut off her words, using my lips to cover hers.

Leigh

I surrendered to Kelly's kiss: the sensations of her lips against mine, her body against mine, surrounding me, making me feel like I was drowning. I clung to her for what felt like life or death. Her palms cupped my face, causing heat much, much lower in my body. I wrapped my arms around her back, aligning our bodies together, mouths to hips.

I've never felt anything like this. Damn it. I should have. I've made love with probably a dozen men, made two beautiful children. Yet Kelly's touch, her kisses, produced an out of this world experience.

As Kelly's mouth unfastened from mine and trailed instead down my throat, a moan of pleasure was an inadequate expression of the feeling. My heart pounded so hard in my chest I was gasping for breath. My center throbbed in time with it, and I could already feel an orgasm building.

I cupped Kelly's ass in my hands and lifted, rubbing my crotch against her, welcoming the heat even as I found no familiar firmness to rub against.

She cried out, lifting her mouth from my collarbone. The sound suddenly ranked near the top of my list of favorites. I pushed my body into hers, causing the sound again.

I nuzzled my face into her hair, gasping, breathing deep, and absorbing the scents of her hair and skin, a mix of citrus and something else. She didn't smell like any man I'd ever known. Was this unique to Kelly, or women in general? Whatever it was, it was driving me insane and making my arousal nearly unmanageable. I needed to come. Right now.

I shifted and my thighs opened. I ground my hips, welcoming the pressure against my center. I threw my head back and Kelly's arms supported my back. Her mouth found its way to a breast. I don't even remember my top slipping down, but now I felt the stretched fabric pinning my upper arms.

The sensations were too incredible to let logic or reason back in, so I simply flowed with it. And flow I did. Kelly's teeth trapped a nipple. I cried out, shuddering, and felt the liquid heat pool between my thighs. My knees buckled. Instead of falling into a graceless heap on the floor, I felt Kelly's arms tighten around me, guiding me to the couch. She cupped my cheek, caressed my face, and kissed my temple. Every contact made me quiver.

'Leigh,' she murmured, pulling my head into the curve of her shoulder and stroking my hair.

'Kel . . .' was all I could manage, my throat working to pull moisture to my mouth.

I relaxed into her embrace. I'd always thought Jack had made a nice match with Kelly. Though she had no experience with children, she made an effort with ours. She was prickly, though, in a way that felt unconsciously territorial, often resenting my presence in her life.

I knew about her past. Jack had told me about the distant father and the mother who died when Kelly was six. But she was always trying to get the parenting thing right with Jack Jr. and Sara. I appreciated that, even when we argued about the exact solutions to each problem.

She felt strong here now, yet delicate as we rested against each other. I've always gone for men bigger than me, because I like the feeling of their strength surrounding me. But the delicate feeling of Kelly made me wrap my arms around her, actually offering her my comfort in return, something I'd not done with any male in my entire life. It felt good – amazing, actually. I squeezed her lightly to try to convey this.

She drew back. Her gaze, a deep, dark brown that had caught my attention the first time Jack introduced us, searched mine. 'You, um, wanna talk about this?' Kelly asked, sweeping a lock of her hair behind her ear.

Yeah, I did, but then again, I didn't. I did want to say something, however. 'Talk, um, doesn't seem to be a strong suit with us.'

'I'm willing to give it a try,' Kelly said.

'Maybe when your head's clear,' I diverted.

'Maybe you're right.' She rubbed her temple, and I found myself resisting the urge to rub it for her.

'You gonna say anything?' I asked.

'Who am *I* gonna talk to about *this*?' Kelly gestured between us.

'Then it's agreed.' I felt ultimately frustrated, not sure exactly what I had wanted to hear, but knowing that dropping this wasn't it. My weak knees were gone. I stood, straightened my clothes, pulling my blouse back above my breasts, and strode out the front door. I pulled it shut behind me with a satisfying slam.

Kelly

Tell someone? What was she, nuts?

My train of thought abruptly halted at the slam of the front door.

I stretched out on the couch. My nose caught the scent of sex lingering on the leather cushion. I pushed up, brushing a hand over the warm spot Leigh had just left. I smiled and in that instant my heart swelled with pride. I chuckled.

I kissed a girl.

And I made her come.

Pandora's Box

by Cheri Crystal

For twenty not-so-terrible years, I took pride in being a successful juggler. I was a married working mom. Michael and I raised twin teenagers, Shannon and Jared, who I'd give my life for, and the change-of-life baby I'd wished for, my sweet toddler, Jessica.

Nobody told me being a mom meant everyone else needed, and felt entitled to, a huge chunk of me. Didn't I crave being wanted? But how much of my self-worth did I have to part with in order to maintain harmony at home? I was becoming a slave to the snooze alarm, with thoughts of taking a hammer to the darn thing to silence the buzzer once and for all. I knew I needed time for me, but I couldn't fathom how to fit it in or what to do with it once I found myself alone – until I found catharsis in writing.

There was no escape into work. Where once I had looked forward to my job, now employment in a nursing care facility meant sicker patients, overwhelming responsibility, endless paperwork, and less staff than necessary to do what was required. Reduced job satisfaction and feeling abused by the system had me believing the stress of being a nurse was bad for my health.

At night, when I could finally catch a breather, Michael was planted in our bed with the remote. I could walk around naked with tassels hanging from my tits and Michael wouldn't notice. He'd lost interest soon after Jessie was born and in the two years since then, we went from having sex four nights a week to three times a month, if I was lucky. Not a satisfactory sex life by any standards. Further depleting my self-esteem, he only commented if the house was a mess, his dinner cold, or someone interrupted his ball game.

I discovered late in life that I could add a little spice and keep my sanity by reading and writing lesbian erotica on the sly. When I started to write saucy tales without a single episode of real life experience, my cyber-buddies warned if I traveled that road it would open a Pandora's box.

One dreary day at the end of January, with the holidays a distant memory, the windowpanes fogged and rattled as a result of frigid winds, ice, and snow. We were headed for the snowiest winter in years. Nostalgic visions of Michael keeping me warm were quickly replaced with those of him playing with his brand-new snow blower instead. I turned my attention toward getting ready for play group.

Twenty active two-year-olds and adults converged weekly at the local church for Toddler Time. I looked forward to it probably more than Jessie. She needed lots of prompting to switch gears between activities. I had all sorts of tricks, but the battle of wills grew tiresome. At forty-six, I didn't have the stamina I had when the boys were her age. I lifted Jessie out of her car seat, not easy with a bulky winter jacket and a death grip on her car toys.

'Jessie, honey,' I cajoled, 'you love play group.' I untangled the belt, only to get it caught in her hood, trying not to take her head off as she squirmed. 'Come on, it's a brand-new session. You'll meet lots of new friends.'

'Nooo, don' wanna.'

'We can't stay here all day. You'll miss juice and cookies.'

'Tookie, tookie.'

'No tookie, ugh, cookie unless you be Mommy's best girl.'

'Me best girl.' She lifted her arms and grabbed my neck. With her weather-induced runny nose, she wiped her snot on my face. Before gathering my pocketbook and diaper bag, both filled with enough junk to sell in a local thrift shop, I made noisy kissing sounds on her chubby cheeks while she succumbed to a fit of giggles. Finally, Jessie and I were on our way toward the building, thank goodness.

Other moms with toddlers scurried toward the door, which blew open as if it'd pop right off the hinge. Jessie's excitement kept me warm, but imagine my shock when I grew hot just peering into the bluest eyes I'd ever seen. She had stunning hair so black in contrast to her pale complexion that I was tempted to touch a silky-looking lock as she wrestled with her feisty son.

'Here,' I said, switching Jessie to my other hip so I could grab the door. 'Let me help you.'

'Thanks, but I can manage.' She spoke with an accent

I couldn't place, but the sound and inflection complemented her exotic appearance.

'Damien, *fronima se parakalo, kane ipomoni ftanoume se ligo.*' Just then Damien kicked his way out of her arms. By sheer luck, I had enough time to drop my bags and grab his sleeve before he bolted into traffic.

I handed the child back to his grateful mother and waited while she scolded him in what sounded like Greek to me, and probably was Greek. Meanwhile, Jessie demanded freedom. I placed her down, holding her hand firmly as the children interacted. Damien spoke in the same English as Jessie and their gibberish was music to my ears.

The Greek goddess – an author-inspired title befitting this regal woman who stood approximately ten inches taller – was decked out in a black tailored hip-length pea coat with a crimson turtleneck sweater showing. I involuntarily cruised her long length and took in the effect her slightly flared, neatly pressed jeans and stylish boots had on her shapely legs. She had done nothing to shelter her face from the elements and yet her unspoiled features remained alluring, although as frozen as my gaze upon her shimmering eyes, high cheekbones, and kissable red lips. The natural blush from cold air drew my eye to her cheeks. I made a mental note to model my next character after this beauty, praying I could remember every detail. I hoped my perusal wasn't obvious.

'Hallo, and thank you. He is quite a handful, no?'

'I have twin boys and know all about energetic young males.'

She smiled. I swallowed my unbidden lust, worrying if I drooled, ice crystals might form. Her shoulders were hunched practically up to her earlobes. She sported many earrings along the rim with a shiny hoop pierced through the cartilage on one side. She had to be at least ten, maybe fifteen, years my junior. Most of the moms were younger. I got used to being one of the oldest parents in this crowd and thanked genetics for my youthful appearance with only a little effort.

'I'm Janice. What's your name?'

'Melina.' She held the door, nodding for me to go first. Our children, still fascinated with each other, followed us into the warm hallway where everyone awaited the group leader.

I raised my voice to be heard above the noise. 'Melina is a lovely name. Nice to meet you.'

'Likewise.'

'I love your accent. Where are you from?'

'A small village in Greece.' Her earlier enthusiasm waned like a tire with a slow leak. 'My mom recently passed away.' Tears formed and clung to her dark bottom lashes. Had one droplet escaped nothing would have stopped me from wiping it away.

'Oh, gee, I'm so sorry.'

'Thank you. We remained in Greece while she was alive. The cancer quickly spread but, thank God, she only suffered at the end and it was short. Once she was gone, I couldn't bear to stay . . .' She cleared the emotion from her throat, and I wanted to hug her so badly. I touched her sleeve in a small gesture of comfort.

'Forgive me,' she said.

'It's okay,' I murmured, feeling her pain.

'I agreed to move here. My husband always wanted to come to America to be closer to his brothers, but I would not leave my mom. I have no brothers or sisters and his family is my family, I guess.'

'How long have you been here?' I was intrigued at her candor with a complete stranger.

The kids grew restless and the moms did their best to keep them from running around lest they get hurt. An elderly lady emerged from the office to inform us the facilitator would be late. 'Miss Marcia apologizes for her delay,' she said, but by then the crowd was too busy interacting to take much notice. I repeated my question.

'When did she . . . how long have you been here?'

'Only a few months.' As tears fell, I wiped them away and pulled her in for a hug. I would have held her longer if the kids hadn't intruded.

'I didn't mean to unload all this on you,' she said, finally able to get a hold of herself. I located tissues in my diaper bag and handed her a tissue.

'I wish I could take away your pain, believe me.'

She smiled through her tears, which reminded me of a field of flowers after a sun shower. I wanted to kiss her that instant, protect her from any storm.

'Thank you. I don't know what came over me.'

'You're in mourning and understandably so. I'd lose an important part of myself if I lost my mother.'

'You two have a good relationship?'

'Yes, she's my best friend.'

'Mine was too.'

'She'll always be with you right here.' I patted the place between her breasts and the innocent touch was too much for me. I withdrew my hand.

'I can tell you're going to be a very good friend,' she said.

'Good, because I can always use another one.' I changed the subject before she had me crying or confessing I thought she was gorgeous. 'Your English is impeccable.'

'I studied English literature.'

It was my turn to be impressed and God help me for hoping against hope I'd found someone who shared my love of literature right in my own neighborhood. Could I tell her I wrote lesbian romance? I decided no. That would probably kill any budding friendship.

Her diamond-studded platinum thumb ring sparkled when she ran her sleek fingers through both sides of a silken center part, showing off more of her face before her hair fell back into place. I managed not to swoon and got a pang of intense longing deep inside. I was falling for her.

I told myself to extinguish these dangerous notions immediately, if not sooner. It wasn't as if secretly lusting for women in film, on television, in books, or in my fertile mind was acceptable either. I was married to Michael and pretty sure I said 'I do' to commit until death do us part. I enjoyed sex with him very much – when I could get it. He could be quite the competent and caring lover – when in the mood. But the longer Melina and I conversed, the more my body laid its own plans, superseding anything my brain decided.

Jessie yanked at the bottom of my jacket repeating, 'Uppy, uppy.'

'Don't you want to stand up like a big girl and play with Damien?'

She poked her finger at Damien's chest. 'Play 'mee-an."

Melina and I shared a maternal moment, which further sealed my fate. She was too pretty for words and appeared all dressed up, even in the casual wear.

That morning, I had tugged on my favorite faded well-worn jeans. The hem had frayed a bit, but this was play group, not a fashion show. I wore a teal waffle henley beneath a plaid flannel button-down for layered warmth.

With Melina staring intently into my eyes, a shade I used to appreciate, but now a pale green in comparison to her electrifying blue, I wished I'd worn the cream mohair cowl-neck sweater that flatteringly hugged my voluminous breasts and slim waist. I've been told my hourglass figure was my best feature, next to thick, strawberry blond curls, even if I always hated being called 'Red' and thought my butt, hips, and thighs could use a good shearing. Too bad the sweater was in the wash pile. I hoped I didn't look like a ragamuffin and contemplated keeping my coat on. Unfortunately the church felt like an oven, and we weren't even bouncing around to the latest kiddie craze yet.

I stole my eyes away from Melina's for a moment to see what my girl wanted next. 'Tookie, tookie.'

'Soon, baby, soon.' I fingered her flyaway blond hair, only to get caught up in static electricity. 'Ouch,' I reacted, hoping Jessie hadn't felt the shock too. 'Sorry, Jessie.' But she didn't seem to notice.

'Jessie is a nice name for a girl. I like it.'

'Thanks, it's short for Jessica. Her brothers chose her nickname and it stuck.'

'How old are your boys? You said they were twins?'

'Seventeen.' Now I knew my age was showing.

'You must have been less than that when you had them.'

'Hardly, but flattery will get you far, dear Melina.'

'You can't be old enough to have teenagers, surely not,' she adamantly added. Conviction looked exceptionally good on her. Everything did.

'You want to make a bet?'

Just then the facilitator bustled in, bringing with her much-needed cold air to cool off the hot flush creeping its way up my neck. Moisture dripped between my breasts. I had to take off my coat or die from a heated rush.

When I did, I caught Melina unabashedly checking me out. My breath caught. She undressed me with her eyes, and the blue of her irises were nearly black. I knew this look. I wrote about it plenty, for heaven's sakes, but I feared I would faint dead having it turned on me. I could barely speak but managed to grasp Jessie's hand as we haphazardly lined up double-file to march down the few steps towards our classroom. I was behind Melina, leading her well-behaved little boy. I wished I understood what she had said to quiet him and figured it was a bribe. Damien was only two and already bilingual. He also got to hold her hand. Jealous of a toddler; imagine that.

With no choice but to stop fantasizing about how she made me want to weep from want, I joined in as we assembled in a circle with our children on the inside. No matter what we were told to do, I couldn't help glancing over at Melina frequently. She was as openly affectionate with her son as I was with Jessie. The more I discovered we had in common, the more enamored I became with my Greek goddess. We really connected during our wait, but there was so much more I wanted to know.

To entice the children to join in, we all danced around like lunatics. I was too busy watching Melina to feel silly singing *Head, Shoulders, Knees, and Toes* with moves to match. I really loved the way Melina did the *Macarena* and nearly landed on my ass tripping over my daughter because I wasn't paying attention to her missteps.

When the hour was over, I commented aloud how fast the time went. Jessie was easily persuaded to get back into her jacket for the trek to the car after I promised her two favorite DVDs. So young and already she was negotiating with me.

The wind blew the top layer off the snowdrifts, across the cleared surfaces of the parking lot, and all the way to the other side. The sky had grown dark for midday. Going home to a messy house didn't hold appeal. With only one weekday off, I had to weigh priorities carefully, and spending quality time with Jessie held the top spot. Reading or writing was a good second, followed by enjoying a peaceful meal, or just relaxing in front of the television catching up on my Netflix stash. Housework, well, there's no surprise where that landed on my to-do list.

One of the moms commented her weather forecast app showed we were headed for a blizzard.

'Is the weather always this brutal?'

Melina startled me. I turned and found us a hair-width apart. I inhaled a hint of mint amid an earthy fragrance I was hard-pressed to name, but would never forget.

'Not usually, but it's supposed to be wetter to make up for the drought we had over the summer.'

'Oh, I see,' she said in a sultry whisper while she maintained eye contact. Her proximity made me desperate to kiss her supple lips, if only to prove my theory that she was probably a great kisser. I had a sixth sense about these things.

I'd often dreamed about what a lesbian kiss would be like. All sorts of salacious scenarios entered my mind and writing them down cemented my obsessive quest. I'll never forget the first time I heard Katy Perry sing lyrics surely written for me. Heck, I even found myself humming the tune at work, when nobody was around.

Here I was, literally dripping with desire, imagining Melina melting the glacier inside my loins, when she interrupted my delicious reverie. 'Are you going food shopping?'

'No, I have tons of stuff on hand for emergencies. What about you?'

'My husband is away this week.' Her eyes glistened with a hint of sadness. 'It's just me and Damien.'

I wanted to invite her over, but I worried she'd notice my relaxed housekeeping skills. It seemed like she was fishing for an invitation and the more I hesitated, the further she withdrew. A gnawing ache burned a hole in my empty stomach as lunchtime approached. The resulting gurgle from my gut made us laugh and broke the tension. It would be wonderful to have lunch with her, but I couldn't get up the nerve to ask. I guess she couldn't, either.

'Well, it was nice meeting you, Janice. See you.' She lifted her son, now putty in her arms, and bundled him – jacket, hat, mittens, and all – under her jacket.

'You'll freeze like that,' I warned.

'I'd rather he stay warm. I'm not worried about myself.'

'Okay then, bye.' I waved as she dashed to her car. I watched her get into an SUV and ventured over to mine. I hugged Jessie and didn't realize how tight my grip was until she fussed. 'Sorry, baby, Mommy has it real bad.' I doubted she understood and saying the words aloud sent smitten feelings circulating in my veins.

It was going to be a long week until next Wednesday.

The roads had started to ice and driving was slow going until I pulled into our driveway. I left my bag in the car and took a now cranky Jessie into the house, dropping my keys on the credenza, running to answer the phone. Michael said he was staying the night in a motel and would dig out as soon as he could. The moment I hung up with him, the school called about early dismissal and closing the next day. This was going to be some blizzard. I prayed we wouldn't lose power, but decided to get the defrosted chicken in the oven as soon as possible.

Although busy, I couldn't stop thinking about why I hadn't invited Melina. I wanted to smack myself silly. Since when did I give a hoot about my housekeeping? I knew perfectly well why. Her lusty gazes in my direction and the way she watched my every move held the promise of things I dared not think about. We could be friends

– nothing more. A true friend was someone who came over to see me, not my house. I was tempted to fetch my class list and call her, but I had to get dinner ready and do laundry, in case of a power outage.

The house was too quiet except for the DVD. I glanced down the stairs to the den. Much to my relief, Jessie, wrapped in her *blankie*, was fast asleep on the floor. The sight of her angelic face and her adorable tush high in the air melted my heart. Maybe she hadn't given up her naps. The phone rang and Shannon asked if he and Jared could chill with their friends. They were good boys, responsible, but I reminded them to be home for supper and to be especially careful. I wished they had worn their boots, but teens were stubborn to a fault when it came to looking cool rather than staying warm.

'Call me if you need a lift.'

'We can walk.'

'Love you,' I said. Call-waiting signaled another call. I got it just in time. 'Hello?'

'Hallo, Janice?'

I knew her voice in an instant, my heart rate escalated and my mouth went dry.

'Hi, Melina!'

'How did you know it was me?'

'By your sexy accent.' I couldn't believe I said sexy. Yikes.

She laughed, a hearty sound I was growing to adore. In the next moment, I extended an invitation just as she asked if I wanted company. We both laughed.

'Yes, please come over but drive safely.'

'Don't worry, I have four-wheel drive.'

'Good. Jessie's asleep but she'll be happy to see Damien.' Then I remembered. 'Oh, and please excuse my house. I work and –'

'I'm not coming to see your house, Janice. I'm coming to see you.'

I was happy she felt that way and gave her directions. The moment we disconnected our call, I scurried to get the sweet potatoes in the oven; it would add a welcome home-cooked aroma. I tossed a salad and remembered I had a pre-baked apple pie and ice cream in the freezer for dessert. My restored exuberance helped me straighten up the house and prepare a full meal.

Responding to a knock at the door, I peered out the peephole and loved what I saw. The moment I opened up my home, I relieved her of one sleepy little boy while she stamped the snow off her boots before stepping indoors and removing them.

'Come in, come in.'

'What a delicious smell.'

'I'm making dinner and hope you'll stay. Michael is stuck at work, and the boys won't be home till later.'

'I couldn't intrude.'

'You're not. I'm glad you're here. Let me take your jacket.'

'I feel as if I invited myself.'

'Nonsense. Now please, make yourself comfortable.' Damien fell asleep in my arms. His jacket pleasantly held the scent of his mommy's perfume. I hoped it would rub off on me.

'I'll take him,' she said, her arms out and ready.

'Do you think he'll sleep in a porta-crib?'

'Yes, he's a good sleeper. I worry he sleeps too much.'

'He's very active. I bet he just wears out his batteries.'

'You're a smart mom. He's my first. I never had siblings and feel I am learning as I go. My mom helped with him, but you know.'

'Yes, I do. My mom saves me all the time.'

'I always wanted a big family. You're lucky.'

'Your husband has brothers.'

'Yes, but their wives are, I don't know the English word, they're . . . they keep to themselves, and I often feel left out.'

'That's too bad. I can't imagine anyone not welcoming you with open arms.'

'You Americans are funny.'

'How so?'

'You speak your mind and make me say far more than I would have dared.'

'I've been told I'm much too honest for my own good,' I admitted.

'That's an endearing trait.'

I wondered what she'd say if I disclosed what I was thinking. With Jessie sleeping on the rug and Damien comfy in the crib, I was ready to snatch her pretty face and press our mouths together so I could explore her with my tongue. I shivered.

'Are you cold? It is nice and warm in here.' With her eyes cast downward, she added, 'I can't turn the heat high enough to feel as warm and comfortable as I am here with you.' She looked up with her dark, thick lashes, and I melted on the spot.

'You're welcome . . . anytime.'

'Good, because I like you already.'

'I like you already, too.' I had to sit or fall. 'Come into the kitchen. Have you had lunch? Do you want coffee?'

'Yes, coffee, although American coffee doesn't compare. Oh sorry. I'm used to coffee back home and well . . . oh, no, I didn't mean to offend you.' She was floundering. I stifled a grin, loving this too much to rescue her, but alas, I couldn't see her suffer.

'I know what you mean. No apology needed, but I have fresh beans to grind and a coffee press. Why don't you judge for yourself if my brew meets your standards?'

'If it comes close, I'll marry you.'

Taken aback by her remark, I was sure as shit going to make the best darn coffee in New York. With bated breath, I waited for the verdict. Her mouth opened, she blew on it before resting her lips on the cup. Then when I was sure I'd die, she took a taste and let out a most satisfied sigh before exclaiming, 'I like my coffee light and sweet but yours doesn't need cream and sugar. It's perfect. Marry me.'

'I'd love to!' A glance at her puzzled look had me desperate to sweep her up in my arms. 'I'm glad you like it,' I amended. 'There's more where that came from. In fact, why don't we add something stronger? Do you like liqueurs in your coffee?'

'Absolutely.'

'Come help me choose the best accompaniment.'

'With pleasure.'

She followed close behind. I feared I'd trip over my own feet.

'I adore your hair.' She captured a healthy handful, playfully wiggling her fingers through it. I stood, immobilized. 'Has anyone ever told you how beautiful you are?'

'No.' Where was she going with this? I prayed she wouldn't stop. My usual reply would be something to refute her claim, but she had my tongue and stomach all tied up in knots, hoping beyond hope she'd elaborate or shut up and just kiss me already. She appeared as if she wanted to kiss me. I'd never felt surer of anything, and I couldn't hide my desire anymore than she could. I wanted her, and I'd bet anything she wanted me, too.

'Well, you're striking, truly.' She continued to play with my hair and I let her. 'Your husband is lucky,' she purred. 'I bet you make love every night.'

I shook all over. She ran a finger along the side of my face. I faltered and encircled her hand with mine. 'Such lovely skin, I could kiss your freckles, one at a time,' she said, and my knees buckled. There was no shame in her tone. Her confidence was as hot as hell. I wanted what she had. I needed to taste her skin with my tongue. I imagined her breasts filling the palms of my hands, her clit. I wanted her to come in my mouth.

My breath heavy with desire, I practically pleaded, 'Kiss me, please.'

She cradled my head and leaned in, her lips moist, inviting.

The second her mouth closed over mine, my heart leaped with joy.

I opened my mouth wider and explored her with my

eager tongue, marveling at soft skin not marred by stubble. I couldn't get enough of her nor she of me.

When our breasts met, my body ignited with more yearning than I'd had in a very long time, if ever, in fact. Her kiss far exceeded anything I had ever penned or even dreamed.

'You taste wonderful,' she said.

I would give anything if she'd promise never to stop touching me. I wanted her to touch me everywhere. I had to rid us of our clothing. Mere thoughts of lying naked with her titillated my senses. If I didn't have her soon, I'd die.

I nibbled on her ear, followed by kissing every spot my mouth could reach. 'You're gorgeous . . . so soft . . . so perfect.'

'Make love to me, Janice, please.'

Heedless of consequences, I grasped her hand and led her to the guest room where, like extra food, I had a bed ready – just in case.

Throwing off the bedspread, I helped her onto the bed. I climbed on top of her, my knees on either side of her hips. I couldn't stop kissing her. Her moans of pleasure spurred me on.

I worked my way down to her breasts and fondled them. As soon as I brushed against her breasts her nipples hardened. She scooted up enough to remove her sweater, revealing a red lace bra. Her nipples protruded, ready to pop right out, so I reached behind her back and unhooked her bra. Together we cast it aside and she helped me shed my top.

Her breasts were round and perky, more than a handful and perfect for a mouthful.

'Your breasts are magnificent,' she said, kneading mine. She drew a nipple into her mouth and it stiffened. The glorious feeling radiated down my body and settled in my crotch.

'Oh, Melina, keep that up, and I'll come in my pants.'

'Then we should remove them right away, no?'

'Yes.'

With haste, we helped each other strip. I gasped in delight at the dark, lush, and full neat triangle between her slender thighs compared to my auburn curls.

She flipped me over on my back with surprising strength and grace. I could look up into her cerulean eyes for centuries and not tire of the sight. Sprawled atop of me, she grasped my wrists above my head, rendering me useless while she explored my body with her tongue.

Her mouth neared my core. I whimpered. Pools of desire seeped out and my clit stood erect.

'Oh, heavens, Melina, kiss me there, please.'

'I intend to do that and so much more.' Her kisses, licks, and sucks rapidly brought me close to climax, but I forced myself to slow down, to enjoy the journey.

'You're so good at this.' My hips jerked to meet her mouth. My clit was about to burst, but I ignored it. 'Like you've done this before.'

'No, you're my first woman.' She let go of my wrists to open my pussy lips wider, carefully inspecting my clit in the most wanton way.

'Mine, too.' Then there was no holding back. I let the

orgasm reach its peak once more before letting go of any inhibition, save one. I stifled a scream so I didn't wake the kids, and came hard. My body quaked. She eased her ministrations until there was nothing left but me lying there motionless and sated.

When I regained my strength, I sat up, kissed her, and let her know it was my turn. She smiled her response, and I delighted in pleasing her as she did me. Making her come was even better than my own climax had been.

Snuggled in each other's arms in post-coital bliss, we were warm and safe.

'I never knew a kiss could feel like this.' Melina couldn't keep her hands from my hair, and I loved the way she teased me with her talented fingers.

'It was better than I imagined.'

'Have you imagined it, then?'

'Yes,' I couldn't lie, not after surrendering and opening myself up so completely. 'Many times.'

'Me too.' She pulled me in tighter, and I knew we'd delve deeper into this topic when the time was right. I didn't want to ruin the tranquil mood by commiserating about the effect our lesbian liaison and sordid kisses would have on our husbands. Worrying about the children would only make me cry.

The buzzer, signaling my chicken was fully cooked, woke the kids. We hurriedly dressed and flew down the stairs, breathless, but giddy.

Jessie ignored us while she showed Damien her toys and the twins called asking permission for a sleepover at their friend's. After one glance out the window, I consented.

When I hung up, I informed Melina she was sleeping over because I couldn't let her drive home in good conscience. It didn't take much persuasion and when the children weren't looking, we stole another sensational kiss. There was so much to discuss, but I was content enough to enjoy a family meal with Melina, Damien, and Jessie, before tucking the kids into bed so the grownups could play.

This was one story I wouldn't have to write because something told me I'd be too busy living it.

Love Thy Enemy

by Alexandra Rowan

Leah still tasted Vicki's lips on hers and the flavor was breathtaking. She couldn't believe she could admit that, not even to herself, but it was true. No one had seen the kiss at least. And she was positive they'd been out of view of the library's security camera when it'd happened. If Tom ever found out, she didn't know what she'd do.

Vicki had a live-in boyfriend named Dan who would no doubt be livid that her lips had brushed against anyone's but his, but screw her and him. She didn't give a damn if her boyfriend shit a brick over it, and she didn't give a damn about Vicki, period.

And why the hell should I? Their relationship at the Buffalo Public Library had been frigid at best over the past five years. Leah blamed herself for none of their professional woes because she understood a protocol for behavior and work ethic must be followed, and she couldn't help it if Vicki had conceded to none of them.

Whenever she'd raised the point to her colleagues, she'd been met with answers like, 'Oh, you'll never change her,' and 'If she gets in shit with the powers that be, that's her problem.' But those answers had been simply insufficient for Leah. She worked her fingers to the bone, and she expected her co-workers to at least carry their own weight.

She'd taken charge of that sentiment last December when she'd caught Vicki surfing the Internet at the circulation desk. Leah loathed that habit more than anything, and Vicki was a seasoned professional at it. So she'd leveled an official complaint with the library director's office. Rumor had it that Steve had gone easy on Vicki, but had threatened to write her up should the event ever repeat itself.

Vicki had refused to speak to her for a month following the fiasco, and Leah supposed she'd known who'd blown the whistle on her. Co-workers had regarded her with a manner of disgust, which had been part and parcel of working in a union shop, she supposed. Yet she saw herself as a woman with convictions who had done her duty by reporting Vicki.

And Vicki had achieved retribution in some respects. Leah had run an evening film program, and had been short on volunteers, which led to everything going haywire. She'd snapped at Vicki when she hadn't stepped lively enough to help her serve the crowd. The spat – or temper tantrum, as her colleagues had dubbed it – had triggered her own meeting with library director Steve. The meeting had yielded the same results as Vicki's Internet-gate episode.

In spite of her colleagues' insistence that she'd been in the wrong – she'd taken every opportunity to bitch about it at the office – she couldn't believe that anyone could defend that woman for any reason. Vicki should have been fired eons ago, and in any other workplace she would have been.

Then Leah had taken her turn to serve up some cold-shoulder treatment. She'd managed to perform every duty that concerned Vicki, sans excess verbiage. In fact, she'd said nothing to her at all except when she'd not been able to help it.

When she'd been asked to cover the circulation desk for an evening shift, she'd been required to relieve Vicki at five o'clock. An abrupt dinner hour had forced her to be five minutes late, by which time Vicki had walked off the desk, leaving it unattended. Leah had chased her to the back and confronted her.

'Excuse me, but you can't just walk off the desk like that!' Leah shouted. 'What if someone has an accident?'

'Sorry babe,' Vicki answered, 'but when five o'clock rolls around I'm done for the day. Up to you to be here on time.'

'Oh, that's a great attitude.'

Vicki raised her fingers as if to rebut, but instead their arms opened up and they took each other. Leah's lips tasted magnificent meshed with hers, and she loved being pressed against her firm, round breasts. Vicki's tongue burrowed into Leah's mouth. She didn't object. Then her fingers combed through Vicki's fiery red hair.

When their lips parted, Leah felt like duct tape had been torn off her mouth at light speed. They stared at each other, stunned, wiped their lips and darted in separate directions.

Leah arrived at the library early in response to Vicki's phone call requesting a private meeting. *She probably just wants privacy to tell her she was going to level a sexual harassment complaint.* But she couldn't really do that. It hadn't been she who'd motioned for the kiss. But then, Vicki hadn't precisely lunged at her either. Who had made the first move seemed terribly unclear.

The tremors in Vicki's voice suggested to Leah that she might have been scared Leah would level a complaint of her own. Leah wasn't ready to do so just yet, but it never hurt to keep that trump card tucked away.

When the back door clicked open, Leah jumped, and she spotted Vicki. She looked ashen, as though she hadn't slept a wink in the fourteen hours since the kiss. Leah herself had tossed and turned and had been unable to look Tom in the face. Plus, the suspense was boring a hole through her.

'Last night was just a –' Leah started, but Vicki unleashed the same phrase before they both stopped dead.

'I just want you to know that what happ – '

Again, Vicki cut her short. No doubt the bitch had been rehearsing lines too. 'Who are we kidding?' Vicki said. 'It was bound to happen sooner or later.'

'It was?'

'Of course it was. I remember boys in school that got on my nerves . . . boys that I absolutely *hated*. But on some level, I liked them. I *wanted* them. It wasn't like a crush. They just created a deep, heated desire in me, you know?'

'I can't believe I'm hearing this.' Leah frowned. 'I won't.'

Even Leah would admit to herself she threw up that kind of resistance as a defense mechanism. Judging by Vicki's plain expression, she wasn't buying it.

So when Vicki inched up on her and brushed her lips

against Leah's, Leah collapsed into her arms. This time, she was welcomed by more than just Vicki's breasts. This time she felt Vicki's nipples, hard and sharp, ready to rip through her shirt. The feeling made her own nipples grow rock hard and tension consumed her clitoris.

Then Vicki enveloped her. Leah lacked the strength to take the initiative a second time. Their arms hooked around each other's necks and their tongues burrowed into each other's mouths.

It was happening all over again. They were getting fresh with each other in the workplace, which was so very wrong, inappropriate and unprofessional. Leah couldn't bring herself to continue such down-and-dirty behavior – yet she could.

Their lips parted. Vicki wrapped her arms around Leah's waist and hoisted her onto the nearest desk. Shoving papers aside, Vicki hauled her shirt over her head to free her braless breasts, which left Leah breathless in the truest sense of the word. Leah's chest heated up as she found herself turned on by something that'd never sparked her desire before. Not only was she turned on, but she felt too wild to stop herself.

Vicki inched forward to feed Leah her nipple. Leah cupped Vicki's right breast with both her hands and sucked it like drinking from a jug of milk. All the while Vicki rubbed Leah's crotch.

Leah could see the hunger in Vicki's eyes, the desire. This woman knew what she wanted in the bedroom – or wherever she chose to fuck – and she was determined to have it sooner than later. Vicki's boyfriend was a very lucky man, indeed.

Vicki gripped Leah's blouse and tore it open too fast to hear the buttons pop. Leah jumped into the act by unhooking her bra and tossing it over her shoulder. Vicki slipped off Leah's pants and panties, burrowed her face between her legs, and flicked her clit with fast, sharp strokes.

Leah shouted from the abrupt pleasure. She'd never shouted when her own husband did that, or anything else for that matter. Pleasure had been a quiet and private state to her until now. But when Vicki licked her pussy, she thought she would erupt with the most monumental orgasm of her entire life. Vicki must've known that. Like any good lover, she knew how to pleasure her mate, but also when to turn down the heat so she wouldn't come before they reached their crescendo.

Then Vicki grabbed her own office chair, sat down, and spread her legs. Leah had never even fantasized about this before, but she dropped to her knees and flicked Vicki's clitoris with her tongue, first to experience the taste, and then to savor the experience. When she rolled her eyes up, she noticed Vicki's head thrust back and her fingers clamped down on her nipples. The woman was putty in her hands, and she needed only to continue to push her over the edge. So she continued flicking Vicki's clitoris and worked her fingers into her sex.

Vicki wrestled Leah to the floor, which seemed like the perfect spot for them. Down and dirty. Vicki was teaching her to love her sex that way. Then Vicki's legs burrowed between hers until their pussies met. When their labias meshed together, Vicki took charge, grinding, pounding, gyrating.

Leah exploded with so many orgasms she lost count, while Vicki's grunts and groans told her she was experiencing the same rush of pleasure. When they finished, they collected their clothes. Leah reeled from an experience that she didn't regret.

Leah's lips parted, as she meant to thank Vicki, but Vicki stopped her. 'You know this can't happen again, right?'

Leah paused. She didn't know it wouldn't. She was certain that Vicki would piss her off again, that she would piss Vicki off likewise, and that they both would need to relieve some serious tension.

Maybe Leah would do something just to piss her off. Make a mess around her desk or get extra snippy when something went wrong. And certainly Vicki would piss her off too. She was certain of it.

Ketchikan Connection

by Regina Perry

The ache between my legs gnawed at my soul. It tickled and churned, mocking my self-esteem. Then it tugged at my heart until it defeated what hope I had left. My exhaustion of the past eleven hours, flying from one airport to the next, compounded my loneliness. One more stop before landing in Juneau. With any luck, I should be in my own bed within six hours. My bed – alone.

It'd been five months, seven days since Derrick had left. But who's counting? I'd insisted he leave. His drinking was destroying us both. Countless times he'd tried to quit. Countless times he started again, drinking more than he had before. I'd decided maybe *I* was the problem. Last time I heard from him he'd been sober for thirty-three days. Guess I was right.

'Flight 785 to Ketchikan will begin boarding in a few minutes. Would Group One please proceed to Gate 34?' an Alaskan Airlines's clerk announced in the Seattle terminal.

I raised the handle of my carry-on and readied myself

for next call. As the announcement for Group Two came over the loud speaker, the girl behind me tripped over her bag and thudded into my back.

'I'm so sorry,' she gasped. 'My foot caught in the strap.'

'No problem.' I reached to steady her as she detangled herself from her luggage.

'I'm always tripping over something.' She chuckled. 'It's my parents' fault. They named me Grace.'

'I guess you don't believe in the Law of Attraction.'

'No, I believe in it. I just think it has a sarcastic sense of humor.'

I burst into laughter. 'Well, I can certainly see you have a great one . . . sense of humor, that is. It's fun meeting you, Grace. I'm Laura,' I said, extending my hand. I guessed her to be about my age, mid-thirties.

'It's a pleasure to meet you. You stopping in Ketchikan or going all the way to Juneau?'

'I'm afraid I'm in for the long haul. You?'

'Me too. Where did you start?'

'D.C.'

'And I thought I had it bad. I'm from L.A.'

'So you're just visiting Juneau?'

'Yes, business. Goldbelt, it's one of the Alaska Native Corporations. Have you heard of it?'

'Heard of it? I work there, and it's why I was in D.C.'

'Wow, what a coincidence. So Juneau's home now?'

'Yes, for six years.'

'And you like it?'

'I used to love it. Maybe the long, dark winters are starting to get to me.'

'I think I could get used to the darkness if I had someone to cuddle up to.'

'True.' I sighed. At the attendant's bidding we worked our way to the gate and down the jet way. 'You're welcome to sit with me if you like.'

'They don't mind if we don't sit in our assigned seat?'

'Not usually. It's not a full flight.'

The two-hour flight to Ketchikan passed quickly. We discovered we not only worked for the same company, but also had kayaking and tennis in common. She'd also experienced a break-up the year before and had been alone since.

Horrific turbulence battered the plane as it began the descent into Ketchikan. We could see snow whirling past the windows and feel the howl of the wind. When the plane dipped, she clutched my hand. The next plummet, her nails dug into my palm. I placed my other hand over hers.

'We'll be all right. Alaskan Airlines' pilots are used to flying in these blizzards.'

'I hope you're right,' she said, her eyes closing.

I hoped I was too.

At the approach, the plane slid onto the runway, the tail swerving left. Grace squeezed her eyes and screeched a hum through her lips. I feared she was going to draw blood on my hand before the brakes took hold. At last, the plane skidded to a stop and the passengers heaved a gigantic sigh in unison.

By the time we'd taxied to the gate, it was evident to

everyone we wouldn't be flying to Juneau tonight. Once inside the airport, the loudspeaker informed us there were vacancies at The Landing Hotel.

'What is *this*?' Grace exploded, as we slid down the ice-covered gangplank to the ferry.

'We have to take a ferry to the mainland.'

'Why?' She was almost in tears.

'You know that bridge-to-nowhere Sarah Palin liked to brag about?'

'Yeah.'

'Well, she must have never been caught in a Ketchikan connection. It would have connected the island, where the airport is located, to the mainland.'

'Oh my God.'

Standing in line at the lodge, Grace turned to me. 'Want to share a room?'

'If you want to. Sure.' I was surprised she'd asked. After all, the company would have paid the expense.

'After that flight, I'd just rather not be alone tonight. That must really sound stupid, I know. I'm sorry.'

'You have nothing to be sorry about. It was harrowing. No reason to be embarrassed.'

A blazing fire greeted us as we walked into the room.

'The staff must have heard about our landing,' Grace squealed. She dropped her bags and ran to the fire, holding out her hands to soak up the warmth.

'That's just Alaskan hospitality.' I smiled at the sight of

her crouching over the fire. She had a childlike innocence and playfulness that was quite attractive. It matched her curly blond hair and petite figure. I hung my coat and began to unpack my toiletries.

Returning from the bathroom, I noticed the bed. Yes, the bed. I'd been so engrossed by her antics at the fireplace I hadn't noticed the room only had one bed. 'I guess they were sold out of doubles.'

'Huh?' Grace turned and saw what I was talking about. 'Oh, I guess so. Do you mind? I could bunk on the floor in front of the fire.'

I was taken back by her kindness. 'Don't be silly. I'm not afraid of you.' I laughed.

While Grace was in the bathroom, I hurriedly undressed and slipped my flannel-lined pajama top over my head, not bothering to unbutton. I hadn't packed the bottoms, preferring my bare legs against the sheets. Crawling into bed, I wondered what Grace had packed to sleep in.

I was hoping I'd be asleep before she came back, but I couldn't stop thinking about her, wondering what it would be like sleeping in the same bed with another woman. I hadn't done that since sleepovers in junior high. A blizzard raged outside, but I wished I was wearing something filmy and sexy. *Am I that lonely*?

Grace opened the door and tiptoed to her suitcase to put away her cosmetic bag. I stared at her midnight blue, see-through teddy. It was form fitting with cutouts at her sides, creating an hourglass of fabric, front and back. Her butt cheeks pressed against the fabric as she dug around in her suitcase looking for her toothbrush. Once found, she clamped it in her cheek and whirled around. Her nipples seemed to poke through the sheer voile. She stopped short and removed the toothbrush. My eyes must have been bulging.

'Sorry. I didn't pack anything decent to sleep in. I like to pretend I have a lover, even if I don't.'

'Doesn't bother me,' I lied.

While she brushed her teeth, I felt for the ache between my legs and discovered a pool.

Soon, she slipped between the sheets and stretched her toes, forward and back, forward and back. 'This is how I unwind,' she explained.

'I should try that.'

'Not as effective as some other things I can think of, but a girl does what a girl has to do.' She turned on her side, facing me. 'You're really pretty. Classy looking. Not like me. I'm more of a tomboy.'

'You're adorable. Cute and sassy,' I said, still lying on my back, my face turned toward her.

'Really, you think so?' She raised, cocked her elbow and rested her head on her hand.

'Of course. I can't believe you haven't had your share of men.'

'I've had a few. But it's not easy finding that right one, you know?'

'Yes, I do.' I rolled to my side to face her directly.

She extended her free hand, and ran her fingers through strands of my hair. 'I love your long, straight auburn hair. And I swear, your eyes are actually sapphire blue. I don't think I've ever seen eyes quite that color before.'

'Daddy's eyes.'

'Daddy? You still call him that?'

'Yeah. But he's gone now . . . died seven years ago. Guess I always had this fantasy of being Daddy's little girl, so I never let go of calling him that. He used to sing that song to me.'

'What song?'

Daddy's Little Girl.

'Ah, how sweet. But was it true?'

'Not exactly. How'd you know?' I asked, tucking my arm beneath my pillow.

'You did say 'fantasy.''

I sighed and smiled at her perception. There was more to this cute little pixie than I first realized.

'Anything you want to talk about?' she asked.

'He loved me as much as he was capable. He had his own issues. What human doesn't?' I attempted a laugh to lighten the mood.

'Isn't that the truth? All families are dysfunctional, just varying degrees of it.'

She arched her back and stretched. Again, my gaze fixed upon her full breasts pressing against her teddy. Since the afternoon I'd discovered Daddy's *Playboy* magazines in the end table next to his recliner, I'd been fascinated by women's breasts. It's probably not an accident that mine are so sensitive. I can orgasm from nipple play alone.

'Yeah, if anyone thinks their family was perfect, they

just haven't discovered the skeletons in the closet . . . yet,' I said.

'I agree. Every family has its problems.' She yawned. 'Sleep tight, Laura. Glad it was you I fell into today.' She stretched again and closed her eyes.

'Me too, Grace. Night.'

Sometime during the wee hours, or mid-morning – one can't tell in Alaska – I was startled awake by arms and legs wrapped around me. My muscles froze until I could assess my situation. *Where am I? Who's in bed with me?* Realization flowed through my body, and I relaxed like a deflating balloon, then realization struck again and I tensed. I listened to gauge her breathing to see if she was sleeping. Her deep, steady breaths assured me she was. She must have become chilled in her sleep. No surprise, with what she was wearing.

She stirred and squeezed against me. My body, with a mind of its own, reacted and pushed its buttocks against her front. Once my brain caught up with my involuntary action it joined forces and wiggled my ass. *You hussy. What would she think if she woke up?* She didn't. My mind took flight, fantasizing what could happen next, forgetting the angle I'd extended my butt to maintain contact with my unexpected bedmate.

Floating, spinning, delirious – the mythical orgasm played out in the gut of my brain. Grace moved her arm, her hand grazing the underside of my breast, and I was jolted alert, holding my breath and cursing thick, flannel pajamas. Her strong, steady breaths convinced me she was still asleep. I reached to the placket at my neckline and slowly, carefully began to unbutton. One, two – and my hand brushed against hers. She stirred, then settled into me – her leg tighter, her hand higher. I clamped my hand over hers, which was now cupping my tit. The sensation beneath her touch had my nipple agonizing in a whirl of tingle and ache.

In minute increments, I tugged at the flannel barrier between her hand and my skin. Tug. Wait. Tug. Wait, until her warmth radiated my orb, my nipples stood erect, and the sensation quivered down through my core and into my pussy. When the agony reached unbearable proportions and I was ready to bolt, her index finger hinted at movement. A moan escaped from my throat and the hint became deliberate, circling my areola. Her breathing quickened. I wagered she was conscious, and turned slightly toward her.

Her hand slid to my other breast and I continued rotating until I could see her face. Embers in the fireplace provided enough glow to see the glisten in her opened eyes. She not only didn't stop but intensified her massage of my breast. As she moved to unbutton my top, I cupped her cheek and moved toward her, stopping within an inch of her lips – silently asking permission. She answered by lifting her mouth to reach mine.

Our lips met, held, parted. Tongues circled our own lips, then touched, tongue-to-tongue. I pulled back and questioned her eyes once again. She responded by leaning in and fully, firmly locking her lips to mine, pressing, sucking, coming up for air, circling, alternating angles, kissing, kissing, kissing.

Slow motion converted to swift. She pulled my sleeve

over my shoulder and down my arm as I rose to be rid of the hated flannel. I, in turn, slid her teddy off her shoulders and down her body. Then I stopped. She lay before me in naked splendor. I'd never been within inches of female nakedness. Even though I'd spent hours examining my own body with mirrors from every angle and varying degrees of magnification, fretting how I compared to other women, it was as if I'd never seen the female body before. I marveled at her beauty in the flickering light. I revered the miracle of a woman. She appeared fragile and soft. I touched her so very lightly, fearing she'd shatter like porcelain.

Recognizing my apprehension, she took charge, thrusting her front to mine. She girdled my buttocks with her arm and pulled me into her as she began to rock her pelvis. Our mons ground into each other, and with each plunge she managed to maneuver lower and deeper.

I didn't know how to respond. *What should I do next?* I just knew I wanted to be devoured, ravaged. My desire for her fingers, her lips, her body consumed me. Lust has no patience.

I felt a finger slide through my creases. I pushed against it, craving its pressure. She pulled her body away to focus on ministrations with her hands and fingers – spreading, examining, parting, circling, flicking. Once aroused, I've always become an exhibitionist. I yearned to expose. I relished being seen. I desired the attention. And I loved every moment of her scrutiny.

Her investigation concluded with the discovery of my pearl. Having found her treasure, she doted on it. I could feel her lightly touch it, inspect it, tilt it. I found my legs and projected my torso higher to present her with my jewel. Then she licked her index finger and circled her prize, claiming possession.

With her other hand she inserted a finger and tickled me, like *come hither.* I squirmed and my g-spot ignited. Grace continued to fondle my clit, gradually working toward more direct stimulation. *Why hasn't anyone known to do this before?* This dual-trigger effect had me immersed in ecstasy. I beat the mattress, then grasped the sheets as my head reeled from the most intense pleasure of my life.

I reached for her. I wanted her close, pressed against my bosom. The urgency to meld overpowered me. She came to me, snuggled into my extended arms, and laid her head onto my heaving chest.

Holding her kindled a spark to give her the same joy and exhilarations she'd given me. I stoked her body. She responded to my flittering fingers with writhes and groans. I feathered my strokes across her arms and down her legs. She rolled to her back. I twirled a finger around her navel, enlarging each circle until it brushed against her breasts and tickled the triangle that parted her legs. Her abdomen and hips rolled in waves of pleasure, begging for more. Her eyes pleaded with mine. But I was merciless.

I savored her desire – never wanted it to end. I shifted my weight and concentrated on her feet, teased her legs, brushed her inner thighs. As I neared her flower, I quickly reversed my stroke before beginning the ascent again. She parted her legs wider and wider with each approach until I was drawn into her fountain. At contact, she shuttered and screeched, drawing up her knees. Overcome by passion, I fell beside her and tucked my arm beneath her neck to cradle her. My hand reached to massage her folds – outer and inner – running my fingers up and down, in between the creases, while I kissed her eyes, cheeks, chin, lips.

I explored her petals with the lightest of touches, knowing the frustration of being overpowered. Her reaction told me when I'd reached her bud. I circled and tickled it until her legs stiffened, her back arched, and she screamed her delight before sinking into the cocoon of my arms, quivering with sporadic jerks.

The rising sun peered through the window and revealed the flush on her cheeks. *After eight o'clock.* The morning flight to Juneau wasn't scheduled until eleven thirty.

I smoothed a flaxen curl from her cheek and tucked it behind her ear. The corners of her mouth upturned as my finger traced her jaw line, but she didn't open her eyes. She sighed, shifted her weight, and began nuzzling her face against my chest. Before I realized her strategy, she latched onto a nipple and suckled my breasts like a newborn. Currents, like lightning bolts, streaked through me, reverberating throughout my core, settling in the sacral chakra.

Gaining strength, she rolled me to my back and slid headfirst to my nether region, her body aligned on top of mine, her dripping pussy positioned over my waiting mouth. I licked the nectar from her folds as I clamped her butt checks in my grip. I wanted to devour this delectable fruit.

Grace wrapped her arms around my legs, slid her hands

up the underside of my thighs to lift my knees and spread my legs before burying her face at my Y. She stationed her lips within my lips – sucking, licking, even slurping my juices. She cried out, sending me vibrations and messages of her eagerness and joy.

I reciprocated, clutching her hips to settle her above my face. I wanted to view her sex, examine that tiny organ of her ecstasy. She scooted her knees forward to support her weight and free my hands. I spread her labia and gently pulled back her hood. I rose and tentatively tapped it with the tip of my tongue. She didn't flinch, so I wiggled it, gradually increasing the pressure.

Her attention shifted to what I was doing. She raised her upper body and rolled her hips giving me more access and better position. 'Oh . . . my . . . God!' she screamed, nearing the pinnacle. I wondered if anyone was in the room next to us but didn't care. She jerked away, collapsed beside me, and begged for mercy. 'I . . . never . . . thought . . . I'd . . . say this,' she huffed, 'but I don't think I can take any more. My brain might burst.'

I continued to lie, spread beside her. I stretched my arm to her waist, pulling her closer and massaging up and down her side, before sliding my hand between her legs and applying counter-pressure to her secret garden, which she'd so graciously opened to me.

'You'd better look out, Missy,' she panted. 'You've got a tongue lashing comin' your way.'

'Mm.' I smiled and felt tiny little men – or maybe it was women – performing somersaults in my lower abdomen.

She rolled over and crawled between my legs and

positioned herself on her knees. She placed her hands beneath my ass and lifted me to her lips and delivered her promise. I squirmed and screamed and thought I might pass out. She confirmed my suspicions that this wasn't her first time. *How lucky for me?* Just when I was so sated I thought I might explode, she mounted me, sex to sex, our legs forming an X. It was the most incredible feeling, wet against wet. She ground against me, rode me, fucked me, and timed her crescendo to mine. In unison we reached new heights.

She cuddled beside me. I embraced her and pulled her close. Within minutes, she was fondling my nipples again.

'What are you doing?' I giggled and twittered her nips in return.

'There's no end, baby. We can just keep going and going. There's no reason *we* have to stop.' She winked.

As realization registered, my eyes widened and my mouth flew open. 'That's right!'

'This really was your first time, wasn't it?'

'It wasn't for you?' I waited, wondering if she was going to admit it.

She feigned innocence – a demure look, puppy-dog eyes, and pouty lips that were oh, so sexy.

'I think I just got seduced.'

'I didn't hear any complaints,' she teased.

The morning was consumed making love – avant-garde experiences and explorations I'd never imagined. We existed somewhere between oblivion and utopia until Grace flung her arm in a motion of bliss and knocked the clock radio off the nightstand.

'It's twelve thirty-eight! We've missed our connection,' she yelled, picking up the alarm.

'Seriously? You really believe that?'

Recognition flooded her face as a smile radiated from the corners of her lips to her eyes. 'Oh . . . no . . . no, not at all.'

Also available from Black Lace:

All You Can Eat

Emma Holly

Sex, lies and murder . . .

Frankie Smith is having a bad day: her boyfriend has just dumped her and she's just found a dead body behind her café.

Still, things look up when sexy local detective, Jack West, turns up to investigate. And when stranger turns up at the diner looking for work, Frankie soon finds herself juggling two men and an increasingly kinky sex life . . .

Explicit, erotic fiction from the bestselling author of *Ménage*

Also available from Black Lace:

I Kissed a Girl

Edited by Regina Perry

Everyone's heard the Katy Perry song,
but have you ever been tempted . . .?

If so, you're not alone: most heterosexual women have had same-sex fantasies, and this diverse collection of short erotic fiction takes us way beyond kissing.

An anthology featuring kinky girl stories from around the globe and women from every walk of life and culture who are curious and eager to explore their full sexuality . . . with each other.

***Black Lace Books*: the leading imprint of erotic fiction by women for women**

And available digitally, a brand new collection in our best-selling **'Quickies'** series: short erotic fiction anthologies

Quickies: Girls On Top
Emma Hawthorne

This new collection of sensational, sexy stories will arouse and, occasionally, even shock you. This volume contains brand new stories from women who ignore the rules, unleash their sexual fantasies and find out just how wildly delicious sex can be when you take it to the limit – and, sometimes, beyond . . .

Includes:

Darkroom – Jen and her boyfriend explore group sex

Doctor in the house – Debbie's visit to A&E results in a romp with a doctor which gives a whole new meaning to the term 'bedside manner' . . .

Mistress Millie – when Millie meets fit farmhand Jake she knows exactly how to put him in his place . . .

Juicy – Samantha is about to discover her husband and his best friend are hiding a sexy secret . . .

Festival Fever – Leanna shares a tent with her friends Dee and Mar. And they get up close and very personal . . .

Top Brass – She's the boss's wife and Cindy knows she shouldn't say no to any of her demands . . .

Also available:

The Dark Garden

Eden Bradley

Surrender has its own rewards . . .

Rowan Cassidy likes to be in charge – especially in her personal life. At Club Privé, the most exclusive S&M club on the West Coast, she can live out her dominant fantasies safely, and with complete control.

Then she meets Christian Thorne. Self-confidant and sophisticated, he's a natural dominant and makes it clear he wants to be Rowan's master. He makes Rowan a daring proposition: she must give herself over to him for thirty days and discover her true nature . . .

Also available:

The Ninety Days of Genevieve

Lucinda Carrington

He is an arrogant, worldly entrepreneur who always gets what he wants.

And what he wants is for Genevieve to spend the next ninety days submitting to his every desire . . .

A dark, sensual tale of love and obsession, featuring a very steamy relationship between an inexperienced heroine and a masterful and rich older man.

Praise for *The Ninety Days of Genevieve*

'This month's essential reading . . . For fans of the renaissance of erotic fiction comes Lucinda Carrington's tale of love and obsession' *Stylist*

'sizzling . . . It's full of expertly written sex scenes that will appeal to any woman who has ever fantasised about bondage, lust, exhibitionism and voyeurism! . . . an excellent plot, well written characters and heaps of charm' *Handbag.com*

Also available:

In Too Deep

Portia Da Costa

Lust among the stacks . . .

Librarian Gwendolyne Price starts finding indecent proposals and sexy stories in her suggestion box. Shocked that they seem to be tailored specifically to her own deepest sexual fantasies, she begins a tantalising relationship with a man she's never met.

But pretty soon, erotic letters and toe-curlingly sensual emails just aren't enough. She has to meet her mysterious correspondent in the flesh . . .

Praise for Portia Da Costa

'Imaginative, playful and a lot of fun'

For Women